PLOUGHSHARES

Fall 2000 · Vol. 26, Nos. 2 & 3

GUEST EDITOR
Gish Jen

EDITOR
Don Lee

POETRY EDITOR
David Daniel

ASSISTANT EDITOR
Gregg Rosenblum

ASSOCIATE FICTION EDITOR
Maryanne O'Hara

ASSOCIATE POETRY EDITOR
Susan Conley

FOUNDING EDITOR
DeWitt Henry

FOUNDING PUBLISHER
Peter O'Malley

PLOUGHSHARES, a journal of new writing, is guest-edited serially by prominent writers who explore different and personal visions, aesthetics, and literary circles. PLOUGHSHARES is published in April, August, and December at Emerson College, 120 Boylston Street, Boston, MA 02116-4624. Telephone: (617) 824-8753. Web address: www.emerson.edu/ploughshares.

ASSISTANT FICTION EDITOR: Nicole Hein Kelley. EDITORIAL ASSISTANTS: Kelly Kervick and Stephanie Wilder.

FICTION READERS: Darla Bruno, Laurel Santini, Elizabeth Pease, Kathleen Stolle, Wendy Wunder, Geraldine McGowan, Eson Kim, Hannah Bottomy, and Emily MacLellan. POETRY READERS: Sean Singer, Christopher Hennessy, Jill Owens, Tracy Gavel, Joanne Diaz, Kristoffer Haines, Aaron Smith, Michael Carter, Jennifer Thurber, and Scott Withiam.

SUBSCRIPTIONS (ISSN 0048-4474): $21 for one year (3 issues), $40 for two years (6 issues); $24 a year for institutions. Add $5 a year for international.

UPCOMING: Winter 2000–01, a fiction and poetry issue edited by Sherman Alexie, will appear in December 2000. Spring 2001, a poetry and fiction issue edited by Heather McHugh, will appear in April 2001.

SUBMISSIONS: Reading period is from August 1 to March 31 (postmark dates). All submissions sent from April to July are returned unread. Please see page 236 for a description of the guest editor policy and for detailed submission policies.

Back-issue, classroom-adoption, and bulk orders may be placed directly through PLOUGHSHARES. Microfilms of back issues may be obtained from University Microfilms. PLOUGHSHARES is also available as CD-ROM and full-text products from EBSCO, H.W. Wilson, Information Access, and UMI. Indexed in M.L.A. Bibliography, American Humanities Index, Index of American Periodical Verse, Book Review Index. Self-index through Volume 6 available from the publisher; annual supplements appear in the fourth number of each subsequent volume.

The views and opinions expressed in this journal are solely those of the authors. All rights for individual works revert to the authors upon publication.

PLOUGHSHARES receives support from the Lila Wallace–Reader's Digest Fund, the Massachusetts Cultural Council, and the National Endowment for the Arts.

Retail distribution by Bernhard DeBoer (Nutley, NJ), Ingram Periodicals (La Vergne, TN), and Koen Book Distributors (Moorestown, NJ). Printed in the U.S.A. on recycled paper by Capital City Press.

CONTENTS

Fall 2000

Cover painting:
Brown Trout Rising by Garry Mitchell
Alkyd on canvas, 21″ x 17″, 1999
Collection of Laura Von Rosk

Ploughshares
Patrons

This nonprofit publication would not be possible without the
support of our readers and the generosity of the following
individuals and organizations.

COUNCIL
Denise and Mel Cohen
Eugenia Gladstone Vogel
Marillyn Zacharis

PATRONS
Anonymous
William H. Berman / Houghton Mifflin
Jacqueline Liebergott
Turow Foundation

FRIENDS
Anonymous
Johanna Cinader
H. Bruce McEver

ORGANIZATIONS
Emerson College
Lila Wallace–Reader's Digest Fund
Massachusetts Cultural Council
National Endowment for the Arts

COUNCIL: $3,000 for two lifetime subscriptions and
acknowledgement in the journal for three years.
PATRON: $1,000 for a lifetime subscription and
acknowledgement in the journal for two years.
FRIEND: $500 for a lifetime subscription and
acknowledgement in the journal for one year.
All donations are tax-deductible.
Ploughshares, Emerson College,
120 Boylston St., Boston, MA 02116

Introduction

A certain college professor used to say that one sits down to write ABC, but in the process discovers—ah!—DEF! He was talking about writing nonfiction, but there is DEF in fiction, too. We discover through writing that we know more than we know— hopefully, if we're writing with honesty and without gimmickry, with respect for tradition but distaste for convention—much more. And we discover that much of what we know is not knowl- edge, exactly; that much is not described by fact; that in fact, facts miss life's essence; and that we take unreasonable satisfaction in the capture of that essence. Why do we care so about the heft of things? About patterns, rhythms, certain chill pleasures? Why do we care what it means to reach; how it feels to be mortal; what tri- umph of sorts is to be found in words? We just do. The grimmest truth is lightened by accuracy of expression, and yet fiction is more than accurate. It is wildly intimate, the human mind at large. We are differently human, in this age of techno-wow, than we were in the age of *Beowulf.* Never mind the machine in the garden, it's the computer in the garden we must contend with now, not to say the camera. Screens have infiltrated our dreams, all manner of visuals. All the same, we are passionate, we are brave. We have dragons to slay. We seek to answer death with glory; and we love stories. Why will no doubt be explained, in due time, by clever use of a brain scan. Certain areas of the brain will light up, and a researcher will announce, There! That is the *storius lovicus,* which distinguishes human gelatin from that of other creatures. But of course, he or she will have only translated human truth into scientific truth, brilliantly.

I write all this because while editing this issue, I happened to find myself on a panel entitled "What Can We Learn from the Arts that We Can Learn Nowhere Else?"—a subject I would not have thought worth expounding upon. To ask such a question seemed to me to be like asking "What can we learn from children that we can learn nowhere else?" As if there were a point to having children; as if they were an educational experience, like Outward Bound. On the other hand, children are, of course, an education, too. We do learn things from them, as we do from literature. One of the great uses of literature today—often mistaken for its point—is its social use. How should we feel about the use of art as artifact? Much of the panel discussion revolved around this subject. Everyone agreed that real art is not didactic; that it has no express agenda; and that it is not intended to be useful. So, good. But what if it concerns society, as fiction often does? What if it sheds light on what it means to live a particular life in a particular time and place? What, then? A. E. Housman said, "If I were obliged, not to define poetry, but to name the class of things to which it belongs, I should call it a secretion..." Fiction, too, is in large measure secreted; should we be dismayed if the secretion turns out to be medicinal?

A number of the pieces in this issue might be construed to have some medicinal use, and yet they retain a secreted quality, a wild intimacy. They are unpredictable. Not so much incorrect as acorrect, they achieve a balance between form and utterance that I find beautiful. Editor friends tell me that while there has always been bad fiction, multiculturalism has engendered a particularly painful sort of bad fiction, full of the pieties of racism sexism classism—fateful maladies for societies that often prove fatal for fiction. I know what the editors mean. In much of the fiction of claracexism there's no DEF. The authors end where they begin, with ABC. Their writing is sentimental.

All of the pieces of this issue, in contrast, multicultural or not, potentially medicinal or not, get to DEF, even G. They discover themselves.

In the interests of diversity, I include an essay from the true "other" of the writing community, a critic. I do not agree with everything this particular curmudgeon has to say, but do think he provides valuable food for thought. That we may go on and on, inventing and reinventing, we writers need our amiable irritants: Here's one.

ANN BEATTIE

Hurricane Carleyville

Carleyville left late because of the rain. That morning the phone had finally been disconnected, after a ridiculous argument with the phone company, when the supervisor he was finally connected with agreed to disconnect after asking a series of questions he could not possibly answer. With his credit card, his "code" was his mother's maiden name, but what security precaution had he come up with a year before for the phone company? What had happened to this country, that a citizen needed a magic word to turn off the telephone? Finally the woman had settled for his social security number, information about other occupants of the house (none, unless you counted the animals), and his assurance that he would put his request in writing and fax it to her before the end of the day. He had a fax, but the thing wasn't working: it spewed out page after page of blank paper for every incoming page, all marked with a deep black line. The broken machine would be Daley's problem now.

Hitched together, his moving home was a wonder: truck pulling trailer pulling horse carrier. The cat, Adventure Kitty, rode in the truck's cabin with Carleyville. That gave Coon, the dog, the use of the trailer—the space shared with the birds and the two chickens, all of which were suspended in a cage he'd improvised from the laundry basket and some nylon netting that hung above the floor, away from Coon's restless tongue. Secretly, Carleyville hoped that the ride would shake up the birds' insides enough that they'd stop laying eggs. He'd left two birds with Daley for Daley's daughter—a sort of early Christmas present— and lost two more, with not bad timing, when they poked their heads far enough outside the cage to peck the paint on an exposed pipe and died (he presumed) of lead poisoning. He and Daley had disposed of them in a backyard burial a few days earlier—Daley had done the digging, because Carleyville was trying to sort out the insurance company's failure to pay for x-rays he'd had taken months ago when, walking across a street in the dark, he'd broken his ankle in a hole down which Alice could have easily tumbled into Wonderland. As the two bird-stuffed Styrofoam cups with plastic tops (leftover from Chai tea to go) were lowered into the ground for a decent burial, a rather amazing thing happened: birds making an early migration passed overhead, the long line uninterrupted until they passed directly above, the birds in back suddenly slowing, as if the gap conveyed a symbolic goodbye, a respectful enactment of emptiness, for their fellow birds. *Two less critters for Coon to bark at,* Daley had commented. And then commented, again, *bark at,* because in spite of the holistic remedy Carleyville had insisted he try, he still suffered from echolalia.

At the end of the street, where the school bus turned around, Carleyville made his final swing, missing a maple tree by a fraction of an inch, settling for letting the horse bounce around for a few seconds. He was always too attuned to her mental state. The guy who ran the organic farm at the end of the road was nice enough, but a worrier: the whole rig might bust apart, he'd said nervously, inspecting it the night before; the horse could move around enough to get hurt, in his opinion. Finally, he and the guy had exchanged firm handshakes, and Carleyville had reminded him that undiagnosed hypoglycemia could cause both sweating and anxiety—Malcolm Curry was a sweatbox, winter and summer—and Malcolm had kidded Carleyville one last time about the pumpkin suicide—a reference to the time a really *enormous* pumpkin had fallen off the back of a truck in front of Carleyville, providing months of what Malcolm called "punkin' postmortems": pumpkin soup, pumpkin flan, manicotti stuffed with pumpkin, pumpkin spice cookies, and of course traditional pumpkin pie. Being a farmer, Malcolm had respect for Carleyville's appreciation of vegetables. Carleyville would miss him, but not his wife, who stood looking grimly out the kitchen window.

Dangling from the rearview mirror was a tail feather from a blue jay the cat had mauled in the front yard—the yard whose lawn was now much healthier as a meadow—and two or three other trinkets or memorabilia, whatever you'd call them, from moments of adversity that Carleyville had triumphed over or, just as important, come to terms with. These little mementos included the rubber finger his former girlfriend had left on the bathroom counter one morning, along with her note saying goodbye (was he ever right about not marrying her!), along with a splash of watery ketchup and a big knife from the kitchen, the sight of which almost made him faint...yep; more than once he'd picked a real crazy. Imagine doing that when things were going fine between them simply because he'd told her there would be no engagement ring on her finger. Imagine waiting two days, purchasing the finger (apparently), never telling him how angry she was, plotting all the while. This was in June, too: not around Halloween. So goodbye to all that: goodbye, Christie, goodbye, phone company with its sky-high rates, goodbye, landlord from Hell. He and the feather and the finger would sustain each other on the ride to Maine, on the way to Jimmy and Fiona's house.

The truck lost significant power on hills, but that was to be expected. As were the assholes behind him. What did they think? That their flashing lights would send photoelectric vibes, causing the rig to clear the road by ascending directly into the universe, on the principle of *The force be with you?* Let *them* try to drive a rig like this. They'd end up a big metal turtle on its back, while he had experience guiding his slithering snake. He had experience, he knew what he was doing, so horns and flashing lights be damned.

He was miles away when he remembered the fish. How had he forgotten it? Probably trying to struggle out with the dog on its leash and his computer in the other hand, plus various odds and ends clamped under his armpit. His thumb had been in the fishbowl, but apparently he had forgotten to pick it up again, once he set it down to close the door. He patted his pocket and felt the cheesecloth he'd brought to put over the top of the fishbowl, and the rubber band—damn! He'd thought of the rubber band in the middle of the night, then forgotten the whole fishbowl. Though the maleficent landlord would no doubt be around immediately to find excuses not to refund the security deposit (he'd probably cut the grass himself and deduct a hefty sum), so, sensitive soul that he was, he would doubtless take the fish.

The force of the rain would not be good for the fish, though if he'd left it under the overhang, everything would be all right. If not, the fish could spend some time dancing in a watery disco.

He used the gauze to wipe the inside of the window, which had fogged up in spite of the defroster being on high. In front of the truck, a squirrel dashed across the road and made it to the other side. Seeing it reminded Carleyville of the days when he and his friends had hunted gophers in Texas, where his grandfather lived: the high-powered slingshots they'd fashioned; the metal bottle caps—in those days that was all there was; metal, not plastic—launched from slingshots. When his foot suddenly plunged into a gopher's hole—the same damn foot he broke again, wouldn't you know, crossing the mothering street—Carleyville's slingshot had misfired as his friend Timmy turned to see what all the noise was about, bull's-eyeing Timmy in his right eye. Timmy—wherever he was now. Wherever so many of his buddies were.

Thirteen hours later, Carleyville was so tired he could hardly keep his eyes open. If the radio worked, that would have helped, but only the darkened scenery of Erie, Pennsylvania, was there to keep him awake, and it wasn't exactly tantalizing. Since it was time to let Coon out of the trailer, anyway, he pulled into a rest area and hopped out, leaving the window half down on the passenger's side because the rain that had chased him from state to state was making sure that the truck windows stayed perpetually fogged. It was colder than he expected, and his legs were stiffer than he thought they'd be. Getting out, he knocked over the water jug he kept next to Adventure Kitty's cage. He thought he'd screwed the cap back on, but no such luck. Water splashed into the cat's cage and produced a shriek he had never before heard, and this cat was big on histrionics. "It's just water," he said. He lifted the cage and tilted it slightly. Adventure Kitty slid forward. Water splashed to the floor. The cat seemed to be soaked. One paw clawed the mesh of the cage. Time for some TLC. He opened the glove compartment and pulled out one of the catnip sticks he'd made after drying the year's catnip crop and poked it into her cage. The cat did not sniff the catnip; she only glared at him.

What happened next he had no explanation for: he was reaching for the water jug, its cap silver-dollar bright as it lay on the floor, when he got a stitch in his side and jerked forward, his ribs pressing into the cage. It was like pleurisy, though he no longer had pleurisy. But still, it was that same searing pain. He took a few breaths, then forced his body to right itself, though in the process he knocked over the jug again. He cursed Adventure Kitty—despised her for making what were already pain-filled, unbearable moments even more excruciating. The cat was capable of sending up a sound like a Skil saw. Sweating, he kept his hand clamped to his ribs and slowly, awkwardly, bumped out of the truck, lowering one leg, the distance to the ground seeming interminable. As he finally stood on both feet, another car entered and swept over him with its headlights. He turned to block the glare, and as he raised his arm he felt the pain shift into his groin. What the hell! He walked tentatively, the pain gradually easing, toward the cinder-block bathroom. Inside, he glanced in the mirror and saw that he had forgotten to shave. The wasp bite on his cheek gave him the look of a half-painted doll—one of those cutesy crafts-fair specials with apple-red cheeks and marble eyes: Grandpa with his mouth puckered like an anus. Those junky crafts fairs where Christie used to try to sell her stained glass—those all-day, exhausting gatherings, where people looked and exclaimed and did not buy, and afterwards you spent too much money consoling yourself with expensive roadside food.

So who should he have been involved with? A lady stockbroker?

He sat on a toilet in one of the stalls, but the pain had passed. Try explaining that to a doctor: sudden, unprecedented pain, and then nothing. Not even a crap. They'd put you through every test in the book. That, or write you off as mental. He decided it had been some bizarre muscle spasm, probably the result of days of packing and hauling cartons to the van, aggravated by tension when the water tipped over. The last of his spring water was now soaking the floor of the truck. Time to get some water to the horse and the dog. Enough of impersonating The Thinker, with his pants around his knees.

Outside, a kid with a white skunk streak in his black hair asked him if he had a match. The kid was sitting on one of those folding stools, like an old-timer at a parade. What the kid thought the spectacle might be, outside the restrooms, when it was almost midnight, he couldn't say. "No, sorry, I don't smoke," he said, but the last word was not entirely out of his mouth before he tripped. Too late, he saw in the dark the narrow end of a black guitar case. He stumbled badly but kept himself upright, though for a moment he was almost nose-to-nose with the kid, who looked at him impassively and said nothing. No apology, nothing. Just one of God's children, out for a pleasant evening of putting invisible obstacles on the ground. Mothering punk: just set up outside a rest area bathroom, kick back with some Absolut Currant, some Absolut *Asshole,* stretch your feet. If the guitar case doesn't do it, maybe the big Nike'd foot will. "You got a problem?" the kid said. Punk, with his dyed hair and his Just Do It shoes. Kids were a new breed now: purposeful, in spite of their mock passivity; unflinching. Everybody had become a malcontent with attitude, a *mock Marine.*

He went back to the truck and let Coon out of the trailer. Coon had been staring at him out the window, his golden eyes glinting like a hologram as Carleyville approached. There was a dog with dignity: none of that scratching and whining. He'd had a bad life, had a leg that had healed so poorly after a break he'd gotten before Carleyville found him that he'd saved up and gotten him an operation, wondering whether that experience wouldn't traumatize the poor beast even further, but Coon had come back from the vet's a new dog. His loyalty to Carleyville even intensified, though he'd still had to work on him for a year to get the dog to make eye contact.

"How you doing, old boy?" Carleyville said. The dog jumped out of the trailer and ran to the trash receptacle and peed for a long time. Carleyville sensed that the punk was watching, but it was too dark to see, and he was too tired to get himself more agitated. If sodas didn't cost a dollar a pop (a pun!), he would have bought himself one, his throat was so dry, in spite of the fact that they screwed up your metabolism. With the dog at his side, he went back toward the restrooms, where there was a water fountain.

"Hey, pooch," the punk said, as if nothing had previously transpired between them.

Carleyville got a drink from the fountain and put his hand to his throat as he swallowed. It was almost as if the water was hot, it burned so going down. Carleyville tested the fountain with his finger: cold water. Okay: so another unsolvable mystery. Something made him go into the bathroom a second time, to check in the mirror; when he did, he saw that his Adam's apple was swollen. Allergies, maybe, if he was lucky. Again, he regretted not shaving, but what did it matter at this hour. When he exited, he saw the punk in a sleeping bag, under a tree. He flashed forward to Coon running up to him, raising his leg to piss the last few drops. The fight that would ensue. Then he shook his head—thank God Coon had good sense—and trekked to the rig to begin tending to the horse. She was lucky to be Coon's best buddy, rather than his dinner. A horse like Cleopatra would have been shipped off to the slaughterhouse if not for him—if not for Malcolm telling him she was about to be Alpo-ed by people two farms over—so in spite of the rocky ride, she should still thank her lucky stars. He had a sack of food for her to eat in the trailer, which he decided to dish out, rather than drag to the ground. But the dishes were all packed, and there was no telling which box contained the bowls. He took a guess, but the tinny sound he'd heard inside one box turned out not to be metal bowls, but Christie's trophy cups: trophies she'd won playing golf, that he'd felt bad about leaving behind. Eventually he'd ship them back to her. He settled for scooping food into the dish drainer, which wasn't boxed. Some fell out, but most of it made it to the ground, where he set it down. For the third time he returned to the restrooms, filling a bucket he *had* left accessible as the dog salivated at his side. "Hey, what am I thinking of?" he said, setting the bucket on the floor of the bathroom. "Thinking of Cleo and not about you, hey, old boy?" The dog lapped up the water until its head was almost stuck in the bucket. "Hey, we don't want you pissing a river in the trailer," Carleyville said, lifting the bucket. He refilled it and headed back. He noticed that the punk was no longer under the tree. A thought went through his head that amused him: maybe it had been a space alien, not a real person. Maybe that was why he'd been so strange, perched on his stool outside a bathroom, with his surliness and his skunk hair. There'd been some skit on *Saturday Night Live* years back about questions to ask to find out if somebody was a space alien; if they couldn't answer, you knew they were. There was some hilarious scene with one of the actors cornering his mother-in-law, firing off the names of bands, about which, of course, she was completely ignorant. The Butt Hole Surfers. That sort of thing.

Getting ready to spring the horse's door, he went into a spasm of coughing, with his damned dry throat. It had been Christie's opinion that he was allergic to animals, but that was just because she didn't like them. In any case, he was taking an antihistamine.

The chickens had set up a real ruckus as soon as he stopped in the parking lot. The next morning he'd get some food for them—they'd been fed once, for God's sake. For the moment, he began to assist in the backwards exit of Cleo the Horse.

He awoke before dawn, coughing his way to consciousness, and decided to get a jump on the day. The Martian never reappeared—probably off passing for a New York City cop, or whatever it was Martians did to be puckish these days. Carrying a bomb into a stadium, maybe. Cleo had backed right over his hand the night before, and it was badly swollen, his knuckles gray-blue with contusions. The hand—wouldn't you know it would be his right hand—was half again its normal size. If he knew where the contents of his medicine cabinet were, he could bandage it, but there was no chance of finding them. All his possessions, for the umpteenth time, somehow eluding him.

The day before he'd forgotten to send the fax he'd promised the telephone lady, though he'd awakened during the night, smugly proud because he'd dreamed he'd sent it. What would she have done but lose it, anyway? She was probably no longer even working there. If you talked to somebody one day they'd be gone an hour later, and you'd be back to square one, spelling your last name and playing the *as in* game: the new, monotonous world of "B-as-in-Boy." Then, when the deaf moron had that down, you could start touching your toes, or whatever else they wanted you to do.

He did a few jumping jacks to jazz up his system. The finale was too enthusiastic and made his hand hurt. Though he'd more or less given up caffeine, the idea of coffee still floated across his mind some mornings—although today was not a day he'd want to pour a hot beverage down his throat. Could it be strep? He watched Coon run around sniffing things, then clicked his fingers for the dog to come. Back in the cabin of the truck, Adventure Kitty clawed at the cage. He got the leash he'd fashioned for her out of a bandanna made rope-like with knots and a length of left-over sailcloth he'd been saving for another project and opened the top of the cage. She stared at him, just on the verge of hissing, though she did not. He slipped it around her neck—nasty swipe from her paw; just what his sore hand needed—and slid his other hand under her belly and lifted her. Probably busting with piss, so maybe it would come out her ears if she pulled her usual shit and wouldn't do it while she was on the leash. He was too smart in the ways of living with cats to let her walk around unleashed on the grass outside a rest area, that was for sure.

On the grass, the cat gagged, dislodging a small ball of fur. The cat proceeded to stand there, wouldn't even walk, let alone pee. After five minutes of tugging her forward in increments, he decided to put her back in the cage. He told her to remember that she'd had her chance. And let the damn horse stay in its carrier until they got to Maine; it would have what it wanted soon enough. Lucky not to be dog food. He'd stop for some food for the chickens—maybe something he could get for himself that they could share.

But the engine wouldn't start. How do you like that? Is that good? Just click-click-click. And, for good measure: click-click-click-click. Still interested? Then click-click-click-click-click. He'd traded his redwood lawn chairs for Daley's extra battery only a week before. What he needed was a jump, but the rest area was deserted. He'd either have to hike out and see if there was a gas station or wait for somebody to pull in, and then you could bet that person would either be a woman, and therefore too afraid to even roll down her window, or some macho truck driver who wouldn't have the inclination, so he'd claim he couldn't take the drain himself. And who knew: maybe Jesus Christ would pull in and have all the time, and all the good inclinations, in the world. That's "J-as-in-Joker."

He got out of the truck and slammed the door, leaning back and staring into space, trying to keep calm—and, having thought of Jesus Christ, made a bargain-prayer: If you get me out of this parking lot in the next ten minutes, I'll send the phone lady a fax *and* a bunch of roses.

And so it came to pass. In the form of a woman, all right, but led into the lot by a guy on a motorcycle. Dawn just breaking, and there was this pale little blond thing driving a little white Toyota, Harley thundering in front of her with a Wonder Warthog guy gripping the handlebars. "Use some help, bro?" the motorcyclist shouted.

He nodded. This was happening: no dream. "Weak battery," he said.

"Cheryl," the motorcyclist shouted into the Toyota's now open window, "back it up a little."

The Toyota rolled backwards.

"I've got cables," Carleyville said.

"Got my own right in the trunk," the man said. Cheryl switched off her engine and got out. She smiled faintly, hurrying toward the bathroom.

"We'll get 'er goin'," the man said.

"Thanks for the help," Carleyville said. The last word didn't make it; it came out a painful croak. He opened the hood. The man was already dragging cables toward the car. "Yeah, anybody moves around without these, he probably don't know to bring a beer cooler, either," the man said. "And that would be *some stupid*."

Carleyville nodded. The man was taking charge, placing the clips. His hands were greasy, as if he'd been doing this before. "Get in," the man said, gesturing with his elbow.

Right. Carleyville had forgotten the part about being inside, turning on the ignition.

It started right away. Hummed like new. As he gave the thumbs-up, he noticed that the overhead light was on. Could he have slept all night with the light on, after he'd turned it on to check the map before doubling up the sleeping bag on top of the cat's cage for a pillow?

"I'm no good with thank-yous," the man said. The look in his eye let Carleyville know he shouldn't insist on any further exchange. It was a look Adventure Kitty might have if he'd left her in the cage for a month. Carleyville nodded and gripped the man's hand, which was difficult to do, since he had to shake left-handed.

He was on his way again. It took him a while to realize that he shouldn't obsess about sending roses to the phone lady, because he wouldn't know where to send them. People who answered the telephone never used their real names, so who was she, really? Even if he remembered her name, it would have been a made-up name, her work address one he wouldn't know until he unpacked and found a phone bill with the address on it. Of course, he could call and ask—but that might begin to seem like he was hassling her. Roses probably cost too much, anyway, and his credit card was pretty much maxed out. That, however, was a thought he did not want to dwell on.

The house was right where Jimmy circled the map: on the corner of Battsbridge Road and Route 91, four miles from the highway. Or he supposed it was four miles, since it seemed a good stretch. The odometer was broken. He'd overshot, at first, and finding a place to turn around had taken him a couple of miles out of his way.

Fiona, pulling weeds in front of the big brown house, stood slowly, frowning at the caravan pulling onto their street. She looked so much like the birds—she held her head at such a birdlike angle—that he cocked his own head, taking it in. Fiona was adorable. A worrywart, but cute. He tapped the horn, but to his surprise, the horn didn't make a sound. The sun glinted off the window, which must have been why she couldn't see him waving. It was murder trying to round the curve and get the horse carrier off 91; expressions of friendship were going to have to be momentarily put on hold.

He sideswiped their mailbox, but it didn't go down; only minor damage had been done to the pole. Cheap metal thing, anyway: he'd fashion them a better one.

"Nelson!" he heard Fiona call. Shrill voice: that was the downside to Fiona.

Fiona rushed to the rig. And the damned window would hardly go down. He had to settle for saying hello through a three-inch crack at the top.

"Is that really you?" Fiona was squealing. "You said September."

"I had to get out of there," he said. "Mr. Rogers was having a breakdown." He smiled at his new nickname for the landlord.

"Where will you park this?" she asked, more hushed than shrill.

Across from Fiona was a dirt road cutting through a field. Jimmy had described their five acres accurately: not much land where the house stood, but a nice amount of acreage across the way. Carleyville jerked his thumb to the right, pointing out the obvious. Fiona nodded. How the rig was going to make the turn onto such a narrow road was another matter…but suddenly Jimmy, in sweatpants and T-shirt, was rushing to Fiona's side, so he threw open the door to give his old buddy a hug. In fact, the door flew open too quickly, but Jimmy jumped back in time. Fiona had to steady him. Carleyville hopped out and embraced both of them—a mistake to squeeze with his right hand; he let Jimmy's back-thump pass unreturned—telling them, all at once, about how he'd thought he might be broken down for good in a rest-area parking lot, but that he'd gotten out by making a silent promise to God concerning a woman he'd never met.

Jimmy said to Fiona: "That's Carleyville—saved, every time, by his incurable romanticism."

Two days later, clouds were gathering and an impressive wind was blowing up. Jimmy had gone out at daybreak to join two of the guys he worked with, who were racing against the impending hurricane to finish a roof. The rig was going to be fine. There wasn't a tree for a hundred yards. At Fiona's insistence, Adventure Kitty had the run of the house, and the birds were hanging in cages inside the garage. Both of the chickens ran off the day they were put in the pen he'd made for them, and Jimmy had told him—straight out; no nonsense—he'd seen one pancaked just up the road. From Fiona and Jimmy's living room window, he could see Coon curled up outside the trailer. Coon would never run away or otherwise cause trouble like Adventure Kitty by being piteous and gagging and staggering in the presence of a fairy-tale lady who could rescue her and put her inside her big, beautiful castle, where she served *sardines*. Coon would have disdained being renamed *Precious Little One*.

"It's the waiting that gets to me," Fiona said. "I can't stand simply waiting around."

"It's better when you don't have the television on," he said. "They're in the business of exciting you."

"I know, but I'm just all jittery, waiting."

"You'll feel better when you have some lunch," he said. He was chopping vegetables. Already missing Malcolm's organic carrots and turnips and beets. "You drink so much coffee, you could do with a B-complex, Fiona. Coffee leaches vitamin B right out of your system."

"But I just don't believe in all these vitamins, Nelson. Too many can be worse than not enough."

"You're a Brit," Carleyville said. "Why aren't you drinking tea in the first place?"

"Let's not have any harmful stereotyping," she said.

She had started chopping with him. She chopped vegetables the way hopeless girls threw softballs: tentatively, and entirely without will.

"Did she get a job?" he said, knowing Fiona would know who he meant.

"Right away. She said there was a terrible shortage of nurses. She could have been at work while the ink was drying on her signature."

He spent a few seconds trying to imagine Christie—wash-and-wear, no-nonsense Christie—writing with a fountain pen. Though considering the bad business trades she made, maybe she'd traded a stained-glass lampshade she'd worked weeks on for a fountain pen. Outside, trees were swaying in the wind. Fiona said: "Well, we've got flashlights and candles, plenty of candles. I suppose if we lose power we can still have light."

"You know," he said, "after lunch I think I'll go over and pitch in on that roof."

"Oh, I think you have to have insurance. Be insured, I mean. I don't think—"

"Well, maybe my good intentions will get rained out," he said.

The lights flickered. He finished scooping vegetables into the wok and ran for the front door, to get Coon. But Coon was already headed his way, he saw, when he threw open the door. He clicked his fingers, urging the dog to speed it up, though Coon always pretty much moved at his own pace, even with a hurricane brewing. His clicking fingers could not be heard, anyway, because of the force of the wind.

"You know, I can't get that story out of my mind that you— look at it out there! Where do you think Jimmy is? Hello, Coon. You come right into the kitchen and stay safe with us," Fiona said, patting his side. She started her sentence again: "That story you told about forgetting the goldfish. I mean, you *are* funny. Though I'd never tell such a story on myself."

"Fiona," he said, "don't you know that old ploy? If you're really self-loathing, no one will listen to you. So you tell them little things, you point out the road markers, rather than talking about the big wreck on the highway."

"Oh, you can't be serious," she said. "You're teasing. I mean, I think it's *terrible* you forgot the goldfish. I really do. But one doesn't know what to do but see the humor in it."

"I tell things for laughs. I want people like you to fall into the trap. It's a skill of mine, very self-serving. Not everybody's Jimmy, who can act like whatever happened the second before never happened."

"Oh, he's haunted. That's all talk, and you know it. He's seen psychiatrists half a dozen times, you know that. He has night sweats. He could use with a little of your ability to back off from the unimportant things, and see life as a comedy." She looked at him. "As a mixture of comedy and tragedy," she amended.

"It isn't. Jimmy's right, and we're kidding ourselves."

She shook her head, disagreeing.

"Tell the truth," he said. "That time I went to bed and forgot I'd left the pressure cooker on. You were furious, weren't you? You didn't think how funny it was the plum puddings were on the ceiling, did you? You were as mad as I've ever seen you."

"Well, I'm not proud of my reaction. You can't take a compliment, Nelson. All I was saying was that your perspective can be helpful. Especially when a thing's already happened."

Lightning seared into the trees at the back of the property. There was a deep rumble of thunder.

"Times like these you think you might be missing your cue and the special effects are there to help turn you into Frankenstein," Carleyville said, staring out the window. "But Jimmy and I have already done Frankenstein, so now we spend the rest of our lives figuring out an encore."

She looked at him, frowning. Finally, her voice more gentle than her eyes, she said: "I know how politically incorrect this is to say, but it still surprises me that a woman wrote that."

"To me," he said, interested in his thoughts, "every day is special effects. Except that there's no transformation. It rains, it snows, it's sunny, there's a hurricane—it's like background music in a movie to create emotion, but the movie's over and there was no plot. Fiona, I ask you: is there any reason I should be alive, and other people should be dead?"

"That's an unanswerable question, and you know it," she said. "The war is over, Nelson, and you've moved on."

"To your field."

"You're just visiting," Fiona said. "You can be so scathing about yourself. You've only come for a visit."

He thought he detected the ripple of a question in her voice. It was mean to be cynical with Fiona. Truth was, she thought of him more, did more for him, than Jimmy did.

Rain lashed the house as another burst of thunder thudded from the sky.

"I'd think he'd have been back ages ago," Fiona said.

"Maybe I should drive over and see if there's a crisis or something."

"Oh, Nelson, *of course not*. We're having a hurricane. It's bad enough *he's* not back."

The stove was gas-burning, so there would be no trouble cooking lunch. He decided to start, to distract her.

"Where did the cat go?" she said, as if snapping out of a fog.

"You know what the cat did one time?" he said. "She got in the tub and curled up right over the drain. Nobody would believe a cat ever did that."

"The tub?" Fiona said, getting up. "You think she could be in the tub?"

She came back a few minutes later, Adventure Kitty curled in her arms. "She was on a shelf of the linen closet," she said. "Someone left the door ajar."

"I hope a handful of kittens didn't follow her out."

"Oh, Nelson, really! You had her fixed, didn't you?"

"I was going to, but I had to put the money into truck repairs."

As Carleyville sautéed, the delectable odor of onions and carrots began to permeate the kitchen. He reached in his pants pocket and took out a small plastic container of dried mint, placing it on the counter. He stirred for another minute, then added green pepper and mushrooms. On top of this he placed shrimp to steam. With his favorite lacquer chopstick, he stirred everything together, gave it another thirty seconds, then reached in the bag and took out a big pinch of what looked to Fiona like anemic mouse shit. "What is that?" she couldn't resist asking.

"Lecithin granules," he said. "Lowers cholesterol."

"Well, I hope there's no harm to it; I mean, half these natural food things, there's—"

"It's good for you," he said. "Here I am optimistic about something, and you try to make me skeptical." He opened the other container and sprinkled mint on the food.

With the next clap of thunder, the cat jumped from Fiona's arms, landing on the dog, who sprang up, scaring the cat even worse.

"Oh!" Fiona said.

Carleyville did not respond to her, but to the scrabbling animals. "Remember this, you assholes," he shouted: "Every cat and every dog must take responsibility not only for himself, but also for his buddy."

They were without power that night and all the next day. In the morning it was still sprinkling rain, and there were enough gusts of wind to have blown Cleo's blanket off, although it had been secured with two belts. Carleyville and Jimmy took a walk to assess the damage. A big tree had gone down across 91 and was being worked on by a yellow-jacketed work crew who stopped cutting to call out that they should be careful because of downed wires. The wires were obvious, like spaghetti dumped on top of drumsticks. Like a really bad meal in a really bad restaurant. Nice of them to pipe up, but, Carleyville thought, he and Jimmy had experienced a few worse dangers.

The second-floor shutters of a Victorian had fallen to the ground. "Made pick-up sticks out of those," Jimmy said, gesturing through the rain. The glass on a downstairs window also seemed to be cracked.

"Hey, there's live wires around the bend," a red-faced man in a telephone truck stopped to holler.

"Okay," Jimmy said.

"Why don't we walk down and take a look at the river?" Carleyville said. He hadn't seen the river, but Jimmy had told him it was there.

"Yeah, good idea." He and Jimmy sank to their ankles in somebody's wet lawn, side-stepping the downed wires. Someone had put a flashing light near the tangle. A car approached, stopped, and went into reverse, taking the only other option: a fork in the road.

" 'But took the other, just as fair,' " Carleyville said.

"Fair? What's fair?" Jimmy said.

"No, I said, 'took the other, just as fair,'" Carleyville said. "Just to let you know I'm not some schmuck out walking around, I'm an educated man."

"Never doubted that," Jimmy said.

What? No return wisecrack? "You can be my Boswell," Carleyville said. "'Of a pile of fallen telephone wires, Dr. Johnson was said to have observed...'"

Jimmy continued walking. He said: "There weren't any fucking telephones then, Carleyville. No fax, no e-mail, no Dr. Johnson@aol.com."

The roses. He had never sent the fax or the roses.

"Why don't you go back and finish your degree? Stranger things have happened to old guys like us," Jimmy said. "Fiona and I were talking about that."

"Hey, Jimmy, you know me: I'm not too big on the concept of going back." Carleyville inspected a dead snake on the road. "Going back is more or less a concept useful for scaring you in science-fiction movies."

"I like the ones that catapult you into the future."

"Most of them do both," Carleyville said. "That way, they spook you with either thing you fear. Sound familiar?"

"We'd have been lucky if that had just been a science-fiction movie," Jimmy snorted. "Then that wall in Washington could have just been the credits rolling."

Jimmy joined him in looking at the snake, until his attention shifted to a big house beside them, and another set of shutters that had blown to the ground. "Maybe it's God's will that people redecorate," Jimmy said.

Around the bend, Jimmy gestured for Carleyville to take off his hiking boots—Jimmy himself had worn topsiders—so they could cut through a marshy field. They immediately sank a foot deep into the mush. Jimmy hopped one-legged to roll up his pants. "Muddy clothes make Fiona bat shit," Jimmy said.

"She told me you told her I was spinning out," Carleyville said.

Jimmy picked up the pace, to get back to Carleyville's side. "We worry about you," he said.

"So what you've come up with is the idea that the prodigal son should go back to school?"

Jimmy looked at him. "We're the same age," he said.

The house they were passing, an acre or so behind a larger house that faced the main road, was a barn that had been renovated by yuppies. A gravel road led to it. They'd done a nice job: redwood shutters, front door with leaded glass. Lucky that sucker didn't blow out in the hurricane, Carleyville thought. He wasn't up for the maintenance of a house anymore. The leaded glass reminded him of Christie's stained glass, and he wondered what her life was like as a nurse in Montana. There was someone who did believe in the concept of going back—she'd bailed and then gone back to her previously despised career.

They were soaked, except for the areas the rain parkas protected—though Carleyville hadn't zipped his until it was too late. More of a wind was coming up. Out in the middle of the field was a muddy dress or robe or something that had blown away. It looked like the most out-of-place thing in the world—or, at least, Carleyville imagined it would to anyone who hadn't already seen plenty of things out of place, including arms and legs.

Ahead was the river. They were coming at it across people's backyards; as they moved closer to the water the fields tapered into suburban lawns. A few had docks. The damage varied: only one seemed to be intact. For whatever reason, some people had left their boats moored in the harbor, though most must have either gotten them to land or transported them to a safer place. He looked at a sailboat with a broken mast. Who would worry so little about damage that they'd just leave the thing out there? Maybe people who were away. People who already lived in a vacation spot, who were off taking a vacation elsewhere.

Jimmy began doing a sort of dance, lifting his muddy feet in something that resembled a Scottish jig and tai chi at the same time. He couldn't help smiling. Jimmy was shedding the parka, pantomiming that he'd let it fly away to join the dress or whatever it was that kept getting airborne behind them. But then he hung it from the branch of a tree—maybe he was going to let the wind decide for him—and Carleyville understood Jimmy's odd dance. Of course; it was the most logical thing in the world: a swim in the river. In a minute they were bobbing around like mad—strange, strange sensation—wearing only their underwear. Carleyville quickly shed his, figuring that this was the perfect opportunity to discard his overload of clothes. Clothes crept up on you: no one needed as many clothes as he had.

As they drifted toward the bridge, a woman stopped her car, and her son got out to look. An enormous truck was coming from the other direction, so the woman backed her car off the bridge and then, when the truck passed (UPS! You had to admire them), joined her son at the rail, cupping her hands over her eyes as if sun shone directly in them, though there was no sun. Carleyville left it to Jimmy to pantomime that they were okay. Jimmy stuck out his tongue, one hand raised to make a corkscrew curl by his ear. Though he smiled, Carleyville could see that the woman did not, as the tide caught them and they shot under the bridge. They went with the flow until they managed to latch onto the roots of a big tree that Jimmy gestured to in front of them. If Jimmy thought it was stopping time, why not? Carleyville swam toward shore, and the snaggled roots, to join his buddy.

Lips pursed, Fiona was putting dinner on the table. Carleyville had contributed the spinach-tofu dish she removed from the oven. The refrigerator wasn't working, but she thought that since the dish did not contain meat, it would be safe to eat. Jimmy had set the table, putting all the silverware on the napkin, which drove her mad.

"Fiona, this is not something he could help," Jimmy said. "This is the sort of thing that could happen to anyone."

"Jumping into a river during a storm?"

"Okay, we might have restrained ourselves, but the rest of it was only bad luck, Fiona: bad luck to get cut by some rusting-away trash can some jerk threw in the water."

"Perhaps better not to jump in at all, when the water is churning and *a person can't see.*"

"Boys will be boys?" he said.

Her jaw was set. "At least he got diagnosed," she said. "Imagine the pain he must have been in with his thyroid gland burning up."

"That's just a figure of speech. 'Burning out'—overactive—was actually what the doctor said."

"So go get him! I've called him twice!"

Adventure Kitty rubbed against Fiona's ankles. She had just finished a meal of canned chicken, to which Fiona had added cream.

"You're nice to his pets, Fiona. Have a little patience with him."

"He has no sense of time. I do everything I can. I tell him an hour before the meal's being served, and then I remind him a second time. Then just when he's supposed to come down, I hear the bathwater being drawn."

"I'll get him," Jimmy said. He turned and, taking a flashlight, walked upstairs. Behind him, the kitchen was lit by an oil-burning lamp.

"Carleyville," he said. "Haul your ass outta there or she's gonna bust a gasket."

"Oh, sorry, dinner," Carleyville said from behind the closed door.

Jimmy shone the light in front of him, heading back downstairs.

"And I want you to bring up the phone call," Fiona said. "You must, Jimmy. I don't want to be involved, though heaven knows, I should know better, by now, than to pick up my own phone."

As soon as phone service was restored, they had gotten a call from Daley, who had made a good guess about where Carleyville had gone. Daley had been none too happy, and had been sarcastic to Fiona, which had made her angry at him, at Carleyville, and at her husband, for knowing both of them.

"I hardly know that Daley person," Fiona added. "Really, except for coming upon him pissing in the bushes at a picnic, I have no memory of him at all."

"That'll do," Jimmy said.

They sat down without Carleyville. Fiona had left the oil light glowing in the kitchen and lit three candles on the table. Fiona began to dish up the tofu. When she was done, instead of handing her plate to Jimmy, she purposefully put it down in front of her and began to eat. Jimmy stood and dished up his own dinner without comment.

"I do feel sorry for him with his thyroid burnout, or whatever it is," Fiona said, after a couple of bites. "I'm sure we would never have gotten him to the hospital if it hadn't been for the cut. And imagine him wanting to sew it up himself, left-handed. It boggles the mind. Jimmy—*it really does.*"

"He's not going to like hearing about money problems," Jimmy said. "He feels awkward about our having paid cash in the emergency room. That's why he's hiding upstairs."

"Well, but he's been called to dinner," Fiona said. "What does he think? That we're going to try to collect, three hours later?" She added: "It makes no sense that you two would have gone into the river. None at all."

"Give me your dream scenario. He passes up the swim and he..."

"Disappears from Earth," Fiona said. Though he could tell from her tone of voice that she didn't mean it.

"Hello, everybody," Carleyville said.

"Hello," Fiona said, when Jimmy said nothing. "Did you take one of those codeine pills the doctor gave you?"

"Yeah," Carleyville said, sitting down. Fiona looked at him, skeptically. His eyes did not meet hers. Fiona pushed her chair back, and dished up some food for him.

"Because there's no reason to suffer, if some medicine will make you feel better," Fiona said. Her voice softened. "How long did your throat—"

"It was nothing," Carleyville said. "I just thought that as long as I was paying the guy—"

"Well, it's good you brought it up. To have your thyroid malfunctioning and not—"

"It wasn't like I was losing my leg and I didn't get myself to the hospital," Carleyville muttered, head still averted. "It was activity inside a gland."

She was staring at him. She said: "You might have lost your leg in the river, but you escaped with only twenty-five stitches and a tetanus shot. Just a minor matter, I'm sure."

" 'Nothing is, but thinking makes it so,' " Carleyville said.

"The river *is* churning and *is* filled with debris, which anyone knows," Fiona shot back.

"We got a phone call from Daley," Jimmy broke in. "He wants us to try to get you to accept responsibility for the failure of the business. He also wants to be reimbursed for cleaning up what he said looked like a 3-D Jackson Pollock. It seems you left behind a bunch of birds that flew around the office shitting all over everything. According to him."

Carleyville put down his fork. "The phone's working?" he said.

"I don't feel that this involves me," Fiona said. "I want to say that I think he was overstepping his bounds to call us."

"You've got no head for business," Jimmy said, with a shrug. "So apologize to the guy about the bird shit and send him a check." He did not add: *If you've got any money.* "The failure of the business you can sort out later."

Carleyville reached for the salt. His arm brushed the candlestick, knocking the candle to the tabletop. Carleyville grabbed for it, but it rolled onto the rug, and Carleyville had to stomp out a small fire.

Fiona jumped up. "What is it?" she said. "What is it that makes everything so *precarious* if you're anywhere near it? You walk into a room and you knock over a table. You turn to pick it up and you step on the cat's tail. I've never seen anything like it! I understand *completely* why Christie left. We ought to send *you* outside and let the damned *hurricane* in." Fiona turned and walked quickly out of the room. She toppled nothing. The cat was not nearby.

They stared after her. The rain had ended, but outside, trees still swayed in the wind. There was a moon; otherwise, even the outlines of things would be difficult to see.

"She's a little worked up. Believe it or not, it was the thyroiditis diagnosis that put her over the top. Concern for you, I mean."

Carleyville folded his hands on the table. He looked at Jimmy.

"Listen, Daley's not gonna stay mad at you forever," Jimmy said. "Send him a check. Put your finger in the dam. That stupid vitamins-by-mail stuff was never gonna work. You've got to have a movie star to promote your friggin' vitamins, nowadays. Newsletters about double-blind tests..." He couldn't continue.

Carleyville pretended to have a better view of the trees than he did. He could see some leaves, occasionally, highlighted in the moonlight. When lightning lit up the sky, though, he saw something else: the outline of his truck, much lower than he expected. He stared until lightning flashed far in the distance, then realized what he was seeing: everything had begun to sink in the sodden field.

"If I just don't move, everything will stay the same," Carleyville finally said. "Very important, magical thinking. You must have done it yourself. Everybody did. If I run fast enough. If I make it to the tree. If I zig left and right and agree that my mother can die. My wife. Anybody."

"She's gonna be sorry as hell she jumped down your throat. You know she already is," Jimmy said.

"But she was right."

"So in the future be more careful. Come on—she's all to pieces because she thinks you're self-medicating and doing it all wrong. You saw how upset she got at the hospital. It was actually sort of funny, that young intern seeing her taking it so hard that you had a thyroid infection. 'He doesn't tend to anything!' I forget I'm married to a Brit half the time, and then she comes out with 'He doesn't tend to anything!' like you had a flock you were supposed to tend."

"I do. It's part of my traveling road show. The birds; my former chickens; the cat; the dog; the horse. Fiona's appropriated the cat, so I won't have to think about her anymore."

"Well, man, you're just going to have to simplify. That menagerie would be too much for anybody. You're like a magnet for other people's problems, which often take the form of having paws and hooves and being covered in fur." Jimmy got up and took a second helping of food. "She's upstairs trying to figure out how to apologize," he said. "Trust me. Fiona is your friend. If she wasn't, she wouldn't have gotten so bent out of shape at the hospital."

"Codeine makes me funny in the head. I didn't take it," Carleyville said.

"I didn't suspect for a minute you did." Jimmy shifted in his chair. "Listen, if it's a matter of writing Daley an apology . . ."

"He had all his money in the business. He doesn't care about bird shit."

"Well, you didn't twist his arm and force him to put his money in the business."

"It was my idea."

"He was interested. He talked to me about it. He thought it was a good idea."

"The war's over, as Fiona always says, but I convinced Daley to do magical thinking, anyway," Carleyville said.

"Stop blaming yourself. Magical thinking, bargains with God— if you want to think that's what it was, fine. It worked. But in peacetime, you've got to have a different M.O. You've got to realize you can accomplish things through your own efforts, not because you've got the right incantation or because you've held your breath until the wheel stopped spinning."

There it was: Jimmy's insistence on the future. And maybe it was wallowing, to go back to the time when he had avoided booby-traps because of his ESP, moved through minefields like a gazelle. Back then, he'd moved in a protective bubble of blessedness. The bubble had stretched over him Trojan-size, making a big prick out of him—that was funny: a medic as a big prick; a big, animated schlong coming at you in what might be your last few seconds... in the end, the bubble was so tight he thought he'd suffocate, but then he was saved: the last time into the field, the last maneuver accomplished, helicopter hovering for an immediate, absolute, final evacuation—that helicopter, like a big asterisk that could eventually footnote the whole friggin' war: *This all made no sense.* Though it might have, if you believed in colossal, malevolent jokes. Years later, the time had still not come to lean back and have a good laugh. He had once been fleet. Fortunate. He had lived, and certain other people—Daley's kid brother among them—had not. Then began the revenge of the ordinary world, and of inanimate objects: the corner of a table nicking his thigh where he'd once been grazed by a bullet; falling on ice, the simple contents of his grocery bag raining down on his head—the ignominy of being pounded by bananas and grapes, instead of artillery fire. During the war, he had escaped friendly fire, though Fiona's helpful criticism might be seen, now, as a new, benign form of that.

It was true: he was still back there, running—was there any lesser speed?—making his bargains, hedging his bets, endorphins in a race with adrenaline. He'd made it across the finish line, arms flung high not in surrender, but in victory: a lucky sprinter pulling the ribbon, instead of his intestines, with him.

Fiona was standing in the doorway. She had on a blue terry-cloth robe and silly slippers that made it look as if she'd plunged her feet into armadillos. She looked chagrined. She was backlit from the oil lamp, and with her enigmatic gaze she looked vaguely Madonna-ish: the real Madonna, not the dyed-blond money machine who dangled a cross.

Jimmy held out his hand. She walked forward, and took it. Jimmy said to her: "Nobody ran faster. Nobody did it better. *He* did it better long before the James Bond theme song. Nobody was faster, or braver, or more inventive than Carleyville. But everybody's only got a particular ration of luck, and to be perfectly honest, I think it might pretty much have run out in his case."

Fiona looked at Carleyville. "I apologize for losing my temper," she said.

"You could do me a favor," he said.

She looked surprised. "What?" she said.

"Do you know a good florist?"

She half-smiled, suspecting the beginning of some joke.

"I know it exasperates you to hear my notions about karma, but I owe somebody something, and until I deliver, my karma's going to stay jeopardized."

"Flowers?" she said.

"Right. Getting some roses to a woman I was supposed to send a fax to. A woman who works for the phone company."

"Who is that?" Jimmy said.

"Some woman who helped me out," Carleyville said.

"Well, actually, I have a catalogue from a place that delivers very nice flowers," Fiona said. She turned and left the room.

Good, Carleyville thought. That left only the question of what her name was . . . if he'd written it down . . . her name, her alias . . . and then the address to send them to. That would be something he could call and ask, since he wouldn't know where to begin looking for an old bill. It seemed destined not to work; he didn't require ESP to figure that out. "Scratch that," he said suddenly. "Scratch the phone lady. I know what to do."

Fiona reappeared with a catalogue. He flipped through, stopped when he saw an interesting flower. *Birds of Paradise;* maybe she'd see the significance in that. More amusing than roses. An improvement on the roses idea. A little pricey, but his credit card wasn't maxed out yet. He went to the phone—the miraculously working phone—and dialed the toll-free number. Twenty-four-hour flowers—great. Always open, like a hospital. Like a church.

He gave the operator the information: Birds of Paradise were to be sent to Christie Cooper in Billings, Montana. Her address (he fumbled) was written down on the top of a traffic ticket he'd gotten for parking approximately ten seconds too long at some voracious Pac Man parking meter, the day before he left. He'd jotted down her address just in case. On the off-chance he might decide to get in touch. In extracting his wallet, though, half of the inside of his pants pocket came with it. What next? Scarves? A rabbit? Adventure Kitty brushed against his leg from behind, and he kicked reflexively. The cat scrambled backwards, mewing loudly. He felt awful, actually apologized to the cat, but in moving toward her, the phone toppled to the floor. The cat dashed from the room, and Fiona rushed after her. Only Jimmy was still there, looking at him with willed composure.

He gave the operator his credit card information—good thing he'd never notified the credit card company to change his billing address—and felt much better, as if the bad black karma cloud had lifted, and lo and behold, it was only a gray day. "Sign it, 'Forgive me, Carleyville,'" he said softly.

"C as in calm?" the operator said.

Where What Gets into People Comes From

Lily Stark's mother had just said the facts of the murder were too horrible to repeat. But Lily's father insisted a story as awful as how Mr. Sam was slaughtered would teach Lily something about this world.

"I don't care about the world you even mean," Lily said. For a long time Lily had been looking for a cause for her wildness. She'd just found it. So she felt like she could tell her father off. And they were in front of neighbors, so he wouldn't slap her.

It was the day of Mr. Sam's funeral. The man *had* been murdered in the most degrading way imaginable. There were thirty or forty people standing around, some in line with the Starks, waiting for the coconut cake, others over with Methodist ladies in navy-blue crepe dresses pulling out their small handkerchiefs, giving condolences to the Cobbs' living children. There were men and boys in between, staring out, eating deviled eggs off glass plates. It was 1967, a small town in eastern North Carolina. Lily Stark was fifteen. She could hardly stand being alive.

Earlier that day at the Cobbs' plot, Lily had noticed the headstone of Mr. Sam's first son, Archie, who had died the day she was born. August 19th, 1952. When he was twenty-seven years old. Lily had lived next door to the Cobbs her whole life, but she had never known there was an Archie.

As soon as they had come back to the home, Lily had gone to ask Zachary, who had been hired for the day to serve the food for the mourners and wash up. Zachary worked freelance: bartending, butlering, throwing weddings and funerals. He knew things that went on in white people's houses. He said that when Archie Cobb got home from the war back in 1948, he took a job at a state hospital outside of town "to be near the dope." By and by Archie fell for a nurse, who saw his withered thigh where he'd found the veins. She wouldn't have him. "And he could not be consoled by the Lord or any person, so Archie took his mother's Nash to the Cliffs of the Neuse, drove off the edge, and crashed it

33

to tiny pieces. Died like that. It was August, over a hundred degrees."

"I was born then," Lily said.

"I know," Zachary said.

Archie must have had a second thought as his momma's car was tumbling down to the river, and he came flying out, spirit only, flesh doomed, and there was my mother, pregnant in that heat, sitting outside in a hammock only a few yards away from the Cobbs' back porch. Archie dove right into my girl baby body. I have his soul, so Lily thought.

If somebody had offered her morphine that spring, she would not have thought twice about trying it. Archie had been a reckless man. She herself was a reckless girl. He just wanted to get out. He hadn't made it. So it was Lily's destiny to leave: she'd known this since she was little. This even explained why her mother couldn't stand her—her mother always said the Cobbs were low. And Lily had no respect for the solid things in life, to hear her father tell it, but Lily could appreciate the flight of Archie's soul over town because of the terribleness of lost love, hoping to leave and looking to land at the same time. She adored the image of poor Archie overhead, she could even feel how the sky felt, the soft heat of the heavens. Then she told her father what she thought of the world he meant.

He said: "Listen to me. You mind what can be seen, touched, counted otherwise—"

"What?" she asked, not really caring to know, not anymore. "Why didn't anybody ever tell me about Archie Cobb, how he died? The day I was born? Nobody ever tells me what *I need to know.*"

"You want to end up like Sam Cobb? Or his son?"

Lily refused to see the parallel. She stood there, in line for the coconut cake. She knew what she knew. What mattered.

In eastern North Carolina the land appears at first too low and dull for any feature as remarkable as a deep river and a steep drop, so the Cliffs of the Neuse are a shock. But when you follow the folds of the plain from where the Neuse River starts to its destination— the Cape Fear, the Atlantic—it's clear that what at first seems overly dramatic for that landscape in truth cannot be helped.

Fayton was a town like other towns on that plain, so small all kinds of people were close at hand. There were twelve houses total on the block of Winter between Park and Locust, one mansion, several proud Queen Annes with towers, and the rest little houses, like the Starks' place and the Cobbs'. People lived in each other's porches and backyards and parlors then. There was some vigilance, but sooner or later every secret saw the light.

Lily's father's house and the Cobbs' right beside it started out in the twenties as plain bungalows, white frame and mute, raised on piers with seven stairs up the front and thick half-brick pillars that supported the roof of the porch. They each had two gumball trees in their yards, and across the street from both of them were the brick walls of finer houses with generous gardens, which were opened every spring so everyone else could peep into them, and wish.

When he was young, Sam Cobb was slender but muscled, dark, considered handsome. In high school in the early twenties, he liked to act in plays. Eventually he became a salesman. He bought the house on Winter after he married in 1921. This was during the days when people thought the town of Fayton would amount to something: a ten-story building was put up, two five-and-dimes were built, then a hotel with an imposing lobby. There was a bus station, a train station with a train that came into it and left for Danville, Virginia, and three cab companies. Mr. Sam was excitable, but he was a working man. Up to a certain point in his life, he was an Elk, a Methodist, a fair earner, a charmer, a good father.

Mrs. Geneva, his wife, was a practical nurse, a kind woman with a sweet tooth, stout, and a great baker. Her specialty was big white cakes. She used boiled icing, the kind that hardens and makes a cake a monument. The hair about her head was cotton candy. There were burst veins in cheeks. Archie was Mrs. Geneva's first son, born 1925, and the best looking. His hair was dark and slightly curly. His chin had a dimple. Raleigh, who came much later, in 1937, was stout, after his mother's side. His whole life he would never get rid of the name Rolley. The third boy, Jimbo, was born during the Second War, 1944. Wild red hair. Soon as he was walking, all of Winter Street said there was something wrong with him.

In 1954, when he was seventeen, after his brother died, after his daddy set out upon his second life, Rolley Cobb eloped with

Isabel Odom, runner-up to homecoming queen, who was pregnant. Her people were upstanding, but they'd lost everything in the thirties. Everybody still thought she had married down. So she got Rolley to make her promises.

Rolley's worst flaws were his weakness for his mother's cakes and the fact he went after his living brother with whatever was near at hand—a belt, a big shoe, a plank of wood. He believed in the beating. Jimbo had to be tamed, it was true—anything in the world might get into him. The boy shot at birds with BBs from his own little blind in the backyard, and he missed, killing squirrels, terrorizing the neighborhood dogs and cats. He came sneaking around after Lily Stark and her friends in the yard with a garter snake dangling from the handle of a hoe. Mrs. Geneva never intervened, on either side, Rolley or Jimbo. That was what living with men was like, she said. Stop them from one thing they will do something else, pretend it is the opposite, but it will be just as bad.

Through the early years, the fifties, due to her father's efforts and her mother's demands, Lily Stark's family's bungalow took on dormers, and wrought iron like people had in New Orleans so it didn't match Mrs. Geneva's exactly anymore. Her mother got creeper with little leaves to cover the grassless yard because she said she couldn't stand the sad sight of that white East Carolina soil. It wasn't even soil. It was sand.

All this time the Cobbs' got shabbier. It sorely needed paint, repairs to the porch. But it turned out that the fact that the two houses looked less and less alike had no effect whatsoever upon Sam Cobb and his ways.

Long after midnight one night when she was four years old, Lily came downstairs for water and saw the front door was open. Rolley Cobb was standing just beyond the screen under the yellow bug light. It was a summer without air-conditioning, only fans. The Starks didn't keep their windows closed or their doors locked. Nobody did. Lily's father finally let Rolley in, but still for a while they stood there looking at something, not doing anything. Rolley's striped pajamas were turned over at the waist. She could see the exhausted elastic. He had stubble on his round face, and ashy hair that fell into his wide blue eyes. Rolley had moles. All the Cobbs had moles.

Eventually Lily put her head around to see what the two men saw: on her mother's slipcovered couch against the wall lay Sam Cobb half-curled up in a ball, his head thrown back at an angle, his mouth open, snot puddled on his upper lip. Her mother was going to be furious, furious. Rolley, who was large so people assumed he was strong, assumed he could play football well, for example, when the fact was he couldn't, made the first move. He lifted his daddy's head, then reached under the arms and dragged him down, causing the body to unfurl on her mother's wall-to-wall carpet. Mr. Sam would wake up, Lily hoped. She came out from hiding, and her daddy didn't see her, but Rolley looked right at her. He was in awful pain, she could see that. Rolley was married, but he was not a real daddy like Lily's, he was not one who had been through the war, seen action in the Pacific, suffered, bled, saved people's lives and had his life saved. Rolley didn't have a store like Lily's daddy did. Rolley was a teenage father with barely a job and a father in the wrong living room, and he lived in a tired house the shame of the neighborhood, and in his face even Lily could see how terrible he felt even to exist.

Finally Lily's father stepped forward and took Mr. Sam's limp ankles. With Lily's father moving forwards, Rolley going backwards, they carried Mr. Sam, whose arms hung down on his sides, across the porch, down the stairs, over her mother's creeper, across the Cobbs' dirt yard. At the other end Mrs. Geneva was holding the door open. For all the disturbance nobody said very much. The next morning Lily's father said Mr. Sam didn't care anymore about who he was or what he was, didn't give a damn, always had been a dreamer. Now he was worse.

After Dora, Isabel had a son, Beverly, people called Bit. They still all lived in that house. Rolley went to work selling cars.

In 1958 Lily's mother hired one of the brilliant gardeners who worked across the street to set in rows of bulbs in her backyard that took turns blooming, and azaleas, and behind them flowering plum trees. They built an arbor for grapes. In March, Isabel invited herself over with Dora and Bit to sit on a blanket, and Lily joined them. It felt like everybody's garden. Lily was conscious of spring, of the beauty. She said to herself, I am alive. I am six years old.

Isabel seemed proud Rolley had started moonlighting doing home additions, small jobs. He paid a crew to paint his parents' house. Crisp, sharp white. Green shutters. Wood houses were white then; it was like a law. You didn't have anything too grand, too gaudy; it might make people covet. Rolley was finally making some money.

When she was about eight, Lily started wondering about God, what He could possibly have been thinking. Her father's father had been a preacher, a poor man, some people said crazy. Her mother said crazy. Her father always took her to church. Her mother wouldn't go. Lily was bored by most of the ceremonies and the sermon, but there was something about praying.

Every so often Mr. Sam would still stumble into the Starks' in the middle of the night, and Lily's daddy would call next door. When Rolley came over, that was all Lily saw of Rolley. He was selling cars or he was doing renovations those days. Eventually Rolley put in a walkway of slate around the side of the Cobbs' house leading to the rear, and installed a light. After that, Mr. Sam slept it off on the back porch, not in the Cobbs' house proper. He mostly stopped showing up at the Starks'.

When Lily was nine, Rolley took a few lots at the edge of Fayton, next to nothing, cheap land, other side of the train tracks, and built three little houses on speculation. They were all alike, with choppy yards and few trees. People bought them right up.

Mr. Sam took up drinking with white cab drivers whose records were so bad they could only work for the colored cab company. He went with the men who ran numbers and moonshine and made deliveries for the homegrown gangsters, men left over from Prohibition, white men and Indian men and light-colored colored men who wore boots and hats even inside a store. Sometimes they wore their old striped suits from the thirties, so they looked like people in the TV show *The Untouchables*. Everybody had a TV by that time, although some had been quite reluctant. Many said it was a fad and would pass, not to take it to heart.

Lily started walking to the library by herself when she was nine. It was in an old house way downtown. She read about religions there. She liked the Christian heresies. She read she lived in a fallen world. The ones who made it hadn't got it right, and they were falling or fallen, too, and terribly sorry about it. She could see that. She read how everything has its cause in the soul's life. She practically memorized *The Encyclopedia of Superstition:* in

Bohemia when a person is dying they open a window. Let the ghost get where it's going. In the Baltic countries it is widely believed that animals always see the spirits of the dead.

The fall she was ten, Lily could hear the Cobbs arguing if she lay awake at night. Isabel wanted to find a bigger house. Everybody could move, Mrs. Geneva, and Jimbo, the whole crowd. Mrs. Geneva said absolutely no. In the end they didn't do it. Isabel was furious. Rolley had to make it up to everybody. He bought his mother a dog, Cookie, whom Lily soon fell in love with. He promised Isabel a new brick house, just for her, himself, and the kids, in a subdivision he was going to start, out across the highway. Everything spanking. He said he would borrow the money. Become a real developer. Then they would move. Isabel said if he didn't keep his word she wasn't sure what she would do.

Christmas 1963, Mrs. Cobb sent over three pounds of pecan divinity in a tin, so Lily's father said they were calling on them. Her mother wouldn't go. Nothing was good enough that year for her mother. She'd gotten a Cadillac and didn't like driving it.

For a long time at the Cobbs', it was just Rolley and Lily's daddy, and Mrs. Geneva and Isabel and the children, and of course Jimbo there impersonating a human being, Lily thought, a short clip-tie on, a jacket with the sleeves too short. Jimbo was a topic all over Fayton by that time. He kept failing tenth grade, held the record, for one thing. He showed up in the middle of the night in people's yards, howling, sticking his face in their windows.

It was as if nobody thought of Mr. Sam as missing until he appeared in the archway by the dining room. He made a slow, tentative entrance. He had on a shirt and a coat as if he'd been to church—Lily knew he hadn't. He began looking around and saying sweet things to his grandchildren, whom he reached for, but didn't truly touch. In the center was the tree with so many gifts Rolley had bought underneath. Mr. Sam said nothing, but there was a place for him on the couch, as far away from the tree as possible, and he seemed grateful for it. Mr. Sam took a chocolate Millionaire Lily's father had brought and chewed it with his mouth open, the way even older people did tobacco. Seeing Mr. Sam and how his clothes hung off of him made Lily notice Rolley had become a real fat man. Lily had heard at Sunday School that Mr.

Sam was drinking with the hands from the bright leaf tobacco warehouses who came through in August. He drank with oyster shuckers and flounder cleaners from the fish market, with men who worked around the bus station, which still did a fair business.

The train had stopped stopping in Fayton, but Lily figured this out that following summer: you could get on a bus in Fayton and get off the very same one in New York City. It started in Savannah as a local, and it went all the way. After Richmond, it was even an express. But whenever Lily charted it out, made plans to run away, something told her it couldn't be. Fayton was the sort of town, when you were in it, there was no way out. People you met believed this even though they would agree a person might leave if you asked them twice. The truth made no difference in the long run, though, to what people believed. No difference at all.

In seventh grade, she made a new plan. Boarding school. She was rough, she needed finishing. They weren't going to send her, so she could shut up, her mother said. I'll finish you, her mother said.

Rolley and Isabel were building their dream home by then, something other people thought was a marvel. Lily's mother was thinking about one, too, and on Sundays they'd drive out into the country, and look at land to buy.

The year Lily became a teenager, something went right. The Army took Jimbo. After that Rolley and Isabel and Bit and Dora moved across the highway, into their mansion, which was up on a clay rise in Rolley's new subdivision. People were amazed by it: a huge brick negotiation between a ranch and a Georgian with a wide yard and large rooms all on one floor. Lily went to see it. The kitchen had thick-doored cabinets, all milled and built up and stained, not painted. There were exposed brick walls in the den, and a new sort of wood floor, plastic-shiny, and central air conditioners, not in the windows, outside the house. The inside Formica was inspiring in its way, as was the sunken pit for watching the TV. Dora told Lily her grandmother couldn't ever leave that house in town because she was worried her grandpa wouldn't find his way home if she moved. Dora thought this was a secret.

After six months, the Army sent Jimbo back. Mrs. Geneva took him in. She had Cookie, she said. He'd never do anything to his mother. He was worse than ever, wrecking cars, spending time with dangerous people. When he was bored he ran outside naked in the daytime holding his BB gun, doing a rebel yell: it took a lot to get Lily's attention by the time she was in eighth grade. She went over and told Mrs. Geneva to get him to stop. Mrs. Geneva's lips trembled a little—she was trying to keep from smiling. Lily could not imagine what was in Mrs. Geneva's mind, behind her little teeth. Rolley tried putting Jimbo in an apartment, but Jimbo came home to his mother after a few weeks. What was he going to eat?

Lily heard tales from the wild boys she french-kissed and went half the way with. Mr. Sam was riding the rails, camping out with the hobos, carrying on. As far as Lily knew, Mrs. Geneva never filed a report on her husband. She never kicked him out formally. She never refused to let him come to his hammock.

Once, Mr. Sam stayed gone for two months straight. Then, it was a morning in January, when Lily went to get Cookie to take a walk, that the old man shocked her, more a ghost by then than a person, nearly bald and long-jawed, sleeping on the floor of the back porch. She sat there, listening to his thready breathing, watching him so long he started to look innocent. She was fourteen then, nearly grown. She remembered him that way, after.

When Mr. Sam woke he saw Rolley's workmen fixing the door screen. He told them to go to hell. What was the use, he said. He always cursed his son's crews. Nevertheless, piece by piece, Rolley had completely renovated the exterior of the house. He had destroyed the original front porch on piers and lowered it to the ground. Instead of the half-brick California bungalow pillars, he put up plain, stained wood columns. He had painted the house Williamsburg green, which was daring. He paved the entry area with flat aged bricks, and sealed it. The whole front looked rather stately. Even Lily's mother admitted it: Rolley had managed to make Mrs. Geneva's house seem older, and also newer, and larger, and more imposing, than Lily's house. But when you were inside, nothing had changed: Mrs. Geneva's afghans and her old kitchen stove.

That next summer Lily's mother announced they were really going to get away from that place. She had two decorators, an architect. Start over from scratch. A new life. Where? Lily asked, full of hope. They'd go out in the country, away from it all, into the most expensive subdivision. Moving, which everybody was doing, was a piss-poor excuse for getting out, she said to her mother. Her mother told her to get out of her sight. Let me go, Lily said. Let me go really go.

The next April, Jimbo had got a girl pregnant. She was gritting her teeth and marrying him, so Jimbo took a job banging nails into two-by-fours for his rich brother. Mrs. Geneva had found out she had diabetes—she had to stop baking. Cookie barked at things that weren't there, because he was blind, people thought.

Mr. Sam had been away one of his extra-long stretches. It was a day right after Easter, around noon, that Cookie, who was sleeping on the new brick front porch where it was cool, suddenly woke up and went around the back of the house in the waddling way he had been walking lately. He started barking at Mr. Sam's empty hammock. Mrs. Geneva opened the door for him. But Cookie didn't come into the kitchen to eat, his custom. Neither Mrs. Geneva nor Lily could get him off the subject of the hammock for the longest time.

Two days later the police found Samuel Cobb's body in a warehouse in the oldest part of downtown, near the abandoned train station. His companion had risen up and beat Sam Cobb about the head until he died.

This took many blows, with a heavy weapon. When people heard the story, what was peculiar to them was that Mr. Sam hadn't run home, when he was only twelve blocks from his own house. The coroner said he'd been awake for the first five or ten hits. And he was dehydrated, but not drunk.

Sam Cobb's companion left him there to die, in that makeshift encampment where they were living to drink. He took to the rails. They found him in Wilmington by the docks. Every name he gave was an alias.

The weapon was one detail Lily's father held on to. He came back to the murder, that night, after the funeral, after Lily had already told him off once, demanding to hear about Archie the suicide. Her father said the murder was evidence of how far a man could fall, and evidence of this sort, that was ubiquitous when he was a boy, had become rarer and rarer in those days. This was the sixties, and everybody was losing their way. Mr. Sam's murder illustrated that ruin could be just blocks away from you—her father wanted Lily to see this point. Something had gone so terribly wrong with her. He'd worked hard to keep misery from her, but that had drawn her to it: she was talking to crazy people, seeing the wrong boys, smoking cigarettes, being moody and lazy, planning to run off soon as she could.

She didn't need her father to serve her some misery, she said. Everything she saw in Fayton by then broke her heart. Like that girl going ahead and marrying Jimbo. Everybody, everybody, desperate to get out, incapable of leaving, of even seeing over the lip of this tiny, binding world.

Look at it, how bad it can get: a once handsome and lively man with a wife and three sons ends up killed the way someone might kill a cockroach, with the same sort of everyday and kitchen sort of instrument, a rather female instrument. The humiliation. It was a touchstone, a cautionary tale. Lily needed a dose of reality. Here it was. The man gave up, he gave in, he was swallowed. It can happen.

Lily said to her father, "Do you know what was in his mind?"

"His mind was gone," her father said. "What difference does his mind make?"

"He sat there for it. The coroner said so," she said.

"Look at it. In the face. The man failed at life," he said.

"How do you know?" she said.

"You have to have something to live for," he said.

"But all of this you put store by is going asunder sometime. The vain things, things of this world. Mr. Sam knew that. You made me read that."

"You going to make that drunk a hero? Wise?"

"There must be something else," Lily said.

"Well, what is it? What is it?" her father said.

"Was everybody wrong before, to say there was something more?" she said. "What about your daddy?"

Her father looked at her as if she'd shot him.

The day Sam Cobb was going to die, the man who was with him asked for three dollars and twenty-eight cents for liquor. Sam had two dollars and a nickel. The man decided to take it out on him, the one dollar and twenty-three cents, so he picked up a cast-iron coffee pot lying there, and he hit him, again and again.

Early on, the pain got to be too much, so Sam let himself fly right out of his body, out a window, it felt like. He sort of watched the pain as it continued to come to him as a neutral phenomenon, a feeling of a certain density and shape and breadth, but the fact that he was being hurt was something he couldn't identify with anymore. Instead he saw his second son, Rolley, his house up on that red knoll above the highway, attracting other big houses, and money like a magnet. And he saw Jimbo, a baby coming now, would he finally get himself attached to this earth, to practical life. He took a good long stare into that baby's face, the one who hadn't been born yet, Jimbo's child inside that poor girl. He tried to bless him. It occurred to Sam Cobb he was dying then, because he could see many things quite well, past and future, and he knew that in ways his family would be relieved to see him go, and he didn't fault them for that, since he had failed so utterly, for so very long, to show his love for them by any other means.

With every one of the later blows, he saw a wider pattern, the Starks next door, the fussy creeper in their yard, that house away from it all they had decided to build. He saw all the other people in Fayton—how the ones who were different were so close to the ones who weren't. He could hear Cookie barking then, loudly, full of mourning. The second to last one he saw was his wife, the light behind her, standing in the kitchen door, which opened into that house Rolley had so cruelly disguised. So Sam let it be back the way it started in the twenties, just a bungalow, modest and white, Geneva in the middle of everything, the source of everything, there holding one of her high white stiff cakes. And then he turned around and saw something more, and beautiful, a place completely hidden from the ordinary world. He hadn't expected this, but soon as he saw it, he was sure it was where his first and dearest son had tried to coax the morphine to take him. Archie had made an error—it had never been a judgment. A glimpse of this, and Sam let that go, finally, finally, finally, that burden he'd borne so long, his belief that his son had thrown away the life Sam had given him, because he found it worth so little. And then Mr. Sam paused, he had to pause, because of the sweetness, the sorrow, the relief—

These days, Rolley's project is complete. To find the residents of Fayton you have to circle around the edges, and seek out cul-desacs, and hidden grounds of his subdivisions, which form a defense against the old town, the abandoned, rotten parts. Hardly anybody, of any class or race, lives downtown anymore.

Lily Stark turned out to be exactly what her father didn't want her to be. Except she was not a suicide, but she thought of it in her twenties. She tried something else, and then something else, and then something else. Nothing practical, usually nothing expected. She turned her back, she invented herself new more than once. She never could take the tangible life very seriously, even while she longed for comfort. In part, she had been happy.

When she got the call and had to go home, she knew she would grieve, but she didn't know it would feel like drowning. She kept remembering the way her father's face fell that day they buried Mr. Sam, the day she heard about Archie.

"You just want an escape," her father said to her finally after he recovered from looking like he'd been shot.

That was true. He had that right. "And what do you really want? Why do you always turn it into things?"

"Your mother wants them," he said.

"You have spent your whole life on them," she said. "Every hour."

"Why are you so cruel?" he said. "What made you like this?"

"You," she said.

Her father said nothing.

"Talk to me."

He wouldn't.

She slammed the door to her room, to contemplate the soul of Archie Cobb the suicide.

After the ceremony she went back and stood in front of those two old bungalows on Winter Street, both of them faded, with peeling paint, windows broken, no grass, no creeper in the yards, and she remembered how she felt like dying for winning that day with her father, but it had been her father who died first.

Someone who came to the funeral told her that lately a few of the people who live in the developments have been saying something must be missing, maybe they should go back and live downtown. Maybe they could be inside each other's lives, and dwell in each other's secrets, share each other's living rooms and gardens, the way people say they used to do. As if they were kin. She recognized him. He was Jimbo's boy, a sane, and decent man, impossibly.

"Maybe we shouldn't have ever left," he said.

"There never was any leaving, never is," she said, but he didn't understand her, because she was speaking of her dreams: when they were serious she was always in Fayton, even though she was forty-five years old, with her own history, she was still in that garden, where whatever she was before she was born came into her girl baby body. She was with her family or with Mrs. Geneva or Cookie or Dora or Mr. Sam or Rolley or Zachary or with the wild boys she used to try to get to love her. Just the night before, Archie had appeared to her. He was hovering above, invisibly tethered to the garden, which he gazed upon with a longing that was the last thing he'd ever thought he'd feel, so it held him. He gestured toward the lands beyond the town's limits, the Cliffs, the rushing Neuse, the Cape Fear, the ocean. Then he came so close he touched her shoulder, turned her around. What he showed her then startled her, woke her up: both their fathers staring back at them, inconsolable and amazed.

Think of England

On the evening of D-day, the pub is packed. It's a close June
night in the Welsh hills, with the threat of thunder. The
radios of the village cough with static. The Quarryman's Arms,
with the tallest aerial for miles around, is a scrum of bodies, all
waiting to hear the Prime Minister's broadcast.

There's a flurry of shouted orders leading up to the news at six.
Sarah, behind the lounge bar, pulls pint after pint, leaning back
against the pumps so that the beer froths in the glass. She sets the
shaker out for those who want to sprinkle salt on their drinks to
melt the foam. Behind her, down the short connecting passage to
the right, her boss, Jack Jones, has his hands full with the regulars
in the public bar. At five to six by the battered grandfather clock
in the corner, he calls back to the lounge for Sarah to "warm 'er
up." She tops off the pint she's pouring, steps back from the
counter and up onto the old pop crate beneath the till. She has to
stretch for the Bakelite knob on the wireless, one foot lifting off
the crate. Behind her, over the calls for service, she hears a few
low whistles. The machine clicks into life, first a low hum, then a
whistle of its own, finally, as if from afar, the signature tune of the
show. The dial lights up like a distant sunset. The noise around
her subsides at once, and it's as if she has stilled it. She turns
round and for a second looks down into the crowd of faces staring up at the glowing radio.

The men, soldiers mostly in the lounge, sip their beers slowly
during the broadcast, making them last. She looks from face to
face, but they're all gazing off, concentrating on Churchill's shuffling growl. The only ones to catch her eyes are Harry Hitch,
who's mouthing something over and over—"my usual," she
finally understands—and Colin, who winks broadly from across
the room. Colin's one of the sappers who've been working on the
new base they're building near the old holiday camp in the valley.
They've been bringing some much-needed business to the Arms
for the last month, and for the last week Sarah and Colin have

been sweethearts. Tonight she's agreed to slip off with him after work, a date made before D-day, which somehow feels destined now. She hears the English word in her mind, "sweethearts," likes the way it sounds. She listens to Churchill, the voice of England, imagines him saying it gravely—"Sweetheart"—swallows a smile. She concentrates on the speech, thinks of the men on the beaches, and feels herself fill with emotion for her soldier, like a slow glass of Guinness. There's a thickening in her throat, a brimming pressure behind her eyes. It's gratitude, she feels, mixed with pride and hope, and she wonders if together this blend amounts to love.

The broadcast ends, and the noise builds again in the pub. It's not quite a cheer—Churchill's speech has been sternly cautious—but there's a sense of excitement, kept just in check, and a kind of relief. The talk has been about an invasion all spring, and finally it's here, the beginning of the end. Everyone is smiling at the soldiers, even the locals clustered behind the public bar, and calling congratulations. Sarah steps up on the crate and turns the dial until it picks up faint dance music from the Savoy in London. There's a sound like applause and, looking round, she sees with delight that it's literally a clapping of backs. There's a rush for the bar again. People want to buy the men drinks. They're only sappers—road menders, ditch diggers, brickies—but they're in uniform, and who knows when they could be going "over there." Suddenly, and without doing a thing, they're heroes, indistinguishable in their uniforms from all the other fighting men. And they believe it, too. Sarah can see it in Colin's face, the glow of it. She stares at him, and it's as if she's seeing him for the first time; he's so glossily handsome, like the lobby card of a film star.

The crowd in the lounge is three deep and thirsty, and she pulls pints until her arm aches, but when she turns to ring up the orders she sees that the public bar is emptying out. She wonders if it's the sense of it being someone else's party that's sending the farmers home or just that they have to be up early tomorrow. She glimpses her father, Arthur, shouldering his way to the door, shrugging his mack on over the frayed dark suit (Sunday-best before she was born) and collarless shirt he wears when out with the flock. He jams his cap on his head, fitting it to the dull red line across his brow, and gives her a nod as he goes, but no more.

She's been working here for almost a year now, since she turned sixteen, but in all that time she has never once served him on his occasional visits. He sticks to the public bar, where most of the local regulars are served by Jack. It's become the Welsh-speaking half of the pub, while she, with her good schoolroom English, serves soldiers and the motley assortment of new arrivals in the lounge. She would stand him a pint or two if he let her (Jack wouldn't mind), although it occurs to her that this is why her father steers clear. They could do with saving even the few pennies he spends on beer—money is why she's working here at all—but of course that's why he barely acknowledges her. It's not that he's ungrateful, she knows. She's been in charge of the housekeeping money in the old biscuit tin, ever since her mother died three years ago, but only since she started working has he shown her the books, the bank account, the mortgage deeds. It's a mark of respect, his only way of offering thanks. Of course, she had her own ideas of how bad things were all along, but guessing and knowing are different and now she knows; the war is holding them up—the national subsidy and the demand for woolen uniforms. Her father is a proud man—prouder in hard times than good, she thinks—and she's grateful that poverty in wartime is a virtue, something to be proud of. It reminds her of the epic tales he tells of the great strike, though he was only a boy then. But she wonders sometimes, also, what it'll be like when the war is over.

It crosses her mind that the same thought has sent him out into the night early. Still, she's not sorry to see him go, not with Colin here, too. She doesn't want to face any awkward questions, and she doesn't want to tell the truth; that she's stepping out with an Englishman. She catches sight of Colin through the crowd, dipping his shoulders to throw a dart. Beneath the national betrayal is an obscurer one to do with her pride at taking her mother's place beside her father; a sense of being unfaithful somehow.

Pretty soon the pub is down to just soldiers and diehards. She can hear the Welsh voices behind her, wafting over with the smell of pipe tobacco. They're quieter tonight, slower, sluggish like a summer stream. The talk for once isn't politics. This is a nationalist village, passionately so. It's what holds the place together. Like a cracked and glued china teapot, Sarah thinks. The strike, all of forty-five years ago, almost broke the town, and it's taken something shared to stick back together the families of men who returned to work and those who stayed out. The Quarryman's Arms is the old strikers' pub—the hooks for their tankards are still in the ceiling over the bar—a bitter little irony since most of its regulars, the sons of strikers, are sheep farmers now. Their fathers weren't taken back at the quarry after the strike, blacklisted from the industry. For a generation the families of strikers and scabs didn't talk, didn't marry, didn't pray together. Even today the sons of scabs are scarce in the Arms, only venturing up the High Street from *their* local, the Prince of Wales, for fiercely competitive darts and snooker matches (games the soldiers have monopolized since they arrived).

To Sarah it seems like so much tosh, especially now that the quarry is cutting back and barely one in five local men work there. But the old people all seem to agree that the village would have died if not for the resurgence of nationalism in the twenties and thirties reminding them of what they had in common, reminding them of their common enemy: the English. Dragoons were stationed here to keep order during the strike, and in the public bar the sappers are still called "occupiers." It's half-joking, Sarah knows, but only half. The nationalist view of the war is that it's an English war, imperialist, capitalist, like the Great War that Jack fought in and from which he still carries a limp. But tonight the success of the invasion has stilled such talk. Even the laughter of the locals—raucous, intended to be heard in the lounge by the English, to make them understand that they are the butt of jokes even if the language of the jokes themselves is beyond them—is muted. The Welsh nurse their beer, suck their pipes, and steal glances down the passage to where Sarah is serving.

It thrills her, oddly, to stand between the two groups of men, listening to their talk about each other. For she knows the soldiers, clustered around the small round tables, crammed shoulder to shoulder into the narrow wooden settles, talk about the Welsh, too; complain about the weather, joke about the language, whisper about the girls. Tonight, they lounge around, legs splayed, collars open, like so many conquerors.

Sarah wonders if the locals are as filled with excitement as she is, just too proud to admit it. She yearns to be British tonight of all nights. She's proud of her Welshness, of course, in the same half-conscious way she's shyly proud of her looks, but she's impatient with all the talk of past glories. Her father is a staunch nationalist. He's never forgiven Churchill for Tonypandy. But she's bored by all the history. Some part of her knows that nationalism is part and parcel of provincialism. This corner of North Wales feels a long way from the center of life, from London or Liverpool or, heavens, America. And nationalism is a way of putting it back in the center, of saying that what's here is important enough. It's a redrawing of the boundaries of what's worthwhile. And this really is what Sarah wants, what she dimly suspects they all want. To be important, to be the center of attention, not isolated. Which is why she's so excited, as she moves through the crowd collecting empties, stacking them up, glass on glass in teetering piles, by the presence of the soldiers, by the relocation of the BBC Light Program a few years ago, by the museum treasures that are stored in the old quarry workings, even by the school-age evacuees. They're all refugees from the Blitz, but she doesn't care. It's as if the world is coming to her.

And she knows others feel this. The sappers are a case in point. No one quite knows who the base they're building is for, but speculation is rife. The village boys, who haunt the camp, watching the sappers from the tree line and sneaking down to explore the building at dusk, are praying for the glamour of commandos. There's talk of Free French, Poles, even alpine troops training in the mountains for the invasion of Norway. Jack is hoping for Yanks and their ready cash. American flyers, waiting to move on to their bases in East Anglia, do occasionally drop in for a drink. But they're always faintly disappointing. Each time they're spotted sauntering around Caernarvon, getting their photos taken under the Eagle Tower, rumors start that it's James Stewart or Tyrone Power, one of those gallant film stars. But it never is. For the most part the Yanks are gangly, freckle-faced farm boys, insufferably polite (in the opinions of the local lads) with their suck-up "sirs" and "ma'ams." Once, one of them, a tail-gunner from "Kentuck," pressed a clumsily wrapped parcel of brown paper and string on Sarah, and when she opened it she saw it was a torn parachute. There was enough silk for a petticoat and two slips. He'd been drinking shyly in a corner for hours, summoning up his courage. She was worried he'd get into trouble, tried to give the bundle back, but he spread his hands, backed away. "Miss," he told her, and he said it with such drunken earnestness, she pulled the parcel back, held it to her chest. He seemed to be hunting for the words. "You...," he began. "Why, you're what we're fighting for!" She's dreamed of him since, getting shot down, bailing out, hanging in the night sky, sliding silently towards the earth, under a canopy of petticoats.

She wonders if Colin will give her a gift before he leaves. She watches him lean against one of his fellows, cocking his head, as the other whispers something in his ear. Colin shakes his head, grins beneath his mustache like Clark Gable, taps the side of his nose. She could get him to tell her who the camp is for, she thinks, but she won't. Somehow it would be unpatriotic to ask the sappers themselves what they're building: disloyal to Britain (they all know the slogans—walls have ears, loose lips, etc.); but also more obscurely disloyal to Wales. It wouldn't do to give the English an excuse to call the Welsh unpatriotic. Only the Welsh, it occurs to her, are allowed to declare themselves that. But whatever the purpose of the new camp, with its long, low barracks and staunch wire fences, there's been a sense in the village over the last month of being part of something, of the preparations for the invasion (although it's odd, she thinks, that here's the invasion itself, and the camp not occupied). Colin, though, has told her, during one of their hurried trysts behind the pub, that the work's nearly over. "Just waiting for our marching orders, and then we're off out of it."

She looks at him now leaning against one of the stained wood beams, chatting with his mates, the dark, cropped hair at the nape of his neck, where it shows almost velvety below his cap. He laughs at something and throws a glance over his shoulder to see if she's heard, and they grin at each other. She sees other heads turn towards her, and she looks away quickly. She is wearing one of her parachute silk slips tonight, beneath her long wool skirt; she likes the feel of it against her legs, the way it slides when she stretches for a glass, while the soldiers are watching her.

The moment is interrupted by Harry Hitch. "Girlie?" he croons. "Another round, eh? There's a good girl." He's trying to wind her up, and she ignores him as she pours. Harry's with the BBC. He's a star, if you can believe it, a comic with the Light Program. "Auntie," as she's learned to call the corporation from Harry and the others, has a transmitter tower on the hillside above the quarry; the radio technicians discovered the Arms when they were building the tower, and they've been coming up of an evening with their "chums" ever since, six or eight of them squeezed into a battered, muddy Humber.

She sets a scotch before him and then a pint, what Harry calls a "little and large." The glasses sit side by side like a double act.

"Nice atmosphere, tonight," Harry is saying. "Lovely ambulance." It's a joke of some kind, Sarah knows, but when no one laughs, Harry chuckles to himself. "I kill meself," he says. He's already half-gone, she sees, must have had a skinful even before he arrived. Sarah has listened to Harry on the radio, laughed at his skits, but in the flesh he's a disappointment, a miserable, moody drunk, skinny and pinched-looking, not the broad avuncular bloke she imagined from his voice.

"Ta," he tells her, raising his glass. "See your lot are celebrating tonight, too."

"My lot?" she asks absently, distracted by a wink from Colin.

"The Welsh," he says, with a slight slur. "The Taffs, the Taffys, the Boyos!" He gets louder with each word, not shouting, just projecting, and as soon as he has an audience he's off as if on cue. "Here, you know we English have trouble with your spelling. All them *l*'s and *y*'s. But did you hear the one about Taffy who joined the RAF? He meant to join the NAAFI, but his spelling let him down." Sarah only smiles, but there's a smattering of laughter at the bar. Harry half turns on his stool, rocking slightly, to take in the soldiers, their shining faces. "You like that one, eh? On his first day the quartermaster hands him his parachute and Taff wants to know what happens if it don't open and the quartermaster, he tells him: 'That's what's called jumping to a conclusion.'"

More laughter, not much but enough, Sarah sees with a sinking feeling, for a few more heads to turn. She catches the eye of Mary Munro, the actress. "Here we go," Mary mouths, rolling her eyes. Mary's thing is accents, she can do dozens of them. Once she even did Sarah's just for a laugh, and listening at home, Sarah blushed to the tips of her ears, more flattered than embarrassed.

"Oh, but they're brave," Harry is going. "The Taffs. Oh yes. Did you hear about that Welsh kamikaze, though? Got the VC for twenty successful missions. But he's worried, you know. His luck can't hold. Sure he'll cop it one day, so he goes to the chaplain and tells him what he wants on his headstone." He drops into a thick Welsh accent. "'Here lies an honest man and a Welshman.' And the chaplain says he doesn't know what it's like in Wales, but in England it's one bloke to a hole."

The men are all laughing now, stopping their conversations to listen. The snooker players straighten up from the table, lean on their cues, like shepherds on crooks. "Come on, Harry," Mary calls. "It's supposed to be our night off." But she's booed down by the soldiers, and Harry rolls on unfazed.

"Reminds me of the tomb of the Welsh Unknown Soldier. Didn't know there was a Welsh Unknown Soldier, did you?" He winks at Sarah. "Nice inscription on that one an' all: 'Here lies Taff So-and-So, well-known as a drunk, unknown as a soldier.'"

"Takes one to know one," someone heckles from the public bar behind Sarah, but the delivery is halting, the accent broad and blunt. It's water off a duck's back to Harry.

"'Well-known drunk, unknown soldier,'" Harry repeats happily. "That reminds me," he cries and gestures for Sarah to refill him.

"Haven't you had enough?" She's aware of the silence in the bar behind her, the listening locals.

"As the sheep said to the Welshman?"

"Very funny," she tells him.

"Oh, you Welsh girls," he says, wagging his finger. "You know what they say about Welsh girls, dontcha, girlie?"

"No," she says, suddenly abashed.

"Give over, Harry." It's Mary again, her voice, lower this time, warning.

"'Sonly a bit of fun. And she wants to know, don't she? You want to know?"

Sarah is silent.

"Well, what they say is, you can't kiss a Welsh girl unexpectedly." He pauses for a second to drink. When he looks up his lips are wet. "Only sooner than she thought!" There's a stillness in the bar. Harry shoots his cuffs, studies his watch theatrically. "I can wait," he says.

He turns back, and Sarah throws his scotch in his face.

There's a second of shock, and then Harry licks his lips with his big pink tongue, and the laughter goes off like a gun. There's a cheer from the public bar, and she's conscious of Jack standing in the passage behind her.

"Steady on," Colin is shouting over the din. He's shouldered his way to the bar. "You all right?" he asks Sarah, and she nods.

"No hard feelings," Harry is telling her. He holds out his hand for a shake, but when she reaches for it, he raises his empty glass and tells her, "Ta very much. I'd love one."

"Come on, mate," Colin says. "Leave it now." He lays a big hand on the dented brass bar rail in front of Sarah.

Harry looks at his hand for a long moment and then says flatly: "Did you hear this one, *mate*? Do you know it? About the Welsh girl? Her boyfriend gave her a watchcase? Tell me if you've heard it before, won't you?"

Colin sighs. "I haven't. And I don't want to."

"Really? You might learn something. She was right chuffed, with that present, she was. I asked her why. A watchcase? Know what she told me? 'He's promised me the works tonight.' "

Colin shakes his head, puts down his pint. Sarah sees his mustache is flecked with froth.

"Colin," she says softly.

"The works, sunshine. D'you get it? Penny dropped 'as it? Tickety-tock. I can wait. All night, I promise you."

"You're asking for it, you are."

"All we're doing is telling a few jokes. Asking for it? I don't think I know that one, though. Is there a *punch* line to it? Is there?"

Jack is there (limp or no limp, he's quick down the length of a bar), his huge arms reaching over to clamp round Colin, before he can swing, but somehow Harry still ends up on the threadbare carpet. He leans back on the stool, trying to anticipate the blow, and he's gone, spilling backwards. It's a pratfall, and after a second, the bar dissolves in laughter again. Jack squeezes Colin once, hard enough to drive the breath out of him. Sarah hears him say, "Not here, lad, *nargois*," and then he releases him quickly. Colin shrugs, takes a gulp of air, glances at Sarah, and joins in the general laughter.

Harry is helped up by Mary and Tony, one of the sound engineers. "Up you come," Mary tells him. "And they say you can't do slapstick. You're wasted on radio, you are."

"Always told you scotch was my favorite topple," Harry mutters.

Mary leans across to Sarah and says loudly, "Never mind, luv. All you need to know about Englishmen, Welshmen, or Germans, for that matter, is they're all men. And you know what they say about men: one thing on their minds...and one hand on their things." There's a round of whistles from the crowd. "Always leave 'em laughing, eh," she grins at Sarah. She turns Harry towards the exit, but at the door he wheels round and lunges over, almost taking her and Tony down in a drunken bow.

"Ladies and gentlement. I thank you." There's a smattering of sarcastic applause, and when it dies out only Colin is clapping, slowly.

"Piss off," he calls. Sarah wishes he'd drop it now. In his own clumsy way, he's trying to be gallant, she knows, but there's an edge of bullying to it.

Harry tries to shake himself loose, but Mary and Tony cling on. "I did see a bloke in here once," he says, "with a terrible black eye."

"Looking in the mirror, was you?" Colin shouts.

"Actually, no. He was a soldier, this fellow. Told me he'd been fighting for his girlfriend's honor. Know what I said to him?"

"Bloody hell!"

"I said," Harry bawls over him, "it looked like she wanted to keep it."

He's red-faced and suddenly exhausted, and Mary and Tony take their chance to frog-march him out.

Over Mary's shoulder he gives the room a limp victory V-sign as he's carried out, and over Tony's arm, flashes a quick two fingers at Colin.

And then he's gone, dragged out into the darkness.

"Sorry about that," Colin says, and Sarah tells him quickly it's fine. She needs the job. She doesn't need customers fighting over her. Her English is supposed to be good enough to talk her way out of situations.

"You shouldn't have to put up with it," he goes on, but she shrugs. She's conscious of Jack still keeping an eye out behind her. It's a small village. She doesn't want talk.

"Anyhow," she says, "thank you, sir."

"Don't mention it, miss," he tells her, getting it finally, but still a little peeved.

She wipes down the bar, drops Harry's dirty glasses in the sink. She finds herself feeling a little sorry for the old soak after all. Mary has told her that his wife was killed in the Blitz. An incendiary. "You wouldn't think to look at him, but it was true love." It makes Sarah wonder. She's heard Harry telling jokes about his wife on the show: the missus; her-in-doors; his trouble and strife. "Show*biz*!" Mary told her with a grim, exaggerated brightness. "The show must go on, and all that."

The clock strikes ten-thirty. "*Amser, gwr bonheddig. Amser boddio,*" Jack cries, clanging the bell behind her, and Sarah chimes in: "Time, gents. Last orders, please."

She rinses glasses while Jack locks up, pouring the dregs away, twisting each glass once around the bristly scrub brush. They come out of the water with a little belch, and she sets them on the rack. Normally, she'd stay to dry and polish them, but Jack says it's enough. "Only gonna get dirty again tomorrow," he tells her. "Gerroff with you." He reaches over her and switches off the radio, and she realizes, with a little flush, that she's been swaying to the muted band music.

"It's all right," she says. "I'll see to these." But he takes the towel from her and nods at the door. She wonders if he knows.

"Long night," he says, handing on her coat. "Get you home."

Colin is waiting for her round the corner.

"Eh up!" he calls softly, appearing from the shadows of the hedge and pulling her to him. He'd been waiting for her here one night last week, when they'd kissed for the first time. His mustache smelled damp, muddy even, but she'd liked it, and she's met him here every night for a week now. Tonight, she's promised to go somewhere more private with him.

She's been kissed before, of course. Only sixteen, but she feels she's acquitted herself well with Colin, surprised him a little. She was wary of his questions about her age, tried to be mysterious and mock offended—"You can't ask a girl that!"—but the way he'd laughed had made her feel small, childish. "I pull your pints, don't I?" she told him. "There's laws, you know. Can't have kids serving in a pub." But she could see he wasn't convinced, and so she kissed him back. She's practiced with the local boys, but the ones her age are all off now, joined up or in factories. The only one she's kissed lately is David, their evacuee—just goodnight kisses, and one longer one to make him blush on his birthday— but it doesn't count, because he's younger than her, if a bit moony.

Colin clambers onto the bike he's brought and wrestles it around for her to perch herself on the handlebars. She'd been hoping for a jeep, but he is only a corporal. She feels self-conscious raising her bum onto the crossbar, aware of him watching, but then they're off. Colin pedals firmly. She can feel the bike vibrating with his effort as they near the brow of the hill behind the pub, and then her stomach turns over as they start to coast down the far side. Pretty soon they're flying, laughing in the darkness. The wind presses her skirt to her legs and then catches it, flipping the hem up against her waist. Her slip billows in the breeze, as if it remembers its past life as a parachute, and her knees and then one thigh flash in the moonlight. She wants to lean down, to fix it, but Colin has her hands pressed under his on the handlebars, and when she wriggles he tells her, "Hold still, love. I've got you."

She has never been to Camp Sunshine, the old holiday camp, but as a child, before the war, she remembers seeing posters showing all the fun to be had there; pictures of cheerful tots and bathing beauties by the pool. On hot summer days, gathering the flock for shearing from the hillside above, running to keep up with her father's long, loose stride, she would steal glances at the faceted blue gem of the pool below her and imagine its coolness. Of course, these places aren't for locals. Even in better days the most her father could afford was the odd daytrip on a growling char-à-banc to Rhyl or Llandudno. Besides, as he used to tell her, "who needs a pool when there's the ocean for free?" But she hates the sea, the sharp salt taste, the clammy clumps of seaweed. She's only ever seen swimming pools at the pictures, but she thinks Esther Williams is the most beautiful woman in the world. So as soon as Colin coasts through the back gates of the old camp, she asks him to show her the pool. He looks a little surprised, he has one of the empty, mildewed chalets in mind, but something in her voice, her eagerness, convinces him. He props the bike in the shadows behind a dark hut and leads her through the kids' playground. She clambers up the slide and swishes down on her backside, arms outstretched. He watches her from the roundabout, circling slowly. When she bats at the swings, he calls softly, "Want a push?" and she tells him, "Yeah."

She settles herself, and he puts his hands in the small of her back and shoves firmly to set her off, and then as she swings back he touches her lightly, his fingers spread across her hips, each time she passes. When she finally comes to a stop, the strands of hair that have flown loose fall back and cover her face. She tucks them away, all but one, which sticks to her cheek and throat, an inky curve.

"I saw the pool from up there," she tells him, breathlessly, and she pulls him towards it. She can see the water, the surface, choppy, and she wants, just once, to recline beside it and run her hand through it like a movie star. But when she gets close and bends down, she sees that what she has taken for the surface of the water is an old tarpaulin stretched over the mouth of the pool. She strikes at it bad-temperedly.

"For leaves and that," Colin says, catching up. "So it doesn't get all mucky."

"But what about the water?"

"Well, they drained it, you see."

He can see her disappointment, but he isn't discouraged.

"Come 'ere," he says, taking her hand and pulling her along to the metal steps that drop into the pool.

He climbs down and unfastens the cloth where it's tied to the edge by guy ropes. "Follow me." He slides down, his feet, his legs, his torso, until she can see only the top of his head. She notices a tiny, sunburned bald spot, just as he looks up and she realizes he can see up her skirt. She jumps back, snapping her heels together, and he grins and vanishes.

"Colin," she calls softly, suddenly alone.

There's no answer.

She crouches closer to the flapping gap, like a diver about to plunge forward. "Colin?" she hisses.

Nothing.

Then she sees a ridge in the cloth, like the fin of a shark moving away from her, circling, coming back. "What's that?" she says and, as if from a long way off, comes the cry, "Me manhood."

Despite herself she laughs, and in that moment grabs the railing of the steps and ducks below the cover.

It's surprisingly light in the empty pool. The tarpaulin is a thin, blue oilcloth, and the moonlight seeps through it unevenly as if through a cloudy sky. The pool is bathed in a pale, blotchy light, and the illusion of being underwater is accentuated by the design of shells printed on the tiles of the bottom. Overhead the breeze snaps the tarpaulin like a sail. She can just make out Colin, like a murky beast at the far end of the pool, the deep end. She takes a step towards him and finds the world sloping away beneath her suddenly, almost falls, stumbles down towards him.

When she gets closer, she finds him walking around in circles, with exaggerated slowness, making giant O shapes with his mouth.

"What are you doing?" she wants to know.

"I'm a fish," he says. "Glub, glub, get it?" And she joins him, giggling, snaking her arms ahead of her in a languid breaststroke.

He weaves back and forth around her. "Glub, glub, glub!"

"Now what are you doing?" she asks, as he steps sideways and bumps her. "Hey!"

"I'm a crab," he says, sidling off, scuttling back, bumping her again.

She feels his hand on her arse.

"Ow!"

"Sorry!" He shrugs, holds up his hands. "Sharp pincers."

"That hurt," she says, pulling away. She starts to backpedal towards the shallow end, windmilling her arms. "Backstroke!" But he catches her, wraps her in a hug.

"Mr. Octopus," he whispers, "has got you."

For a moment she relaxes, kisses him, but he kisses back with force, this soldier she's only known for a week. She feels him turning her in his arms, as if dancing, and she tries to move her feet with him, but he's holding her too tight, simply swinging her around. She feels dizzy. Her shoes scuff the tiles, and she thinks, *I just polished them.* The pressure of his arms makes it hard to breathe. She moans softly, her mouth under his mouth. When they finally stop spinning, she finds herself pressed against the cold tile wall of the pool. Up close it smells sharply of dank, chlorine, and rotten leaves.

"I'll be leaving soon," he whispers. "We're almost done here. Will you miss me?"

She nods in his arms, pressing her head against his chest, away from the hard wall.

"I'll miss you," he tells her, his lips to her ear. "We could be at the front this time next month. I wish I had something to remember you by then. Something to keep up me fighting spirits."

She feels him picking at her blouse, the buttons. She feels a hand on her knee, fluttering with her hem and then under her skirt—"Mermaid," he croons—sliding against the silk of her slip, against her thigh.

"Nice," he breathes. "Who says you Welsh girls don't know your duty. Proper patriot, you are. Thinking of England." Her head is still bent towards him, but now she is straining her neck against his weight. Between them she can feel the bony crook of his elbow, pressing against her side, and across her belly the tense muscles of his forearm, twitching.

"*Nargois*," she tells him, but he doesn't understand. "*Nargois!*"

She feels pressure and then pain. Colin grunts into her hair, short, hot puffs of breath. She wonders if she dares scream, who would hear her, who might come, wonders if she's more afraid of being caught than what he's doing to her.

She begins to turn her head against the coarse wool on his chest, trying to shake it, and he says, "Almost, almost," but at this she lifts her head sharply, catches him under the chin with a crack, and he cries out.

He steps back, clutching his jaw.

"Are you all right?" She starts to reach for him.

"Cunt!" he says, snatching at her wrist. She doesn't know the word, it's not in her schoolbooks, but she knows the tone, pulls away, curses him back in Welsh.

"Speak English, will you?" he tells her, turning her loose.

She leaves him there, struggling up the slope towards the steps. She thinks of a flirty argument they had over the bar one night last week. He'd wanted her to teach him some Welsh, but then she'd laughed at his pronunciation, and he'd gotten mock-mad. "Ah, what's the point?" he said. "Why don't you just give it up and speak English, like the rest of us?" She'd turned a little stern then, mouthed the nationalist arguments about saving the language, preserving the tongue.

"Oh, come on," he hisses after her now. "Play the game. I didn't mean it. Come back, eh? We'll do it proper. Comfy, like. Get a mattress from a chalet, have a lie-down."

But she keeps going, slipping a little on the tiles, tugging her skirt down, shoving her blouse back in, and she hears him start to laugh. There's a shout from the deep. "Who are you saving it for, eh? Who you saving it for, you Welsh bitch?"

She expects him to come after her then, feels her back tense against his touch, won't run for fear he'll chase. But before she reaches the opening, she hears shouts, a harsh scrape of feet on the concrete above. It's as if she's willed her own rescue into being, and yet she cowers from it. Torch lights dance over the cover of the pool. Despite herself, she turns to Colin with a beseeching look—*to be found like this!*—but he's already past her, his head in the shelter of the tarpaulin, peering out. Frantically, she tries to button her blouse, her fingers fumbling. "Shite," Colin breathes, but the lights and the footsteps are already receding, and she leans against the wall, her heart hammering. The thought of being discovered, the near miss, makes her stomach clench. Her throat feels raw. She looks back at Colin, wanting to share their escape, but he is already scrambling up the ladder, and a second later, gone.

A clean pair of heels, she thinks; the English phrase so suddenly vivid she feels blinded by it.

Her body seems heavy, waterlogged, her arms shaky, too weak to pull her up the metal ladder, and she clings to the cold rail as if she might drown. It's a few moments before she can climb out of the pool. There are shouts at the other side of the camp, where the barracks have been built—the local boys must have broken in again—but she hurries the other way, back over the playground. The seesaw and roundabout are still, the swings rocking gently in the breeze. She finds the bike where he left it, propped up behind a chalet, and climbs on, noticing as she hitches up her skirt that the stitching of her slip is torn. It will take her five minutes to mend with a needle and thread, but she suddenly feels like weeping.

She pushes off, pedaling hard, although she finds it makes her wince to ride. She doesn't care that she's stealing his bike. She'll throw it into the hedge outside the village. She knows he'll never ask about it, and if he does, she decides, staring at her pale knuckles on the handlebars where his fingers have curled, she'll pretend she's forgotten her English.

TOM DRURY

Two Horse Ashtray

Jane and Evan moved to a small city in eastern Ohio and rented an old house on half an acre surrounded by a stone wall. Jobs came easily to them. People could see by their open and unlined faces that something good was happening in their lives.

Evan went to work for an insurance agency, and Jane became a clerk in a school for problem learners. They didn't bring home a lot of money, but they had all they needed.

The man who hired Jane thought of her as a real person in a way that suggested he himself had faded from reality over time. Once he had been real, but not anymore; that was the gist of his thinking.

Jane and Evan were young, twenty-five and twenty-six, and both were dealing with the troubles of strangers for the first time. They would discuss their work late at night while sitting at the kitchen table on either side of the backgammon board.

Maybe someone's car had burned up overnight and no one knew how. Or, given a harmless assignment, a child had written a story full of violence and fear. These were intriguing situations and by talking about them Jane and Evan seemed to understand each other in a deeper way than before.

Meanwhile they played serious backgammon—rolling the dice, hitting the blots, sliding the doubling cube back and forth. Neither one of them liked to lose. Jane was always rolling high doubles while bearing off, and Evan would pretend to be angry at Jane's luck.

And she would only laugh, because she did feel lucky. The house, though mostly empty, the stone wall, on which a fox sometimes walked, Evan, with his strong arms and rough elbows—there was hardly anything in her life that did not seem like an omen of the world's generosity.

One weekend in the fall, the man who had hired Jane—Trayer was his name—cleaned out his attic, happening on a cardboard box with the words TWO HORSE ASHTRAY written on it. The box had belonged to his parents and while he must have seen it before he did not remember it.

He wondered what the words might mean. They sounded like a subtle putdown, or as if the writer had a hard time describing what was in the box. (Trayer suspected that his mother had done the labeling, but the writing style consisted of those block capitals that belong to no one.)

He took out his knife and cut the tape that sealed the box. And when he got it open he saw that the label had been exactly right, if too simple to understand. There was one ashtray, large and copper-plated, with two horses that stood on either side of a glass bowl tinted green. The bowl had cigarette rests pressed into its thick rim and could be lifted from its metal platform for easy disposal of the ashes.

Trayer was on his knees in the attic, holding the ashtray before his eyes, listening to the rain on the roof. The thing seemed a relic of a time in which people smoked so much that they had need of novel settings for their cigarettes. And it meant little to Trayer. He had long ago given up on hanging on to the past in the form of items that belonged to it.

But he thought that Jane, with her dark blue eyes, might like to see it. It was kitsch, wasn't it, and people new to adulthood were thought to like that sort of thing, unless they no longer did.

Trayer took the ashtray to the school for problem learners on the following Monday and left it on the desk that Jane shared with two other clerks. Like the Wooden Horse of Troy, the two-horse ashtray made a stir with its mysterious arrival. The three who shared the desk did not understand whom it was meant for or why. They couldn't smoke in the school or anywhere near it. None of them smoked, anyway.

Trayer kept making up reasons to walk by Jane's desk, and finally he found her sitting there.

"Where did it go?" he said.

"Where did what go?"

"Did someone take it?"

Jane reached down, into the kneehole of the desk, where she and her coworkers had decided to hide the ashtray, in case anyone might suspect them of making light of the smoking prohibition.

"This?"

"Yeah—it's a two-horse ashtray."

"You didn't have to get me something."

Trayer had not meant to give her the ashtray, or perhaps he hadn't made up his mind, but her guess decided the question. He didn't want to embarrass her for assuming a gift where none was intended. And if she didn't like it, if she found it antiquated and stupid, it would be better, somehow, as a gift. So he nodded; it was for her.

Jane carried the ashtray home, set it on the coffee table in the living room, and took a bath. Then she put on clean old clothes and went for a walk on the stone wall.

Walking on the wall always made her feel good. It was easy enough, anyone could have done it, and yet only she did, she and the fox, and she sensed a kinship with the fox and with the red-tailed hawk that glided low over the yard sometimes.

And she thought how she and Evan lived inside the wall, and everyone else in the city lived outside, and she imagined that eventually, if they stayed long enough, they would become known as "that couple with the stone wall." She felt strangely happy, and a little ridiculous, and she knew that there must be a word for this feeling, but if so it would not come to her.

Evan did not notice the ashtray all that night. Mostly he and Jane lived in the kitchen and the bedroom—food, drink, love, and sleep being their only real needs—and they felt false in the living room, or self-conscious, like actors on a stage they were not used to.

At three in the morning, however, unable to sleep, Evan went down to the living room to read. And there it was, the ashtray, with the stoic copper horses, looking away from the davenport and toward the dark windows, but in different directions, like sentinels.

Evan picked up the ashtray in one hand and touched his forehead with the other. It was the accepted gesture of someone wondering what to make of something. The horses had elaborate Western saddles and little chains for the reins. He went out to a cupboard in the hall, took down his wooden dope box, returned to the living room, and rolled a joint. He smoked with amusement, shaping the ash on the glass between the horses. Then he forgot about the ashtray for two days.

On the third day, in the morning, he asked Jane where it had come from, all of a sudden. She told him it was a present from her boss. They were on their way to work but went in to look at the ashtray instead.

Evan said it seemed like a strange gift. Jane shrugged. She did not really know what to make of it, either. A cigarette lay half-smoked in the ashtray. Evan asked Jane if she was smoking now, and she said that she had picked up a pack, yeah, for the fun of it.

Then it was Friday night and they smoked grass together for the first time since moving into the house. They passed a joint back and forth in a clip with a feather on a leather string. They laughed at the notion of being so suggestible that a present of an ashtray would send them on a smoking binge. What if it had been a coke spoon? Or a heroin needle? What was heroin, anyway? Where did it come from?

There was a long pause, following which Evan said that heroin came from poppies. The word seemed especially hilarious.

They brought the backgammon board in from the kitchen, and tried to play their customary game, but the pieces refused to form familiar patterns on the long triangles of the board. It was one of those games without discipline or apparent strategy, in which one or both of the players would wind up with an absurd number of pieces in his opponent's inner table.

So they dropped the game, just like that, feeling pliable and resilient and somehow afraid, like children given the roam of a strange house. And later, upstairs, when they made love in their bed, it was with the wordless passion of two people who are about to be separated for a long time.

Then Evan fell asleep and Jane lay awake, dreaming of what she would do if she owned the house and had a million dollars to make it any way she wanted. This was something she did in her spare time—think of what a million dollars could do.

In her mind she moved walls, added windows, ripped out the kitchen, and above all she wondered if any of these improvements would ever happen. She admired Evan but his dreams seemed small and scattered beside her own. Once she had tried to get him to play the million-dollar game, and he had said, "If we had a horse, we could ride it on Sunday."

What a meaningless response that was. She wished that he were awake now so that she could tell him how it had disappointed her. She was sure he did not know; she had not really known until this moment. She made herself breathe slowly, thinking that the night was over, and thinking also that she smelled smoke. She shoved Evan's shoulder but he only mumbled, "Who is it?" and rolled away.

Jane went downstairs and found that the debris she had dumped from the ashtray had started a fire in the wastebasket in the kitchen. The trash and the wastebasket itself were burning, and green flames rose up against the cabinet that housed the sink. She stood quietly for a moment, blinking and covering her mouth with her hands. There was an unreal and gemlike quality to the fire in the shadowy kitchen, as if it represented not disaster but something precious and unknown.

She took a frying pan and filled it with water and threw the water on the wastebasket. She did this six times, until the wastebasket stood smoking and reeking and melted to half its original size.

Jane sat in a chair and laid the frying pan on the table. Water and ashes spread across the tiles and into the light from the hall. She was not crying but she was very quiet and sad and perhaps still stoned.

Meanwhile, in another part of town, Trayer was putting ceramic vases into a cardboard box. The vases had come from various shops and the house had begun to feel cluttered with them. He would put them away and eventually his wife would find them and set them out again. The vases seemed to stare at him, from inside the box, amazed that they were to be shunted off.

Trayer closed the flaps, one over the next, the last over the first, infinitely interlocking. It was the box the two-horse ashtray had been in. He had no doubt now that his mother had written the words. His father would not have said anything about the horses. They were different in that way. Trayer lifted the box in his arms, and felt a longing for Jane, or his idea of Jane, for he really didn't know her very well at all; but whatever he was longing for, it hurt him right down to his heart.

Sing

Nicky licks my eyelids. He pins me down and licks my eyelids.

You should hear what boys call me always looking for the tongue in my mouth because my lips are the only place on me with any fat like maybe once they got bit. I'm a small town so up go my fists and they scat. Sticks and stones, says me to their skinny shirt-tails, what else you got. Some words aren't worth the breath they're made out of. I'm a wishbone but I don't break. There's this calico cat who sits on the fence making faces because he's mute. Wow goes his mouth opening and closing wow. The bluebirds bite his tail. He feels like corduroy slacks when you pet him, all the long thin veins inside him sticking out through his skin. I'm sorry for him but still I go right up to his face when he's clinging to the pickets his limp face like a lily pad wow I say to him wow and watch the whacking of his ears. They say your other senses get really strong to compensate, there's always this give and take, isn't there, a win and a loss, the only drawback being that you don't get too much choice either way.

Who gave you the fat lip, Nicky says with a smirk. Just from that smirk you know he's asking for it.

My mother buys me halter-tops in the junior department at Strawbridge's. She says they give me a little something up top. There is something nice about the string of a halter-top softing across your bare back. You're a late bloomer, my mother says. She doesn't know about spin the bottle or seven minutes in heaven. My growing shinbones—the tibias, to put words in my mother's mouth—hurt at night while I lie there helpless. The heart rises from a horizon crossing me sometimes it's like a class running sprints, sometimes the only thing inside me is squeaky cleats.

The cat got my dad's tongue a long time ago. His words would rather be whistle. On a good day, you'd swear there was a bird in the house. My dad calls me shy, but he is hello goodbye, like the sky. If I'm ear, he's eye.

Pam is a pinup before her time. She gets quieter and quieter as her body gets louder and louder. I hear it, banging like a band. She's an easy target. Wendy and Lee-Lee and Alison and me, we're slim as hammers, we slit our eyes and stalk the halls. We pick on Pam. It gets out of hand, I'll be first to admit. We sneak up behind her and pluck at the stripe of her bra strap and it goes pop! snap! It's like hopping down the block. We chase her into the boys' room our hands clawing at the yellow hair flowing off her. She slides to the floor with her hands holding the edge of the sink. The principal says we hurt her two ways, feeling and physical. He sighs, he wouldn't expect this of girls. Pam walks around in a daze, her head down and her shoulders curling inward. She moves as if cupped in parentheses. This is what sticks in my mind: Pam on the tile floor of the boys' room, Pam's pale arms and pink freckles folding a soft X across her own self. Tears in her brown eyes. That's my point of view. But looking at it another way, there's me with a stringy ponytail staring down at her, and that picture is labeled with my name first and last and it's filed in her head forever and ever.

You think it's the big events that mark your life but it's not, it's the teensy moments that come back to haunt you.

Before my brother Mattie died they shaved him bald. Here he was a sorry sight coming back to school and on his scalp the blue veins showed through. At recess I pretended I didn't see him, I stuck to the swing-side of the playground, shortsighted and singing I swung and swung stamping the sky. The helmet of his head glowed golden. The sun singing in your eyes. This is what happens that comes back to haunt you.

My other brother sees in me what the others don't. He sees me getting away with murder. He's sick and tired of hearing about me, the baby of the family, the princess and the pea. When my parents' friends kiss me they leave lipstick on my cheeks. They measure my every inch because it helps them feel the flow of time and they shake their heads as if it makes them sad it might be a coincidence how they always say the same thing: oh my we're not getting any younger are we my oh my can you believe how fast they grow? Life is a river a sea and it's weeping out of a tap in me.

Secrets don't smoke like fire. My other brother is a building bearing down on me. He's bricks and stones on the bends of my back. His breath butters the back of my neck. Your big brother is a bully, my mom says, but he's just a boy.

This is my trick: look as if you're having the time of your life especially if you're not.

There is nothing cool about catechism class except that now they're having us come on Tuesday afternoons we sit under the fluorescent lights with a teacher who says let's talk about real life let's see who would like to begin? There's my foot swinging off the shin there's the twitch twitch the peek at the shiny watch face. There are the seconds saying this this who doesn't ever feel that. Instantly I'm looking around for my only friend who happens to be Nicky. You could spot our grins a mile away. A Hail Mary in my mouth I slip out the door and here he comes my friend Nicky. We sneak across the street to the supermarket and climb up for a smoke on top of the Salvation Army dumpster. It's not a bad view because at dusk the street suddenly blazes with lights and everywhere the sea to shining sea of cars. Cigarette smoke goes inside you like a soft mood nothing else is quite like that. Lozenge lips, he calls me and it's no compliment. His chin has a point so sharp it could cut you. Nicky I call him but he says please call me Nick. Nick the dick, I say. His lips are sticky and stick to mine.

With me it's all or nothing. Best friend or no friend at all. I shrug and say take it or leave it. They give in and you end up getting all and they get nothing. That's the equation with me coming after the equals sign. My other brother says someday it will all catch up with me. At some point, he says, the truth will out and you will finally get what you deserve. Truth is this odd thing because most people talk about it like it's something that you can never really know.

In truth or dare I pick dare every time, I'm not giving anything away, I'm looking out for number one. Actions are always safer than words.

Which is why when Nicky dares me the burned out cigarette goes in my mouth and down the hatch ash and all. It tastes like a dead leaf not that I'd know. Which is how I ended up inside the Salvation Army dumpster and closed the door and I let myself breathe it in, the smell of people that stays in clothes and I didn't let my imagination go because it's true that all these thrown-away things were like bodies, soft as moths.

He slips his clammy hand inside my halter-top and his palm holds its breath on top of my ha ha heart.

My other brother says my luck will run out sooner or later, he says people will wise up to my tricks. It's his job to roughen the edges of my life, toughen me up. I watched him eating peas with a soupspoon and I wondered what if just one jumped down the wrong tube. It was just a passing thought because right then his eyes rolled over me like I was this small stretch of sidewalk.

Nicky lives in a pink stucco house behind a tall black gate. Open the front door and you can almost smell the glue drying, his house is that new, the air feels wet inside it. They have plastic slip-covers on the sofas and chairs and lampshades. You have to take off your shoes inside. You have to wash your hands. It makes you feel nice and neat like the best little pieces of you come out on tiptoes. The only snacks they have are carrot sticks and tangerines. He says his mom hates him for being a pint-size version of his dad. My house is a hundred years old, which is more than most people ever dream of reaching. Maybe in its long life my house is like trees but then it might also be like stone.

I'm not one to brood on the bad, this is no pity party I'd be first to say. But my mom has the bright idea to beat this thing into the ground. It's called a year without my brother Mattie. I sit down to write and this is what comes to mind. The summer of the Japanese beetles. They swarm in the leaves buzzing like bees and feasting on the trees. They float like black bullets in the pool. I'm on the diving board, my arms in an X across my chest like Ultraman. He's in the shallow end, he Ultramans me, his arms crossed over ridges of ribs, the gleam of the sun on his shaved head. His head is a polished skull atop the crossbones of his arms. I smack my feet hard on the gritty board and fling myself into the air. The water shatters as I hit the surface and fall through, and fall, thorns of ice raking my skin, the only way I can share it with him the scalpels flashing silver blades inside his brain scooping and scraping and leaving him hollow.

This is what happens when you dwell on the past, when you won't let a thing be, when you worry about who what why when.

Japanese beetles and gypsy moths. Both at the same time. Who would think it possible, Dad says, what are the chances of two blights at once? When it rains it pours, he sighs.

I didn't learn the brain when we studied it in school maybe it was too close to home. On the screen it looked like egg pie served up on plates as you went past the gray matter and got into the ganglion. I got up to go to the bathroom because I felt sick but I just stood and stared down into the toilet while it flushed and imagined millions of neurons and all those sparks and how your head is a bowl and what's it holding but this huge soup you call a soul.

Nicky flicks off the basement light and we go up the steps holding hands. His clammy hands. He turns around at the top and our bodies bump. He wraps his arms around me, his heart peeping at my cheek, he holds me to him and something in me is a wave before it breaks. His parents talking in the kitchen, his mom says, You're pathetic you're a worm. Her heels click on the hard floor. You're over the hill, she says and she clicks into view through the crack and we huddle hidden watching her flash her hands in his dad's face. Nicky shivers in my arms. I can see his dad has already lost, she is sharpened, she'll slash him to shreds, her heels her fingernails the edge of her lips. But he does it anyway, he drops to his knees in front of her, he kneels before her and embraces her legs, he presses his face to her skirt. He cries at her crotch. *Lo siento,* he says. *Lo siento.* He slides to her feet and she steps out of him, she lifts her heels one by one and leaves him on the floor like a crumpled pair of pants. He weeps, silver strands of hair on handpainted Mexican tile. She licks a finger and smooths a curl off her forehead, click click her heels.

In the coils of Nicky's black hair I see the swish of a slinky sliding down some steps. I wish I had hair like that, I say. He sponges black shoe polish on my head, it feels like soggy paws padding across my scalp. My hair turns into greasy tar and Nicky is in hysterics. I laugh with him, I can laugh at myself, and pretty soon he's smudging his fingerprints on my arms and cheeks and down my spine. Because his skin almost glows because he comes from an island because I am ashamed of how my hands sometimes look so white and drained of life because he is so full sometimes I feel scrawny and thin.

His front tooth is chipped. You can see the tip of his tongue through the opening. It makes his smile look untidy without your knowing exactly why. His jeans torn just below the back pocket so of course I look where it shows a scrap of thigh the size of an eye.

This is one thing leading to another. My other brother found me looking for the girls under his mattress and is thinking up a way to make me pay. Back massages are only the beginning. The hot of his hands like sun. The way you chap and crack.

This is what Dad says the summer of the Japanese beetles and the gypsy moths. He says our hair is clogging up the filters and from now on bathing caps are rule number one.

Shoes lined up on the mat inside the door except for hers, she keeps her high heels on because they are clean. In his room we can hear her move and move the cool smooth sound of her shoes click click click on marble and parquet and Mexican tile. She's trapped, he says, listen to her pace back and forth.

A net of crickets surging against the stone walls of my house. It is already tomorrow when my parents turn the locks and slide the bolts. They climb the stairs whispering. Their door shuts softly. Darkness is a draft breathing through my room. Crickets swell and subside, swell and subside. Prayers help push off an accidental death while you swim through sleep. Someone can hear your every thought. If I should die before I wake I pray the Lord my soul to take. Souls are icy stars crucified on the night sky.

His dad gives Nicky a turtle. He says my son needs company and all the better if it's not human company. In my country, he adds with a little wink, *la tortuga* makes good soup. Let's split, Nicky says, before we get the recipe in Spanish. The turtle has stringy legs and webbed feet. You can't make him come out until he's good and ready, Nicky says, he's safe and sound inside his shell, he's a tiny turtle tank. A hammer could crack it open, I say trying to make him laugh. His bangs fall in slats across his eyes, I tilt my head to copy but mine won't budge. The turtle pushes out a telescoping head slim as a pinky finger, it paddles across his palm jerking side to side like a puppet on strings.

The gypsy moths spin thick cocoons in the trees, the branches are dipped in cotton candy. Our heads are pinched in tight elastic caps, our skulls are smooth bulbs planted in the pool, our bodies dangling underwater like spindly roots.

Pam was pink her skin was pink we called her spam.

This is the sound of the gypsy moth summer: sprinklers spraying silvery jump ropes of water across the lawn, a pulsing sst sst sst sst. I hide under the pine tree, the branches so long and thick they drape to the ground. Carpenter ants come crawling up my ankles. It's called putting things in perspective, but I never seem to fit. I'm not sticking around the sick. I am saying this all the time now: why should I stick around the sick? This is the slowest summer of my life, but everything is flying. I can't keep my mouth shut. I can't stand anybody sick. Pine needles are gummy in my fingers and peppery in my mouth. Black charred branches creak and sigh and needles fall and fall and I think about ticks and Rocky Mountain spotted fever, ticks rain on my head, small sharp thumbtacks sticking to my scalp and sickening my blood. You'll be singing the song of sorry, my other brother says, for the rest of your long and selfish life.

We're eating eyeballs in the wine cellar. When you are in my house because it is at the very end of a long and winding lane and because it is big and you are down in the deep ground it is easy to believe that everything lived is quickly lost. Out comes Nicky's tongue past the crooked teeth to show me a cocktail onion sitting there like a pearl. In some countries tongue is a good and rare thing to eat which is probably why it's usually so carefully hidden far inside our razor-sharp chops which is why I wanted to say okay Nicky now put it away please and in my chest I started feeling those fast fast feet.

Dad drives the lawnmower, he lets me ride shotgun. We drive across the lawn, blades chopping beneath us and clouds of grass spitting a wake behind us. He switches gears on the turn and we lurch and tilt and I yell, can't we go faster, and he holds the shift in his hand and I'm bouncing beside him holding on with both hands in a hive of grass clippings, a hive of green and whining saws. When I slide down at the end my knees are elastic, the ground swings like a clothesline, I look up at him and see the pulse in his neck, bits of grass on his face. He surveys the cropped lawn and he doesn't smile but somehow you know he is pleased in a quiet way and his gaze is a hand smoothing across the silky short grass feeling the life pushing crisply against his fingers.

I come up his driveway and see this: Nicky on his hands and knees in the azalea bushes, dirt on his face and his hair a frenzy. She killed it, he says, she killed it and buried it. He's holding his turtle to his chest and crying; she's in butterscotch suede, a shine on her skin and mascara blotting around the eyes, and for a second she looks like him something scared or hurting in the eyes, and then she looks at me, she glances at my hightop sneakers, she says, Would you like a tangerine while Nicky has his tantrum? And she turns, she glides inside the house like an eel the way she moves through life. I feel pulled two ways at once, Nicky sobbing on his knees, his mom gliding inside the house. Maybe he knows it because he looks at me and stops crying long enough to say, Get out of here. All I can think about is his wormy turtle half-decomposed. You shouldn't dig up the dead, I say and I turn and walk down his driveway.

This is my dad: he scoops up the earth in his hand and sifts it through his fingers. He sees the small signs of disease, a ragged hedge, a torn petal, he will turn a leaf over and read it like a palm. Look there, he says and the sadness in his voice makes me freeze. Aphids, he says pinching off a leaf here a leaf there.

This is my mom: she shucks the corn peeling back the stiff leafy sheaves, yanking off the yellow silk. She flicks the worms into the trash. She peels the potatoes and gouges out the eyes.

After dinner Dad sits back and lights a cigar. Well that hit the spot, he says with a big smile and you can feel the fullness in the kitchen and Mom finally sits down still and drinks some herbal tea and he looks at me and says, Didn't that hit the spot? and he looks at Mom, Wasn't that something, he says blowing out blue smoke, he looks at her as if she's the next and best course. Oh, she says squirting lemon into her tea, that was nothing at all.

This is to show how somethings can be made of nothings. His smoke rings spin silver blue halos for our centerpiece.

Next time I'll get a snapping turtle, he says. He snips off the heads of his mother's tulips with sharp scissors. Flowers fall with soft thuds like falling fruit. Red and yellow flowers, waxy as crayons, firm and fleshy. Snapping turtle, he says, snap snap snap, scissoring the thick stems. He picks them up and crushes them in his fist. He smells the crushed petals. He licks a red scrap and it sticks to his tongue. A plastic bag fills with crushed tulip heads. He hands it to me and pulls the cuff of his sweatshirt over his hand like a mitt, he polishes the vases. Don't run with scissors, he says, she told me never to run with scissors in my hand, she said I'd fall and end up stabbed through the heart. Sawed-off stems in vases, I feel a shimmer in the mirror and I look up and see us reflected there, he's behind me, and the mirror is smoky as if the glass has been rubbed with a damp rag or an eraser, he's standing behind me a beam of sunlight on his head, white teeth in a grin, scissor blades slashing. He puts his arms around me and he bites my neck and whispers, I vant to suck your blood, scissor tips sticking into my belly, his breath spilling milkily inside my ear.

My other brother talks about me as if I'm not there. He says to my dad, Do you think she should be spending so much time with Nicky? My dad sips his vodka on the rocks. You can smell the hot jalapeño peppers splitting open in my mother's spaghetti sauce. My other brother takes a whiff and looking at my dad he asks me this: And where exactly does Nicky come from—he's not exactly American is he? On my bedroom door late at night my other brother's knuckles go knock knock. I don't remember before the backrubs I don't know how a girl gets unbent sometimes it makes me sick just watching my family eat.

This is the end of summer number one. This is the end of a year without my brother Mattie. I am getting closer to his eyes. His eyelashes are long and when they flicker they leave purple stains like bruises.

I hear it from my mom but she isn't talking to me, she sighs and I hear a sizzle of butter in the frying pan and I hear her telling my dad, I hear her say, Nicky stuck a fork into an electric outlet, I hear her voice and the exhaust fan ticking in the background and a highball glass set down on the countertop, What, Dad says, her little friend Nicky?

I stand on top of the fence. I hold my arms up, I close my eyes. I am a lightning rod shrieking with static. I jump into the leaf pile. I fall into a soft bed of rotting leaves and I feel my life taking a deep breath and I'm inside it and all I can hear is the crinkling and crackling of dead leaves and the thump of my life going on and on and on.

I dream him charred and sooty like the branches of the pine tree, the hole of his mouth and the chipped front tooth. The sockets of his eyes.

When I hopped in the front seat the door closed on my rabbit coat and what I said was *Fuck* I felt her hit the brakes and my body went bump my mother said what did you say? I couldn't see through her black sunglasses but I pretended I could and aimed a long honest gaze into the place where she might have eyes. Luck, I lied, I was praying for the Irish luck you're not supposed to listen. I was thinking how my rabbit coat was almost alive the fur came up to pet my fingers and take a few puffs of living people.

Just once he calls, he says hi and I say hi and then I hear him breathing. I'm going away to school, he says, and my mom's going to live in France. I'm going to military academy, he says and I hear him breathing. I imagine the hair burnt off his arms. Oh, I say. My dad's selling the house, he says, I might not ever be back. I don't know what to say to somebody who stuck a fork in an electric outlet. Some people are magnets for bad luck, he says and I hear him breathe in deep. I bite off my thumbnail and this is when I understand that I suck up the luck from everybody around me and leave them the bad. Well bye, he says and cuts the connection and I hold on thinking he'll pick up one two three four five seconds I count and I'm still breathing through the wires down the street and up the hill and inside his house and then I hear a click and a pause—as if there's a turning place in every moment where it can go one of two ways—before the line goes dead and the smallest something in you goes quiet and lazy and flies off like a flea.

The Mourning Door

The first thing she finds is a hand. In the beginning, she thinks it's a tangle of sheet or a wadded sock caught between the mattress cover and the mattress, a bump the size of a walnut but softer, more yielding. She feels it as she's lying, lazing, in bed. Often, lately, her body keeps her beached, though today the sun beckons, the dogwoods blooming white, the peonies' glossy buds specked black with ants. Tom has gone to work already, backing out of the driveway in his pickup truck. She has taken her temperature on the pink thermometer, noted it down on the graph—98.2, day eighteen, their thirteenth month of trying. She takes it again, to be sure, then settles back in, drifting, though she knows she should get up. The carpenters will be here soon; the air will ring with hammers. The men will find more expensive, unnerving problems with the house. She'll have to creep in her robe to the bathroom, so small and steady, like one of the pests they keep uncovering in this ancient, tilting farmhouse—powder post beetles, termites, carpenter ants.

She feels the bump in the bed the way she might encounter a new mole on her skin, or a scab that had somehow gone unnoticed, her hand traveling vaguely along her body until it stumbles, oh, what's this? With her shin, she feels it first, as she turns over, beginning to get up. She sends an arm under the covers, palpitates the bump. A pair of bunched panties, maybe, shed during sex and caught beneath the new sheet when she remade the bed? Tom's sock? A wad of tissue? Some unknown object (needle threader, sock darner, butter maker, chaff-separator?) left here by the generations of people who came before? The carpenters keep finding things in the walls and under the floor: the sole of an old shoe, a rusted nail, a bent horseshoe. A Depression-era glass bowl, unbroken, the green of key lime pie. Each time they announce another rotted sill, cracked joist, additional repair, they hand an object over, her consolation prize. The house looked so charming from the outside, so fine and perfectly itself. The inspector said go ahead, buy it. But you never know what's lurking underneath.

She gets out of the bed, stretches, yawns. Her gaze drops to her naked body, so familiar, the thin freckled limbs and flattish stomach. She has known it forever, lived with it forever. Mostly it has served her well, but lately it seems a foreign, uncooperative thing, at once insolent and lethargic, a taunt. Sometimes, though, she still finds in herself an energy that surprises her, reminding her of when she was a child and used to run—legs churning, pulse throbbing—down the long river path that led to her cousin's house.

Now, in a motion so concentrated it's fierce, she peels off the sheet and flips back the mattress pad. What she sees doesn't surprise her; she's been waiting so hard, these days, looking so hard. A hand, it is, a small, pink dimpled fist, the skin slightly mottled, the nails the smallest slivers, cut them or they'll scratch. Five fingers. Five nails. She picks it up; it flexes slightly, then curls back into a warm fist. Five fine fingers, none missing. She counts them again to be sure. *You have to begin somewhere,* the books say. *You have to relinquish control and let nature take its course.*

She hears the door open downstairs, the clomp of workboots, words, a barking laugh. Looking around, she spots, on the bedroom floor, the burlap sack that held the dwarf liberty apple tree Tom planted over the weekend. She drops the hand into the bag, stuffs the bag under the bed. Still the air smells like burlap, thick and dusty. She pulls on some sweatpants, then thinks better of it and puts on a more flattering pair of jeans, and a T-shirt that shows off her breasts. She read somewhere that men are drawn to women with small waists and flaring hips. Evolution, the article said. A body built for birth. Her own hips are small and boyish; her waist does not cinch in. Her pubic hair grows thin and blond, grass in a drought. She doesn't want these workmen, exactly, but she would like them, for the briefest moment, to want her. As she goes barefoot down the stairs to make a cup of tea and smile at the men, she stops for a moment, struck by a memory of the perfect little hand; even the thought of it makes her gasp. The men won't find it. They're only working in the basement and the attic, structural repairs to keep the house from falling down.

In her kitchen, the three men: Rick and Tony and Joaquin.

Their eyes flicker over her. She touches her hair, feels heavy with her secret, and looks down. More bad news, I'm afraid, Rick tells her. We found it yesterday, after you left—a whole section of the attic. What, she asks. *Charred,* he says dramatically. There must have been a fire; some major support beams are only three-quarter their original size. She shakes her head. Really? But the inspector never— I have my doubts, Rick says, about this so-called inspector of yours. Can you fix it, she asks. He looks at her glumly through heavy-lidded eyes. We can try, he answers. I'll draw up an estimate but we'll need to finish the basement before we get to this. Yes, she says vaguely, already bored. Fine, thanks.

Had she received such news the day before, it would have made her dizzy. A charred, unstable attic, a house whittled down by flames. She would have called Tom at work—You're not going to believe this—and checked how much money they had left in their savings account, and thought about suing the inspector and installing more smoke alarms, one in every room, blinking eyes. Today, though, she can't quite concentrate; her thoughts keep returning, as if of their own accord, to what she discovered in her bed. One apricot-sized hand, after thirteen months, after peeing into cups, tracking her temperature, making Tom lie still as a statue after he comes, no saliva, no new positions, her rump tilted high into the air afterwards, an absurd position but she doesn't care.

After thirteen months of watching for the LH surge on the ovulation predictor kit—the deep indigo line of a good egg, the watery turquoise of a bad, and inside her own body, waves cresting and breaking, for she has become an ocean, or it is an oceanographer? *Study us hard enough,* the waves call out to her, *watch us closely enough and we shall do your will.* She has noted the discharge on her underpants—sticky, tacky, scant. Egg white, like she's a chef making meringues or a chicken trying to lay. *Get to know your body,* chant the books, the Web sites, her baby-bearing friends, and oh she has, she does, though it's beginning to feel like a cheap car she has leased for a while and is getting ready to return.

She still likes making love with Tom, the tremble of it, the slow, blue wash, the way they lie cupped together in their new, old house as it sits in the greening fields, on the turning earth. It's afterwards that she hates. She can never fall asleep without picturing the spastic, thrashing tails, the egg's hard shell, the long, thin tubes stretched like IVs toward a pulsing womb. A speck, she imagines sometimes, the head of a pin, the dot of a period. The End—or maybe, if they're lucky, dot dot dot.

But the hand is so much bigger than that, substantial, real. Her own hands shake with relief as she puts on the tea water. Something is starting—a secret, a discovery, begun not in the narrow recesses of her body, but in the mysterious body of her new, old house. The house has a door called the Mourning Door—the realtor pointed it out the first time they walked through. It's a door off the front parlor, and though it leads outside, it has no stoop or stairs, just a place for the cart to back up so the coffin can be carried away. Of course babies were born here, too, added the realtor, her voice too bright. Probably right in this room! After she and Tom moved in, they decided only to use the door off the kitchen. Friendlier, she said, and after all, they're concentrating, these days, on making life.

When she goes back upstairs, she takes the burlap sack and a flashlight to the warm, musty attic, where Tom almost never goes. With the flashlight's beam, she finds, in one dark corner, the section where the fire left its mark. She touches the wood, and a smudge of ash comes off on her finger. She tastes it: dry powder, ancient fruit, people passing buckets, lives lost, found, lost. She leaves the sack in the other corner of the attic inside a box marked "Kitchen Stuff." Then she heads downstairs to wash her hands.

Three days later she is doing laundry when she comes across a shoulder, round and smooth. She knows it should be disconcerting to find such a thing separated from its owner, a shoulder disembodied, lying in a nest of dryer lint, tucked close to the wall. But why get upset? After all, the world is full of parts apart from wholes. A few months ago, she and Tom went to the salvage place—old radiator covers, round church windows, faucets and doorknobs, a spiral staircase leading nowhere. Then, they bought two doors and a useless unit of brass mailboxes, numbers fifteen through twenty-five. Now she wipes her hands on her jeans and picks the shoulder up. It is late afternoon, the contractors gone, Tom still at work. She brings the shoulder up to the attic and puts it in the sack with the hand. Then she goes to the bedroom, swallows a vitamin the size of a horse pill, climbs into bed, and falls asleep.

Whereas before she had been agitated, unable to turn her thoughts away, now she is peaceful, assembling something, proud. But tired, too—this is not unexpected; every day by four or five o'clock she has to sink into bed for a nap, let in dreams full of floaty shapes, closed fists, and open mouths. Still, most days, she gets a little something done. She lines a trunk with old wallpaper, goes for a walk in the woods with a friend, starts to plan a lesson sequence on how leaves change color in the fall. Her children are all away for the summer, shipped off to lakes and rivers and seas. Sometimes she gets a "Dear Teacher" postcard: *I found some mica. We went on a boat. I lost my ring in the lake.* The water in the postcards is always a vivid, chlorinated blue. She gets her hair cut, sees a matinee movie with her friend Hannah, starts to knit again. One night Tom remarks—perhaps with relief, perhaps with the slightest tinge of fear—that she seems back to her old self.

In the basement, the men put in lally columns, thick and red, to keep the first floor from falling in. They construct a vapor barrier, rewire the electricity. They sister the joists and patch the foundation. In her bedroom, she stuffs cotton in her ears to block the noise. She wears sweatpants or loose shorts now, and Tom's shirts. Each time she catches a glimpse of herself in the mirror, she is struck by how pretty she looks, her eyes so bright, almost feverish, her fingernails a flushed, excited pink.

She finds a second foot with five perfect toes, and a second shoulder. She finds a leg, an arm. No eyes yet, no face. Everything in time, she tells herself, and at the Center for Reproductive Medicine they inject her womb with blue, and she sees her tubes, thin as violin strings, curled and ghostly on the screen. They have her drink water and lie on her back. They swab gel on her belly, and she neglects to tell them that her actual belly is at home, smelling like dust and apple wood, snoozing under the eaves. They say come in on day three, on day ten. They swab her with more gel and give her a rattle, loose pills in an amber jar. Tom goes to the clinic, and they shut him in a room with girlie magazines and take his fish. At home, while he is at the doctor's, she finds a tiny penis, sweet and curled. Tom comes home discouraged—rare for him. He lies down on the floor and sighs. She says don't worry, babe, and leans to kiss him on the arm. She would like to tell him about everything she has found, but she knows she must protect her secret. Things are so fragile, really—the earth settles, the house shifts. You put up a wall in the wrong place and so never find the hidden object in the eaves. You speak too soon and cause—with your hard, your hopeful words—a clot, a cramp. Things are so fragile, but then also not. Look at the ants, she tells herself—how they always find a place to make a nest. Look at the people of the earth, each one with a mother. At the supermarket, she stares at them—their hands, their faces, how neatly it all goes together, a completed puzzle.

She knows her own way is out of the ordinary, but then what is ordinary these days? She is living in a time of freezers and test tubes, of petri dishes and turkey basters, of trade and barter, test and track, mix and match. Women carry the eggs of other women, or have their own eggs injected back into them pumped with potential, four or six at a time. Sperm are washed and coddled, separated and sifted, like gold. Ovaries are inflated until they spill with treasures. The names sound like code words: GIFT, IUI, ZIFT. Though it upsets her to admit it, the other women at the Center disgust her a little. They seem so desperate, they look so swollen, but in all the wrong places—their eyes, their chins, their hearts. Not me, she thinks as the nurse calls her name and she rises with a friendly smile.

One day, she moves the burlap bag from the attic to the back of her bedroom closet. It's such a big house, and the attic is sweltering now, and soon the men will be working up there on the charred wood. Before, she and Tom lived in a tiny, rented bungalow and looked into each other's eyes a lot. She loves Tom; she really does, though lately he seems quite far away. Outside, here, is a swing set made of old, splintered cedar, not safe enough for use. But that same day, she finds an ear in it, tucked like a chestnut under a climbing pole. The tomatoes are ripe now. The sunflowers she planted in May are taller than she is, balancing their heads on swaying stalks. In the herb garden, the chives bear fat purple balls. The ear, oddly, is downed with dark hair, like the ear of a young primate. She holds it to her own ear as if she might hear something inside it—the sea, perhaps, a heartbeat or a yawn.

It looks so tender that she wraps it in tissue paper before placing it in the bag.

One night on the evening news, she and Tom see a story about a girl who was in a car accident and went into a coma, and now the girl performs miracles and people think she's a saint. The news shows her lying in Worcester in her parents' garage, hitched to life support while pilgrims come from near and far: people on crutches, children with cancer, barren women, men dying of AIDS. Jesus, says Tom, shuddering. People will believe any-thing—how sick. But she doesn't think it's so sick, the way the vinyl-sided ranch house is transformed into a wall of flowers, the way people bring gifts—Barbie dolls, barrettes, Hawaiian Punch (the girl's favorite)—and a blind man sees again, and a baby blooms from a tired woman's torso, and the rest of the people, well, the rest sit briefly in the full lap of hope, then get in their cars and go home. The girl is pretty, even though she's almost dead. Her braid is black and shiny, her brow peaceful. Her moth-er, the reporter says, sponge-bathes her each morning and again at night. Her father is petitioning the Vatican for the girl to be made an official saint.

Days now, while the men work in the attic, she roams. She wanders the house looking for treasures, and on the days when she does not find them, she gets in her car and drives to town, or out along the country roads. Sometimes she finds barn sales and gets things for the house—a chair for Tom's desk, an old egg can-dler filled with holes. One day at a yard sale, she buys a sewing machine, though she's never used one. I'll give you the instruc-tion book, the woman says. It's easy—you'll see. Also at this yard sale is a playpen, a high chair, a pile of infant clothes. The woman sees her staring at them. I thought you might be expecting, she says, smiling. But I didn't want to presume. As a bonus, she throws in a plump pincushion stabbed with silver pins and nee-dles, and a blue and white sailor suit. It was my son's, she says, and from behind the house come—as if in proof—the shrieks of kids at play.

That night, with Tom in New York for an overnight meeting, she sets up the sewing machine and sits with the instruction man-ual in her lap. She slides out the trap door under the needle, examining the bobbin. Slowly, following the instructions, she winds the bobbin full of beige thread, then threads the needle. She gets the bag from the closet. She's not sure she's ready (the books say you're never sure), but at the same time her body is guiding, pushing, *urging* her. Breathe, she commands herself, and draws a deep breath. She has never done this before, never threaded the needle or assembled the pattern or put together the parts, but it doesn't seem to matter; she has a sense of how to approach it—first this, then this, then this. She takes a hand out of the bag and tries to stitch it to an arm, but the machine jams so she unwinds a length of thread from the bobbin, pulls a needle from the pincushion, and begins again, by hand.

Slowly, awkwardly, she stitches arm to shoulder, stops to catch her breath and wipe the sweat from her brow. She remembers back stitch, cross stitch; someone (her mother?) must have taught her long ago. She finds the other hand, the other arm. Does she have everything? It's been a long summer, and she's found so much; she might be losing track. If there aren't enough pieces, don't panic, she tells herself. He doesn't need to be perfect; she's not asking for that. He can be missing a part or two, he can need extra care. Her own body, after all, has its flaws, its stubborn limits. What, anyway, is perfect in this world? She'll take what she is given, what she has been able, bit by bit, to make.

She stitches feet to legs, carefully doing the seams on the inside so they won't show. She attaches leg to torso, sews on the little penis. The boy-child begins to stir, to struggle; perhaps he has to pee. Not yet, my love. Hold on. She works long and hard and late into the night, her body tight with effort, the room filled with animal noises that spring from her mouth as if she were someone else. She wishes, with a deep, aching pain, that Tom were here to guide her hands, to help her breathe and watch her work. Finally—it must be near dawn—she reaches into the bag and finds nothing. How tired she is, bone tired, skin tired. She must be finished, for she has used up all the parts.

Slowly, then, as if in sleep, she rises with the child in her arms. She has been working in the dark and so can't quite see him, though she feels his downy head, his foot and hand. He curls toward her for an instant as if to nurse, so she unbuttons her blouse and draws him near. He nuzzles toward her but does not drink, and she passes a hand over his face and realizes that he has no mouth. Carefully, in the dark, she inspects him with both her hands and mind: he has a nose but no mouth, wrists but no elbows. She spreads her palm over his torso, and her fingers tell her that he has kidneys and a liver but only six small ribs and half a heart. Oh, she tells him. Oh, I'm sorry. I tried so hard. I found and saved and stitched and tried so hard and yet—

She feels it first, before he goes: a spasm in her belly, a clot in her brain, a sorrow so thick and familiar that she knows she's felt it before, but not like this, so unyielding, so tangible. Six small ribs and only half a heart. While she holds him, he twitches twice and then is still.

Carrying him, she makes her way downstairs. It's lighter now, the purple-blue of dawn. She walks to the front parlor, past the TV, past the old honey extractor they found in the barn. She walks to the Mourning Door and tries to open it. It doesn't budge, wedged shut, and for a moment she panics—she has to get out now; the weight in her arms keeps getting heavier, a sack of stones. She needs to pass it through this door and set it down, or she will break. Trying to stay calm, she goes to the laundry room and finds a screwdriver, returns to the door, and wedges the tool in along the lock placket, balancing the baby on one arm. Finally the door gives, and she walks through it, forgetting that no steps meet it outside. Falling forward over the high ledge, she lands, stumbles, catches her balance (somehow, she hasn't dropped him) to stand stunned and breathless in the still morning air, her knees weak from landing hard.

Across the road, the sheep in the field have begun their bleating. A truck drives by, catching her briefly in its headlights. She lowers her nose to the baby's head and breathes in the smell of him. He's lighter now, easier now. *Depart,* she thinks, the word an old prayer following her through the door. *Depart in peace.* With her hands, she memorizes the slope of his nose, the open architecture of his skull. She fingers the spirals of one ear. Then she turns and starts walking, out behind the house to the barn where a shovel hangs beside the hoe and rake. It's lighter now. A mosquito hovers close to her face. The day will be hot. Later, Tom will return. She buries the baby under a hawthorn tree on the backstretch of their land and leaves his grave unmarked. My boy, she says as she turns to go. Thank you, she says—to him or to the air—when she is halfway home. She sleeps all morning and gardens through the afternoon.

That night (day sixteen, except she's stopped charting), she and Tom make love, and afterwards she thinks of nothing—no wagging fish, no hovering egg, no pathway, her thoughts as flat and clean as sheets. Tom smells like himself—it is a smell she loves and had nearly forgotten—and after their sex, they talk about his trip, and he runs a hand idly down her back. She is ready for something now—a child inside her or a child outside, come from another bed, another place. Or she is ready, perhaps, for no child at all, a trip with Tom to a different altitude or hemisphere, a rocky, twisting hike. They make love again, and after she comes, she cries, and he asks what, what is it, but it's nothing she can describe, it's where she's been, so far away and without him—in the charred attic, the tipped basement, where red columns try to shore up a house that will stand for as long as it wants to and fall when it wants to fall. Nothing, she says, and inside her something joins, or tries to join, forms or does not, and her dream, when she sleeps, is of the far horizon, a smooth, receding curve.

Beasts

"Thank you, beautiful," I said as my six-year-old daughter, Maude, came skipping over from the swings to hand me a warm, wilted bouquet of dandelions. Dandelions, the only flowers no one cares if you pick. Maude smiled at me, then turned and ran screaming back to the playground.

"Stop," she called as she ran, her voice freezing Kyle, her best friend, in mid-motion about to sit on the one free swing. "It's my turn."

"You shouldn't call her that," Bibi, Kyle's mom, said. Bibi was my oldest friend; we'd known each other since college.

"What?" I wasn't really paying attention. I was watching to make sure Maude didn't bully Kyle, who was small for his age, a worrier and easily bossed. Instead Maude turned suddenly gracious and led Kyle by the hand to the playground's other swing set where two cast aluminum ponies hung side by side.

"Damn adjective," Bibi said, raking her long black hair out of her eyes with her fingernails. "Or is *beautiful* an adverb?"

"Adverbs modify verbs," I said, English teacher that I was. "Beautifully is an adverb. As in 'Maude sings *beautifully.*'" Maude, as a matter of fact, took after me and couldn't carry a tune in a great big bucket.

Bibi waved away the instruction. "The point is, Jean, you shouldn't call Maude beautiful." Bibi emphasized *beautiful* in a way that held it out like a dirty sock between two pinched, disapproving fingers. I looked across the playground at Maude. As I watched, Maude's blond hair flew first forward then back as she swung her horse without mercy toward some imaginary finish line. Her eyes looked blue and big and bright even from here. Why shouldn't I call my daughter beautiful? Maude *was* beautiful.

And not because of hair or eye color. In Wisconsin, being blond was nothing special. Two thirds of the kids in Maude's first-grade class were blond. Kyle was so fair my husband, Anders, joked you could read a newspaper through him. And it wasn't her neat, symmetrical little girl chin and nose. She was beautiful because in some way I couldn't quite prove scientifically, she glowed. She spun off energy like a hot, new star.

Not a day went by people in the street or the grocery store didn't notice, didn't stop me and repeat that very *b* word. What a *beautiful* baby, what a *beautiful* girl. At the Mexican restaurant near our house where we stopped for takeout, the señora called Maude *La Linda*. "Beauty," Anders would say, when Maude pitched a fit over some little thing, "and Beast."

"It warps girls," Bibi said, her voice was shaking. She sounded like she might cry. "Take my word for it. I know." Of course, Bibi knew. She was beautiful. And I, I was not. Nice-looking, neat maybe, but not beautiful. "It becomes everything to you. You end up spending all your time trying to *be* beautiful, wondering why no one has called you beautiful yet today, this hour, this minute. You live in fear of the day you'll get sick or old and turn so ugly no one will love you."

"Oh, honey," I said. I put my arm around her and squeezed her shoulder, but at the same time I thought, She's talking about her life, not Maude's.

Bibi accepted the consolation of the hug, but said, "I know what I'm talking about, Jean. You should listen."

I frowned, shifting my focus from Bibi to Maude. My beautiful girl. It seemed so innocent. "Do you really think I'm hurting her?"

"Not if you stop," Bibi said.

I looked toward Maude. Was Bibi right? Maude was spinning Kyle on the merry-go-round, her small sneakered feet raising dust. She was putting her back into it, clearly determined to go faster than childkind had ever gone before. Kyle was hanging on with both hands, squeaking, *No no no*. And then something that sounded like suspiciously like *Sssstttttooooopppp*. Instead Maude jumped onto the flying carousel and stood right in the middle, hands flung up to the sky, a blond whirligig, a Wisconsin dervish. Kyle let go of the safety bar and clung to her leg.

Bibi was looking not at the pale blur that was her son, but at the horizon, at the tall chain-link fence that marked the boundary between playground and park—this side for children, the other for grass. She seemed, for a moment, to have forgotten we were there. She sighed.

"I'd better grab Maude," I said, giving Bibi's shoulder a last, clumsy pat, "before she breaks Kyle in two."

All the way home from the playground, I thought about what Bibi had said. Was she right about Maude? It was hard to know. I thought of Bibi, so bright and, yes, beautiful, sitting on the bench in her red tunic and purple velvet bell-bottoms. I would never have admitted this to Bibi, but I picked clothes to be purposefully neutral. That way if I wore the same sweater three days in a row, people assumed I owned three gray sweaters. Actually, I owned half a closetful.

I thought about what she'd said while I sorted the dirty clothes before dinner. One basket of whites—mostly towels and Anders's T-shirts. One of darks—my grays and Anders's black jeans. In a college town like ours, nearly everyone wore black, the house color of academics. One basket of bright colors—all Maude's. Did beautiful people instinctively crave purples and oranges and reds? Maude had a weakness for chartreuse as well.

Over dinner, Anders told about his trip to our neighborhood hardware store to get brass screws for an installation piece he was working on. Anders was a photographer who taught in the art department at the state university, but lately his photographs had begun to leap, rather inconveniently, off the walls. He cut and arranged them in dioramas and installed them in large impressive pieces of vaguely Victorian cabinetry. He'd even made an inlaid teak projector stand that spun in circles while showing magic lantern slides—"moving pictures." I liked it. It was exciting to watch hand-colored prints of tropical fish spin dizzyingly around the room on the white walls above the furniture. It made me think about all the things I took for granted, real movies, TV, video, computers—miracles too much a part of everyday life to seem miraculous anymore.

These new pieces already took up an amazing amount of space in our small, crowded house, but still Anders kept buying sheets of mahogany, brass pulls and knobs and screws, slowly and quietly building his private World's Fair. "So," Anders was telling Maude, "I was standing in line when this woman comes up behind me and says, 'Aren't you Maude Dahl's father?' and then the old guy behind the counter says, 'Maude's your daughter?'"

Anders laughed. "Isn't that amazing? I thought. My daughter is famous!" Maude shrieked she was so delighted. I smiled.

The old man behind the counter must have been the owner, Mr. Vandergraff. Maude had gone with her class on a fieldtrip to the hardware store just two weeks before and had come home with instructions for how to make birdfeeders out of pop bottles. Obviously, Maude had made an impression on him. Had she been wearing chartreuse that day?

The woman was probably one of Maude's many teachers, at school, swimming, Sunday school, tumbling, ballet. Unless she knew Maude from Anders's pictures. Locally, they were his best-known work. They'd hung in the faculty show at the university, in the biannual survey of who was who among Wisconsin artists, and in a popular coffeehouse near campus where students hung out for hours drinking latte. Over the students' bent heads hung Maude at four months, an upside-down blur swinging in front of Anders's lens, the amazing flying baby. Maude at two, with a jumbo pitted olive on the end of each stubby finger like some mutant half-toddler, half-tree frog.

Anders shaped his face into an extravagantly artificial frown. "Famous on five continents, but I'm nobody in this town but Mad Maudie's dad."

"Oh, Daddy," Maude rolled her eyes. She had taken to pretending offense when he called her Maudie, his baby name for her. The *mad* she didn't mind. But wasn't "mad" as bad as beautiful? I wondered, all adjectives suddenly suspect.

"When you win the Nobel Prize," Anders said, his faux frown losing out to his usual slight, mocking smile, "just remember to thank your old dad."

"Thanks, Old Dad," Maude said, kissing him on the top of his graying, old dad head. That done, she turned to her mother. "Is there a fieldtrip tomorrow?" she asked. I nodded. I'd signed a permission slip for Maude and her fellow kindergartners to be taken to the State Historical Society to see a new exhibit on Native Americans of Wisconsin. I had, as usual, ducked Maude's teacher's suggestion that it was my turn to chaperon. I taught freshman English at the local community college and had forty student essays waiting for me in my bulging book bag. "I want to wear my straw hat, Mom," Maude said.

"Are you sure, Maude?" I said. On family trips, Maude tended to start out with a sunhat and then lose interest. Usually I wound up carrying or wearing it. And none of Maude's teachers looked like the straw bonnet type. Maude, though, looked absolutely stunning in it. When she'd worn it to the farmer's market that past weekend, half the people who passed us hurrying in their search for the perfect pumpkin or heirloom apples or aged cheddar could be heard to remark in passing, *Did you see that beautiful little girl in that lovely/amazing/damn big straw hat?* I was sure Maude had heard them as well.

Maude nodded. "And," she added, "if they're clean, I'll wear my chartreuse socks."

That night after Maude had been steered clear of the treacherous reefs that surrounded six-year-old bedtime and was safely asleep, I lay in bed, trying to summon up some energy for my stack of papers. When I was engaged in my teaching, full of the kind of energy I had rarely been able to summon this fall, I gave my students what I thought of as slightly mad, challenging assignments. Compare someone you love to a wonder of the world. This time I had only told them to compare or contrast two people, places, or things. So I knew without looking I was doomed to comparisons of dogs to cats, Big Macs to Whoppers, Frisbee golf to Hacky Sack, Wisconsin to Iowa or, at best, Illinois.

I gave up on my students' attempt to find meaning in the subtle variations of daily life, and began leafing through one of the many back issues of *The New Yorker* I hadn't gotten around to reading. I glanced at the listings for photography shows. Anders was too busy building his vision of the Past/Future for gallery openings in Manhattan to interest him. I had grown up as an Army brat, moving every four years. Anders had been born in Wisconsin in the same small town where his great-grandparents were buried. He'd left Wisconsin reluctantly to go to grad school in New York, serving time as if in the foreign legion until he could at last return home, return to a place where the people had the innate sense to call all cold fizzy drinks *pop.* His plan, he told me on our first date, was to be like Frank Lloyd Wright, a fellow Wisconsin native, who also hated cities and who had made the world beat a path to his low, well-designed door.

When we met, Anders had been a brand-new assistant professor. He was experimenting with color film, mad with the extravagance of having unlimited access to the department's color processor and printer. He blew up everything he shot to poster-size. He would stay up all night printing what he'd shot, then drag it still wet into class the next morning for his students to see.

After we started dating, Anders begged me to model. If I would, we could spend all our nights together. So I had agreed to pose. But first we'd gone shopping. Even then my wardrobe had been better suited to black and white photography, so we'd gone to a vintage clothing store near campus and bought a big red satin shirt the color of Technicolor lipstick. Then we went to an all-night drugstore and bought the lipstick to match. The first night, he took pictures of me leaping off a chair, a blurry, midair kiss of a woman. Then on other nights, juggling—and dropping—green apples. Then, in an artistic breakthrough, throwing lime Jell-O into the air.

Some of the shots looked like Kodak ads—all color, no content. But some, when I had tired of the games and the endless delays for moving the spots, metering the lights, reloading the camera, when my mouth was a weary smear, my eyes narrowed, my neck bent with fatigue into a slightly odd, painful angle, *voilà*, there was tension and some hint of a story that would forever remain tantalizing and unknowable. There was art.

After the photo sessions, we would make love on the futon that was Anders's only furniture, and then he would leave me to a few lumpy hours of sleep while he went to his darkroom on campus to develop that night's film, make color prints from the negatives he'd taken the night before.

By the end of the semester, it was clear that Anders was going to move his futon into the house I was renting, the one we would later buy. So when Anders asked me to pick up the four-foot party sub he had ordered for his end-of-class party, I agreed. I'd walked through the door carrying this most ridiculous of foods, and the assembled photography students looked up and cried as one, "It's her." As genuinely starstruck as if they had spotted Madonna. "It's the Jell-O Woman." For a moment, I was famous. But where was there to go after fruit-flavored gelatin? I had been relieved when, a little more than a year later, Maude came along to model for Anders.

But how long had it been since Anders had taken a picture of Maude? I tried to remember. Not a roll of holiday snapshots to send my parents, who'd retired to a condo in Sarasota, but an honest-to-God photo as Art? I couldn't remember. Last summer? Earlier this fall? At any rate, before Anders bought a table saw and began building his mahogany boxes.

Anders came to bed, crawling over me to get to his side, picking up a magazine on the way. Anders actually read the long *New Yorker* profiles of people you never knew existed until you saw the columns of tiny type about them. I propped myself up on one elbow. "Why don't you take pictures of Maude anymore?"

"What?" Anders was flipping through his issue, squinting at the cartoons. "Oh." He blinked, as if he hadn't really realized he had stopped. "No reason. Just that last time, it didn't work out. She posed too much."

"What do mean?"

He shrugged. "She didn't know what to do with her hands, with her mouth. She kept smiling like she thought she should smile in a picture." He turned back to his magazine. "You can't be yourself if you're worried all the time about being beautiful."

That's it, I thought, as we settled down to sleep. I was going to go cold turkey on all words, adjective and adverb, that referred to the illusion we call our bodies, bodies that were bound in the course of things to grow sick or old. No more beautifuls or lovelies. Not even a stray little *don't-you-look-nice.*

Thursday was Bibi's and my annual night out to celebrate our birthdays, which fell a mere ten days apart. Our tradition was to go to a bar we'd never been before, get good and drunk, exchange small gifts, sometimes break into fits of inappropriate song or dance. Once we got bounced from a bar for doing an imitation of the Rockettes, high-kicking and singing "New York, New York," in my case shrill and off-key. Then, our birthdays duly celebrated, we'd take taxis home, where families and hangovers awaited us. In other words, for one night we acted like we were still in college. Anders and Bibi's husband, Lloyd, had seen the ritual enough times that they kept the aspirin handy. This year we'd chosen the town's first martini bar. We found a table, then we each pulled out our presents and set them in front of us. Mine for Bibi was in a small gold gift box that had obviously been wrapped at the store, Bibi's present for me in a red handmade paper bag pulled shut with rough twine.

Bibi and I had known each other as undergraduates, floor-mates in a large, rowdy coed dorm. But we hadn't started this tra-dition, hadn't become best friends until we were in grad school. Bibi in her first semester of art and me working on my master's in English, already teaching freshman composition, though I hadn't known then I had stumbled into my future. At that first birthday party, Bibi had handed me a scroll tied up with gold ribbon. I un-rolled it, expecting to see words—maybe a hand-set poem or a Zen koan done in calligraphy. Instead, the paper was blank. I turned it over, looking carefully at both sides. It was odd paper, as blue and fuzzy as dryer lint. I looked up at Bibi, trying not to look too puzzled. "I made it," Bibi said, "in my papermaking workshop. You whiz snips of old blue jeans in a blender with water and Elmer's Glue, then spread it out to dry on an old win-dow screen."

It is lint, I thought. "It's amazing," I said, knowing it had prob-ably taken Bibi hours to make.

"I'll show you how to frame it." Bibi smiled lovingly at the first piece of paper she had ever made. She, too, had found her life's work.

I still had Bibi's first gift and her second, a blank book. I, on the other hand, doubted Bibi still had the first gift I had given her, a literary guide to Wisconsin. Bibi had flipped through it, peering at the foldout map, at the black and white photos of authors and their houses. I didn't know then that Bibi was badly dyslexic, could hardly read, and so had good reason to prefer her books blank. It was me, crazy English major, who liked them dense with type.

The second year, I made a better choice, I gave Bibi a pair of earrings. Big purple glass grapes, a bunch for each ear. That set the pattern. Every year was a paper anniversary for Bibi. I, on the other hand, worked my way up from glass to silver. Last year, I'd even sprung for an odd bobbing pair of fourteen-carat gold plumb weights. This year, though, I'd broken with tradition. Instead of earrings, I had gotten Bibi a pin. A single smooth nugget of amber the size of a baby's heart bound with a band of silver, a sharp dagger of a pin set in the back. It looked like some-thing a Goth might have used to close his rough woolen cloak. I couldn't wait to see Bibi pin it to her bulky lime-green and orange sweater.

Before we opened presents, we always had at least one drink. Bibi got her martini with vodka and a pickled baby Vidalia onion. I, ever the more conservative, went for gin and an olive. But after the first glass of pure alcohol, I loosened up. Bibi talked me into ordering something off the specials board for my second. When it arrived it was a lovely, sad blue. What liquor turns a martini aquamarine? After one sip, I felt like crying. Then I was crying, not from sadness, really, but a sudden acute sense of time slipping past me. I could hear it rushing like water. I remembered our first birthday bash—our skin had been peach-perfect. I remembered Maude in my arms for the first time, a red-faced blue-eyed little radish. Where were any of us headed? Suddenly, time made me dizzy. I wanted to stop the relativity train and get everyone I loved off before we all came to some terrible end.

"Are you okay?" Bibi put her hand on my arm, her concern touching and genuine, though she knew from experience I was a maudlin drunk.

I nodded, wiped my eyes with my cocktail napkin.

"Hey," Bibi said, picking up her present, "may I?"

I nodded. "Tear away."

Bibi tore into her birthday gift, shredding the wrapping. She had a casual attitude toward machine-made paper. She held the amber up to the light and let out a long, happy *oooooh*.

"Be careful," I said, reaching out to touch the brooch's silver pin. In my martinied state, I misjudged this distance and pricked myself. As if in fairy tale, a single drop of red blood appeared on the white tip of my finger.

"Close your eyes," Bibi said, unknotting the string on her pre-sent to me. I did, and heard a soft *whoosh* like moths fluttering past me. Bibi put something over my head, placed it gently around my neck. Could you knit scarves out of paper? I opened my eyes. This year, Bibi had given me jewelry. A necklace of folded paper strung on a silver cord. A lei. Aloha, I thought, my mind ever the dictio-nary, a word that means both hello and goodbye. I reached slowly up to touch it, almost afraid the paper might startle and fly away.

"It's *beautiful*," I said.

Bibi gave a wry laugh. "Oh, I almost forgot," she said, position-ing the amber over her left breast, then stabbing the silver pin into her sweater. "Can you watch Kyle for me on Saturday?"

I noticed my finger was still bleeding. It had left a red smear on my cocktail napkin and probably, though I couldn't see it, on the paper necklace as well. "Sure, what time? Maude has swimming lessons at eight-thirty, but we can be home by nine-fifteen if I tell her Kyle's coming. Otherwise she takes forever in the shower."

"No rush," Bibi said. She was signaling the waitress for our tab. "I'll drop Kyle off around ten. I have to go in for another biop-sy—this time on my right breast. Lloyd's going to drive me. I should be home by two-thirty at the latest."

I started to say something, I wasn't sure what, but Bibi put a finger across my lips.

"Later," she said. "No matter what they find, they won't do any-thing. Not then."

Saturday, Maude was up before the alarm went off, digging through her drawer for her bathing suit and goggles. We had taken the summer off from swimming lessons, and now she was eager to start again at the Y. She had forgotten last spring's tears over her inability to float on her back. I made a pot of coffee, toasted a bagel. Friday morning after my night out, I had been wretched, as sick as I had ever been in my life. "Think of it as nature's way of keeping you sober," Anders had said, shaking his head. This morning I still felt a little shaky. This is what age did to you, I thought. Throw a little party, and it took a week for your liver, cranky old housekeeper, to clean up the place. Maude, a healthy six, ate three heaping bowls of Cheerios.

Maude swam with great splashing enthusiasm, cheerfully ven-turing in over her head. It made me nervous to watch her, but her teacher was full of praise. He moved her up from Minnow to Fish. "The spirit's there," he said, when the class was over and the kids ran shivering for the showers. "Her body will catch up."

In the locker room, Maude's class struggled into their clothes as the next class wriggled into their suits. Lockers banged, and girls shrieked. A baby, sibling of some young amphibian, cried at the top of her lungs. I felt yesterday's hangover in the base of my skull, clearly planning a comeback. I was pretty sure I had some Tylenol in my purse, and I desperately wanted to wash them down with Diet Coke, that perfect shot of caffeine and Nutra-Sweet. Maude, sensing where her mother was headed, begged a quarter off me for the gum machine. I hesitated. Anders disapproved of gum. It stuck to your shoes and wasn't even food, but then again, he wasn't here. I opened my change purse and dug out a quarter for Maude. That and a few pennies were all the change I had, but I knew from Maude's past swimming lessons the Coke machine took dollar bills.

What was Bibi doing, thinking right then? I wondered as I dug through my wallet for a bill that wasn't too wrinkled. They wouldn't let you have breakfast, even before a minor surgical procedure. She must be starving. Bibi always ate a good breakfast. Maybe she was brushing her teeth, over and over. That was okay as long as you spat and didn't swallow. She wasn't worried, she'd told me the night before. This was her third biopsy in as many years. Her mother had been the same way, Bibi said. Biopsies every year and never anything but harmless fibroids. And now with mammograms, every shadow made the docs jump. They'd be negligent not to follow up.

I fed a bill into the Coke machine. It sucked it in halfway, then spat it out. Damn. I smoothed it, running the bill back and forth across the sharp corner of the candy machine. I had had only one lump, one biopsy. It happened just before I met Anders. The scariest thing had been the changing room at the university hospital, a locker room full of women coming in for biopsies, women getting the news from ones already finished, still others on their way to a dose of chemo or radiation. No privacy. In the corners, women wept. Bibi said it wasn't like that now. Each woman had her own little curtained cubicle with a La-Z-Boy recliner to lounge in while the nurse started her pre-op IV.

The Coke machine emphatically and finally rejected my dollar bill. I turned my back on the idea of liquid refreshment other than water. Maude was sitting on the couch by the door, looking glum. Wasn't the gum machine working, either? "What's the matter, sweetie?" I said.

"I swallowed it."

"The gum?"

"The quarter."

I didn't know what to say. I had heard plenty of jokes over the years about kids swallowing things, about parents keeping watch over toilet bowls to get back diamond engagement rings. Surely, surely swallowing change was not that serious. Maude looked okay. We could afford the quarter. Maybe we should just go home and see what Anders thought.

"It hurts, Mom," Maude said, pointing at a place just below her heart. Now, suddenly there were tears in her eyes. "It hurts right here."

We went to the emergency room. There the triage nurse was openly concerned. "You didn't call 911?" she asked me.

I shook my head. The nurse frowned, then turned to Maude. "Tell me what happened, dear. How did you swallow the quarter?"

Maude looked embarrassed. At six, she knew she was old enough to know better. "I don't know," she said. "I didn't have pockets so I put it in my mouth, then I was just standing there looking at the gumballs and I forgot and swallowed it."

It made sense, I found myself thinking, drawn in by Maude's slant logic. I had noticed how few clothes made for girls Maude's age had pockets. Boys' pants always had pockets. What were little girls supposed to do, carry purses?

"Did you cough or choke?" the nurse asked. She was writing all this down.

"No," Maude said. "I tried to spit the quarter out but it was too late."

"Are you having trouble breathing?"

"No," Maude said, "but it hurts." And she looked like she was going to cry again. I put my arm around her.

"It'll be okay, sweetie," I said. The nurse, I noticed, looked less sure.

"The peds doc will probably want an x-ray," she said. She put us in a cubicle to wait for the pediatrician on call. A cubicle similar, I imagined, to the one where they would put Bibi. *Bibi.* Had I told Anders that Bibi was going to drop Kyle off? I had forgotten my watch, but surely it was ten already. There was a phone on the wall beyond where Maude lay on the narrow examination table, paper sheet pulled up around her neck, but it was a blinking maze of buttons. I ran my hand over Maude's damp hair. "Does it still hurt?"

"A little," Maude said.

"Rest, sweetie," I said to my daughter. "I need to call Daddy." I stuck my head out of the curtain. "Excuse me," I said to a nurse, not our nurse, behind the desk. "How do I get an outside line on this phone?"

The nurse made a sour face, as if all the indigent moms in town came in here to make phone calls. "Press nine," she said, "then your number."

"He's here," Anders said about Kyle. "He's watching me stain plywood. Where are you?" I told him. "What does the doctor say?"

"We haven't seen one yet, but Maude seems better." Actually, Maude now had the paper sheet pulled over her head. "I'll call when I know something. We may be a while." I hung up the phone and peeked under the paper covers at my daughter. "Are you okay, Maude?"

Maude was crying again. "Why did you have to tell him? He'll think I'm stupid."

I sighed. We were in the adjective swamp again. And *stupid* didn't seem an improvement on *beautiful*. "I had to tell him," I explained. "He was worried. Besides, just because you do something stupid doesn't mean you are. Your father knows that. Everyone does stupid things sometimes." I patted Maude's paper-covered knee. "I certainly have."

"Knock, knock," a woman called, then flung back the curtain. "I'm Barbara. The doctor sent me to take you to x-ray." The woman spoke directly to Maude, not looking at me. You let your daughter swallow a quarter, I thought, and they all know what kind of mother you are. The x-ray technician held out her hand, and Maude hopped down off the table and took it. "Where does it hurt?" she asked Maude.

"Right here," Maude said, pointing.

"Her esophagus," I heard myself say.

The technician looked at me as if she were surprised to find me there. "Are you a medical professional?" she asked.

"No," I said. Just a person with a passing knowledge of body parts, I wanted to say, but didn't. "I'm an English teacher."

"Oh," the technician smiled. "In that case, I'd better watch my grammar." She started to lead Maude down the hall. I began to follow. The technician waved me back. "We'll only be a minute," she said. "And Maude's a big girl, aren't you?"

Maude nodded emphatically and abandoned me, the mother who had given her the ill-fated quarter, without a backward glance.

Actually, they weren't gone long. Maude reappeared with two heart-shaped stickers on her purple turtleneck. The first read *I Got An X-ray Today!* and the second *I Was Brave!* "She was super," the technician said, holding up the black and gray picture of Maude's insides. She snapped it under the clip on the light box. "I'll go get the doctor," she said, and left.

"They make you hold your breath," Maude said, hopping back up on the table. She was taken with her stickers. "Just like in swimming class." I wanted to sneak over and flip the switch on the light box, illuminate Maude's irradiated bones, but before I could move the doctor was there.

"Dr. Jorgenson," he said, holding out his hand. I shook it. He looked about the same age as my students and his palm was almost as soft as Maude's. "So," he said, "let's see where the foreign object in question, the"—he glanced at the notes the nurse had taken—"quarter has gotten to." He flipped on the light. And there was the missing quarter, floating like a bright, full moon in the night that was Maude's chest.

The doctor pulled at his smooth, young chin. "How long ago did she swallow this?"

I peeked at the doctor's watch. It was nearly ten-thirty. "A little over an hour."

"Hmm, it's sitting right where the esophagus opens into her stomach. A tight squeeze for a quarter," he said. "Let me go talk to the pediatric gastroenterologist on call. We may have to go get it."

"Operate?"

Maude was excited. "Will I have a scar like Madeline?" she asked. The doctor looked puzzled.

"It's a children's book. The heroine has her appendix out."

"Oh," Dr. Jorgenson said. "No, no scar. We have this long rubber tube, an endoscope. We slip it down your throat and grab the quarter. Bring it up, good as new."

"Yech," Maude said. Thinking, I imagined, about where that quarter had been, but the doctor thought Maude meant the idea of the endoscopy.

"You'll be asleep," he said. "You won't even know when it happens." Maude nodded. "Be right back," he said to me.

Maude sat swinging her legs. I wondered if now was a good time to check in with Anders—I didn't like the "asleep" part—but Dr. Jorgenson was back before I had chance. "Dr. Gert says Maude should rest here for a while. Give her own muscles some time to squeeze that quarter through. We'll take another x-ray in thirty minutes, okay?"

I didn't like the idea of more radiation, either, but it sounded better than anesthesia. "Okay," I said to Dr. Jorgenson.

He patted Maude's foot. "Relax," he said.

After he was gone, Maude asked, "What did you do that was stupid, Mom?"

I almost said, "You mean besides start this conversation with my six-year-old daughter?" But it was too late to back out now. I thought of the time I had eaten a large dose of hash in sloppy joe mix. For a week, I'd thought my roommates were planning to kill me. Then of the time I slept with my Theory of Composition professor even though I knew he thought my teaching was hopeless. But those didn't seem quite the right examples for Maude. "Well," I said, "last year I backed out of the garage too fast without really looking and knocked the sideview mirror, *bam,* right off the car."

"Really?" Maude asked.

I nodded, not adding that I had told the insurance company someone had hit me in the grocery store parking lot. Or that I sometimes dreamed a big guy in an Allstate jacket was chasing me, calling me a liar and a lousy driver. "What else?" Maude asked.

"I jumped off the garage roof and broke my collarbone." Maude nodded. She knew that story. "I swung a baseball bat without looking and hit a kid standing behind me in the nose." Maude lay down again.

"It's really hurting now, Momma," she said, touching the same spot under her ribs. If only, I thought, I'd given Maude a dime. Maude turned over on the examining table, clutching her wrinkled paper towel of a sheet.

"Shhh," I said, stroking her hair. If Maude got any worse, I was going to fling back that curtain and go find Dr. Jorgenson. I put my face next to Maude's on the little paper pillow. "Then there was the time..." I had gotten as far on my list of stupid-things-I-did-as-a-child as the time I'd given the family dachshund a crayon to eat, when the Barbara, the x-ray technician, reappeared.

This time Dr. Jorgenson brought Maude back himself. He snapped the x-ray into place on the light box, flipped it on. I couldn't see through him—he was no x-ray—but I didn't have to. Dr. Jorgenson took one look, then whooped and made a fist, pulling victory down from the air. "Way to go, Idaho," he said to Maude. Then he stepped back, and I could see the full moon of the quarter was much lower and off to one side, no longer centered over the orderly ladder that was Maude's spine. "Into the stomach and on its way home," Dr. Jorgenson said.

Maude poked at her ribs. "It doesn't hurt anymore," she said, as though that surprised her.

"You know, kid," Dr. Jorgenson said, still admiring the x-ray. He tapped Maude's faint curving ribs. "You've got a *bea-ut-i-ful* set of bones here." He stretched out the word I had banned from our lives into four comic syllables. "You must drink a lot of milk."

"Ice cream," Maude said seriously. "The secret is ice cream."

"Really?" Dr. Jorgenson said. He stuck his hand into the pocket of his lab coat, drew out a prescription pad and some children's Motrin samples. He shook his head and tried the other pocket. "Then you'd be a good candidate for one of these." With a flourish, Dr. Jorgenson handed Maude a slip of paper. It read, *Rx: one ice cream cone to be taken internally. Fill this prescription at the University Hospital Cafeteria. ASAP.*

"Please, Momma?" Maude said. Part of me wasn't sure girls who swallowed quarters for a main course deserved dessert, but I was so grateful to have Maude unsedated, unintubated, I nodded.

"Sure," I said. "But remember, Kyle's waiting to play so we can't take all day." Would Anders have heard from Lloyd about Bibi yet?

We found the hospital cafeteria in the basement—weren't they always in the basement? It smelled unpleasantly like dishwater and overcooked broccoli, but the lunch rush, if there was one, hadn't started yet, and the large woman in the hairnet working the food line was happy to scoop Maude out a very large cookie dough cone. I grabbed a stack of napkins and followed Maude to a table near a row of dusty plastic plants. "Work on it a little," I told Maude, watching my daughter digging the chocolate chips out of the ice cream with her tongue. "Then we'll risk taking it in the car."

I spotted a pay phone on the far wall. "Stay right here, sweetie. I'm going to tell Dad you're okay." I got change for my wrinkled dollar from the cashier. The quarters looked huge in my hand. Would I ever look at one the same way again? A woman with a stroller beat me to the pay phone, and I stopped short, trying to signal I wanted to make a call, but not wanting to seem like I was listening in.

Luckily, it was a short conversation. "No. No. Okay," the woman said. "All right, then, pick us up out front." I smiled at the woman, looked into the carriage to smile at her baby as well. As a mother, I felt obligated to do that kind of thing. But the child in the carriage was much older than a baby, would have been a toddler if he had been able to walk. Twin oxygen tubes ran into his nostrils from a tank at his side. A blank rubbery expression filled his round face. I forced myself to smile anyway. The mother nodded at me as she pushed her son past.

I felt dizzy, but I made myself reach up to the receiver of the pay phone. Then I leaned forward, resting my forehead on the cool metal of the coin return. After a moment, I straightened. Maude was still sitting at the table, working hard on her cone. This was the first time Maude had ever been to an emergency room. She had never had more than a cold. Anders nothing worse than the flu. We had been living, were living, on the lucky side of the planet. *Lucky,* another word you couldn't trust. We were lucky. The other people in this room—some trailing IVs from tall T-shaped stands, others just sitting wearily over Styrofoam cups of coffee, waiting for news that was not likely to be good—they, clearly, were not.

But if beauty could desert you, then so could luck. Was Bibi, across the highway in ambulatory care, still one of the lucky ones? I thought of the boy in the baby carriage, then of blond, sweet, perpetually worried Kyle. I knew Bibi would say she had been lucky so far. Maybe that was the best any of us could say.

I dialed my own number. "Hello?" Anders said.

"We're coming home," I told him.

At the house, Kyle ran to greet Maude. No kid's idea of a good time is spending Saturday with someone else's parent. I told Anders the good news. "It might take as long as two weeks," I said, repeating what Dr. Jorgenson had told me. "But unless Maude starts throwing up or running a fever, the quarter can be considered safely on its way."

"Two weeks?" Anders said. "After that long, it should come out two dimes and a nickel."

I nodded, then belatedly realized he was making a joke and tried to smile. I hadn't done anything all morning except sit around and wait, but I felt exhausted. "Did you hear from Lloyd?" I asked. "Do they know anything yet?"

"Yes," Anders said, "and yes." He looked over his shoulder. Kyle was sitting on the living room couch. Maude was standing in front of him, tracing the path of the quarter with her finger. Anders lowered his voice. "It's malignant. Lloyd said they want to do a lumpectomy, probably tomorrow."

God, I thought, *lumpectomy.* What an ugly word. I knew, though, there were uglier ones.

"Then," Anders was saying, "Bibi will to have choose between chemo or radiation. Apparently it's her choice. I told Lloyd I'd help him do some research on the Web tonight."

I shook my head. Printouts about odds would never help Bibi decide what to do. Bibi was Bibi. I imagined her flipping a big gleaming quarter—heads I chose death rays, tails poison cocktails.

Anders looked at his watch. "Lloyd said he'd be by for Kyle as soon as he got Bibi settled at the house."

Kyle was looking at us, looking even whiter than usual. He knows, I thought, somehow he knew. For a chronic worrier, it must make a kind of perfect sense. He'd been preparing for bad news all his life, and now it had arrived.

"Dad, Dad." Maude was pulling on Anders's arm. "I need you to put on some music."

"What?" Anders said, for once not on his daughter's six-year-old wavelength.

"Kyle's playing audience, and I'm going to dance."

"What kind of music?"

Maude shrugged. "Dance music." Anders put on the Supremes. Then, at Maude's insistence, he sat on the couch next to Kyle. "*Stop, in the name of love.*" Maude was wiggling around, mouthing the words.

"No, no," I said, "like this." I spun into the routine I'd learned from Bibi in our dorm days, one she and I had done in a sports bar on the memorable occasion of our first birthday night bash.

"*Stop!*" I held my hand out like a school crossing guard. "*In the name of love.*" I crossed my heart. Maude threw herself into it, wagging her finger along with me. "*Before you break my heart.*" I heard footsteps on the front porch.

"Come on in, Lloyd," Anders called over the wall of sound.

"Nice moves." It was Bibi, standing next to Lloyd, looking as if nothing had happened to her on this Saturday that hadn't happened a thousand times before, as if under her sweater were no fresh stitches and, beneath them, no tumor, hard and hungry and growing.

"Auntie Bibi," Maude said, catching her hand, pulling her into the middle of the room. "You dance, too. We're a girl group. We're..." Maude paused, frowning with the effort of making up a name. "We're The Beautiful Girls."

Bibi didn't flinch when Maude said *beautiful.* Instead she smiled, began making the hand motions I remembered so well from the early years of our Beautiful Girl lives. As one, the three of us pivoted and turned and mouthed Diana Ross's words as if nothing in this world could ever be less than lovely. As if there were no tragedy or loss, no unlucky quarters in stomachs, no blank-faced children who couldn't breathe or walk, no ugly cancerous lumps. As if the world were all beauty and no beasts. Kyle and Anders on the couch gaped in amazement. Lloyd still standing, the long folds of his face damp from tears, sang along. Their girls were breaking their hearts. "*Stop,*" we girls sang. "*Stop.*" But, for now, there was no stopping us.

Intramuros

I. The City

> How deserted lies the city, once so full of people!
> How like a widow is she, who once was great
> among the nations! She who was queen among
> the provinces has now become a slave.
> —Jeremiah, Lamentations 1:1

Manila suffered during the war. How many times have I heard this? There are tales of the city weeping in the dead quiet that followed MacArthur's triumphant entry and of her shame at the rubble which greeted him. She wept in pain as bombs blasted away the monuments that marked her time as mistress to the Spaniards and destroyed the infant democracy, a gift from when she bedded the Americans. She mourned for the loss of Chinese and Indian baubles, and for the surrender to the Japanese—her Malay features disfigured by a history of rape and failure. Why would she suffer this degradation?

The image of Manila fleeing down the southern tip of the island of Luzon comes to mind. She bears great stone churches perched on her shoulders, universities in her arms, commerce belted about her waist, and a host of barrios tangled in the hem of her skirt. In pursuit are a plague of tanks and sword-wielding conquerors of the co-prosperity sphere. I picture an *indigena* Lady Liberty warily dipping her toe into the South China Sea.

A city does not suffer. A city knows no pain, nor can it shrink from it. She merely waits for someone to liberate her, and if the liberation is successful, the war recedes into the pages of history. I shall return Manila to her rightful place at the mouth of a great bay. She curls around it with an arm flung to the east. Her legs snuggle the southern coastline, her sorrowful gaze aimed towards the Bataan and Corregidor—if a city could gaze, which it can't any more than it can suffer. Walls are rebuilt, buildings constructed, people reenter the city carting the memories back, much as in the previous year they carted off the dead.

II. Intramuros

The Japanese did not march into Manila. They came quietly—more like the Chinese merchants than the Spanish soldiers. Intramuros—which was a neighborhood bound by stone walls, the legacy of the Spaniards—did not have a history of being hostile to outsiders. My family was of mixed blood; they ate the Chinese moon cakes and blasted firecrackers, learned Spanish, harvested rice in the provinces, and remembered all the pagan superstitions. They believed that the Jesuits were second only to Christ himself and were hospitable to the Japanese merchants who set up their bodegas in the Walled City during the twenties, side by side with the churches, mumbling their rolled *l*'s at the brown-robed friars who purchased soap and bags of sweets there. The old city, with its rat-infested canals and crumbling monuments, was such a mess of humanity that it would have been hard to single out the Japanese. They crept in like everything else and were patient and persistent, just like the succulent vines slowly tearing at the wall itself.

III. My Grandmother

There's a story about my grandmother refusing to leave Intramuros. Most of her children had already been shipped off to Nueva Ecija, where the rice fields were. The Japanese had already occupied Manila, but she didn't want to leave her house. She would stand in her kitchen looking at all the pots and pans, thinking, I don't want Mr. Matsushita getting his hands on these. This is the Mr. Matsushita who probably sold her all the pots in the first place and one fine morning appeared on the doorstep of his shop in full military regalia. Long live the Emperor and all of that. I wouldn't want him to get his hands on my pots, either. One day a Japanese soldier who was not much taller than my grandmother (and she was four-eleven) informed her that the house was needed by the Emperor. My grandmother didn't much like the idea of her house being a collaborator, but the Emperor's representatives insisted that it was not her choice, nor the house's.

I picture her with one hand fixed firmly to the doorknob of the kitchen door (hand-carved in the likeness of St. Joseph's face) and the other wrapped tightly around the wrist of her smiling baby, who can't tell the difference between visitors and invaders.

My grandfather, a sweet, irresponsible doctor who spoiled my mother to the point that she is still hard to live with, was standing knee-deep in water in Fort Santiago with other members of the Philippine elite and his fourteen-year-old son. The Japanese had informed the doctor that he could not leave in much the same tone as they'd informed my grandmother that she could not stay. My grandmother and baby Isabel moved into the church, ate leaves, and occasionally ventured over to the American POW camp, where her father-in-law, a Texan left over from the Spanish American War, would pass her handfuls of rice through the bars.

IV. Granddaddy

Granddaddy would not leave the Philippines. He'd left Texas at sixteen and never returned. The story is that he was riding his horse to buy a loaf of bread—something I'd like to believe, but has the stamp of Filipino romanticism of the Wild West all over it— and never came back. Next he was in Houston. Next he was cooking huge vats of beans on a Naval vessel bound for Manila. Then there was something about a railroad that has since mysteriously disappeared. Then he married, had a son, never left. He didn't want Mr. Matsushita to get anything, either. I'm not sure when Granddaddy switched residences, but I imagine the Japanese took him first. Finding him must have been a happy surprise for the sons of The Rising Sun: the enemy, drunk and old, wandering around in his house yelling obscenities. They stripped him naked, poked at him with their rifle butts, and had a grand old time.

Granddaddy ended up with the Americans in Santo Tomas, where his son had received his medical degree in the twenties. Granddaddy would joke about it—son, class of '25, father, class of '45. Things were bad then. In fact, the only up side of internment seemed to be that you met famous men like General Wainwright, a cavalry man with a heavy limp, whom MacArthur had left to hold the fort. Granddaddy had some questions for the general— for example, "Is MacArthur returning?"—but the fall of Bataan seemed to have left Wainwright with little to say.

Granddaddy would save his food and pass it through the bars to his daughter-in-law and granddaughter. He wrapped it in banana leaves. They ate the food. They ate the banana leaves. He would look at little barefoot Isabel in disbelief—an angel shot out of the sky and stuck in hell. He would say, "Any news on Raymond?" And my grandmother, with her hard, Spanish mouth and sad eyes, would simply shake her head. Granddaddy would watch them leave as they made their way back to the church. She was a brave woman, he thought, with a faith he envied in a God he didn't understand. "Isabel and I are safe," she said. "We're sleeping under the altar."

V. Uncle John

One day, an American soldier named John Strawhorn was wandering through the old city carrying some important piece of paper, and a little boy ran up to him and begged him not to bomb the church because it was full of civilians. John Strawhorn ran through the streets like he'd never run before, his heart pounding and tears streaming down his face, and he reached the man with the maps and the authority and told him, "Don't bomb the church!" Who would believe that John Strawhorn—with his Southern accent and thinning blond hair that stood up like a wheat field—would return to Maryland and have a daughter named Mary Lee, and that this woman would marry my uncle Jappy?

VI. Uncle Jappy

My uncle Jappy survived the war, got a degree in medicine (Santa Tomas '56), moved to the U.S., and began introducing himself as "Carlos." I knew him as Uncle Jappy. The more Spanish-influenced in the family called him Tito 'appy. He was not Japanese, nor was he a collaborator, being a mere five years of age when the war started and hardly a man when it finished. His only guilt was in his genes, which expressed the Chinese blood of my family to a startling degree—he could have passed, perhaps, for Japanese. I cannot explain why the family thought it was a joke to call him Jappy during the war, and even more difficult to explain why they used that appellation with all the love and affection implied by nicknames when the war was over. We called him Jappy until the day he died, which was long after his father and brother had left this earth, escorted into the afterlife by the Japanese.

VII. Lolo Raymond and Narding

My grandfather and Narding, my uncle, lived out their lives in

Fort Santiago. Who knows what happened? The records are murky. In fact, we only knew that they were in there because someone saw them. How could anyone see them? So many collaborators in those days of hopelessness. Our city, their war. Survival is easy to justify. My aunt Isabel was then two. She'd made it out to the province where the rest of her siblings were crashing around, wondering when they'd have to go back to school. The story goes something like this: Everyone was in the dining room eating, and Isabel decided that she needed to pee, although her mother did not have time to attend to her. She got left in the bathroom for quite a while. When my grandmother finally got around to getting her cleaned up, my aunt informed her that a man had come to visit her. He just stood there smiling, and Isabel was not afraid, even though she didn't know who he was. He was wearing khaki pants and a jacket made out of similar stuff. He looked like her brother Ray, only older, a lot older. He had just kind of disappeared and not through the doorway. That's how my family found out that my grandfather, Lolo Raymond, was dead. There is no way of knowing how much time he and his son were incarcerated.

I imagine my grandfather with his arm around his son, holding him close, while young Narding's heavy eyes looked to him for an answer. "The general said he was coming back," is all that he can say. He wonders if his wife is all right, whether her obstinacy has worked for or against her. He wonders if his father is still alive and prays that the other six children have made it out to the province.

VIII. *Uncle Joe*

Uncle Joe and Uncle Ray escaped Manila in a truck full of Japanese soldiers headed for Cabanatuan. At first they were confused by the generosity, but after a soldier insisted that they were to stand at the back of the truck and stay visible, they saw that they had earned the ride. Two mestizo teenagers were more than a good luck charm against guerrilla attacks and American snipers. Cabanatuan was where the Americans who weren't at Santa Tomas were imprisoned. Gapan, the town where the family kept the provincial home, was less than ten miles away.

My uncle Joe worshipped MacArthur. My uncle Joe thought he

was a hero. Uncle Joe left the Philippines for the land of MacArthur shortly after the war. Granddaddy took him on a ship away from his country, just as he'd taken him from my grandparents' house when he was a baby, determined to make him as American as he had once been. Granddaddy returned to Manila. Uncle Joe never did. He joined the all new American Air Force. He married his blond, blue-eyed sweetheart. He joined the John Birch Society. He ran for congressman on the Libertarian ticket. He's so American that I—who am half-American—cannot comprehend him. "MacArthur," says Uncle Joe, "defines glory." As far as I'm concerned, "glory" is "gory" with an *l*.

MacArthur's at the battle of Bataan facing fully armed Japanese troops, gets all the Filipinos together—most of whom are farmers and don't even have shoes—arms them with sticks, tells them to go into battle, and then gets mad when they break rank. Some didn't break rank, and that was a far greater bungle. Bravery and stupidity are not the same thing. I have another theory—Americans pronounce "Bah-tah-ahn" as "B'tan," which sounds completely different. I wouldn't be surprised if all the Filipinos got confused and went somewhere else.

IX. Tio Jack

If they did, they were lucky. My great-uncle Tio Jack (Joaquim was his real name) was in the wrong place at the wrong time, and soon found himself being marched north with a bunch of American GIs. This stroll through the countryside is now known as the Bataan Death March. I'll bet they were cursing MacArthur, imagining the Aussie steaks and fried eggs he had for breakfast every morning. Survival was improbable. A man stooping to sip water from a dirty puddle usually found himself face down in it and on his way to the afterlife. The only choices that presented themselves seemed to be modes of death: shot in the head, dehydration, decapitation, or starvation—you make the call. Dizzied with sickness and exhaustion, the prisoners made their way, teetering a hundred miles along the edge of the grave. My Tio Jack somehow managed to sneak away. He lay down hidden in a boat, and some villagers, with little thought of their own lives, managed to secret him away. In later years as Tio Jack—a jovial octogenarian—recounted the tale, he would say, "Others escaped. They learned the Japanese were crazy about staying clean. They threw, you know, you know, you know, at the guards." In my family, three "you knows" means shit. "So these GIs just pitch it at them, and the Japanese, who would take a grenade in the face for the Emperor, go running and screaming. You should have seen it, it was so damn funny." Tio Jack was a great man. He could tell you about the Bataan Death March and make it funny. All of his stories were funny, even though half of them weren't.

X. Benito

A lot of them were about the war, and since he spent the majority of the war with his cousin Benito, a lot of them were about Benito.

Benito, who was not known for his stellar intelligence, is hanging out in front of this building that has been "liberated" by the Japanese, and the locals are busily "liberating" it of everything of value. Benito lucks out. He gets a bicycle. He stands there, full of pride, watching all the guys leaving with typewriters (no ribbon has been available for the past three years), banker lamps (same thing goes for electricity), and other junk—files, paper weights, rubber stamps. He thinks he might want a rubber stamp, or a dried-out inkwell. Listen, he wasn't too bright. He sees this man standing by him, pleasantly smiling in his direction, a realm of focus that not only contains Benito but also the bicycle. Benito did not question the man's generosity when he offered to watch the bike while Benito went in to get more stuff... Somehow, this story is only funny when told by one of my relatives over sixty. Or maybe only people over sixty find it funny, although I found it funny the first thirty times or so I heard it. What I think is odd is that I find myself telling that story, often to people who don't really understand the war or the Philippines or Benito, and therefore have a slim chance of finding it amusing. I've decided that there must be some kind of "Benito story gene" that expresses itself randomly yet powerfully throughout my family members. I find myself telling that story to my mother, who I inherited it from in the first place.

XI. Some Family History

She's a war story in herself. All that crap in the basement, draw-

ings from when I was five, every doll, every toy I ever owned—
even the ones I never liked. Childhood pictures that I'd like to
have, but that she'll never let go. Clothes that haven't fit me since I
learned to walk. School uniforms bearing the monograms of religious orders that only have two living members left. Three-
pronged adapters to convert currents to levels acceptable only in
Australia. Betamax machines acceptable nowhere but Manila.
Moth-eaten sweaters that have crossed the Pacific four times,
never worn at any port. Shoes with buckles. Shoes without buckles. Shoes that ought to have buckles but lost them twenty years
ago when I still wore a children's size 11. Even the boxes—proud
"Mayflower" relics from the first move, when we left Pennsylvania
in 1969. Dust and dirt, ghostly smells, odd chills rising when a
neglected box is disturbed. Monument upon monument to the
past reminding one of nothing more than how very dead the past
is. My sister and I discovered recently that we both got insomnia
over thinking about all that junk; late at night we think about that
mountain of memory and wonder what we'll do when our mother dies. Morbid, maybe, but this happens in families where those
absent by untimely deaths play as much of a role in day-to-day
existence as the living. Death, among my people, is the inability
to disagree.

XII. Tita

My mother tells me sometimes of the beautiful dolls that her
father bought her, Shirley Temple—the genuine article—with
real golden curls; the eyes closed when you laid her down, and
they hadn't forgotten anything, not even the dimples. Where was
Shirley now? Where was my mother's beautiful sharkskin dress
with the pleats—very tailored, not like a little girl's dress at all.
Her father had bought her a paper doll one day. Over the course
of my childhood I received about fifty. And guess what? They're
all in the basement. My father has trouble with the basement—he
says it's a fire hazard—but I don't really expect him to understand. From what I gather, his experience of war was ping-pong
parties in his basement and blanketed windows around Boston.

I think of my eight-year-old mother and of that jeepney. It was
headed for Nueva Ecija, the provincial home. My grandfather
stood with her and Narding, surveying the interior. There was

just one space for a child. He did not see the gravity of his decision. How could he know when he waved my mother onboard that he was consigning his beloved son to a fatal companionship? My mother did not want to leave her father and her brother. She did not want to make the journey without them, but my grandfather said, "Tita, you go. If Narding goes with you, the two of you will fight." They never fought after that. I think, in all sympathy, that people tend to feel the most guilt over things for which they are not responsible. My mother ended up in the country, far from the staccato of the rifles and booming mortar.

XIII. Her Daughter

When I was little she would tell me of this time when she would wander in the peaceful garden singing a song. It went something like *"I can't stop blowing bubbles..."* and she'd waltz around the bushes, beneath the shade of the tamarind tree with her head full of Gregory Peck and Vivienne Leigh. Thinking about that now, watching this scene played out from twenty years ago when I, a big-eyed, black-haired child smiled as she danced, I get an odd chill, like I'm watching a scene out of *Whatever Happened to Baby Jane?* with an Asian Bette Davis. I hate myself for all the times I've been angry at her.

XIV. My Lola

For some odd reason, I can't remember my grandmother telling any war stories, and she lived it in the old city shoulder to shoulder with the Japanese. From listening to her, you'd think the war had been one big diet.

"Granddaddy was very, very fat. Then he got very, very skinny."

"General Wainwright was big, then he got skinny. They called him 'Skinny Wainwright.'"

"I was not so fat, but I got skinny. Very skinny."

Then she would say, "Ija, why are you so skinny?"

XV. Uncle Ray, S.J.

My uncle Ray, the Jesuit, visited us in Maine last summer. He stayed for a month. He was on sabbatical. He and my mother regressed to the point that at different times I wanted to say, You cut that crap out, or you'll have hell to pay. If he's bugging you, why don't you just go into the other room, et cetera. They talked about the different maestras who had shown up in the prewar years to teach them Spanish. They talked about Narding, who had been an angel his whole life and who, as far as they knew, was doing the same thing, only in a better place. They talked about those Japanese shopkeepers who had slipped them pieces of candy in the thirties then taken their father in the forties. Then one day, during this odd summer of reminiscence, my mother spun around from the sink, where she was up to her elbows in suds, and said, Remember the heads? And my uncle nodded for a few seconds. His eyes crinkled at the edges, and little nervous laughs began escaping his mouth. My mother got hit by the same humorous wave. She squatted down in front of the sink so overcome by laughter that she was silent other than the sharp sound of her inhalations. I walked around them both, going, What? After my sixth "What?" went unanswered, I gave up and starting laughing anyway. Finally, I'd been laughing for so long that not only did I feel like I was about to have a heart attack, but I had to go to the bathroom. When I came back, neither of them was laughing; in fact, they both looked a little disturbed. The next morning, over a cup of coffee, my mother informed me that the heads had appeared shortly after the Americans plowed through Manila. They were hanging from every public building, decorating every tree. They were the heads of the Japanese. You learn to laugh, she said. She was not apologetic, and I understood.

The Japanese, she told me, would not surrender. To be a prisoner of war meant that you didn't have the courage to die for the Emperor, you were less than a dog. The idea was to keep fighting and never to ask why.

XVI. A Japanese Soldier

This sounds an awful lot like MacArthur. *Dulce et decorum est pro patria mori.* If you were a soldier and not of that opinion, he would help you on your way to glory whether you liked it or not. Such a disposition was good for MacArthur because it gave him insight into the Japanese warrior.

What about the last Japanese soldier? You know the one. He was wandering in the jungles of Guam all the way into the sixties, carrying his gun and the love for his Emperor, and these two things along with some grubs and wild banana had kept him going. Then they found him and sent him home, maybe with a stack of old newspapers—a lot of newspapers. Never mind, he must have had a good deal of reading time in the hospital. That's a myth, actually, not the soldier, but the fact that they found him. For one thing, Guam isn't that large, and it seems more likely that they noticed him than anything else. Besides, if they were looking, they would have found many more people. I know that jungle well. Somewhere, behind a clump of bamboo, is Granddaddy and Tio Jack. In a dark cave is my grandmother, my mother, some uncles and aunts. And if they'd bothered to look at all, they would have found me, because we're all in that last stronghold of the Pacific Campaign or the Co-prosperity Sphere, as much a part of the jungle as that Japanese soldier or a banana plant or a mosquito. And the jungle is a part of my family. The war lives and breathes like a congenital virus manifesting itself when one is weak. Some of us are less susceptible than others.

XVII. My Aunt Pina

I will use my mother's eldest sister as an example. In her mind, people die and that's okay. During the war, lots of people died, which wasn't okay, but they would have died anyway. In addition to that, we're all Catholic, so aren't we supposed to want to die? Don't we envy the dead their proximity to God? Besides, the more of the family who are dead, the more people there are to intercede on our behalf.

I'm not sure what Aunt Pina was doing during World War II. If her behavior now is any indication, she was probably dispensing wisdom and making sure everyone had something to eat. She married shortly after the war when she was eighteen years old. The man she married—a mestizo doctor—was forty-three. He built her a house, far from the rubble that had once been Intramuros, with a fountain and a garden and graceful Corinthian pillars. He took her to Spain, where she bought chandeliers that hang in the sala. He commissioned their life-size portraits that hang in the drawing room. She lived with her mother-in-law, Feliza, and Granddaddy, who spent his final years in a sprawling apartment in the basement of Aunt Pina's house. Aunt Pina and her husband, Uncle Pitoy, prospered. Or they squandered. It's hard to say, but they never seemed short of anything. They had five children, the youngest of whom died of a kidney ailment in the sixties. Uncle Pitoy died five years ago. He was in his eighties. His death had nothing to do with the war, but rather a stomach cancer, which, true to the nature of stomachs, consumed from within.

Grief

Harris was walking his usual route to work, up Beacon Street and past the State House, when half a block ahead he saw their stolen car stopped at a red light. It was their missing car, all right—a white '94 Honda Accord, license plate 432 DOG, easy to remember—and it was still pumping out pale blue exhaust, portent, Harris remembered thinking, of a large muffler bill and so much grief.

He quickened his pace to get a look at the driver leaning against his door, the driver's fingers drumming impatiently on the wheel as if he had better things to do with his time and Harris's car than wait for the light to turn green. Or maybe the police cruiser idling two cars behind was making him nervous.

Harris ran back to the cruiser and rapped sharply on the window, passenger's side. It scrolled down at a snail's pace. Pointing, Harris told the cop, "See that car two cars ahead? The white Honda. That's my car. It was stolen two weeks ago. See it? That's my car." As the light turned green, the Honda pulled away with the rest of the morning traffic. Bursts of adrenaline shot through Harris—the first thing he'd felt in the year since his wife's death.

The cop looked after Harris's disappearing Honda and then back at Harris, as if trying to decide if he was a nut. "Okay, mister, get in," the cop said. For once Harris was grateful for the respectable-looking briefcase his wife had given him on their twenty-fifth anniversary.

Harris yanked on the door handle, but it was locked.

"No, in back," the cop said. "Get in the back."

Harris threw his briefcase onto the back seat and slid in behind what was surely a bulletproof window between him and the cop, taxi-style. Siren blaring, they crept down Beacon Street in a low-speed chase and swung right on Tremont. Cars parted for them reluctantly—giving up feet, not yards.

Thirty seconds later they were bumper to bumper with Harris's stolen car, and the cop was strongly suggesting on his loudspeaker that the driver pull over. Harris was sitting forward, his nose inches from the scratched plastic divider. "That's it, that's my car," he said.

"You wait here," the cop said, as if Harris had foolishly been planning to accompany him on the dangerous stroll to the stolen car. Unbidden images came to Harris's mind. He pictured a stash of cocaine or a weighty little handgun the new owner had tucked under the driver's seat or hidden among their maps of New England. If the thief had noticed all the hiking guides, he probably wondered why Harris needed a car.

Now the cop was standing outside Harris's car, legs spread in cop-stance, no doubt asking to see the driver's license and registration. Good luck. The registration was in the glove compartment where it belonged, but hidden—his wife's idea—inside a paperback mystery involving root vegetables. The cop car's siren and flashing lights had drawn a business-suited crowd, which gathered at a safe distance from any anticipated mayhem.

Knowing Boston, Harris had never hoped to get their car back—and still road-worthy. He'd merely expected to come home to some message from the police on his answering machine saying they'd found his car trashed and wired on the campus of Tufts or MIT or abandoned in a bad part of town. The day after his wife died, he'd driven an hour west on I-90 until he came to a rest stop with an outside phone booth. He'd pulled the folding door shut against the outside world, and he'd called home over and over to hear her voice say, "Hello, please leave a message. We don't want to miss anything." Then he'd saved the tape and left a message of his own.

"No license on him," the cop said as he dropped into the front seat. "Says he left the registration with his sister cause she's trying to sell the car for him." He punched 432 DOG into a black box on the dash. Seconds later, like a fax—maybe it was a fax—out scrolled a sheet of paper with not much written on it, but the cop studied it thoroughly. He verified Harris's name, address, and when he'd reported the car missing. Then once again he told Harris, "Wait here," and approached Harris's stolen car, where he motioned for the driver to get out. The crowd drew back.

The driver's Red Sox jacket had a ripped sleeve, and his jeans were faded to a pale blue. Short and stocky, he was this side of forty, a limp ponytail hanging off a bald rump of a dome.

The cop spun him around and told him to lean against the car, his legs spread apart, then he patted Ponytail down movie-style before clamping handcuffs on his wrists. Satisfied, the cop pointed to where Harris sat waiting and gave Ponytail a slight nudge toward him. Soon Ponytail was peering in at Harris on one of those fake freeze frames Harris would trust in any movie from that moment on. His gaze was cool, not giving anything away. Real static hissed on the cop's radio as the dispatcher asked if the cop wanted backup. "Nah," the cop said through the front window, "I'm bringing him in."

Somehow Harris couldn't picture himself and Ponytail locked in, side by side, in the back seat of this cruiser. He tried to roll down the window, but it wouldn't budge.

The cop nodded for Harris to get out—what else could his nod mean? Harris gathered up his briefcase and waited for the cop to open the door. Harris's peripheral vision assured him that Ponytail and he were not going to do anything rash like make eye contact a second time.

"The car's all yours," the cop said. "Keys are in it."

All three of them looked at Harris's car, helping the police cruiser hold up traffic. Their bottleneck was doing a bad job of channeling three lanes of angry drivers into two.

"Thanks," Harris said. Then, "You mean I just drive it away?"

"Anywhere you want," the cop said. "I can't take custody of him and your car at the same time. He's coming with me. I guess that leaves you with the car." His mustache twitched with humor, impatience, and pride.

"Sure thing," Harris said, something he knew he'd never uttered before in his life. "Well, see you around." Feeling a bit ridiculous, Harris took possession of his car. He moved the seat back and adjusted the rearview in time to see Ponytail disappear into cop-car-land, the cop's hand on the back of Ponytail's neck to make sure his head cleared the doorframe. The cop pulled out and around Harris, no siren, but his lights still flashing.

Slowly, Harris drove back to his apartment and parked in front, in the same spot from which his car had been stolen. For the first time, he assessed its state—then set to gathering up Dunkin' Donuts cups, McDonald's cartons, and candy wrappers, and stuffed them into a white Dunkin' Donuts sack. The paperback mystery—*Roots of All Evil*—was still in the glove compartment and, just as his wife had predicted, had disguised the registration well. The walking guides and maps were still under the seat; there was no handgun. And when Harris got home after work that night, there was no wife to tell the story to.

Three days later, he was matching socks and watching the six o'clock news when the phone rang. He hoped it wasn't the solicitous new tenant from the upstairs apartment, a woman whose roast lamb and braised chicken tempted Harris to emerge from his solitary gloom—a gloom he always returned to well-fed but even more despondent. She had probably noticed his car in the street and wanted to hear how he'd got it back, perhaps help him celebrate. He didn't know how to tell her that more than the car was still missing. When he said "Hello," he felt instant relief that it was not the woman upstairs, but a man's gravelly voice. "You got my TVs," the voice said.

Harris told him he had the wrong number.

"No I don't," he said. "I want my TVs."

Harris hung up and went back to sorting socks. Mostly black, they were draped over the back of the couch, side by side, toes pointing down, the way his wife used to line them up. Now, fewer and fewer of them matched. The phone rang again. It was probably the guy missing his TVs, and Harris thought, Let him.

Next night, about the same time, the phone rang. Harris was sitting on the couch beside the leftover socks, again dreading the cheerful voice of the woman upstairs. A man's gravelly voice said, "They're in the trunk of your car."

"The TVs?" Harris said.

"See, I knew you had them."

Harris matched the man's TVs with his own stolen car. Ponytail. Knowing Boston, what made Harris think that Ponytail would be arrested, indicted, convicted, put away? The cop never suggested to Harris that he should press charges, a failure pointed out by his cynical colleague in the accounting firm where Harris spent his days. "The cop probably dropped your Ponytail-guy at the next corner," Rentz had said. Clearly, Ponytail wasn't calling

Harris now from some jail. Lord, Harris didn't need this. "Look—"

The man cut him off. "You got your car back safe and sound. No harm done. I just want my TVs."

"How did you get my number?" Harris asked.

"Information," the man said. "AT&T."

"Someone's here," Harris said. "Can we talk about this another time?"

"You'll talk TVs tomorrow?"

"Tomorrow," Harris said and hung up, picturing Ponytail carless, standing in some phone booth near a bus stop or subway, figuring his chances. Harris put a Stouffer's lasagna in the oven and headed out to visit his car.

The car was where he'd parked it when he got it back four days ago. In the beam of his flashlight, he unlocked the trunk and found three TVs wedged in tight, just like the man had said. Harris had to admire the way he packed. With a sharp pang of regret he recalled his annoyance that his wife insisted on packing up the car for their camping trips. She'd assemble everything outside by the car, eye it thoughtfully, then begin with the large items first—the tent, the kerosene stove. At the end, there'd be no extra space, but nothing left behind.

The TVs weren't new, but newer than Harris's, with large blank screens. All of a sudden he felt very tired.

The next night he waited for the call, not sure what he'd say. He turned the news on with no sound. The back of the couch was free of socks, the socks put away. Who said they had to match? When the phone rang Harris was ready with a gruff hello, but this time it was the woman upstairs calling to say she'd just slipped a stuffed free-range roasting chicken into the oven and it was far too much for one person. It would be ready in about two hours. Cornbread and onion stuffing, she said, and quite a bit of tarragon. Harris's wife had always used sage and rosemary. For what must have been the fifth or sixth time, Harris thanked her and said he'd bring a bottle of wine. He imagined the new photographs his upstairs neighbor would show him, her son's gourmet peppers, or alarming images from her daughter's latest assignment with Doctors Without Borders—a daughter who had his neighbor's same pale hair and deep-set, discerning eyes. He could hear his neighbor's stories of Sip, her cat, who carefully coated his trousers with hair, her hints about a new movie she'd like to see at the theater down the block. He wouldn't tell her, and she couldn't know, that his wife and he had held hands in every movie they ever saw—her hand in his, their fingers changing pressure in her lap of wool, or denim, or silk. Often now, his hands felt empty. His neighbor couldn't know he was afraid, no, terrified, that in a moment of high emotion or fright at the images on the screen, he might reach for her hand—her perfectly good, but achingly unfamiliar hand. He'd bring a bottle of red wine, he said, because he didn't know how to say no. Then he clicked off the silent news and hauled out his briefcase. Two hours was enough time to get through tonight's office work.

Ponytail called five minutes later.

To Harris's surprise, he found himself taking part in complicated, delicate arrangements to give back the TVs. Of course, this was after Ponytail explained that they had once been in dire need of repair, but now they were ready to be returned to their impatient owners. "I pick up and deliver," he said. "This won't take long. You got any TVs, toaster ovens, anything giving you trouble?"

"Just the TVs," Harris told him. They said goodbye.

Ten minutes later Harris was driving to the appointed place, wondering if he really would go through with this maneuver. He didn't feel prepared for anything since his wife died. He probably wouldn't be meeting Ponytail if his wife were at home waiting for him, worrying. They would have talked it over, together come up with a plan. It saddened him that he didn't know what she would have wanted him to do.

As arranged, Ponytail was standing on the corner of Government Center, near the subway stop, only a few blocks from the spot where Harris had been given back his car. Neither of them had suggested Ponytail come to Harris's house. Though the September night was warm, Ponytail's hands were tucked into the front pocket of his Red Sox jacket. This made Harris a little nervous. He pulled to the curb and beeped his horn twice. Ponytail glanced at Harris's car, and then, as if to shield himself from a brisk wind, he slowly turned full circle to light a cigarette behind cupped hands. Clearly, he was looking for a trap, and somehow

his caution made Harris feel a little better. Finally, Ponytail saun-
tered over and leaned down as if to make sure it was Harris, then
casually he flicked away his cigarette and tugged on the handle of
the passenger door. It was locked; Harris had made sure it was
locked before setting off. Ponytail didn't seem to find the locked
door strange and stepped back with a nod. Harris, embarrassed
by his own unaccustomed display of caution, got out. His car
idled in a light cloud of blue exhaust.

Across the roof, Ponytail squinted at him, straight in the eye.
"Like I said on the phone, this won't take long. An hour maybe."
He took his hands out of his pockets and placed them flat on the
car's roof—as if to offer Harris, with this gesture, his assurance
that he was not going to do anything rash. No doubt he was
counting on the same from Harris.

"Okay," Harris said, thumping the car's roof with the flat of his
palm. "Let's do it." Once again, adrenaline was pumping through
him as it had when he first spotted his car. He slid behind the
wheel, leaned over to unlock the passenger's door. Ponytail got in,
the first passenger to ride in his car since his wife died. Although
he'd never thought of his wife as a passenger. Ponytail's knuckles
were white, and his fingers drummed on worn denim knees.

"Where to?" Harris said, belatedly thinking he should have told
someone—maybe the woman upstairs—where he was going.

"Get onto Storrow and head up Route 1." Ponytail buckled his
seatbelt and slouched against the door, eyeing his side mirror, his
ponytail a wisp on his solid shoulder. Stealthily Harris rubbed the
back of his neck, unable to imagine securing his hair with a rubber band, unable to feel a ponytail swishing against his collar, surprised even to consider it.

Once they were on the open road, Ponytail said, "Hear that rattle? Oil needs changing."

Harris glanced down at the dash, which was reassuringly dark.
"A light usually comes on if—"

"Them lights don't know nothing."

"So, you think it's the oil?" Harris said.

"I was gonna do it."

"Yes, well, thanks," Harris said.

"You probably know about the muffler," Ponytail said.

Harris told him he did. Then, "You been repairing TVs long?"

Ponytail thought for a moment. "Nah. Not too long. What do you do?"

"Mostly tax returns," Harris said.

"Repairing tax returns long?" Ponytail said.

Harris had to wrap his mind around this one, but finally he said, "Not too long." They settled into silence as the neon of roadside small businesses flashed by. After a while Ponytail told Harris to turn off Route 1 and take the overpass, then make a right at Cappy's Liquor. Three streets over they were in a neighborhood of two-story houses, lanky trees, and sloping cracked sidewalks. Aluminum siding glowed in the evening's dusk, and one house had a horizontal freezer on the front porch, another an old-fashioned gas oven. Harris had seen such things on porches before, but now they seemed strange and menacing. He tried for a little light-hearted humor. "Okay, first stop coming up," he said. But it turned out—and why was he again surprised—that all the TVs were going to one house. Ponytail's house.

"I said it wouldn't take long," Ponytail said, as if he was doing Harris a favor by consolidating the deliveries. They pulled into a narrow driveway bordered on one side by a chain-link fence. Lights were on in the downstairs of the house. A green pickup on cement blocks loomed off to the side. Now it was Harris's turn to think about a trap as Ponytail got out and slammed the car door. A jungle gym took up most of the small backyard.

Harris guardedly emerged from the car. Clothes flapped on a clothesline in the skinny side yard next to the driveway: blouses or shirts, workpants, kids' clothes, socks, and a long red dress or robe of some shiny material that caught the light from the streetlamp. Ponytail followed Harris's gaze. "Damn dryer's broken," he said. "Wife's been nagging me to fix it. I keep forgetting to order the part." At the fence, beneath a window, he gave a sharp whistle.

Harris backed up fast till he was flat against the car door with thoughts of taking off, TVs and all. Why on earth was he here? As if on cue, a woman came to the window and peered out through the screen. She was jiggling a kid about two on her hip. Absurdly, Harris found himself noticing that her blond ponytail was fatter than her husband's.

"Hey," Ponytail called out to her, his thumb jabbing the air in Harris's direction. "He's gonna help me put the stuff in the garage." Another kid, not much older, butted his head under her arm. "Bring in the clothes when you finish," she said without acknowledging Harris, then smartly wheeled the children away.

"Let's do it," Ponytail said. His voice startled Harris, who had been imagining what it would be like to park in this driveway, to live in this house. Reaching down, Ponytail heaved up the garage door and turned on the light. "They're going in there," he said. With a jerk of his head, he indicated four sawhorses covered with boards at the rear of the garage. This makeshift table sat under a large, neat wall-board display of tools—most of which Harris didn't recognize—and three small blue cabinets of tiny drawers labeled screws and nails and nuts and bolts. To one side, Harris could make out the sturdy shapes of five microwaves still in their shipping boxes and four spiffy new leaf blowers. Ponytail swiped the table with a rag—it was a kind of "no comment" gesture, and Harris was grateful for it.

Together, they hoisted the first TV out of the trunk. Hobbling sideways, they carried it up the driveway, arms wrapped under and around it, foreheads almost touching across its top.

"Set her down—right—here," Ponytail panted, wiping his face on his jacket sleeve. The TVs were heavy. After the second one, Harris was sweating and huffing; his arms burned. He flexed his fingers and bent to wipe his face on his shirtsleeve, out of shape from no exercise, no long hikes for over a year. They trooped back to the car for the last delivery.

"Done." Ponytail patted the last TV. Carefully, he spread a brown tarp over the TVs and microwaves, then turned off the light. Harris stood off to the side while he pulled down the garage door.

"Well—" Harris said. Because he didn't know what else to say, he turned toward his car. It had probably been parked on and off in this same driveway for three whole weeks. The candy wrappers must have been from the kids. Beyond the fence, the shiny robe or dress was fluttering back and forth. It was actually a bathrobe, and Harris could see now that the hem was a little ragged and one of the elbows had a hole in it, but it was still of use. Without thinking, he walked past his car to the clothesline and reached up to undo the clothespins holding the robe in place. The robe was red; it was light and slippery as he folded it over his arm.

Ponytail touched his shoulder. "Hey, man, you don't need to do that."

On the way home, Harris forced himself to drive slowly even though the upstairs neighbor was waiting for him. She'd want to know all about his getting the car back, so over dinner he'd recount how he'd spotted his car in traffic, and his surprise that it was still road-worthy. He'd tell her about the telephone calls, the tense drive up Route 1, the wife and kids at the window, the garage full of companionable leaf blowers, microwaves, and TVs. He'd tell her how, as he was pulling out of the drive, Ponytail had slapped the side of his car, hard, and Harris had jumped like he'd been shot, but Ponytail only wanted to tell him to remember and check the oil. Then maybe somewhere along toward dessert, Harris would tell her more about his wife.

JESS ROW

The Secrets of Bats

A lice Leung has discovered the secrets of bats: how they see without seeing, how they own darkness, as we own light. She walks the halls with a black headband across her eyes, keening a high C—*cheat cheat cheat cheat cheat cheat*—never once veering off course, as if drawn by an invisible thread. Echolocation, she tells me, it's not as difficult as you might think. Now she sees a light around objects when she looks at them, like halos on her retinas from staring at the sun. In her journal she writes, *I had a dream that was all in blackness. Tell me how to describe.*

It is January: my fifth month in Hong Kong.

In the margin I write, *I wish I knew.*

After six, when the custodians leave, the school becomes a perfect acoustic chamber; she wanders from the basement laboratories to the basketball courts like a trapped bird looking for a window. She finds my door completely blind, she says, not counting flights or paces. Twisting her head from side to side like Stevie Wonder, she announces her progress: another room mapped, a door, a desk, a globe, detected and identified by its aura.

You'll hurt yourself, I tell her. I've had nightmares: her foot missing the edge of a step, the dry crack of a leg breaking. Try it without the blindfold, I say. That way you can check yourself.

Her mouth wrinkles. This not important, she says. This only practice.

Practice for what, I want to ask. All the more reason you have to be careful.

You keep saying, she says, grabbing a piece of chalk. E-x-p-e-r-i-m-e-n-t, she writes on the blackboard, digging it in until it squeals.

That's right. Sometimes experiments fail.

Sometimes, she repeats. She eyes me suspiciously, as if I invented the word.

Go home, I tell her. She turns her pager off and leaves it in her

131

locker; sometimes police appear at the school gate, shouting her name. Somebody, it seems, wants her back.

In the doorway she whirls, flipping her hair out of her eyes. Ten days more, she says. You listen. Maybe then you see why.

The name of the school is Po Sing Uk: a five-story concrete block, cracked and eroded by dirty rain, shoulder-to-shoulder with the tenements and garment factories of Cheung Sha Wan. No air conditioning and no heat; in September I shouted to be heard over a giant fan, and now, in January, I teach in a winter jacket. When it rains, mildew spiderwebs across the ceiling of my classroom. Schoolgirls in white jumpers crowd into the room forty at a time, falling asleep over their textbooks, making furtive calls on mobile phones, scribbling notes to each other on pink Hello Kitty paper. If I call on one who hasn't raised her hand, she folds her arms across her chest and stares at the floor, and the room falls silent, as if by a secret signal. There is nothing more terrifying, I've found, than the echo of your own voice: *Who are you?* it answers. *What are you doing here?*

I've come to see my life as a radiating circle of improbabilities that grow from each other, like ripples in water around a dropped stone. That I became a high school English teacher, that I work in another country, that I live in Hong Kong. That a city can be a mirage, hovering above the ground: skyscrapers built on mountainsides, islands swallowed in fog for days. That a language can have no tenses or articles, with seven different ways of saying the same syllable. That my best student stares at the blackboard only when I erase it.

She stayed behind on the first day of class: a tall girl with a narrow face, pinched around the mouth, her cheeks pitted with acne scars. Like most of my sixteen-year-olds she looked twelve, in a baggy uniform that hung to her knees like a sack. The others streamed past her without looking up, as if she were a boulder in the current; she stared down at my desk with a fierce vacancy, as if looking itself was an act of will.

How do you think about bats?

Bats?

She joined her hands at the wrist and fluttered them at me.

People are afraid of them, I said. I think they're very interesting.

Why? she said. Why very interesting?

Because they live in the dark, I said. We think of them as being blind, but they aren't blind. They have a way of seeing, with sound waves—just like we see with light.

Yes, she said. I know this. Her body swayed slightly, in an imaginary breeze.

Are you interested in bats?

I am interest, she said. I want to know how—she made a face I'd already come to recognize: *I know how to say it in Chinese*—when one bat sees the other. The feeling.

You mean how one bat recognizes another?

Yes—recognize.

That's a good idea, I said. You can keep a journal about what you find. Write something in it every day.

She nodded vehemently, as if she'd already thought of that.

There are books on bat behavior that will tell you—

Not in books. She covered her eyes with one hand and walked forward until her hip brushed the side of my desk, then turned away, at a right angle. Like this, she said. There is a sound, she said. I want to find the sound.

18 September

~~First hit tuning fork.~~ *Sing one octave higher: A B C. This is best way.*

Drink water or lips get dry.

I must have eyes totally closed. No light!!! So some kind of black—like cloth—is good.

Start singing. First to the closest wall—sing and listen. Practice ten times, 20 times. IMPORTANT: can not move until I HEAR the wall. Take step back, one time, two time. Listen again. I have to hear DIFFERENCE first, then move.

Then take turn, ninety degrees left.

Then turn, one hundred eighty degrees left. Feel position with feet. Feet very important—they are wings!!!

I don't know what this is, I told her the next day, opening the journal and pushing it across the desk. Can you help me?

I tell you already, she said. She hunched her shoulders so that her head seemed to rest on them, spreading her elbows to either side. It is like a test.

A test?

In the courtyard rain crackled against the asphalt; a warm wind lifted scraps of paper from the desk, somersaulting them through the air.

The sound, she said, impatiently. I told you this.

I covered my mouth to hide a smile.

Alice, I said, humans can't do that. It isn't a learned behavior. It's something you study.

She pushed up the cover of the composition book and let it fall.

I think I can help you, I said. Can you tell me why you want to write this?

Why I want? She stared at me wide-eyed.

Why do you want to do this? What is the test for?

Her eyes lifted from my face to the blackboard behind me, moved to the right, then the left, as if measuring the dimensions of the room.

Why you want come to Hong Kong?

Many reasons, I said. After college I wanted to go to another country, and there was a special fellowship available here. And maybe someday I will be a teacher.

You are teacher.

I'm just learning, I said. I am trying to be one.

Then why you have to leave America?

I don't, I said. The two things— I took off my glasses and rubbed my eyes. All at once I was exhausted; the effort seemed useless, a pointless evasion. When I looked up she was nodding, slowly, as if I'd just said something profound.

I think I will find the reason for being here only after some time, I said. Do you know what I mean? There could be a purpose I don't know about.

So you don't know for good. Not sure.

You could say that.

Hai yat yeung, she said. This same. Maybe if you read you can tell me why.

This is what's so strange about her, I thought, studying her red-rimmed eyes, the tiny veins standing out like wires on a circuit board. She doesn't look down. I am fascinated by her, I thought. Is that fair?

You're different than the others, I said. You're not afraid of me. Why is that?

Maybe I have other things be afraid of.

At first the fifth-floor bathroom was her echo chamber; she sat in one corner, on a stool taken from the physics room, and placed an object directly opposite her: a basketball, a glass, a feather. Sound waves triangulate, she told me, corners are best. Passing by, at the end of the day, I stopped, closing my eyes, and listened for the difference. She sang without stopping for five minutes, hardly taking a breath: almost a mechanical sound, as if someone had forgotten their mobile phone. Other teachers walked by in groups, talking loudly. If they noticed me, or the sound, I was never aware of it, but always, instinctively, I looked at my watch and followed them down the stairs. As if I, too, had to rush home to cook for hungry children, or boil medicine for my mother-in-law. I never stayed long enough to see if anything changed.

Document everything, I told her, and she did; now I have two binders of entries, forty-one in all. *Hallway. Chair. Notebook.* As if we were scientists writing a grant proposal, as if there was something actual to show at the end of it.

I don't keep a journal, or take photographs, and my letters home are factual and sparse. No one in Larchmont would believe me—not even my parents—if I told them the truth. *It sounds like quite an experience you're having! Don't get run over by a rickshaw.* And yet if I died tomorrow—why should I ever think this way?— these binders would be the record of my days. Those and Alice herself, who looks out of her window and with her eyes closed sees ships passing in the harbor, men walking silently in the streets.

26 January

Sound of lightbulb—low like bees hum. So hard to listen!

A week ago I dreamed of bodies breaking apart, arms and legs and torsos, fragments of bone, bits of tissue. I woke up flailing in the sheets, and remembered her, immediately; there was too long a moment before I believed I was awake. *It has to stop,* I thought, *you have to say something.* Though I know that I can't.

Perhaps there was a time when I might have told her, *This is ridiculous,* or, *You're sixteen, find some friends. What will people think?* But this is Hong Kong, of course, and I have no friends, no basis to judge. I leave the door open, always, and no one ever comes to check; we walk out of the gates together, late in the afternoon, past the watchman sleeping in his chair. For me she has a kind of professional courtesy, ignoring my whiteness politely, as if I had horns growing from my head. And she returns, at the end of each day, as a bat flies back to its cave at daybreak. All I have is time; who am I to pack my briefcase and turn away?

There was only once when I slipped up.

Pretend I've forgotten, I told her, one Monday in early October. The journal was open in front of us, the pages covered in red; she squinted down at it, as if instead of corrections I'd written hieroglyphics. I'm an English teacher, I thought, this is what I'm here for. We should start again at the beginning, I said. Tell me what it is that you want to do here. You don't have to tell me about the project—just about the writing. Who are you writing these for? Who do you want to read them?

She stretched, catlike, curling her fingers like claws.

Because I don't think I understand, I said. I think you might want to find another teacher to help you. There could be something you have in mind in Chinese that doesn't come across.

Not in Chinese, she said, as if I should have known that already. In Chinese cannot say like this.

But it isn't really English, either.

I know this. It is like both.

I can't teach that way, I said. You have to learn the rules before you can—

You are not teaching me.

Then what's the point?

She strode across the room to the window and leaned out, placing her hands on the sill and bending at the waist. Come here, she said, look. I stood up and walked over to her.

She ducked her head down, like a gymnast on a bar, and tilted forward, her feet lifting off the floor.

Alice!

I grabbed her shoulder and jerked her upright. She stumbled, falling back; I caught her wrist, and she pulled it away, steadying herself. We stood there a moment staring at each other, breathing in short huffs that echoed in the hallway.

Maybe I hear something and forget, she said. You catch me then. Okay?

28 January

> *It is like photo negative, all the colors are the opposite. Black sky, white trees, this way. But they are still shapes—I can see them.*

I read standing at the window, in a last sliver of sunlight. Alice stands on my desk, already well in shadow, turning around slowly as if trying to dizzy herself for a party game. Her winter uniform cardigan is three sizes too large; unopened, it falls behind her like a cape.

This is beautiful.

Quiet, she hisses, eyebrows bunched together above her head-band. One second. There—there.

What is it?

A man on the stairs.

I go out into the hallway and stand at the top of the stairwell, listening. Five floors below, very faintly, I hear sandals skidding on the concrete, keys jangling on the janitor's ring.

You heard him open the gate, I say. That's cheating.

She shakes her head. I hear heartbeat.

The next Monday, Principal Ho comes to see me during the lunch hour. He stands at the opposite end of the classroom, as always: a tall, slightly chubby man, in a tailored shirt, gold-rimmed glasses, and Italian shoes, who blinks as he reads the ESL posters I've tacked up on the wall. When he asks how my classes are, and I tell him that the girls are unmotivated, disengaged, he nods, quickly, as if to save me the embarrassment. How lucky he was, he tells me, to go to boarding school in Australia, and then pronounces it with a flattened *a, Austrahlia,* so I have to laugh.

Principal Ho, I ask, do you know Alice Leung?

He turns his head toward me and blinks more rapidly. Leung Ka Yee, he says. Of course. You have problem with her?

No sir. I need something to hold; my hands dart across the desk behind me and find my red marking pen.

How does she perform?

She's very gifted. One of the best students in the class. Very creative.

He nods, scratches his nose, and turns away.

She likes to work alone, I say. The other girls don't pay much attention to her. I don't think she has many friends.

It is very difficult for her, he says, slowly, measuring every word. Her mother is—her mother was a suicide.

In the courtyard, five stories down, someone drops a basketball and lets it bounce against the pavement; little *pings* that trill and fade into the infinite.

In Yau Ma Tei, Ho says. He makes a little gliding motion with his hand. Nowadays this is not so uncommon in Hong Kong. But still there are superstitions.

What kind of superstitions?

He frowns and shakes his head. Difficult to say in English. Maybe just that she is unlucky girl. Chinese people, you understand—some are still afraid of ghosts.

She isn't a ghost.

He gives a high-pitched, nervous laugh. No, no, he says. Not her. He puts his hands into his pockets, searching for something. Difficult to explain. I'm sorry.

Is there someone she can talk to?

He raises his eyebrows. *A counselor,* I am about to say, and explain what it means, when my hand relaxes, and I realize I have been crushing the pen in my palm. For a moment I am water-skiing again at Lake Patchogue: releasing the handle, settling against the surface, enfolded in water. When I look up, Ho glances at his watch.

If you have any problem you can talk to me.

It's nothing, I say. Just curious, that's all.

She wears the headband all the time now, I've noticed: pulling it over her eyes whenever possible, in the halls between classes, in the courtyard at lunchtime, sitting by herself. No one shoves her or calls her names; she passes through the crowds unseen. If possible, I think, she's grown thinner, her skin translucent, blue veins showing at the wrists. Occasionally I notice the other teachers shadowing her, frowning, their arms crossed, but if our eyes meet they stare through me, disinterested, and look away.

I have to talk to you about something.

She is sitting in a desk at the far end of the room, reading her chemistry textbook, drinking from a can of soymilk with a straw. When the straw gurgles she bangs the can down, and we sit, silently, the sound reverberating in the hallway.

I give you another journal soon. Two more days.

Not about that.

She doesn't move: fixed, alert, waiting. I stand up and move down the aisle toward her, sitting two desks away, and as I move her eyes grow slightly rounder and her cheeks puff out slightly, as if she's holding her breath.

Alice, I say, can you tell me about your mother?

Her hands fall down on the desk, and the can clatters to the floor, white drops spinning in the air.

Mother? Who tell you I have mother?

It's all right—

I reach over to touch one hand, and she snatches it back.

Who tell you?

It doesn't matter. You don't have to be angry.

You big mistake, she says, wild-eyed, taking long swallows of air and spitting them out. Why you have to come here and mess everything?

I don't understand, I say. Alice, what did I do?

I trust you, she says, and pushes the heel of one palm against her cheek. I write and you read. I *trust* you.

What did you expect? I ask, my jaw trembling. Did you think I would never know?

Believe me. She looks at me pleadingly. Believe *me.*

Two days later she leaves her notebook on my desk, with a note stuck to the top. *You keep.*

1 February

Now I am finished
It is out there I hear it

I call out to her after class, and she hesitates in the doorway for a moment before turning, pushing her back against the wall.

Tell me what it was like, I say. Was it a voice? Did you hear someone speaking?

Of course no voice. Not so close to me. It was a feeling.

How did it feel?

She reaches up and slides the headband over her eyes.

It is all finish, she says. You not worry about me anymore.

Too late, I say. I stand up from my chair and take a tentative step toward her: weak-kneed, as if it were a staircase in the dark. You chose me, I say. Remember?

Go back to America. Then you forget all about this crazy girl.

This is my life, too. Did you forget about that?

She raises her head and listens, and I know what she hears: a stranger's voice, as surely as if someone else had entered the room. She nods. *Who do you see?* I wonder. *What will he do next?* I reach out, blindly, and my hand misses the door; on the second try I close it.

I choose this, I say. I'm waiting. Tell me.

Her body sinks into a crouch; she hugs her knees and tilts her head back.

Warm. It was warm. It was—it was a body.

But not close to you?

Not close. Only little feeling, then no more.

Did it know you were there?

No.

How can you be sure?

When I look up to repeat the question, shiny tracks of tears have run out from under the blindfold.

I am sorry, she says. She reaches into her backpack and splits open a packet of tissues without looking down, her fingers nimble, almost autonomous. You are my good friend, she says, and takes off the blindfold, turning her face to the side and dabbing her eyes. Thank you for help me.

It isn't over, I say. How can it be over?

Like you say. Sometimes experiment fails.

No, I say, too loudly, startling us both. It isn't that easy. You have to prove it to me.

Prove it you?

Show me how it works. I take a deep breath. I believe you. Will you catch me?

Her eyes widen, and she does not look away; the world swims around her irises. Tonight, she says, and writes something on a slip of paper, not looking down. I see you then.

In a week it will be the New Year: all along the streets the shop fronts are hung with firecrackers, red-and-gold character scrolls, pictures of grinning cats, and the twin cherubs of good luck. Mothers lead little boys dressed in red silk pajamas, girls with New Year's pigtails. The old woman sitting next to me on the bus is busily stuffing twenty-dollar bills into red *lai see* packets: lucky money for the year to come. When I turn my head from the window, she holds one out to me, and I take it with both hands, automatically, bowing my head. This will make you rich, she says to me in Cantonese. And lots of children.

Thank you, I say. The same to you.

She laughs. Already happened. Jade bangles clink together as she holds up her fingers. Thirteen grandchildren! she says. Six boys. All fat and good-looking. You should say live long life to me.

I'm sorry. My Chinese is terrible.

No, it's very good, she says. You were born in Hong Kong?

Outside night is just falling, and Nathan Road has become a canyon of light: blazing neon signs, brilliant shop windows, decorations blinking across the fronts of half-finished tower blocks. I stare at myself a moment in the reflection, three red characters passing across my forehead, and look away. No, I say. In America. I've lived here only since August.

Ah. Then what is America like?

Forgive me, aunt, I say. I forget.

Prosperous Garden no. 4. Tung Kun Street. Yau Ma Tei.
A scribble of Chinese characters.
Show this to doorman he let you in.

The building is on the far edge of Kowloon, next to the reclamation; a low concrete barrier separates it from an elevated highway that thunders continuously as cars pass. Four identical towers around a courtyard, long poles draped with laundry jutting from every window, like spears hung with old rotted flags.

Gong hei fat choi, I say to the doorman through the gate, and he smiles with crooked teeth, but when I pass the note to him all expression leaves his face; he presses the buzzer and turns away quickly. Twenty-three A-ah, he calls out to the opposite wall. You understand?

Thank you.

When I step out into the hallway I breathe in boiled chicken, oyster sauce, frying oil, the acrid steam of medicine, dried fish, Dettol. Two young boys are crouched at the far end, sending a radio-controlled car zipping past me; someone is arguing loudly over the telephone; a stereo plays loud Canto-pop from a balcony somewhere below. All the apartment doors are open, I notice, walking by, and only the heavy sliding gates in front of them are closed. Like a honeycomb, I can't help thinking, or an ant farm. But when I reach 23A the door behind the gate is shut, and no sound comes from behind it. The bell rings several times before the locks begin to snap open.

You are early, Alice says, rubbing her eyes, as if she's been sleeping. Behind her the apartment is dark; there is only a faint blue glow, as if from a TV screen.

I'm sorry. You didn't say when to come. I look at my watch: eight-thirty. I can come back, I say, another time, maybe another night—

She shakes her head and opens the gate.

When she turns on the light I draw a deep breath, involuntarily, and hide it with a cough. The walls are covered with stacks of yellowed paper, file boxes, brown envelopes, and ragged books; on opposite sides of the room are two desks, each holding a computer with a flickering screen. I peer at the one closest to the door. At the top of the screen there is a rotating globe and, below it, a ribbon of letters and numbers, always changing. The other, I see, is just the same: a head staring at its twin.

Come, Alice says. She has disappeared for a moment and reemerged, dressed in a long dress, silver running shoes, a hooded sweatshirt.

Are these yours?

No. My father's.

Why does he need two? They're just the same.

Nysee, she says, impatiently, pointing. Footsie. New York Stock Exchange. London Stock Exchange.

Sau Yee, a hoarse voice calls from another room. Who is it?

It's my English teacher, she says loudly. Giving me a homework assignment.

Gwailo a?

Yes, she says. The white one.

Then call a taxi for him. He appears in the kitchen doorway: a stooped old man, perhaps five feet tall, in a dirty white T-shirt, shorts, and sandals. His face is covered with liver spots; his eyes shrunken into their sockets. I sorry-ah, he says to me. No speakee English.

It's all right, I say. There is a numbness growing behind my eyes: I want to speak to him, but the words are all jumbled, and Alice's eyes burning on my neck. Goodbye, I say, take care.

See later-ah.

Alice pulls the hood over her head and opens the door.

She leads me to the top of a dark stairwell, in front of a rusting door with light pouring through its cracks. *Tin paang,* she says, reading the characters stenciled on it in white. Roof. She hands me a black headband, identical to her own.

Hold on, I say, gripping the railing with both hands. The numbness behind my eyes is still there, and I feel my knees growing weak, as if there were no building below me, only a framework of girders and air. Can you answer me a question?

Maybe one.

Has he always been like that?

What like?

With the computers, I say. Does he do that all the time?

Always. Never turn them off.

In the darkness I can barely see her face: only the eyes, shining, daring me to speak. *If I were in your place,* I say to myself, and the phrase dissolves, weightless.

Listen, I say. I'm not sure I'm ready.

She laughs. When you be sure?

Her fingers fall across my face, and I feel the elastic brushing over my hair, and then the world is black: I open my eyes and close them, no difference.

We just go for a little walk, she says. You don't worry. Only listen.

I never realized, before, the weight of the air: at every step I feel the great mass of it pressing against my face, saddled on my shoulders. I am breathing huge quantities, as if my lungs were a giant recirculation machine, and sweat is running down from my forehead and soaking the edge of the headband. Alice takes normal-sized steps, and grips my hand fiercely, so I can't let go. Don't be afraid, she shouts. We still in the middle. Not near the edge.

What am I supposed to do?

Nothing, she says. Only wait. Maybe you see something.

I stare, fiercely, into blackness, into my own eyelids. There is the afterglow of the hallway light, and the computer screens, very faint; or am I imagining it? What is there on a roof? I wonder, and try to picture it: television antennas, heating ducts, clotheslines. Are there guardrails? I've never seen any on a Hong Kong building. She turns, and I brush something metal with my hand. Do you know where you're going? I shout.

Here, she says, and stops. I stumble into her, and she catches my shoulder. Careful, she says. We wait here.

Wait for what?

Just listen, she says. I tell to you. Look to left side: there's a big building there. Very tall white building, higher than us. Small windows.

All right. I can see that.

Right side is highway. Very bright. Many cars and trucks passing.

If I strain to listen I can hear a steady whooshing sound, and then the high whine of a motorcycle, like a mosquito passing my ear. Okay, I say. Got that.

In the middle is very dark. Small buildings. Only few lights on.

Not enough, I say.

One window close to us, she says. Two little children there. You see them?

No.

Lift your arm, she says, and I do. Put your hand up. See? They wave to you.

My God, I say. How do you do that?

She squeezes my hand.

You promise me something.

Of course. What is it?

You don't take it off, she says. No matter nothing. You promise me?

I do. I promise.

She lets go of my hand, and I hear running steps, soles skidding on concrete.

Alice! I shout, rooted to the spot; I crouch down, and balance myself with my hands. Alice! You don't—

Mama, she screams, ten feet away, and the sound carries, echoes; I can see it slanting with the wind, bright as daylight, as if a roman candle had exploded in my face. *Mama mama mama mama mama mama mama*, she sings, and I am crawling towards her on hands and knees, feeling in front of me for the edge.

She is there, Alice shouts. You see? She is in the air.

I see her. Stay where you are.

You watch, she says. I follow her.

She doesn't want you, I shout. She doesn't want you there. Let her go.

There is a long silence, and I stay where I am, the damp concrete soaking through to my knees. My ears are ringing, and the numbness has blossomed through my head; I feel faintly seasick.

Alice?

You can stand up, she says, in a small voice, and I do.

You are shaking, she says. She puts her arms around me from behind and clasps my chest, pressing her head against my back. I thank you, she says.

She unties the headband.

6 February

Man waves white hands at black sky
He says arent you happy be alive
arent you
He kneels and kisses floor

El hombre que yo amo

from a memoir in progress

1. El hombre que yo amo

The night before I left my mother, I wrote a letter. "*Querida* Mami," it began. *Querida,* beloved, Mami, I wrote, on the same page as *el hombre que yo amo,* the man I love. I'd struggled with those words, because I wasn't certain they were true. I didn't know why I was running away from home with a man a year older than my mother. Mami understood love, so I used the words and hoped that they were true. *El hombre que yo amo. Amo,* which in Spanish also means *master.* I didn't notice the irony.

I sealed the envelope, addressed it formally to Sra. Ramona Santiago, and placed it in the mailbox. It was a Tuesday, the mailman would come in the early afternoon, and by then, I'd be in Florida with my lover, *el hombre que yo . . . amo.*

I carried very little. A battered leather bag once used for dance costumes now held a couple of changes of clothes, a bikini, a toothbrush, comb and hairpins, a pair of shoes and sandals, underwear, pajamas. I left my tights and leotards, stage makeup, the showy jewelry I'd collected to add spice and color to the characters I created onstage.

When I stepped onto the sidewalk, I resisted the urge to look back, to run back into the building where my mother, my grandmother, my ten sisters and brothers, my aunt and cousins slept. The stairs to the train station, a long block from our front door, were under my feet sooner than I would have wanted. Once I took the first step into the subway out of Brooklyn, I knew my life had changed inexorably. Were I to turn around and run back into my mother's house, into the safe, still warm space next to my sister Delsa, it would have been too late. When I wrote the words *el hombre que yo amo,* it was already too late. I had made a choice—a man over my mother. Even if I didn't follow him to Florida, I'd taken the first step, a week after my twenty-first birthday, into the rest of my life.

* * *

I knew little about him. He was Turkish, lived alone in a luxury apartment building a block from Bloomingdale's, wore expensive suits in muted colors with finely detailed pleats and creases. In addition to his first language, he spoke fluent German and French, but his English was heavily accented and hesitant. He'd won the Golden Bear at the Berlin International Film Festival for a black and white movie he'd directed and starred in, made in Turkey, which he was desperate to distribute in the United States. He was a hard worker, and ambitious, I'd noticed. I'd spent hours watching him reedit his film, add new music, create subtitles in English, reshoot pivotal scenes with an actress who looked like the original star, half a world away in Istanbul. He'd traveled extensively and boasted that he had friends all over the world.

His name, Ulvi Dogan, sounded so foreign in my tongue, that it was sometimes difficult for me to pronounce it. That initial vowel made it awkward—not the rounded Puerto Rican *u* nor the puckered, sharp English *u*, but something halfway in between, a strangled diphthong.

"Hi," I'd say when I called him on the phone, "it's me." I'd never say my name, because he'd christened me something else: Chiquita, little girl. Having grown up with a familial nickname, Negi, and being an official Esmeralda everywhere else, his pet name for me felt as foreign as his name on my lips. When I tried to give him a nickname, he refused. "Ulvi," he said. "Just Ulvi." He would not let me call him darling, either, or dear, or honey, or sweetheart. Not even any of the lovely Spanish words that express affection—*querido, mi amor, mi cielo*—would convince him. Just Ulvi, he insisted. Ulvi.

With this man I barely knew, whose name reshaped my face every time I spoke it, I left my mother's home. I sat next to him, my forehead pressed to the window of the airplane, and swore I could see Mami's house, way down there in Brooklyn, the tiny square of cement that was our backyard, the larger playground directly across our door, which we were forbidden to play in because there was always the danger that a fight would break out over the outcome of a basketball game. In the distance Manhattan's spires pierced the sky, while Brooklyn's rectangular roofed buildings seemed to push against it, defying the clouds.

I turned to Ulvi, who leaned over me to look at the city we had left behind. "This is only the second time I'm ever on an airplane," I said.

"Really?" He leaned back, fiddled with the controls on the armrest, pushed his seat back, and closed his eyes. The air around me grew cold, and I rubbed the goose bumps from my arms, turned again to the tiny rectangular window as the plane droned through cotton candy.

Days earlier, when I'd told him Mami would never give me permission to go with him to Florida, Ulvi had said: "You must take the bull by the horns." I'd never heard that phrase, had no idea what it meant. He spoke less English than I did. Where did he pick it up? He didn't want me to run away with him. "Talk to her woman to woman," he'd said. "Explain the situation." But I couldn't face her, couldn't imagine the hurt in her eyes when I told her I'd had a choice, and I'd chosen him.

"When was the first time?" Ulvi's voice was so soft, I thought at first that it came from inside my head. I turned to him. Still leaning back, his heavy lidded eyes looked at me as if he'd just met me, a stranger on the seat beside him on a plane to an exotic destination.

"Seven years ago, when we first came from Puerto Rico."

"Hmm," he said and closed his eyes again, turned his face toward the aisle. His thinning black hair had picked up static from the seat cushions, and fine strands fluttered languidly up, like soft antennae. I pressed my spine against the back cushion and tried not to think, not to imagine Mami's face as she read my letter.

"What did your mother say when you told her?" Ulvi asked, and heat rose to my cheeks.

"I didn't." I closed my eyes, afraid to see his, the anger I knew was there. He thought it was wrong that I hadn't told her about us, but he also refused to meet her. She will understand, he had assured me. But he didn't know Mami.

"That is not good, Chiquita," he said. "It is not good."

I would not open my eyes, did not answer. I heard him turn away from me again, and imagined the tiny hairs drifting toward the plane's low ceiling. Below us New York was becoming a memory, but the words I'd struggled with, *Querida Mami* and *el hombre que yo amo,* floated around my head, every dot over the *i*'s, every downstroke, every loop, fine threads that twisted in and out between who I was and who I had become.

The apartment at the Gateway Arms was huge: a bedroom, a living/dining room, a bright kitchen with dishwasher and an electric stove. It was completely furnished, down to matched towels on the racks, extra linens in the closets, and landscapes on the walls. There was a telephone on the table between the two twin beds. Ulvi picked it up and smiled when he heard a dial tone. Another telephone with an extra-long cord was tacked on the wall in the kitchen. Thick, mustard-colored shag covered every room but the kitchen and bath, which were vinyl-tiled. A glass slider off the dining room led to a narrow second-floor balcony overlooking a weedy lot and, beyond, the fenced-in backyards of several one-story houses surrounded by lush gardens.

The building belonged to Ulvi's partners, who were letting us use the apartment while Ulvi had a hernia operation at Fort Lauderdale's Holy Cross Hospital. According to Ulvi, his partners were also paying his medical bills and had bought our airplane tickets. I found their generosity impressive, but Ulvi dismissed it. The reason they were being so nice to him, he argued, was to protect their investment. They had put money into the American edition of his Turkish film with the idea that, once it found a distributor, they would share in the profits that were sure to come. Unlike him, they were not artists, and, therefore, not generous and softhearted. They were businessmen who had financed one movie starring Gina Lollobrigida and were planning to make more with award-winning art film directors like him. To them, he was a commodity, nothing more.

"You must not believe when people too nice, Chiquita," he said. "Usually they want something else."

"You don't really believe that, do you?" I asked. He smiled, wrapped me in his arms, kissed my hair.

"Ah, Chiquita, you are innocent. The world is not so good like you imagine." In his arms, the world was a wonderful place, soft and warm and clean-scented. He lifted my face, sought my eyes. "Is not always what it looks."

"I know that..."

"Shush, shush, do not argue. I will teach you everything. But you must listen what I say. Okay?" He waited for me to nod my head. "Okay, then."

We unpacked our belongings into the dressers, one for each, the drawers lined with floral paper. He pointed to my side of the walk-in closet, and I hung up the two dresses I'd brought, placed the sandals side by side on the floor, across from his leather shoes, toes facing toes across the mustard shag.

We were about to go out for some lunch when there was a knock at the door. Ulvi answered it, and a tall, blond woman accompanied by a squat, ruddy man stood in the glare, their arms laden with groceries.

Ulvi greeted him with a handshake and her with a kiss on each cheek, then turned and introduced them to me as Leo and Iris, no last names. Iris went into the kitchen and started putting things away. With a look and a nod, Ulvi let me know I should follow her while he led Leo to the sofa.

"You didn't have to do this, it's so kind of you...," I burbled.

"Oh, I know, we didn't have to, but we wanted to. I only wish we could have gotten here sooner." She moved around the kitchen with confidence. "I'm sorry if I seem like I'm taking over," she smiled. "We've had many guests here, and I'm familiar with where everything goes."

She spoke English easily but with a pronounced German accent. Her lips puckered into coquettish smiles whenever she looked toward the men in the living area. From time to time, she flicked back her shoulder-length platinum hair, which was combed straight to frame a narrow face with wide, blue-green eyes, a long nose, thin lips frosted pink. Like Leo, Iris wore a lot of gold jewelry: bracelets, rings, neck chains. They both smelled newly showered and perfumed, his thick black hair matted wetly to his skull.

We returned to the living area. Iris sat, crossed her long legs, and, in one movement, flipped her hair to one side, placed it gently over her breast, and leaned close to Leo, who shifted toward the armrest. To me, Iris's sinuous movements seemed designed for Ulvi, not Leo, and a possessive knot formed in my stomach.

Ulvi held his hand toward me and drew me onto his lap. The tension inside me eased as I leaned against him, conscious of Iris's eyes. I could see her question "Whatever do you see in her?" I was nothing, Ulvi had told me many times. "You are poor and naïve. But I like you are young and innocent. I can teach you everything." Iris, in spite of her perky appearance, was closer in age to Ulvi than to me. And even to my inexperienced eyes she looked like a woman who had little left to learn.

Leo told us about Jim, who also lived in the building and was another associate. "Different business from the movies," he chortled, but didn't explain. He pushed Iris away and stood up abruptly. "Well, we have to get going," he said. "We'll pick you up around six, and we'll go eat." He led the way to the front door, opened it, and guided Iris through before she had a chance to exchange more cheek-to-cheek kisses with Ulvi. He waved at us, and closed the door behind them.

I tried to exchange a look of surprise with Ulvi, but he was already moving toward the kitchen. Their visit and the promise of a meal in a few hours seemed to have eased his hunger a little, but he still wanted a snack. "Let's just have some tea," he offered as he rummaged through the cabinets. "Come, Chiquita," he said, "this is your job."

"My job?"

"Make us something to eat," he said with a grin as he pulled a tea kettle from a cabinet under the electric stovetop. He set the kettle on the counter. "I have to make some calls." He went into the bedroom and closed the door behind him.

I was instantly aware that, in the twenty-one years I'd been alive, I'd never been in a kitchen alone with someone depending on me for a meal. At home, my mother or grandmother always cooked for me, my sisters and brothers and whatever relative or friend happened to drop in just as the pots were going on the stove. Both Mami and her mother, Tata, were excellent cooks who delighted in always coming up with a good meal even when the only thing to be found in the refrigerator or pantry were bits of this and scraps of that. I now faced several cabinets filled with canned and boxed food, a refrigerator stocked with fresh fruits and vegetables, milk, butter, eggs, and orange juice, luncheon meats in tight plastic bags, and didn't know how to begin preparing "something to eat."

Mayonnaise, I said to myself, I'll make us a sandwich. But a sandwich seemed like such an American meal that I didn't want to make that as the first thing I ever prepared for Ulvi. Rice and beans, the staple in my diet, would take the better part of a day, if I started by soaking the beans, as Mami did, overnight. The image of my mother easily moving from stove to refrigerator to the sink back to the stove brought tears to the corners of my eyes. It was mid-afternoon. By now my sisters and brothers would be coming home from school, the mailman would have made his delivery, and Mami might be sitting at the kitchen table, reading my letter.

"All right, Chiquita?" Ulvi came out of the bedroom, his face bright, as if he'd just received a marvelous compliment. He scanned the counters and dining table with nothing on them. The tea kettle was still where he had left it. "Are you crying?" he asked when he saw my expression.

"I was thinking about my mother," I said and burst into sobs.

"Come on, Chiquita," he said, "you must be strong girl."

"I should have told her. It was cruel to just leave a letter."

"You left a letter, Chiquita?" He pronounced the double *t*'s in *letter* forcefully, and I felt them like a slap to the cheek. "Did you mention my name?" His voice dropped to a whisper, as if the violence of the word *letter* had frightened him, as if telling my mother his name were dangerous.

"I . . . no, I don't think so. Not your name." *El hombre que yo amo* seemed relieved.

The restaurant was on the highway, across the street from a long, sandy beach. Leo and Iris were greeted by the owner with vigorous handshakes and a toothy smile. We were introduced, Ulvi by his full name and relationship to Leo, who referred to him as his director. I was "Chiquita, his girlfriend."

We were led to a large round table in the center of the room, already occupied by two men and another stately blonde, younger and curvier than Iris. Janka was with Jim, the associate in a "different business from the movies." Francis, Leo's partner and the only other person in the group who seemed to know Ulvi, stood up to shake hands. He was handsome in the way Charles Bronson was handsome, with narrow eyes that squinted beneath thick, arched eyebrows, and fleshy lips that covered dazzling white teeth. The way he squeezed my hand and looked me in the eyes, the half smile, the slight nod of the head, the way he pulled out my chair and waited until I was settled between him and Ulvi before he sat down, relaxed the tension that had been squeezing my shoulders toward my ears. He had a deep voice, which carried across the large round table when he spoke in a near murmur to deferential silence from the rest of the party. Within minutes it was clear to me that Francis was the boss, Leo the second in command, and Jim, like Ulvi, was an employee who spent the rest of the evening trying to impress Francis with his sense of humor.

Ulvi reached under the table from time to time to squeeze my hand, or to get my attention so that I would watch him. He was teaching me how to eat European style, which he said was the proper way. This meant holding the knife and fork in the opposite hands from the way everyone else did it. He also thought that I should slow down. "You eat," he'd told me, "like somebody will take the food from you before it gets inside your mouth." That moment between plate and lips had become the most important part of my meals, a few hesitant seconds which he controlled by insisting that I eat at his speed, to get used to the timing. I was to drink when he drank, to eat when he did, to blot my lips, "never wipe," he'd said, when his were wet.

The men talked business. Gina Lollobrigida had been in New York the previous week, and Francis and Leo had met with her and discussed another movie they wanted to produce. "She's a beautiful woman," Francis murmured. "Striking." He turned to Ulvi. "Do you know her?"

"We met," Ulvi said, "in Cannes." Francis and Leo exchanged a satisfied look.

Jim was in town for a couple of weeks, but he and Janka would be on the road soon. From the conversation I gathered that Jim was a representative for a line of portable saunas that Francis and Leo produced. He'd been having trouble selling them for use in private homes because they took up a lot of space. Then he had an idea.

"It came to me on I-95," he said. "You get a big girl like Janka here, put her in a bikini, stand her next to the sauna, and bingo! The unit looks smaller." The men laughed, and Leo reached behind Iris to pat Jim's back. Janka laughed, too, stood up to demonstrate how tall she was, at least six feet, easily the tallest person at the table.

"You're a genius," Iris purred, rubbing Jim's thigh. Jim's face went slack, and his eyes sought Leo's, who nodded his head to one side in a gesture that seemed to mean "Don't worry about it." Iris finished her drink and looked around for the waiter, who appeared the minute Francis lifted his finger.

Ulvi sipped his glass of wine, smiled mysteriously when he wasn't being addressed, listened attentively to whatever Francis said while remaining deferential to Leo, who watched him carefully. A couple of times Francis or Leo addressed a question to me, and I stuttered through an answer, aware that they were doing it to be polite, that I, like Iris and Janka, was there for decoration, not conversation. At the end of the evening, they knew no more about me than they had at the beginning.

Jim drove us to our apartment. He was staying in another of the units, on the first floor—"So I can roll out of bed and dive into the swimming pool," he laughed. He drove a burgundy Lincoln Continental, cushy as a feather bed. As I cuddled next to Ulvi in the back seat, it was hard to believe that less than eighteen hours earlier I'd left my mother's house to walk, frightened but determined, into this life of luxury cars and roomy apartments with swimming pools, dinners at expensive restaurants, businessmen who could move an army of waiters with a raised finger, clever marketing strategies, Gina Lollobrigida at the Cannes Film Festival, and the man who now stroked my shoulder, his fingers slowly making their way toward my breast.

2. *Not Swimming*

The light in Fort Lauderdale reminded me of the clear yellow of a Puerto Rican morning. It had been seven years since I'd been back to the island, but the memory of its warm sun returned the moment I stepped onto the balcony overlooking the pool at the Gateway Arms. New York, even at its brightest, always seemed gray and shadowy, the unreal sky far above, a sheet of silk stretched between skyscrapers. New York had felt like a deep box, the façades of buildings enormous labyrinthine walls that prevented any semblance of a natural world. Even Central Park, where Ulvi and I spent many afternoons, was an artificial environment bounded on all sides by Gothic buildings and the distant throb of Harlem. But here, in the soft yellow light of Fort Lauderdale, I closed my eyes and remembered Puerto Rico.

If I kept my lids shut, I could see the barrio in Toa Baja where I'd grown up. It was shaped like a funnel, the open end at the two-lane road that led east to San Juan and west to Arecibo. Macún. I couldn't pronounce the word without wondering what it meant, where it came from, who had thought up such a strange name for a place. It was near another barrio called Candelaria, which meant Candlemas, across from Pájaros, which meant birds. But Macún had no meaning. It was as foreign in Spanish as it was in English, an African word, perhaps, or a fool's utterance elevated to language. A nonsense place where my early life resided, locked away in my imagination, seldom talked about, but never forgotten.

Lying on a plastic lounge chair in Fort Lauderdale, I, a twenty-one-year-old woman, recalled a childhood that didn't seem so very long ago. An ocean lay between me and the girl called Negi who had climbed Macún's trees, ran up its hills, bathed in the first rains of May believing they brought good luck. I was now Chiquita, and the man who had renamed me didn't like to talk about my past.

The sun licked my skin, a quiet breeze rustled the ornamental bushes along the walkways that led to the apartment. The swimming pool rippled in sparkles. I didn't know how to swim, but I tried to enjoy the feeling of idleness that just being poolside generated. I wondered if this was what being rich felt like—a warm body under a hot sun, a cool pool at my feet, nothing to do but relax in a plastic lounge chair. At the same time I asked myself how anyone—no matter how rich and idle—could possibly just lie there. The thought made me anxious for something to do, but there was nothing. I'd left my book upstairs and was afraid of the water.

Ulvi slid in and began to do laps, his arms stretching along the surface of the pool, grabbing, pushing, propelling himself toward then away from me. His brown body shimmered like that of a hairless sea creature, and when he turned his head to breathe, his mouth twisted to the side of his face, distorting it. It was mid-morning. In an hour, he would be going to the hospital, where he would spend the night. The surgery would be early the next day.

"No, you do not come," he'd already warned. I protested that it was my duty to be there, waiting the outcome of the surgery, but he contended that there was nothing I could do. "The doctors are in charge," he said, and I gave up trying to convince him. "You come," he suggested, "after the operation."

Watching him glide across the clear blue water, I wondered what would happen to me if Ulvi died during surgery. I would probably have to return to the grayness of New York. But maybe I could stay beneath the warm Fort Lauderdale sun. I could find a job in one of the office buildings we'd passed last night on the way to the restaurant. I could pay my own rent, perhaps maybe even here at the Gateway Arms.

"Let's go up." Ulvi stood at the foot of my chair, glistening, his black hair plastered to his forehead. He looked healthy and vibrant and not at all like someone about to undergo an operation. For the first time since he'd told me about it, I believed that it would be minor surgery, not life-threatening. He would go to the hospital and in a few days he'd be back and we'd continue our life together. But I couldn't picture what that life would be like. We'd known each other ten months, but last night was the first we'd spent under the same roof. "A honeymoon," he'd teased, and I'd been happy because the word sounded like a promise.

"Make us some breakfast, Chiquita," he said as we entered the apartment, and again I felt the panic of the day before. This time, however, I brushed nostalgia aside and concentrated on boiling water for tea and on toasting slices of bread. I found jam and cheese in the refrigerator and silently thanked Iris for bringing us groceries.

"Would you like an egg?" I called to Ulvi, who was changing in the bedroom. It was a relief when he said no, just something light. He came out dressed and ready, nodded approval at the set table, the crisp toast cut in triangles, the pot of tea, the jam spilled into a small bowl with a spoon inside.

"Very good, Chiquita," he said and kissed my cheek. We sat opposite one another, he fully dressed, me still in my bathing suit. "While I am gone," he said in between sips of tea, "do not answer the telephone."

"Why not?"

"In case it is business. You will not know what to tell."

"I was a secretary..."

"It is how I want it, Chiquita. Do not answer." He stared me down until I dropped my gaze and mumbled okay.

"Can I call out?" I tried not to sound defiant.

"Who do you know here?"

"I might call home."

"Yes, of course you can call your mother." He spread strawberry jam from one end of his bread to the other. "You are with me of your own will, Chiquita," he said after a while. "You can go home anytime."

The world caved beneath me. "I don't want to go home."

"That's good," he murmured standing, pulling me up from my chair and embracing me. "Because I want you here, with me."

I melted into the smell of him, into the soft black hair on his chest, and tried not to cry. He held me for a few minutes, caressed the panic that had made me sound hysterical and childlike. "You be good girl while I'm away," he said into my ear, and it was then that I sobbed. He thought I cried for him, but those tears were for me.

He left in a taxi, and the minute it pulled away from the Gateway Arms I felt lighter. Guilt made me look in the direction the taxi took, as if Ulvi could have read my mind, could have felt my relief. I could not have explained the change. A few minutes earlier I'd worried that he'd die on the operating table. Now that he was gone, I was happy not to have his gaze upon me, his constant attention to every little thing I did. I needed a chance to think things through without having to explain myself to him.

I planned to call my mother and tell her where I was, to apologize for causing her pain and worry. But when I got up to the apartment and faced the phone, I stared at it for a while, imagining Mami on the other side, hysterical, or angry, or so hurt that my own heart would crack in two just to hear her voice. I paced from the kitchen to the bedroom, feeling the space, the emptiness of the apartment. Back home our rooms were rarely empty. One of my sisters or brothers was always there, my grandmother, an aunt or uncle or cousin. It was never possible to stand in a room as I was now doing and feel the uninterrupted distance between two walls.

I pushed the coffee table into the sofa to make the floor bigger.

The space created was as large as some of the dance studios in New York where I had spent all my spare time and money—before Ulvi saw me dance and told me I looked ridiculous.

There was no radio in the apartment, no television, nothing to give sound to the controlled movements I performed from memory, the Indian classical dance routines I had so painstakingly learned and practiced for hours on end, often, as now, with no music to guide the gestures. I could hear it all inside my head—*di di tei, di di tei, di di tei, tah*—the syllables used to mark the choreography. *Dum didi tei, dum didi tei, dum didi tei tah.* I danced until the air-conditioned room felt as hot as the outdoors, until my skin gleamed with sweat, until my legs, arms, and back throbbed.

Afterwards, I showered and lay down. The night before, Ulvi had insisted that we push the beds together to form one huge bed, but the narrow gap in the middle still made it feel as if there were a boundary between us, his land closer to the bathroom, mine nearer the window. I stretched out on the bed, my left arm and leg spread over the gap into his side. It was luxurious to have two whole mattresses to myself. Two pillows. Two sheets and blankets. I rolled from one side of the bed to the other, anticipating the middle gap, which now felt less like a depression and more like a long, sharp hill. Up one side, down the other, my eyes closed, my legs stretched, toes pointed, my arms above and around my head. I established a rhythm, back and forth from one bed to the other until a sharp ringing stopped me midway. I pushed onto my elbow and watched the phone, its black face banded with white circles, upon which shiny, blacker numbers and letters appeared stark and businesslike. I counted four, five, six rings. The face showed every number in its proper order, the letters like eyebrows over them. But the combination necessary to make this particular phone ring was missing from the yellowish moon in the center of the dial. Eleven rings. I itched to pick up the receiver, to know who could be so sure someone was there that they would let the phone ring so many times. It stopped, and I did pick it up, as if the ringing were insufficient proof that the phone worked. The minute I set it down, it started again. Fifteen this time. I imagined it was Ulvi calling, to see if I would pick up the phone. But maybe it was one of his business associates. Or it could be my mother, who had somehow discovered where I was. But how could she? Even I didn't know exactly where I was or the number of the apartment. Another pause. Then six rings. And finally silence. The austere circle in the center of the dial now looked like an eye watching my reaction. I threw one of the pillows over it.

I was certain that the person at the other end knew I was there and was daring me to pick up the phone. But then it occurred to me that maybe it was burglars checking to see if anyone was home, and they would be, that very minute, making their way to what they thought was an empty apartment. I dressed quickly, found the keys, and left the apartment with no particular idea of where I would go. I just wanted to get away from there, telling myself my life was more important than whatever burglars might find in the spare apartment. But I knew that the real reason was to avoid hearing the phone ring while I stood by, forbidden to answer it.

It was midday, the sun high overhead, the air heavy with moisture that pressed into my clothes. I remembered the mall we'd passed the night before, just a few blocks down the avenue, and headed for it, hoping to find an air-conditioned bookstore where I could linger among the stacks. But the stores all displayed pastel-colored tops and dresses or showy jewelry like what Iris and Leo wore. In New York I'd called fashion like this "blond people clothes," because they seemed designed for pale skin and hair. If I wore those colors, my café con leche complexion turned ashen, and I felt conspicuous, as if the soft shades made me stand out more than the vivid colors I favored. The one time I dared enter one of the stores, the saleswoman hovered behind me, as if afraid I would run off with the merchandise. Her wariness camouflaged behind an obsequious smile, she jiggled hangers from front to back of this rack or that, trailing my every move with pointless activity. I was offended by her attention, but didn't have the nerve to tell her and walked out, humiliated by her suspicions but not knowing how to challenge them.

That night I slept alone in the enormous bed in the vast apartment, conscious that the world outside the locked front door was huge, unknown, and mysterious. I felt so inconsequential that Chiquita seemed like the perfect name for me. I slept fitfully, waking up several times to reach out for Delsa, Norma, or any of my always-nearby siblings, only to discover the solitude around me. I promised myself that I would call Mami the next morning and let her know I was all right. By then, I imagined, she would have cried enough and might accept that, at twenty-one, I was old enough to make my own choices and lead my own life. I tried to picture what that life would be like, but came up against murky, incomplete images of Ulvi gracefully sliding across a shimmering pool while I stood on the edge, invisible even to myself, paralyzed by my inability to swim.

3. Echándole todo en cara

Never having had to find a taxi anywhere but in New York City, I set out along the Sunrise Highway expecting that any moment a yellow Checker cab would go by. For over a half hour I was the only person walking along the road. Everyone else was in a car or pickup truck, and some looked curiously in my direction, their eyes scanning around for the reason I was on foot. A couple of men pulled over to offer me rides, and I waved them away with a thank you and walked in the opposite direction. Finally, a police cruiser stopped, and the officer asked if everything was all right. When I explained that I was waiting for a taxi, he told me that in Fort Lauderdale one had to call ahead, and pointed to a pay phone a few yards away where a thick, dog-eared directory dangled from a chain. He drove by a couple of times after I made my call, and each time waved at me as if he were making sure I was okay. But I was a dark-skinned Puerto Rican from the outer boroughs of New York City, and his attention was not welcome. I was certain that he, like the saleswoman the day before, was watching me so that I would not steal something.

When the taxi finally came—not a yellow Checker cab, but a plain white sedan with bold red letters on the doors—I was feeling as if I *had* done something wrong, even though my only crime had been to be on foot on the Sunrise Highway. The driver was sullen and preoccupied, so I didn't try to make conversation, but watched the flat, low landscape speed by in a flutter of pink, green, and turquoise. Again I was reminded of Puerto Rico, but these streets, unlike those of my childhood, were richer, the homes surrounded by neat hedges and thick, well-tended lawns. The streets were deserted, except for the occasional mailman or bouffant-headed woman walking a dog.

The hospital was set back from the road and looked new. Inside, the floors and walls were shiny, the halls patrolled by women in white habits. The nun at the reception desk directed me to one of the upper floors. The squeaky tiles, the gleaming walls, the flowing white nurses' uniforms, gave an impression of cleanliness and virtue to the place. Ulvi's room was the last door before a tall narrow window that shed bright light on the long hallway. As I walked, it felt as if I were floating on a shaft of light toward the sun, and I had to squint as I came nearer his door. It took me a few seconds to focus my eyes once I entered his dim, cool room. To the right was Ulvi's high hospital bed, and Ulvi wrapped in white sheets, his mournful eyes staring at my mother, who sat on the only chair in the room, her hands clasped over her purse.

"What are you doing here?" I screeched.

"I came to bring you back home," she said, standing up, her face flushed, her eyes bloated from lack of sleep or tears or both. She bristled with anger, and I was afraid she would lift her hand and hit me in front of my lover.

"I'm not going back with you," I screamed. A nun appeared at the door, and Ulvi lifted his arms weakly from under the white sheets and made a gesture as if to shoo us out of the room. He was still drugged from the surgery, his features slack, which made him look older. Even through the haze, he managed to slur out, "You should have told her, Chiquita."

The nun glowered at me and Mami. We stood side by side now, facing Ulvi's bed, for the moment unable to face each other.

"Mr. Dogan needs his rest," the nun said. "Please leave." She settled the sheets around him, and I walked out, followed by Mami, who carried a small bag.

I couldn't speak, couldn't cry, couldn't see where I was going, but yet managed to retrace my steps down the sunlit hall. Every once in a while a nun passed us, and I felt dirty and sinful. Mami's anger was like a weight that dragged on me, even as my own anger and humiliation propelled me forward. I felt dizzy, and wished I could faint so that Mami's worry over me would replace her rage, which was as solid and transparent as the hospital's gleaming glass doors. I kept seeing Ulvi's face, drawn and dark over the stark white sheets, the displeasure on his drug-slackened lips, his gesture shooing us both out of the room. The nun's long fingers had pulled the covers up around his shoulders and trapped his arms inside, while her translucent face scowled at me and Mami. The nun in her virginal robes, Ulvi wrapped in white sheets, stood in stark contrast to me and Mami, both of us practically glowing with fury, disappointment, and humiliation. We climbed into a taxi that was, through some miracle, waiting at the curb, and I gave the driver the address. In silence Mami and I were taken to the Gateway Arms, each looking out a different window, our backs to one another, waiting for the privacy of a locked door.

No sooner had we entered the apartment than I began to yell at Mami. Didn't even give her time to settle her things or to look around. Didn't try to speak calmly, "woman to woman," didn't try to "take the bull by the horns." Or maybe that's what the phrase meant. I was a toreador and she was a bull and I goaded her, made her angrier than she was by being disrespectful, offensive, and insolent. How could she do this to me, I began, to show up unannounced, to sit scowling in front of a man who had just undergone an operation? What made her think I would return with her? What would I be returning to? A crowded house in a ghetto, no privacy, no room to breathe, welfare.

Mami was stunned. Her face fixed into a frown, her eyes narrowed, she stared at me as if seeing me for the first time. I was out of control and felt it. I'd never spoken to her this way. Since we'd arrived in the United States, I'd been so conscious of how hard she worked to make sure that my ten sisters and brothers and I had what we needed, that I hadn't dared complain about how the move had affected me. I now told her that silence hadn't meant acceptance, that every little humiliation I'd suffered in the United States was her fault. That leaving Puerto Rico had been her idea. That we hadn't progressed much beyond who we were in the barrio where we'd last lived. That I would have much rather stayed with my father in that remote primitive barrio than endure the daily degradations of being a Puerto Rican in New York. I screamed that getting a good education was not worth the price of losing myself in the process. That our lives had not improved, as she had promised, but had gotten worse.

How much resentment had I stored over the previous seven years? Enough to wound my mother so that she was unable to answer my tirade with anything more than a hurt look and trembling hands. When I took a breath, she opened her mouth, hesitated, then yelled back.

"After all I've sacrificed for you, this is how you repay me."

"For me? For me?" I screeched. "I have nothing. I am nothing. I'm lucky a man like Ulvi took interest in me. Just look around here," I said, "look at where I am. A huge apartment with a swimming pool! This is better than anything you ever gave me! Just look! Have we ever lived anywhere like this?"

And Mami did stop and look around at the enormous apartment, at the picture window leading to the narrow balcony, at the shiny new kitchen with dishwasher and garbage disposal.

"For this," she said, her voice tight, "you gave yourself to him?"

I couldn't answer, didn't know if what she said was true or not. "I love him," I finally whimpered.

"He's taking advantage of you," she warned. And I responded that if he were, it was all right with me. What else had I to give him but myself? The hurt look returned to her face, but she wasn't about to be silenced by me.

"What kind of man will take you away from your family and not marry you?" she asked, and I screamed that marriage hadn't seemed so important for her with the three men she'd lived with. She slapped me, and I fell on my buttocks and covered my head with my hands. She stood over me. "Don't you ever speak to me like that again. I don't care how old you are, even when you're a grandmother you are never to talk to me like that. Now pack your things and let's go!"

"I'm not leaving! You can't make me!" I screamed. "I'll kill myself." I ran to the kitchen and pulled out a knife, a butter knife with a serrated edge, but a knife nevertheless. Had I tried to cut my wrists, as I threatened to do, I would have merely scratched the skin. But Mami fought me for it as if it were a machete, and took it from my hands.

"You would kill yourself over him?" she asked with a mixture of wonder and disdain. The minute she spoke those words, I stopped fighting. I leaned against the wall, my hands over my face, and sobbed. I had not only disappointed Mami by choosing Ulvi over her, I was choosing him above life. In that instant I was certain that the latter was the greater shame.

"Go away!" I screamed. "Go away!" Mami picked up her bag, her purse, opened the door, and slammed it behind her. My heart grew so large that it threatened to explode through my chest. I sobbed with my whole body, had to sit on the floor and hold myself so that I would not break into pieces. Crumpled on the shag rug, I felt how completely alone I was now that my mother had left. Had Ulvi walked in that instant, his presence would not have compensated for her absence, and it was clear that, had she walked in the door, the world would not have felt as big and frightening as it now did. I sat on the floor for what seemed like a long time, crying until my eyes were so swollen, I couldn't see through them.

There was a knock, followed by Mami's voice, soft and not at all angry. "Negi, *por favor, ábreme la puerta.*" I stood at the door, my hands on the knob, uncertain whether I should open it. "I'm not going back," I said, and even as I did, I hoped she'd make me.

"It's all right," she said, "you don't have to go back. I understand." I opened the door and fell into her arms, and shed tears I didn't think were left in me. She let me cry, then led me to the sofa, where we sat a long time, both of us weeping. I wanted to comfort her, but didn't know how, which saddened me even more. There was no way to take back what I'd said, no way to return home now that my real feelings had been revealed. My invective had changed both of us, had distanced me from Mami more than I ever expected. Until that afternoon there had always been a layer of respect between us, mutual, silent admiration for what the other achieved against terrible odds. But my words had torn that wall down, had diminished her achievements. I hadn't chosen Ulvi over Mami, I had rejected her. He just happened to be there when I did. She understood the difference much sooner than I did. It would be years before I realized that, by not fighting me anymore, she was seeing something I was blind to. Ulvi was not the reason I had left my family. I'd been leaving for a long time. He just provided the opportunity.

Mami helped me lie down on the sofa and went to the kitchen. Cabinet doors opened and shut, the refrigerator door hissed, pots clanged against the counter, water ran. Within minutes, she was cooking something that, even through my clogged nose, I recognized as the fragrance of love.

We went for a walk after dinner, to the same mall I'd been in the day before. Both of us were swollen-eyed and tense, our conversation sparse, each of us determined to avoid mentioning the reason we were both in Fort Lauderdale. We ambled up and down the corridors, looking in store windows, never going inside, both of us disdainful of the clothes and showy jewelry. As it was getting dark, we headed back, swatting mosquitoes that buzzed in thick clouds near the waterway. Back at the apartment, we showered and prepared for bed. I offered her Ulvi's side, closest to the bathroom. As I drifted into sleep I heard what might have been crying or might have been chortling.

"What is it?" I asked. "Are you all right?"

"Don't they have taxis in this town?" she asked.

"They don't just show up," I answered. "You have to call them."

"I felt like a fool out on that road waiting for one," she said. She turned over and was soon asleep. I lay awake a long time listening to my mother's breath fill the room. I fell asleep to the sound of it, to the deep, slow drafts of air that made her body rise and fall like a wave in a still ocean. I wondered how she'd found us, how she'd managed to find Ulvi, whose name she didn't even know. She'd gone to great expense and effort to bring me, her eldest child, back home, and I wondered if it would be as humiliating for her to return without me as for me to return with her.

The next morning, while the air was still damp and the light from streetlamps battled the encroaching daylight, I stood in front of the Gateway Arms and helped my mother put her bag into the back seat of a cab. I dreaded the moment when she'd ask me again to come home, but she didn't say anything but goodbye. We hugged long and hard, and when we separated, we were both crying. She looked out the back window of the cab at me standing among the lush greenery, her eyes so sad I felt once more as if I would break into pieces. When the cab took the corner I returned to the apartment and crawled back into the still warm bed. I was weighed down with a sorrow so immense that I couldn't move. My limbs curled up to my belly, my hands against my face, I lay there for hours, unable to cry and yet choked beyond speech, thoughtless yet filled with images that confused me and sent me deeper under the covers, as if the cotton blankets could protect me from my past, as if they were armor against the rest of my life.

Help

In our battle against the Beatles, it was my uncle Willie who threw the first punch, and for that, he said, he should have been knighted. I didn't argue.

We fought them in 1966, the year they played Araneta Coliseum in Manila, to a crowd of over one hundred thousand people. Their visit was quick; they were scheduled to leave two days later, and as director of Manila International Airport, it was Uncle Willie's job to make sure the Beatles' travel went smoothly, that no press or paparazzi detain them. But the morning after their concert, Imelda Marcos demanded one more show: a Royal Command Performance for the First Lady. When reporters asked the Beatles for their reply, they said, supposedly, "If the First Lady wants to see us, why doesn't she come up to our room for a special exhibition?" Then they walked away, the newspapers wrote, laughing.

Uncle Willie took it hard.

Later that same evening, he called JohnJohn, Googi, and me. "It's an emergency," he said on the phone. "Come quick!" Except for the six-pack on my bedroom floor, we had nothing better to do.

"Be right there," I told him. We drank the beer, then headed out.

When we arrived at Uncle Willie's apartment, he was sitting at the kitchen table, the ceiling fan spinning slow over his sweat-beaded head. His fists were clenched tight atop his lap, and the wrinkles at his eyes seemed to deepen with anger as he recounted the Beatles' lewd remarks. "They were insulting the whole of Filipina womanhood!" His face fell, and he shook his head, still in disbelief. "Oh my goodness."

"What exhibition were they talking about exactly?" Googi asked, seating himself across from Uncle Willie. He was the oldest of us, three months shy of twenty-one, but the slowest. "What did they mean by it?"

"What do you think they meant by it?" Uncle snapped at him. "What do you do in the bedroom in the first place?"

JohnJohn wouldn't let his brother answer. "It was a joke," he said, lighting a cigarette. He reached into the refrigerator for a San Miguel (Uncle Willie kept his refrigerator well-stocked in case any of us should drop by unexpectedly) and pried the cap off against the edge of the kitchen counter. "A few laughs. No harm done." He drank his beer fast, then gave me a look that said it was my turn to calm the old man down.

"Take it easy," was all I could say.

Uncle Willie got to his feet. Nothing, he insisted, was funny about Imelda Marcos. "She is the face of our country!" he said, pointing to a framed black and white picture of her on top of the TV. He brought it over to us and held it close to our faces. His fingers were pressed so hard against the glass I thought it might crack right over Imelda's face and cut his skin. "Don't you see?" he asked. "Don't you see?" In the picture, Imelda was seated in a large wicker chair frilled with ribbons and flowers, staring out into the distance, her queenly face shaded beneath a parasol held by an anonymous hand.

"Yes," I finally said, "I do. I see it." Googi agreed with me, nodding. JohnJohn shrugged his shoulders and let out smoke.

That was enough to make Uncle Willie believe we were on his side. "Okay," he said, "good. Then the Beatles will pay for their insolence." He sat back down and put his elbows on the table, his forehead slumped against his clasped hands like he was in prayer. His face was hidden, but I could see the strands of his thinning gray hair, hard and slick with pomade, almost shiny beneath the kitchen lights. Even the short, slight hairs on the back of his neck had gone white.

JohnJohn looked at me, his face impatient, almost angry. I knew what he was thinking. He'd been volunteering at the student paper at the university, reading up on Imelda's questionable dealings. He clipped out articles about the workers who died in the heat building a statue of the President and the First Lady under her orders. The week before he showed us photos of families living in city dumps after Imelda had their homes bulldozed to make space for a nightclub that was never built. JohnJohn was the first person I knew who called Imelda Marcos a phony.

I kept my eyes on Uncle Willie. He was mumbling so softly that I only heard "Mrs. Marcos" and "those hateful Beatles" whispered in his mix of English and Tagalog, and then he went silent, motionless. For a second I thought he'd fallen asleep, and in the next second I thought something worse. I almost reached out to him, but his head suddenly came up, and he was with us again. "I will need your help," Uncle Willie announced. He rose from his chair, dimmed the lights, and drew the curtains, as though someone were watching us through binoculars or telescopes from afar. "Listen carefully to me, okay, guys?" My cousins said of course, absolutely, no question. But they paid attention for their own amusement, for the sake of hearing Uncle Willie speak the ridiculous with heartfelt seriousness, with all the passion a man his age could muster. They didn't mean to be cruel.

"This is how we will defeat the Beatles," he went on. He revealed an intricate plan, one that required him to take advantage of his position at Manila International Airport. He would divert the Beatles' security and send the group to their gate, where we would be waiting, dressed as airport personnel, ready to pounce. "Nothing injurious, just enough for them to get the message," Uncle Willie assured us. He mapped out the scene with his finger, drawing invisible X's and arrows, showing who would stand where and who would do what when it was time to strike. But where he saw battle plans I saw only fingerprints streaked over the glass tabletop. My cousins' serious faces were fake, but I tried to make mine real, tried to see things the way Uncle Willie could. I owed him that.

He finished his plan. "And that," he said, "is how we will defeat the Beatles." He turned his head from left to right slowly, reading our faces to see if we were ready for the fight.

"So what you're saying," Googi said, "is that we get to meet the Beatles."

"To defeat them, yes," Uncle Willie answered. "Of course."

"But we get to meet the Beatles," JohnJohn checked again.

Uncle Willie nodded slowly, as if they were the ones who didn't understand what was really being said.

My cousins looked at each other, then to me. "I'm in," Googi beamed. "I'll help you."

"Me, too," JohnJohn said. "To beat them up, of course."

Uncle Willie turned to me. *You're my uncle,* is what I should have said. *Of course I'll help you.* But I didn't. I looked past him instead, at a newspaper on the floor, and I saw the headline BEATLES RULE ARANETA COLISEUM, 100,000 SCREAM FOR MORE. My cousins and I had so badly wanted to see that show, but we convinced ourselves that trying would be pointless, that there was no way any of us could afford even the cheapest of tickets. We'd accepted that they would come and go, that the most we could hope for was a muffled radio broadcast. I didn't want to admit that this was a once-in-a-lifetime opportunity. "Yeah," I said, finally. "Okay."

Uncle Willie reached out and squeezed my shoulder, smiling. "Good boys," he said.

He went into his bedroom and came out with pillows and sheets stacked upon his arms. "Bedtime soon, guys." We would need a good night's rest, he said, if we were to defeat the Beatles the next day.

But only Uncle Willie went to bed; my cousins and I stayed up, gambling away what little pocket money we had in our own version of poker. "I think Paul's autograph will be worth the most," Googi said, shuffling the deck. "I want it to say *To Guggenheim, man of the world and dear, dear friend.*" My cousin changed his name to Guggenheim when he turned thirteen, believing that if you were named after someone great, you might become someone great, too. But our grandparents couldn't pronounce it, so he got stuck with Googi instead, and he only used Guggenheim for special occasions like graduation or confirmation.

"So you're going to deck Paul McCartney then ask him for an autograph," I said. "Makes sense."

"We want to *meet* them, not beat them," Googi whispered.

"This is the Beatles we're talking about," JohnJohn said. "You want to meet them as much as we do."

Googi nodded. "Do you think Paul would sing to me if I asked him to?" he asked.

JohnJohn socked him in the arm. "Don't be such a queer. Quit talking like that."

"You can't ask for autographs," I told them. "That isn't why we're doing this." They looked at me like I was crazy, but they didn't say it. "We have a job to do, right?"

"To hell with Imelda," JohnJohn said. He shook his head, looking at her framed picture, which was still on the table. He laid it flat, then mashed his cigarette against it, leaving glowing ashes on the glass. They looked like fireflies dancing around her, and it made her look like some sort of fairy-tale queen, friend to all creatures great and small. I flicked them off with my finger. "Filipina womanhood, my ass," he said, lighting another cigarette.

"Just one song, that's all I'd ask for," Googi whispered to himself, still rubbing the spot on his arm where he was hit.

A light was still on in Uncle Willie's room. "Just deal," I said.

In less than an hour JohnJohn and Googi were giggling drunks, and they had all my money. I was tired of letting them cheat. I finished my beer and got up from the table, a little tipsy, and went to check on my uncle.

He always called it the second floor, but his bedroom was just three steps up from the back of the kitchen. Despite his good pay, he lived modestly—he never bought a house, and he'd lived in that small one-bedroom apartment for as long as I'd been alive. "I like my things to be close together," he said once. I stood at the bottom step, watching him through the hanging strands of beads in the doorway as he ironed his work clothes for the next day. His arm was slow and steady over wrinkled white sleeves, and steam spouted up from the iron, coating his face. "Still awake?" I said, to let him know I was there.

"You should be in bed."

"So should you."

"I'm old. I don't need sleep. But you're still growing." He warned me about staying up too late, telling me that my mother would not approve if she knew I spent the last and first hours of the day drinking and gambling with my cousins.

"I'm nineteen now," I reminded him. "I'm not a kid anymore. And there's not much she can do from an ocean away, right?" Uncle Willie shook his head, then told me to come in.

I sat at the foot of his bed. Across from me were the faces of Imelda, tacked and taped on the bedroom wall. There were articles and pictures everywhere, headlines which read IMELDA TAKES PARIS BY STORM and IMELDA LOVES AMERICA, AMERICA LOVES IMELDA. It was like a page from a giant scrapbook, full of airbrushed eight-by-tens and photos carefully torn from glossy magazines. But the wall was only half-covered, as though the other half was a reserved plot for the rest of Imelda's life. In my head I filled the empty space with articles about Uncle Willie's victory against the Beatles, and I imagined an accompanying photo of him, his arm in a sling, his face bruised black and blue with pride. A soldier still smiling after the battle, despite the hurt. "Will Imelda be there tomorrow?" I asked.

"*Mrs. Marcos*," he corrected me. "Certainly not. She doesn't have time to waste on those scrawny British rascals."

Uncle Willie unplugged the iron, then slipped the shirt into an armor-gray blazer hanging on the closet door. Instead of the black tie he normally wore for work, he pulled from the top drawer a handful of ties I never knew he owned. Strips of bright silk spilled out between his fingers, and one by one he held them to the collar of his shirt, waiting for the right match. "Any of them will do," I said, but all I really noticed was the fuss Uncle Willie was making over himself. He was in his early fifties by then, and we had all given up hope for an end to his bachelorhood. But as I watched him testing tie after tie, when I saw a newly opened bottle of cologne on top of his dresser, I thought he might be trying to put an end to that. I could smell Uncle Willie, the change in his scent. It was on his clothes, his skin, the air around him. I was only nineteen, but I thought that this must be love, that if something could change you so much then maybe, in the end, it was worth fighting for, even if you weren't going to be loved back.

He reached for another tie but set it down, laughing at himself like he was being silly. "Simple is best," he decided. He looped the black tie around the collar.

"No. This one works better." I took it away and replaced it with a turquoise tie patterned with silver paisleys. "It goes with the gray."

Uncle Willie took a step back, studying the outfit like someone trying to understand a strange piece of art. "Okay," he said. He sat on edge of his bed and bent over, wiping away a bit of dust from his shoe. He stayed that way for a moment, then asked, "Do you think I'm crazy?"

"What?"

"Do you think I'm crazy," he said again. It was the kind of question that most people ask with an answer already in their heads, the kind of question you ask only to see if the answer you get is the one you're hoping for. But when Uncle Willie looked up at me, his face was blank; I really don't think he knew what the answer was, and whatever I said he would be willing to accept.

"I think you're dutiful," was what I finally told him. He didn't know what it meant. "Dutiful," I repeated. "It's like the obedient son who does what he's told. Or the knight who enters a battle without asking why." This was the best definition I could give him. The answer seemed to please him.

But I couldn't leave it at that. "I just don't understand why the Beatles mean so much to her. What have they ever done that's so great anyway?"

And that was enough to get him started. No one, he said, should ever second-guess the First Lady's intentions, not after all she had done for our country. He insisted that because of her, the world looked at us differently. "She dazzles and inspires," he said. "How many of us are able to do that?" His voice was breaking, but he continued, reminding me that no matter how famous Imelda Marcos became, no matter how many times she flew off into the world, she always came back. "She belongs to us," he explained. "She will never leave us. It is our duty as men to protect her good name."

"Right." I looked past him, at an autographed photo of Imelda beside his bed. *For Willy,* she misspelled, *who keeps me safe in the sky. Always, Imelda.* "It's getting late," I said. I told him goodnight and exited through the hanging beads. At the bottom step I turned around, and I saw him kiss his finger then press it against her picture; not on the lips or on the cheek—that wouldn't be appropriate for someone of his station—but on a spot near her shoulder, just above her heart. That part of her was sore, Uncle Willie once read, from all the corsages that had been pinned there during her travels abroad. "You see what she does for us?" he'd said. "It aches her to leave us, even for just a short while."

Then from behind me a clumsy two-part harmony started up. *"You're gonna lose that girl, yes yes you're gonna lose that girl,"* my drunk cousins crooned to Uncle Willie, *"you're gonna loooose that giiiirrl."*

"Leave him alone," I told them, pushing them back into the living room. "He's fine."

* * *

The dozen San Miguels hit my cousins hard; JohnJohn was passed out on the couch, and Googi was on the recliner, giggling in his sleep, talking back to his dreams as he always did. It was almost three a.m., and I was wide-awake on the floor, listening to the slow turn of the ceiling fan as it tried to cool the air.

It wasn't the Beatles that kept me up. Though we were going to meet them the next day, nothing felt different about that night before; even if Uncle Willie hadn't called on us, we still would have ended up at his apartment, drinking too much, playing bad poker, trying to ignore the dullness of life. We had been spending nights at Uncle Willie's ever since we were kids. Whenever we needed an easy escape from our parents and their rules, Uncle Willie was always there for us: if we didn't want to go to Sunday mass, he would let us hide in his apartment, then drive us to meet our mothers when it was over, telling them that he found us seated on the balcony level, praying hard; in middle school, we persuaded him to buy cigarettes for us, and he gave us garlic to chew to hide our ashy smell. "I do not approve," he made it clear, "but someone should supervise at least." Our every small rebellion he willingly indulged, and I was never ungrateful, but I hoped that one day we wouldn't need his help, that my cousins and I would venture out to somewhere far away. But after high school we all ended up at small local colleges, and none of us could afford to live in the dormitories. There was no travel, no journey; all I wanted was to wake up, just once, in a different place.

It was dark, but I could navigate my way through the living room easily. Uncle Willie's magazine rack was to the right of his recliner, his footstool next to the TV. I knew where JohnJohn's head was on the couch, where on the coffee table Googi rested his feet. Even in our sleep everything was the same.

There was one beer left on the kitchen table. It was warm, but I opened it anyway, then stepped out the back door into the alley behind Uncle Willie's apartment building. It felt like another normal night—sticky and dark, a sky without stars—but there was music coming from the street. *"Oh you've gone away this morning,"* someone sang, *"you'll be back again tonight."* It was the Beatles, and I walked to it, still barefoot, drinking my beer slowly. On the sidewalk I saw two boys not much younger than me, wearing pegged pants and button-up, short-sleeve shirts, sitting on a vinyl couch that had been left on the street. One played an acoustic guitar, the other slapped his knees like a drum, and they were singing Beatles songs to an audience of three school-aged girls seated on the hood of a rusting jeep that was missing its front right wheel. They played and sang reasonably well, and the girls swayed their heads in time to the music. But their eyes were closed, like they were trying to fool themselves into believing that it really was the Beatles playing before them.

"I'm going to meet them," I told them. "Tomorrow."

The one playing guitar lifted his finger from the strings. "Who?"

"The Beatles. All four of them."

"Liar," he said.

"No," I said, "really. I'm going to meet them tomorrow."

"We know who you are," one of the girls said accusingly. She slid down the hood of the car to the sidewalk. "We've seen you before. You live here, too."

"I live in the next town over," I said, as if it made a difference. "And I'm not a liar."

"You're crazy," another girl said. She spit on my foot. She turned to the girl beside her, and they giggled. They couldn't have been older than ten.

They began again. *"You'll never leave me and you know it's true,"* the boys sang, and the girls swayed and snapped along. I could have kept talking, revealed the plan altogether. But I lost my nerve. Instead I just told them to keep it down, that it was too late in the night and too early in the morning for them to be playing around like that. I walked back into the alley and drank my beer fast, hoping it would help me sleep and keep me still.

A pot of hot Milo and a platter of half-burnt toast were on the kitchen table when we woke the next morning. "Come on, guys," Uncle Willie said, clapping his hands twice. "Eat up. Big day today." We made our way slowly to the table, and he went to get dressed.

The taste of beer still coated my tongue and teeth, but I didn't want Uncle Willie's efforts to go to waste. I took slow sips of Milo and broke off burnt crust from the bread. "Someone help me with this," I said, pushing the toast to the center of the table.

JohnJohn already had a cigarette going. "Not hungry."

"Me, neither," Googi yawned. "Why can't the Beatles come to us instead? Maybe we could schedule an afternoon tea. That's what they do in England."

"How would you know?" JohnJohn blew smoke in his face. "You've never been to England, dummy."

"Someday," Googi said, fanning the smoke away. "Maybe."

"Would someone eat some of this?" I repeated.

"Forget afternoon tea. Let's make it an afternoon drink instead. Run up a bar tab on Imelda's bill." JohnJohn tapped ashes on a saucer, then put his head down on the table.

Uncle Willie came into the kitchen. He'd heard what we had said, and he told us we were just being lazy rascals. To prove his point, he brought out a book called *The Quotable Imelda: Famous Quotes by Imelda Marcos*. I'd seen it before in high school; it was required reading for senior English classes. "Listen to this," Uncle Willie said, opening to a bookmarked page, "and you try to follow her example." He cleared his throat, then shared her wisdom. *"The truth is that life is so beautiful and life is so prosperous and life is so full of potential and life has so much good in it that really, one should not have time to sleep. I have no time to sleep. You only get bored if you are tired. And I only get bored and tired with ugliness, with negativism and evil and all of that."*

JohnJohn raised his head, wanting to speak, but Uncle Willie wouldn't stop.

"I start in the morning and I feel that we all have one thousand energy. In my case, I see a beautiful flower, a beautiful program, a beautiful person, a beautiful smile, a beautiful child, by that time it's midnight. I'm just about ready to take off! I have a million energy, no longer one thousand! Everybody's falling apart and I cannot understand." Then Uncle Willie closed the book gently, solemn as a priest. "Think about it," he said, turning to his room, "and finish your breakfast."

I looked at JohnJohn, and all I wanted was for him to laugh, to make a joke of the sheer stupidity of the First Lady, of our entire situation, anything to break the stone look on his face that stays with me even now. "Everybody's falling apart, and she can't understand," he said, letting out smoke.

"This isn't about her," I whispered. But JohnJohn just lit up another cigarette then left to smoke outside. Googi got up to get ready. I stayed and cleared the table, wiping it clean of our crumbs, our ashes, the smudges and smears of battle plans from the night before.

Uncle Willie walked back into the kitchen. His hair was slick and crisp. His blazer was buttoned all the way up, his oxfords gleamed at their tips, and he smelled like cheap cologne.

The parking lot of Manila International Airport looked like a protest against war: high above the crowds were banners and signs, and all you could hear was the noisy overlap of shouting voices. As our taxi slowly pulled up to the curb, I thought that maybe Uncle Willie was right, that maybe the Beatles really had done something terrible to bring together so many people. But when I stepped out I could understand what they were saying: BEATLES WE LOVE YOU and BEATLES COME BACK were painted in block letters on huge pieces of paper, were screamed in chorus by weeping teenagers. A line of arm-linked policemen held them back.

JohnJohn and I walked toward the entrance, but Googi turned to face the crowd. He threw his arms in the air and blew kisses, like they were gathered there for him. "I'm bigger than the Beatles," he laughed. Uncle Willie, losing patience, scooted him along.

Uncle Willie flashed his ID to security. "They are with me," he gestured to the three of us. Uncle Willie had given us security blazers and nametags, and the guard let us through. It was a rule that only ticketed passengers were allowed inside, but with all the chaos the Beatles were causing in Manila, few people were traveling that weekend, and many of the outbound flights had been canceled. The long stretch of the ticket counter was almost empty, unmanned except for a few bored agents who watched the clock, twirled pens in one hand, put their heads down and napped. I hadn't been to Manila International in four years, and this was the first time I'd seen more excitement outside than inside the airport.

The Beatles were scheduled to depart from Gate 44, which Uncle Willie said was used exclusively for politicians and celebrities and their private jets. "It is where the First Lady waits patiently for her flights, and she was generous enough to let the Beatles use it," he said. "Ungrateful scoundrels."

We walked past the duty-free gift shops, the near-empty waiting areas. At the end of the terminal, Uncle Willie reached for his keys and unlocked a door that read AIRPORT SECURITY ONLY BEYOND THIS POINT. "Let's go, let's go," he said, holding the door open for us. I turned around, convinced we were being watched, maybe followed, but the few people in the terminal made nothing of our presence.

We stepped into a long white corridor, windowless and silent except for the hum of the track of fluorescent lights above. We walked single file, Uncle Willie, Googi, JohnJohn, then me, and no one said a word. I looked back at the white emptiness behind me, and I had the feeling that the farther we went in, the more impossible it would be to get back. "Almost there," Uncle Willie said.

He unlocked another door. We walked out and immediately stepped onto an escalator that took us to Gate 44, a small square of a room furnished with a couch and two wingchairs, a Victorian-style coffee table in the center. To the side was a fireplace that didn't look quite real, and above it was a painting of a life-size Imelda Marcos, her head slightly tilted, her open palms at the end of reaching arms crowned with butterfly sleeves. "Run!" John-John whispered to me. "Before she destroys us with her one million energy!" I told him to shut up, but it really did look like those Imelda-arms were out to pull us into her, either to cradle or strangle us to death.

Uncle Willie called us to attention and reviewed the plan once more. As soon as they arrived, he would escort the Beatles to Gate 44 and have them proceed up the escalator. The three of us would begin the attack while Uncle Willie made sure that the group's bodyguards were properly diverted by his security staff. "And then finally, I will join you up here to crush the Beatles." My cousins nodded as if they were with him each step of the way, but my eyes were fixed on the mess of paisleys knotted at his throat, and how wrong they looked in the daylight.

"But who are we?" I asked. "What are we supposed to be doing when they get here?"

"Just act like you're supposed to be here," Uncle Willie said, pointing to my nametag, "as if you are meant to be here." Then he shook each of our hands, wished us luck, and left.

Standing there, alone with my cousins in a room meant only for the most important travelers in the world, I believed I was answering a call of duty. I kept my fists clenched and my head up, ready for the fight, but the truth was undeniable: we were unprepared and unarmed; all we had on us was pen and paper for autographs, a camera hidden in Googi's pants pocket, and "Ticket to Ride" boomed inside my head.

JohnJohn's watch read two o'clock. An hour had passed since we saw Uncle Willie go down the escalator. Restless and bored, JohnJohn and Googi began taking swings at the air, sparring with each other like martial arts masters. "We must be ready," Googi said, imitating Uncle Willie, "if we wish to defeat the Fab Four!"

JohnJohn stepped up on the table. "In the name of Imelda," he shouted, fist in the air, "die!" He jumped off, slamming a palm on Googi's head upon landing.

I went to the window and looked out onto the runway. There were only a handful of airplanes out that day, and none of them were taking off. Beneath the shade of a wing a group of cargo workers sat on the ground, looking bored and useless, their earphones down around their necks. The day was especially humid, and the heat in the air blurred and rippled the runway and everything on it, like the special effects for a dream sequence on TV. It was as though the planes weren't real, as if the possibility of departure and flight were just an illusion and a hoax.

When I was a kid, Uncle Willie always brought me along to the airport, and he showed it off like it was his. "You see all those people leaving and returning?" he said to me on my first visit. "I am the one who is responsible for them."

"Where do they go?" I asked. I was five years old.

"That way," he pointed skyward, then moved his hand to the side. "Then that way." I always assumed he meant the States.

Uncle Willie lifted me up, bringing me close to the window. The glass felt hot against my forehead, and I could feel the vibrations of the revving engines. But when their wheels left the ground, I had to look away; I couldn't believe that something so big and heavy with metal parts could stay afloat in the air. I thought of emergency landings, of airplanes bobbing in the middle of the ocean. "Will you go, too?" I asked.

Uncle Willie shook his head, promising me that he wasn't going anywhere, that it was his job to stay behind to make sure everything ran just right. I loved him for that. Growing up, I watched branches of my family breaking off as they headed to the States, aunts and uncles taking my cousins and my friends with them. The year I turned twelve, I lost my mother, too. For years she watched her sisters pack up as soon as their husbands' requests for transfer went through. Fighting with my father was how she dealt with being left. *I'm stuck here,* she would say, and she blamed him nightly for it. *Why didn't you join the service like the rest of the men? Where is your ambition? Don't you at least want your son to be somebody?* My mother stood behind me when she said this, cupping my shoulders with her hands, presenting me as an example of my father's failure. He looked at me apologetically, but he never said a word.

But she finally got to go. Her younger sister bought her a ticket, and my mother started packing that same day. *Tourist visa only,* she assured me the morning she left. I wanted to see her off at the gate, but a sign read NO WELL-WISHERS BEYOND THIS POINT, and the guard refused to let me go with her. I wanted to tell him that the sign didn't pertain to me, that I didn't wish my mother well at all, that in fact, I wished her a terrible trip, a time so awful she would take the first flight back to Manila. But my father held me back, and we couldn't find Uncle Willie to get us special clearance. *Tourists can't stay forever,* my father reminded me as we drove home. I took that technicality as my guarantee for her return, but six months later, on the back of a postcard of the Golden Gate Bridge, I learned that the visa had become a green card. *The weather is good for my health, for my skin,* she wrote. *You should see how well I look.* I told my father I didn't know she'd been sick. He said he didn't know it, either. He handed me the card, put on his hat, then left to play mah-jongg with his friends at the corner cantina. But Uncle Willie was there, and he told me not to worry. "She'll be back," he promised, and he looked like he really did believe she would return. He took the postcard from my hand and put it in his pocket. We got into his car, picked up

JohnJohn and Googi, and he took the three of us out for mango milkshakes.

But my fear of leaving turned to envy. When I turned thirteen, Uncle Willie got me a job at the airport helping passengers with their bags. While I dragged and pushed along heavy pieces of luggage, they would walk ahead of me, fanning themselves with their tickets like they were flaunting their travels. I never checked their destinations; all I knew was that they were leaving for someplace far away, and that their eventual return would be a triumphant one, like astronauts coming back from outer space. I wanted that bit of triumph, so I play-acted myself into those airport reunions I saw throughout the day: I would get off the plane and find my family waiting, their arms spread out in welcome, my cousins asking question after question, everyone impressed by the way I changed.

But when I finally took a month-long trip to visit my mother in California for my fifteenth birthday, my homecoming was a disappointment. Only Uncle Willie was waiting for me at the airport, and all he asked about was my return flight, whether or not the service was satisfactory, if I was able to sleep away the long hours to make the trip feel quicker than it was. "It's good that you are back," he said, loading my bags into the trunk of a taxi. He paid the driver and told him to take me home. I rolled the windows down, and the back seat filled with a mugginess, a thick and heavy air I hadn't really noticed before. It clung to me, and all I wanted was to feel cool again, the way I did in California. When I got home, no one was there; my father was out, and JohnJohn and Googi didn't collect their souvenir T-shirts until the next afternoon. For the next month, I slept through the day and paced the house at night, restless and sweaty, my body and mind still on American time. I thought back then that it was the seventeen-hour difference that inverted my days. Four years later, in that moment when Googi tapped me on the shoulder and twice whispered, "The Beatles are coming," into my ear, I knew that jetlag had nothing to do with my ruined sleep.

We heard voices below. From above we watched Uncle Willie direct the Beatles toward the escalator. As planned, there were no porters to assist them with their luggage, and I heard Paul complain about the weight of his bags. "Porter shortage in the Philippines?" he said. His voice was clear and smooth, without the static of the bad reception we always seemed to get in Manila.

"No porter?" Ringo asked. "I'll take whatever's on draft, then."

Uncle Willie hurried them along. As soon as each Beatle was on his way, my uncle looked at us and gave the thumbs up. *It's up to you now,* was what I read in his face, so I shut my eyes, trying to remember his plans from the night before, the X's and arrows indicating who and where we were meant to be. The only image in my head was his thin wrinkled finger, the nail chipped and yellow at the end, dragging across the table.

But even that picture faded away when the Beatles finally came. Until that moment, I'd known them only as a single sound of blended voices among guitar riffs and drumbeats. I would play their records and watch the needle curve along the grooves, then try to work my own voice into their harmonies. I always sang in secret, embarrassed by my voice; when no one was in the house I would sit on the floor next to the stereo speakers, shut my eyes, and belt out their words like they were truths about myself. And now they were here, and they were real, entering my life one by one as the escalator steps rose and vanished into the floor: Ringo then Paul then George and finally John, who was holding a giant seashell to his ear. They were each dressed in bright, loose-fitting shirts that seemed to change color with the slightest movement. When they stepped closer, I realized their skin was the same way; their white English faces held a bit of pink in their cheeks, their necks had faint patches of orange and brown, from the Philippine sun. It was a sign of their travels, evidence of the world, proof that you could move through it and keep it with you. I remember standing there by that fake fireplace, standing between my cousins in our borrowed blazers and fake nametags, thinking, *This is it. This is the real thing. This is what it means to be in the world.*

Ringo was the first to speak to us. "There's no porter shortage at all," he said. He waved hello. I waved back. JohnJohn and Googi waved, too.

"No, but shorter porters they are," Paul said, tapping each of us on the head. "But you can take these onto the plane if you don't mind." He dropped his carry-on luggage to the floor. The other Beatles did the same.

JohnJohn picked up two bags. I followed his lead. But Googi just stood there, sweaty and pale. He was almost reverent in the way he looked at Paul, and he kept swallowing, like he wanted to speak. "My name is—" he finally said, but he was so nervous he mispronounced it.

"Huggengeim?" Ringo said, one eyebrow raised. "Type of cheese, isn't it? All the same, nice ring to it."

"Thank you," Googi beamed.

Paul leaned into us. "You boys ever listen to the ocean?"

We shook our heads no.

"Mean to tell me you live on this island, and you never heard the ocean? Hey, John," Paul said, still looking at us, "give the lads a listen." John looked up, a bit irritated, unwilling to surrender his shell.

"Oh, don't be so chintzy," George said. The other Beatles laughed.

I didn't know what chintzy meant—it sounded French and German and Chinese all at once—but the three of us joined in the laughter anyway, like we were having a real conversation with the Beatles, though I hadn't said a single word myself, never told them my name. It didn't matter. JohnJohn looked truly happy for the first time in months, and even now I'm sure there were joyful tears welling in Googi's eyes. All I felt was a feeling of arrival, that feeling of awakeness that comes with the impact of landing. I wanted to plant myself there, take root in that moment with the Beatles, and never leave it, not ever.

Quick as it was, the picture of it is clearer to me now: the Beatles in a line, facing my cousins and me, a four-on-three standoff that should be in mid-battle. But what Uncle Willie finds when he reaches the top of the escalator is a friendly exchange between his enemy and his allies, a truce he never called. And when I turn to look at him I'm just stuck, like someone ankle-deep in hardening mud, and I can't run or hide or change my traitorous face. I betrayed my uncle Willie, and the woman he loved.

So I acted.

"Now!" I said. I stepped away from the group, then pushed a potted plant over, hoping it would crash upon a Beatle like a fallen tree, pinning him to the ground. But it just landed softly on a wingchair and dirt spilled everywhere, soiling Paul's and Ringo's shoes. I kept going, throwing their bags across the room and into the fake fireplace, and Uncle Willie nodded, like everything was going according to plan after all, and he stepped forward, too. I picked up another carry-on, hurling it onto the Down escalator. *Take that, Beatles,* was the intended message, but it fell slowly like a tumbleweed, and the only reaction I remember was George saying, "That's my bag," and Paul saying, "He wanted to check that in." I ignored them both, and took the gift basket of mangoes at Ringo's feet and kicked it over, the fruit rolling onto the floor, and I picked them up and threw them hard against the ground like grenades. All the while, Googi struggled to work the flash on his camera, and JohnJohn took fast, nervous drags of his cigarette, looking confused in a corner of the room. "Don't just stand there," I said, but as soon as I ran out of things to knock over and throw, all I could do was remove myself from the scene, too.

But Uncle Willie wouldn't stop. He took John by the collar, his head bent back so he could look him in the eye. "So *you* are the rascals who are more popular than Jesus Christ?" he questioned knowingly. John nodded, the shell still at his ear, but my uncle persisted, trying to shake him into submission. He was near tears about Imelda, almost incoherent, and what I saw next was his hand curl into a fist and then the shell drop to the ground. It broke in two, and suddenly there were a dozen other bodies— they looked like real airport security—rushing up the escalator, screaming and cursing the Beatles for defaming the First Lady and the rest of the country. "Come on, everybody!" Uncle Willie called out to them. His back was to me, and I couldn't tell if he'd planned this from the start, if somehow he knew that we would fail him in the end.

The mob closed in on the group. I fought my way in to pull Uncle Willie out, but when I reached for his shoulder he turned and swiped my arm away, telling me to leave him alone, to get out, to go. Then someone shoved me, and I fell backwards to the ground. Next to my hand was a mango, so I picked it up and threw it hard against the painting of Imelda Marcos, hitting her in the center of her chest. An orange, pulpy ooze bloomed like a flower, then dripped down like blood. I wanted to call out to Uncle Willie, to show him what I had done, but my cousins grabbed me, pulling me toward the escalator. "It's over," John-John said. "Let's go." We ran down, and all I saw when I looked back was my uncle vanish in the haze, his old thin arms lost among the shaking fists, his war cry in the name of love dulled down to the background noise of Imeldamania.

We ran through the corridor and headed for the entrance. "What about Uncle Willie?" Googi said. I told him to forget him, that there was nothing we could do. I kept running, my body perspiring in the thick polyester blazer, the nametag flopping up and down against my chest. I finally stopped, hunched over and out of breath, at the long line of police trying to contain with threatening waves of their batons the thousands of fans who cried out, "Beatles, don't leave us, Beatles, don't go."

The three of us took a taxi back to my house. In the end, the Beatles' own security team broke up the fight and made sure the group made it to their plane. No serious harm was done, but the Beatles never came our way again.

"Yes," Googi told reporters, "we witnessed the whole thing." We ended up making the papers, the international news, and for the first time the world came to us, calling us late at night, knocking on our doors early in the morning for interviews. Googi basked in his brief fame, and JohnJohn tried to use the spotlight to expose the corruption in the Marcos government, but reporters just stopped their tape recorders and put down their pens when he spoke. I stayed quiet, letting everyone else remember and tell the story however they wanted.

But Uncle Willie made his role in the attack known, and what he got in the end was a reprimand from the President himself. And Imelda Marcos—essence of Filipina womanhood, face of our country—called the incident a breach of Filipino hospitality, and she offered more quotable wisdom to help the people understand what had happened. *"In life, ugliness must sometimes occur,"* she said. *"But when such ugliness happens, only beauty can arrive, 'to save the day,' so to speak. Despite the ugly events of the past days, beauty has returned, so let's focus only on the beautiful things and let beauty live on."* Ashamed for any embarrassment he brought to the First Lady, Uncle Willie issued an official apology, and resigned soon after.

But he didn't disappear. "I still have one million energy," he said, and he was often seen at the airport, making sure everything continued to run smoothly and that Imelda's flights were on schedule. He remained a fixture there, never quite coming or going, but always floating about. At least that's what people would tell me.

Years later, when I made my final trip to the Philippines from California, I visited Uncle Willie, who still lived alone in his apartment. I was the last, the only one left, and he was anxious for my visit. Googi had run off to Hong Kong with an English businessman years before, and JohnJohn was dead, one of the few to take a Marcos bullet in 1986. Things weren't the same, not really, but when I walked into his apartment, I struggled to find any change: the ceiling fan still creaked when it turned, beads hung in the doorway, our places were still at the kitchen table. The only difference was that Imelda's presence had grown. There were more stories and pictures crowding his bedroom wall, as if she had never left, as if she was still the First Lady.

We did very little that week; Uncle Willie was over eighty years old, and all he wanted to do was nap or watch TV. But late one night, he told me he had something to show me, and he put a videocassette into the VCR. "Watch," he said, pressing the PLAY button. The screen went blue, and suddenly the Beatles appeared on the screen, doing an interview in which they mentioned the incident that we helped make famous. "Do you remember the battle?" he asked from his wheelchair. "How bravely we fought?" I smiled and told him I could never forget.

I turned up the volume. "I hated the Philippines," Ringo said bluntly. George and John agreed, smoking before the cameras, but Paul was more introspective. "It was one of those places where you knew they were waiting for a fight," he said. Uncle Willie nodded, confirming its truth. I stared at the Beatles' faces, and I wondered if they remembered mine, if they would know who I was if they saw me now.

"If I had been an American, like you," Uncle Willie said, "I would have been knighted." I didn't tell him that they only do that in England. In America, you might get a compliment in the papers, maybe a medal for bravery, but nothing that big. You would be the same person as when you started, long before the fight. That much I'd come to know. Still, I told him yes, that most certainly he would have been knighted, and I proceeded to create for him a picture of the ceremony, of Uncle Willie on his knee and Imelda on her throne, a sword in her hand, its blade gentle on his shoulder.

Song for a Certain Girl

In August, the summer after her ninth-grade year, the girl—pudgy, moonfaced, with dull brown hair and new breasts—met the man who became her first husband. Before that, she'd been seeing a tall boy she danced with at junior high graduation, starting with a concentric-circle wheel-dance the chaperons employed to pull the boys and girls from their sniggering packs and make them sway clumsily with one another, parodies of the men and women you see cracking wise on the color TV. After the dance, screened from view by a dumpster, the tall boy kissed the girl. She'd kissed boys before, here and there, no one special. It was the tall boy's first kiss. He was afraid he'd be caught and made fun of. He would grow up and write for TV; she was already grown.

The tall boy was from the west side of their town, the oldest son of unpious Presbyterians who owned a clothing store and a brick home. The girl was from the east side and Baptist, with black people as neighbors. In the center was a courthouse and actual train tracks. She thought she loved the tall boy (she never said so). She wrote songs about him on her grandmother's guitar, songs she didn't let anyone hear. She'd never been in his house, met his parents, or been shown off to his friends. When she came to watch his swimming meets, he didn't talk to her. The day before the tall boy left town for a family vacation, a three-week trip to Disneyland and other attractions in and around Anaheim, California, he called her from a rotary phone in his basement and said it was over.

"I won't let you," she said. "You can't break up with me unless I let you, and I won't."

The tall boy stammered that this wasn't how it worked. "Look, if I start going out with someone else...," he said.

"It doesn't matter," said the girl. "I'll forgive you." She had her blue shirttail balled up in the white knuckles of her fist. A song she liked was on the radio, one about a stubborn woman who pushed through betrayal and loss to find true love. "No matter what you say or what you do," she said, "we're still going together, you and me."

The tall boy said no they were not and hung up. He and his family left for California in their Pontiac Silhouette minivan. The girl went to the BP station, bought a folding roadmap of America, and found Anaheim, California. She herself had been no farther west than Fort Wayne, Indiana, which was an hour away. She'd been as far east as Cleveland (once, she and her mom took a Greyhound there to see Art, her mom's dad; they ate at a Ruby Tuesday's in a mall; her mom and Art argued, and the girl and her mom took an early bus home; the girl never even saw downtown Cleveland, unless a glimpse of the distant gray spires of the Society Building and Terminal Tower counts). She'd been as far south as Gatlinburg, Tennessee, and Great Smoky Mountain National Park (once). She'd been as far north as the party store just over the Michigan line where they sold warm canned beer to anybody. She took a ruler and an ink pen and connected those four points on the map. Then she drew some angled lines, shading in the quadrilateral. She refolded the map and hid it under her mattress. By her math it was 2,448 miles to Anaheim.

Two days later at Sunday church, she played and sang "Jesus Wants Me for a Sunbeam" on her grandmother's guitar. After the service, in the fellowship hall, a man came up and said she'd moved him. He was a friend of a cousin of her mom's. He drove a white Ford truck with boards in back, and he looked like those pictures in her head of the men women sang about on country-music radio. He lived in an even smaller town, thirteen miles east. He worked in a Chinese-food factory there and had his own apartment, up over someone's garage. Their first date was a movie with Bruce Willis in it. Afterward, the man took her to a diner with a big revolving coffee cup on the sign, bought her pie, and showed her off to his friends. He said he was going to grow a mustache like the one Bruce Willis had in that movie. His hair already did look a lot like Bruce Willis's toupee, only it wasn't a toupee and needed a cut. He smelled like Aqua Velva aftershave. He wore brown Dingo boots.

One night when the girl's mom came home from the dinner shift at Pizza Hut, the girl lay on the couch, with her top and bra pulled up, her shorts and her underpants tangled at her ankles.

The man had his T-shirt off, his oily jeans still on; his fingers were looking for trouble. Her mom cleared her throat. If they agreed to speak with Minister Steve, she said, she would not punish the girl. In the minister's mayonnaise-smelling office, the man was moved by the Holy Spirit, or so he said, and proposed to the girl. She thought this was ridiculous, but couldn't say so in front of Minister Steve, who kept looking on, nosy and pleased with himself. She said yes. It gave her a thrill to do a bad thing that Minister Steve, her mom, and all her mom's people would think was good. She could have relations all she wanted, and nobody could say anything. The next week, before that mustache filled in enough to show in the pictures, they were married. Her ring was a band of pure silver.

The wedding was small and in the little white Baptist church, the only one in the county. Her much older half-sister, Janelle, took the photos, using a succession of disposable cameras. The man's parents were dead; the rest of his people lived in southern Indiana and couldn't afford the trip. No one knew how to get hold of the girl's father. Her mom, citing tradition, refused to give her away. That role was played by the organist's surprised husband, who didn't even have long pants on. Shorts, dark socks. The girl wasn't stupid. She understood how this looked. But she held her head high and walked down the aisle with her eyes on the mural of the crucified Jesus. *Please,* she thought. *Please.*

The reception was held under the deluxe aluminum awning of the cousin's doublewide, in the town's nicest trailer court, which happened to be owned by the tall boy's grandfather. (If you enjoy meanwhiles, picture the tall boy riding It's a Small World, fighting with his little brother, Todd, and not thinking about the girl.) The man had told the girl they'd have their honeymoon in the new Ramada Inn up by the Ohio Turnpike, but as they drove there he said it was booked. They'd be staying across the road at the Seashell Motel, which was thousands of miles from any sea. The only time she'd ever been in a motel was that trip to Gatlinburg and the Great Smoky Mountains, when she, Janelle, her mom, and Janelle's daddy (Mr. Dixon, who was back in the picture there for a while) all piled into one room with a king-size bed in a newly remodeled Knight's Inn in Pigeon Forge, Tennessee.

The man parked his truck by their door. He carried in the luggage: hers, an old mint-green piece of hard-sided Samsonite; his, two plastic bags from Kroger's, one with clothes, the other full of sixteen-ounce cans of Bud Light beer. She stood at the threshold, dressed in new beige slacks and a matching knit blouse. She fingered her ring. "Oh, Mr. Man?" she said. "You forget something?"

The man already had the cable TV on, his tie off, his shirt unbuttoned, and was sprawled on the threadbare chenille bedspread, sipping beer and watching the Detroit Tigers play baseball. He moaned and mentioned a bad back that she hadn't known about, painkillers he hadn't told her he was on. But as he begged off, he called her *baby*. She smiled, let herself in, and locked the door behind her.

The place had been built in a time when Formica was dark and plentiful. There was no telephone. The curtains had Southern belles and mansions on them. The air-conditioning was a dripping window unit. Over the bed hung a big-framed piece of cardboard with painted seashells glued to it in the shape of Indian chief head. The room was clean. The girl dragged her suitcase into the bathroom and put the hook in the eye to lock the door. She faced the mirror. She stared into her own eyes as she took off her clothes, applied perfumes and powders and ointments, and decided to leave in the side pouch of the suitcase the diaphragm her mom had insisted she get and that the girl had been humiliated to be fitted for. She was married. God would provide.

She began to cry, though not so loud as to be heard over the sound of the TV and A/C. The girl rarely cried. She'd cried the day after her daddy came into her room one night smelling of whiskey and stood silent and still at the foot of her bed for a long time. She felt a menace she could not name or anticipate, though all that happened was that he finished his drink and left the empty glass on her dresser and got into that Camaro he was so proud of and left town to take a job with a company that did door-to-door baby photos, or so his letter said. The girl was only six then. When she read that letter, that's when she cried. Long sobs that hurt her ribcage. He didn't say where the company was located, and neither the girl nor her mom had heard from him since, during which time the girl found it hard to cry anymore. Even last year when her grandmother died—the woman who cooked for her, watched her after school, and taught her how to play guitar—the girl didn't cry.

Even now, in the bathroom at the Seashell Motel, where many women before her had looked into that small mirror and cried, she didn't cry for too awful long. She fixed her makeup, slipped into the pink nightgown her half-sister had lent her, unhooked the door, and saw the man asleep on the bed.

"Baby?" she said. "Hey, baby." She turned off the TV set, which woke him up.

"Hey," he said. "I was watching that." Then he caught sight of her and said, "Whoa."

The curtains were open. She didn't have the nerve to close them, because of what that meant, but she didn't want to leave them open, because someone walking by might see.

No time for that. They got naked as babies. The man pinned her to the bedspread, didn't even pull down the covers, and the bristles of his thin mustache scratched her lips. Down there he was hard, jabbing, grunting from his failure. The girl had thought she knew what to do, but she couldn't move and couldn't find any words. She closed her eyes. She asked Jesus to make this turn out okay, to help her husband thrust himself inside her, fill her with his seed, so she might know the joys of married love.

Abruptly, the man, her husband, threw himself on his back and said an ugly word. He'd gone soft. He cupped his hand around the back of her head, lifted it up, and pressed it down his chest and his stomach to where he wanted it. She opened her mouth and received him. He kept his hand planted on the back of her head, fingers twined in her dull hair, and she performed for him their first act of love as man and wife. After, he went to sleep. Darkness fell. With the taste of him still in her mouth, she curled up against him, shivering, still atop the bedspread. She kept meaning to get up and close the curtains, but she didn't want to wake him. She did not sleep. At dawn, he awoke, went to the bathroom, came back to bed without brushing his teeth, climbed on her, and they just couldn't. This simple human act, and they couldn't manage to fit themselves together. The girl blamed herself and satisfied her husband again the only way she could think of. Again he fell asleep. Later that morning, he woke up, got dressed, said he'd be right back, and left. She got under the covers. Still she was shivering. He came back with a big jar of Vaseline. He stripped, pulled back the sheets, took a fist-size dollop of

Vaseline, and slathered it over her and inside her. This time when he got on top and poked at her it worked. She could hardly feel him, for all the Vaseline. Only the weight of this grimacing, wiry man on top of her. This stranger, her husband. She looked up at the water stains on the ceiling, looking for Jesus' face or any sort of sign. Then her husband yelled as if he'd been shot and for some reason pulled himself out of her and wrapped his hand around his own penis, pumping it madly while his seed dribbled out, gray pearls that fell onto the adorable paunch of her stomach.

Outside, there was applause and male and female laughter. Someone *had* seen! Her husband stood up, shouted more ugly words, and yanked closed the curtains. Car doors slammed.

"I love you," the girl whispered. She blinked back tears. For a long time the man was quiet. Finally he said, "Back atcha, baby doll." He got her a wet washcloth so she could clean herself up, got himself a beer, switched on the color TV to a game show, and sat there shouting out wrong answers.

They barely touched or talked. They didn't even eat until late that afternoon, when they showered and got dressed and walked over to the Ramada Inn.

"I'm so sorry." He reached his hand across the table. "I'm not as...," he said. "I mean, I know you wanted me to teach you, but..." He looked across the restaurant, as if the sneezeguard at the salad bar were the most interesting thing ever.

The girl squeezed her husband's hand. "It's okay," she said. "Everything will be all right."

He did not look at her.

"But can I tell you something?" Finally, he looked at her. In a whisper, she scrunched her nose and said she didn't like it, that Vaseline. She couldn't wash it completely off. She could still feel it, oozing out of her. "Let's do it naturally." She tried to smile. "We'll learn, together, how to be man and wife, the way God intended."

All the man could do was nod.

When the waitress came he said they'd both have the all-you-care-to-eat chicken. Afterward, he was shocked at the size of the bill. He was the one who'd ordered four four-dollar Heineken beers. The girl just had water. "Here's the first secret I'm telling you, man to wife," he said, getting up to pay. "They weren't booked up here. It just cost too much." He shrugged. "Hope you understand."

"I do," she said, for the second time in two days. She didn't mean it.

They spent another night and day at the Seashell Motel. The more she got to know him, the more he seemed like a stranger. Nothing got better. He lost more and more patience, drank can after can of Bud Light beer. Her jaw muscles burned with pain. Right before they checked out, he climbed onto her and tried again, and again it didn't work, and he raised his fist and looked like he was going to punch her. He didn't punch her. He stopped himself. He slapped himself on the top of his head, again and again and again.

All she said was, "We're through." She knew from watching talk shows that if he raised the fist once, he'd raise it again, and eventually when he lowered it, it would not be his own head he was hitting. She did not cry.

The man, her husband, begged for mercy. Broke into tears and swore it would never happen again. After more of this than she'd have thought he had in him, she relented. They were charged extra for late checkout, which was all the man could talk about on their drive to his apartment, up over someone's garage. Her mom had packed her things—clothes, AM-FM radio, and the guitar— and left them sitting on the wooden steps to the apartment. For- tunately it had not rained. Under her breath the girl praised God for small mercies.

This time the girl did not stand waiting at the threshold. She went inside first. She took out the guitar, and rubbed its warm, battered wood, and sat on a beer-smelling couch, and stared out the window at the main house, where the landlords, she hoped, had nice lives. The phone rang. The man answered. Sure, he said, give him five minutes. He kissed her goodbye with his scratchy mouth closed and left to go meet the boys. She watched his truck disappear around the corner. She tried to write a song, but the words wouldn't happen. Even when she tried singing old songs her grandmother had taught her, the girl kept forgetting the lyrics. She kept thinking of the fist the man, her husband, raised against her. She couldn't sing anything, not even hymns.

* * *

By the time she and the man had failed at love so often they gave up trying and the man had raised his fist once more (though still not hit her) and the girl had canceled her appointment at the doctor's to see what might be wrong with her and instead packed her things, left her wedding ring on top of the TV, and got a ride to her mom's house from her older half-sister, Janelle, and her mom called Minister Steve to see if it was possible to get an annulment but he said sorry, once *does* count—by then, the girl had missed the first two months of the tenth grade.

She reenrolled under her new name, was given a locker surrounded by seniors, and found herself in classes with "general" in the title. The tall boy had a locker among the other sophomores and was taking college-prep everything. Once in a while they'd make eye contact in the hall. He never said anything, but he always smiled and nodded. She smiled back. Seeing him was like opening a dresser drawer and finding a dear, forgotten toy—broken, useless, still there.

She worked hard to catch up. One teacher told her to find a study partner, but her old girlfriends treated her like bad marriage was a virus they could catch from her. Another teacher told her to bear down; high school was a new world, more complicated than junior high. A time when you learn that everything you knew is wrong. She heard this and shook her head. She could teach these teachers some things.

At night she sat in her mom's house with the kitchen and TV-room TVs both on, gnawing ink pens and staring at the route Magellan took around the world or at story problems starring people with names like Jacinto, LaShawnda, and Emiko. She couldn't keep her mind on it. She kept waiting for the man, her husband, to beg her to come home. To say they needed to talk. To say he was sorry. But he never called, never stopped by. Sometime that fall, according to the girl's mom's cousin, he was a no-show at the Chinese-food factory, his things were gone from his apartment over the garage, and that was all anyone knew. Southern Indiana, the girl guessed, where his people were. She took out that BP roadmap. How many trips to, say, the package store right over the Michigan line does it take to equal a trip to let's just say Evansville, Indiana? She never got story problems like this, ones that seemed worth the trouble. Her attention strayed to the TV. Her favorites were the reality shows: rescues, mysteries, heroes, funny videos. She disliked comedies, all those fake, pretty people in fake, faraway cities like New York, Los Angeles, Seattle, and even Cleveland. Her mom made them watch doctor shows, lawyer shows, and, worst of all, those shows where everyone is in high school forever. Luckily her mom was only home two nights a week.

One day, walking home from school, a warm day for early winter, the girl ran into the tall boy coming out of the library. Who knew why, but he said hello, she said hello back, he asked if it'd be okay to walk her home, and she said sure, why not? They talked about the school basketball team and the tall boy's fastest swimming times and what music he hated on the radio (nearly all of it). When they got to her house she asked if the tall boy would like to know what had happened to her. He said he thought he sort of knew. Her new name gave it away.

"Well, I'm getting it annulled," she said, which was still a possibility. Her mom was arguing that man's law is not God's law and that once didn't have to count, that the girl should go to court and forget about that once. "It's different from divorced. It's like it never happened, the marriage."

At that word, *marriage,* the tall boy flinched.

But he followed her into her house. They drank Kroger's-brand cola and talked about small things. When he thought he needed to get home for dinner, he stopped at the door and turned around. She was right behind him. They kissed. She watched him run home. When she saw him actually jump up in the air and kick up his heels, she laughed.

They started seeing each other again, more on the sly than ever. They'd meet at her house, under the crumbling bleachers at Park Stadium, and in groves of pine trees on the edge of town. Sometimes he wrote papers for her or did her math, careful to do C work—though, really, who'd have suspected? No one from the tall boy's life seemed to know the girl existed. Plus, by now, the schoolwork the girl did on her own had improved. But the secret kissing and groping became a habit.

What did they do? Not *it.* The boy wasn't even pushing for it. They ground their clothed bodies together. The tall boy slipped his clammy hands under the girl's ill-fitting bras. At most, he put his finger inside her and, with rank ineptitude, tried to pleasure her; she would let him know, sometimes, that this was sinful. She reached inside his jeans and grabbed him through his underwear and made him come. (He was fourteen; a strong breeze could do the same.) Then the tall boy would clean himself up, and the girl would talk about Jesus, sin, adultery, hell, fornication, and country music songs sung by thin, pretty women. After that, he'd walk home. She imagined him, halfway to that nice brick house where she still had never been, hearing a siren and breaking into a run, thinking she'd called the cops, that the bright future his parents were forcing on him was going to blow up.

He'd once been dumb enough to confess this to her.

As school wound down, the girl got a job at a church camp in the Irish Hills of Michigan, farther north than she'd ever been. That's nice, said the tall boy. He'd be busy, too, what with working in his parents' store and especially the summer swim team. Hovering unstated between them was the fact she was still married. So again they broke it off. This hadn't been a part of their daily lives, after all, just a strange, sweet thing, shiny with guilt, along the edges of what it was to be sophomores in a small town in Ohio.

At camp the girl's job was to serve meals in the dining cabin and to clean up. In exchange, she attended camp for free: Bible study, canoeing, making string-art pictures of Jesus, shooting arrows at hay bales, and sneaking out of the cabin at midnight to smoke cigarettes and drink fortified wine on the beach of a mossy pond and then, the next morning, pray for forgiveness. She told the counselors not to call her *Mrs.*, since her marriage was getting annulled. Word got out, but the idea that a girl in one of those bleak cabins had been married—married!—was hard to believe. When kids asked her, she laughed and said nothing. At the nightly bonfires, she played her old guitar along with the two music majors from a Bible college in West Virginia who'd been hired to lead the singing. She was as good as either of them. She wanted to sing her own songs (it's easy to change a song about "loving him" to one about "loving Him"), but she never got the nerve. She sang her songs alone in the woods behind the dining cabin, in the half hour of free time after she finished the lunch dishes. The last week of camp, she and one of the music majors, a redheaded man with a beard, wrote a song about the camp that mixed names of the counselors and campers in with those of Bible characters.

When they finished, he leaned toward her and kissed her. She kissed him back, then caught herself, pulled away, and reminded him she was married. He asked for forgiveness. She said he had to ask God for that. When it came time to perform the song in public, the girl played guitar and did not sing.

When she got home, she saw in the paper that the swim team had finished third in their championship meet. The tall boy had won two events. She called him. "Congratulations," she said.

"For what?"

"Your swimming."

"Oh," he said. "That."

His voice was so dead she had to think fast, to save face. "My annulment went through," she lied. "Can you come over?"

"What does that mean," he asked.

She could tell he was thrilled and afraid. "It means," she said, "just what you think it means."

There was a long pause. "I'm not sure I think anything."

He was so dumb! "Just come over, okay?"

"I will," he said, "if I can. My parents need me this week at the store."

He did not come by. The girl wasn't sure if she was surprised or relieved.

She'd already lied and told the boy she was annulled. Was it worse to go before the law of man and—advised by her own mom that once didn't count—say the marriage hadn't been consummated?

One afternoon, a week before Labor Day, before their junior year was to start, the tall boy showed up at the girl's house, riding a fifteen-speed racing bicycle. That was just like him, not to get a mountain bike like everyone else. Except the girl herself, who didn't know how to ride a bicycle.

"I was in the neighborhood," he said. "Riding around and stuff."

"I'm sort of busy," she said. She'd been watching a comedy show about a rich man with a butler and three orphans, marveling that anyone, anywhere, had ever found this funny.

The tall boy asked about her summer. She said it was fine. She asked about his. It was fine.

"So," he said. He was still standing astride his bike.

"Want some water?" she said.

He tugged the skin of his throat. "Yeah," he said. "I'm parched."

Parched? That was what it was about this boy. Not just the racing bicycle. No one she knew said *parched.* When he was with her, she let herself think he was a boy who could take her out of their town to a place where people have nice lawns, personal computers, and fragile bicycles, and men don't leave, and everyone has brainy kids who grow up to say *parched.*

The tall boy chugged two glasses of water. They sat on the couch in the TV room and watched a show about crazy people stuck on an island. "A three-hour tour," the boy said. "Why would they have all that luggage for a three-hour tour? Why would they have *any* luggage?"

"Beats me," said the girl. "I've never even been on a boat."

Canoes at the camp, yes. But that wasn't what he was talking about, canoes.

They got back to their old ways. This time when she touched him, it wasn't through his underwear. As he left, he said that his parents and his little brother, Todd, were going away that weekend. "If you want to, like, stop over, that'd be okay."

Saturday morning, the girl got dressed in a yellow bikini that some of the other girls at the camp had said she looked good in. She told herself maybe she'd go for a swim at the public pool, which was on the west side. She pulled tight cutoffs over her bikini bottom and took a towel. It wasn't such a long walk. She went barefoot. It was the end of summer.

The tall boy was in his driveway shooting baskets. He saw her, put the ball away, closed the garage, showed her into the house, locked the door, took the girl in his arms, and kissed her. She asked what he thought he was doing. "Really, I have no idea," he said. "That's the gospel truth."

Was that blasphemous? Or reverent? "I have no idea, either," she said.

The house was just a house, but it was so up-to-date and *nice,* as if, in preparation for her visit, it had been painted, carpeted, remodeled, and spring-cleaned. "Have you read all these books?" she said. One living-room wall was lined with bookshelves, crammed full. At her house, the lone small bookcase was strewn with Avon decanters and commemorative shot glasses.

"Some," he said. "They're my parents' books."

Before they knew it, they were in each other's arms and their clothes were coming off as if peeled by a divine hand. In times past the tall boy had glimpsed of the girl's nipples and had often had her pants unzipped but not pulled down. The girl had seen the tall boy in a tiny Speedo and had her hand on his penis. This was the first time they'd been naked together. It was the girl's second naked and aroused man, the boy's first naked and aroused girl, yet they hardly looked anywhere except into each other's eyes. He pulled her gently down onto the rich gray carpeting, so thickly padded it felt nicer than a bed. "What do you think you're doing?" she whispered.

And the tall boy grimly said, "I have no idea."

By then they knew where this was leading. They rolled around and touched each other. They moved their hands in hapless, fumbling arcs over the curves of their unformed bodies. They kept looking at each other, and it reassured the girl to see fear in the tall boy's eyes. Suddenly, moved by some unseen spirit, the boy rolled the girl onto her back and began to jab himself at her.

"I'm sorry," she said. "I may have a problem."

He was trembling. She told him she'd had problems before, with the man, problems they'd taken days and been unable to solve. The tall boy stopped moving but remained on top of her. Their naked skin pressed lightly together.

"Maybe it's wrong," she said, "for us to do this."

"You mean you never?" he said.

"Once," she said. "Only the once."

He looked lost. He kept starting to say something. They still weren't looking upon their nakedness, just into each other's eyes, and that, probably, was what made the girl reach down and take hold of the boy, inexpertly jabbing herself with his penis. Suddenly he was in. She said, "Oh!" He also said, "Oh!" They looked into each other like the terrified children they were, but now it was too late. She thought to twitch her hips. His eyes were open so wide. Her hips started doing a little more than twitching. The boy was on top, but he was frozen. She slowed down a little, and the boy pulled out and came all over that cute, round stomach.

He rolled over. He had his smooth back to her. The girl looked up at the smooth ceiling. Everything in his world was smooth. He got up and got her a warm washcloth and gently cleaned her. "I'm sorry," he said.

"It's okay," she said.

"No," he said. "I'm really, really sorry."

This time she didn't say it was okay. They got dressed. She wished she'd worn a T-shirt over her bikini top. She found the bath towel she'd brought from home and draped it around her neck.

"I'm sorry," the boy whispered.

She realized that because she hadn't said it was okay he was starting to wonder if he was going to get in trouble. Saying it was okay would make him feel better. She felt womanly not to say it. She got up to leave. The tall boy followed, begging her to tell him what was wrong. She told herself she wasn't going to say anything.

"Please," the boy said. "I don't know why, what I'm feeling but . . ." He asked her to sit down, on a bench in the mudroom. She looked out the window, counted to ten, to make him sweat, then sat.

The tall boy kneeled. "I don't know who to tell," he said. "I don't know who to talk to." He told a story about his best friend, Jason Hartsock, a boy from the swim team and the college-prep classes, whose mother, the tall boy said, was dying of cancer.

The girl hardly knew Jason Hartsock. She did not know that his mother was dying of anything. It was a cheap plea for sympathy. She wanted to go home.

But the boy went on and on about the homemade bread Mrs. Hartsock used to make and give to her friends, and about how great it made the Hartsocks' house smell, and how his mother and Mrs. Hartsock talked endlessly on the phone or, together, over endless cups of coffee, and how Jason's big brother, Bret, had said that if his mother died he didn't see how he could believe in God anymore.

For some reason, the girl was not shocked. Instead, she let the boy rest his head on her lap. She stroked his hair, and he kept talking about how Jason Hartsock had started going to parties and drinking twenty-plus bottles of Little Kings Cream Ale. When anyone said anything to Jason Hartsock about his mother, he'd change the subject and talk about sports, even golf.

The boy started to cry. The girl kept stroking his hair. Who ever saw a boy so big cry so long?

When he finished, he washed his face, and they stood in the mudroom and gave each other a hug. They kissed goodbye. He said goodbye. She said okay.

The girl stopped at the pool, paid her admission, and set up her towel on the cement sundeck. She took off her shorts. She lay there all afternoon in that yellow bikini. No one talked to her. She was happy about that. She tried to write a song in her head, a song about men. She ought to at least get a song out of all this. But it was hard to write anything without her guitar.

And so she got up and, ignoring the lifeguard's shrill whistle, climbed the steps to the high dive. She had never once done this before. For one thing, the high dive was closed except to the diving team. For another she could barely swim. But she was good at floating, more so since she'd become a woman. The swimming instructor at camp had said this was natural.

When the girl got to the top, the lifeguard was screaming at her. She walked straight to the end of the board and jumped awkwardly off, closing her eyes and plugging her nose. She crashed into the water. It felt cold and harsh against her sunburned body.

Underwater, she opened her eyes.

Underwater, she asked God to show her the way.

Can you hear me, God, from underwater?

She felt her feet touch the smooth painted bottom of the diving well. A sharp pounding feeling pushed at her ears. She wanted to stay underwater until she saw her sign. Surely God would at least send the angry lifeguard into the pool to save her? Her lungs began to burn. She felt a kind of gulping spasm in her throat. Her body betrayed her: she began to float toward the bright light of the surface.

Minister Steve was full of it. Courts disapprove of a person under the age of consent avoiding a consummated marriage, but the general rule is to grant an annulment as a matter of right. Allowable grounds include mental incompetency, intoxication, impotence, venereal disease, non-consummation, bigamy, incest, fraud, duress, lack of mutual consent, or that the underage spouse feels he or she made a mistake. Once the girl walked into the legal-aid office, things fell smoothly in place.

The girl was married once more before she finished high school.

She had the baby, went to summer school, and graduated with her class. She is still married. She lives in the small town. Four kids. At that little Baptist church, on the third Sunday of every month, she sings her own songs.

She never saw her father again (he sells new house trailers at a sales lot in a certain suburb of Las Vegas, Nevada, that will remain nameless) or her first husband, either (he died a while ago, off the coast of the Florida panhandle, while trying to save a buddy who'd gotten a little drunk, hooked a tarpon, and fallen overboard). The day the tall boy wept in his parents' mudroom was the last time he and the girl ever spoke. (He is currently writing a pilot for a TV show set in a candy factory in a small town in Ohio; he has not set foot in his hometown since his parents retired to live near his brother, Todd, who is the youngest mayor in the history of one particular suburb of Phoenix, Arizona.) Mrs. Hartsock died a slow, hideous death. Jason Hartsock and the tall boy went to different colleges and lost touch. Bret Hartsock got up in the middle of his mother's funeral, said an ugly word, and stormed out. He no longer believes in God.

Dr. Strangereader: Or How I Learned to Stop Worrying About Suburban Novels and Love International Fiction

In the past, readers and critics expected serious novelists to catch the spirit of the new in their fiction, to absorb the particular experiences of living and thinking in a specific time and place. The form and language of fiction evolved to fit changing times and tastes—sometimes briskly, sometimes slowly—to reflect or critique transformations in technology and culture, the tensions between traditional beliefs and discoveries in science and psychology, the impact of the political on the individual, the ambiguous influences of history. The novel mirrored the nips and tucks in reality, inner as well as outer, with realism mutating into miraculous metaphysical and self-reflexive directions. From the beginning, the novel was nothing if not capacious: critic Viktor Shklovsky mischievously asserted that *Tristram Shandy* was "the most typical novel in world literature."

Today, the artistic virtues of plasticity are no longer paramount in the American novel. For a number of reasons, the essential links between the flexibility of the novel's form and the fluidity of experience are dissipating, the mysterious give and take between the elasticity of words and ever-shifting realities weakening. Contemporary life calls for an imaginative renovation of the novel, but it's a challenge our writers won't or can't tackle. Most new homegrown fiction is hidebound and modest, self-involved and shrewdly commercial, calculated reanimations of nostalgia. The typical American novel is content to be typical, sociologically speaking.

How can that be? In his book *Reading & Writing: A Personal Account*, V. S. Naipaul argues that our reliance on the novel's past makes the form easy to teach in the classroom but inadequate before the growing complexities of modern experience. Stuck in traditional postures, fiction isn't able to penetrate a brave new world overwhelmed by electronic media, a confused global culture that threatens "to be as full of tribal or folk movement as during the centuries of the Roman Empire": "But the novel, still (in spite of appearances) mimicking the program of the nineteenth-century originators, still feeding off the vision they created, can subtly distort the unaccommodating new reality. As a form it is now commonplace enough, and limited enough, to be teachable. It encourages a multitude of little narcissisms, from near and far; they stand in for originality and give the form an illusion of life. It is a vanity of the age (and of commercial promotion) that the novel continues to be literature's final and highest expression." For Naipaul, fiction is a burnt-out case stuck in a rut, serving up a simulation of modern experience filtered through worn, self-regarding molds, missing a genuine encounter with the evolving vicissitudes of history. Notice that Naipaul doesn't want a return to the reassurance of the old but an encounter with the new.

Adding insult to injury, a number of respected writers and critics encourage the American novel's drift by arguing for the merits of the tried and true. Literary magazines and creative writing schools—which should be fighting for artistic and intellectual freedom, for a renewed sense of possibility—thumb their noses at what *New Republic* critic James Wood calls "the risk of thought," choosing instead the comfort of fizzled bromides in popular genres or the suburban blues. Whether fighting for survival in a competitive market or upholding the merits of good gray realism, too many writers are swept up into a whirlwind of cultural forces that promise more (publicity, journalistic timeliness) but demand less: less artistic ambition, less intellect, less peculiarity.

The situation is reversible, though rebellion calls for stretching (or reinventing) boundaries rather than accepting them. The battle is not over shoring up the waning prestige of the novel; no matter how strenuously new fiction is celebrated, books will continue to lag behind the chic celebrity of popular music and the movies. The fight is for writers and critics to accept the necessity of redefining the form to convey shifting circumstances, the hard but honorable task of reshaping our expectations of what a novel is supposed to be. The best fiction transforms the way we picture the world, pitting itself against the leprous spread of the mundane and the bland. For the novelist, creativity's mobility—its chameleonic talent for dramatizing changing notions of consciousness and reality—is crucial. The imagination should serve as an unforgiving goad in the pursuit of the more: the more difficult, the more far-reaching, the more particular. According to Italo Calvino, "literature remains alive only if we set ourselves immeasurable goals, far beyond all hope of achievement."

In American fiction, that expansive conception of the imagination is in danger, not so much because of the tired rhetoric about a country dumbed down, but due to the systematic shrinkwrapping of the novel's potential by those who should know better. Part of the problem is that our writers and critics are too provincial for literature's good: cultural nationalism takes the defensive form of the triumph of self-sufficiency. Thus one way out of this creative paralysis is for American writers to look for inspiration from fiction beyond our shores; international novels in translation offer a sense of aesthetic capacity necessary for a reinvigoration of the form.

Critical opinion-makers play it safe by hopping between chipper optimism and dank pessimism, finding lots of novels to praise while issuing generalizations about the end of fiction. These extremes fit snugly into the commercial and intellectual bubble that surrounds and isolates American fiction. Even analysts savvy about the artistic poverty of American novels are cramped by their nearsighted gloom, their fear the novel may have reached its demise in the cyber age. Naipaul isn't the only critic who fears serious fiction has stalled, perhaps permanently.

Sven Birkerts, in a December 1999 *Esquire* piece titled "The Next Revolution," laments the lack of ambition, the truckload of "mere excellence" produced by postwar authors. He frets over the disappearance of the mysterious inwardness and formal innovation found in the work of James Joyce and Thomas Mann. Birkerts, along with Naipaul, wonders if the contemporary novelist is nothing more than a pale reflection of a past he can't budge out of the way: "Missing is some greater thrusting at ultimates, the quixote factor, as well as the implicit sense that the world is being made and that he is making it. Making it new. Now we are devolved again—golden age to silver to bronze. Everyone is good, even brilliant, but we are self-conscious now, playing in front of the mirror. The legacy of the past seems to overpower our writers;

sometimes it feels as if they're dabbling around in the muddy footprints of giants." Birkerts makes his argument through contradictory images: artistic narcissism versus the bullying accomplishments of history. But the modernist heroes he worships were acutely self-conscious and deeply aware of the past, and they still managed to be innovative.

Throughout the piece, Birkerts wrings his hands, hoping a replacement for a diminished modernism is on the way. Unlike Naipaul, he believes something miraculous may happen, though his flurry of rhetorical questions leads me to suspect he wouldn't bet the farm: "Have we reached terminal saturation? I don't want to believe that." "I believe they are out there—cultures generate the antibodies they need—but where?" Birkerts's anxiety and Naipaul's far-ranging dismissal also reflect fashionable fears of a cultural downturn; books with threatening titles abound, from *Nobrow* to *Faded Mosaic: The Emergence of Post-Cultural America* and *The Twilight of American Culture.* Instead of cutting against the grain of literary business as usual, both Naipaul and Birkerts accept the deterministic assumption that either new realities or too much self-consciousness are spoiling the future of the novel. This belittlement of the novelistic imagination, paradoxically, links these critics with those who believe, in this day and age and cutthroat market, fiction has no choice but to aim low.

Blaming the smallness of the novel on the scary ghosts of modernism or the intimidating density of contemporary life distracts us from a less glamorous but more insidiously realistic cause: commercial forces. Critic Albert Mobilio lays this scenario out in his article "The Genre Generation: Where Did the Novel Come From and Where Is It Going?" in the February 2000 issue of *The Village Voice Literary Supplement.* For Mobilio, a growing number of significant writers are absorbing the conventions of genre fiction; he points to a number of novels, including Jonathan Lethem's *Motherless Brooklyn* (whose detective protagonist has Tourette's syndrome) and Richard Price's drug thriller *Clockers.* After the rigors of modernism, a cerebral cool-down period is necessary, he implies. After all, a retrenchment at this time isn't going to embarrass anyone. "Serious novelists now know that they will lose little literary cachet," observes Mobilio, "yet gain many potential readers if they can package their romp through the uncreated consciousness as a thriller." "In the final analysis," the critic concludes, "socioeconomic factors, not aesthetic ones, may well be the determinant."

Mobilio implies that economics and politics shape our perceptions of which works of fiction should be considered new and worthwhile. The marketplace determines what is novel in the novel rather than the imaginative achievements of writers or the clarion cries of critics. Like many reviewers, Mobilio isn't concerned about fiction's capitulation to small-scale projects. Citizens fried by the electronic age need a rest from demanding prose (his assumption is that these readers waded through the murky waters of modernism in the first place), so the hip writer obligingly lowers the limbo bar: "Set against the vogue for genre's zing and flash, syntactically dense rants like William Gass's 600-page *The Tunnel* may simply prove too much for remote-control-style readers. Perhaps the quick-cut grammar of visual media has so jangled our attention spans we require that stability of expectation that is genre fiction's defining element." Given the onrush of communication technologies, just when will our attention spans expand? It's more likely we are in for decades of coming contractions.

Set Mobilio's "stability of expectation," with its patronizing bow to the techno-frazzled reader, against Naipaul's more radical demand for serious novels. Amnesia and originality are interconnected: "What is good is always what is new, in both form and content. What is good forgets whatever models it might have had, and is unexpected; we have to catch it on the wing." Of course, genre conventions can serve as the foundation for ecstatic imaginative flights, but only when they are beside the point, when either characters or ideas take over and a new compound is created or the genre is exploded. Unfortunately, Mobilio is accurate about today's earthbound fictions. Most American novels are not out to astonish, either by way of style or content. The snug contours of genre cushions the reader's nerves, providing a conservative underbelly—often reassuring and/or moralistic—that prefers the familiar over the surprising.

In that sense, Mobilio's tribute to retrenchment typifies a widespread failure of artistic and critical nerve that seeks to rationalize why the bar must be lowered. Thomas Mann said all of his work could be seen as an effort to free himself from the middle class, a rebellion Lionel Trilling believed was "the chief intention of all modern literature." The chief intention of most contemporary American novels is the opposite; suburban fiction embraces aesthetic provincialism, a narrowness of technique and subject matter that distrusts irony, playfulness, inaccessibility, and complication. Contemporary American novels want to join the middle class, paying ambivalent homage like a moth that can't break free of the flame. This obsessed love/hate (love the comfort; hate the privilege) is trotted out in endless variations on the pieties of the suburban novel, even in the most radical-seeming feminist and multicultural fables. The irony is that novels revolving around characters struggling against the siren call of the middle class have become part of the form's fatal attraction. What could be more neatly bourgeois than alienation?

Novelists have come up with a literary variation on how popular culture goes about renewing itself: writers reupholster the old, though it is the same lumpy sofa underneath. The rise, fall, and rebirth of the suburban novel is a representative case. In the postwar period, the genre focused on the discontent of the middle class; it dramatized the traditional clash between the individual and the collective, between human feelings and social duties. In the seventies that conflict devolved into a standoff between hyperalienated suburbanites and an attenuated society incapable of providing satisfaction. During the eighties the genre sank into a polite nihilism aptly characterized by John W. Aldridge in his 1992 book *Talents and Technicians: Literary Chic and the New Assembly-Line Fiction:* "Over and over again in their fiction these writers tend to treat the personal life as if it were a phenomenon existing totally apart from society and without connotations that would give it meaningful relevance to a general human condition or dilemma." By this time both sides of the seesawing duality, the individual and society, were emptied out. Novelists couldn't stretch smug self-hatred any further—so the genre had to snap back.

The suburban vision remains an ongoing commercial concern, but desperately needs replenishment to seem new again. The latest group of multicultural writers is pumping life into the moribund form. The tensions of middle-class existence remain front and center, but as ethnic groups struggle for their share of the good life, the synthetic hell of the 'burbs takes a back seat to meatier issues of cultural assimilation, shifting identities, and the waning of tradition in the face of contemporary mores. Culture clashes on the turf of the affluent have become trendy literary property. The Orange Prize for Fiction, the richest literary award in Britain, is given to a book by a female novelist. Almost half the finalist novels this year contain "stories of immigration from one culture to another," says the contest's chairwoman, *Guardian* columnist Polly Toynbee. She adds that "after reading them all, you look at mothers begging with babies in their laps—Romanians or whatever—and you think, Those kids are going to write a book someday." These children will be penning books for readers who are less interested in Eastern Europe (when was the last time you read a novel translated from the Romanian?) than in the guilt-inducing struggles of the "Other" in Western society.

In the March 23, 2000, issue of *The New York Review of Books,* Ian Buruma bluntly suggested the price ethnic writers pay for admittance into the middle-class novel: homogenization in the name of universality. Buruma reviews novels by Chinese-American Ha Jin and Korean-American Chang-rae Lee and concludes that "what Jin, [Kazuo] Ishiguro, and indeed Chang-rae Lee have done, given their oddly angled perspectives, is reopen subjects which most Western authors can only treat with irony: marriage, family relations, the boundaries set by social obligations." The catch is that verbal inventiveness and forays into unfamiliar territory are not welcome in the new world fiction: "In this kind of global literature there is little room for the linguistic and cultural playfulness that breathes so much life into books such as *Berlin Alexanderplatz* or indeed Joyce's *Ulysses.* The fact that cultural references are either not shared or deliberately rejected by writers like Ha Jin or Kazuo Ishiguro explains the lack of irony in their novels. But you can get too much of irony and in-jokes." Fatigued by irony, Buruma wants to make an artistic virtue of unencumbered earnestness: "by stripping their stories of irony, cultural allusions, and exotic ornament, writers with complicated backgrounds can restore a classical purity to our languages, and even bring us a little closer to the ground of our shared human condition."

Naipaul's criticism that today's imitative novels "subtly distort" an increasingly unruly contemporary reality has relevance here, once you notice the connections between Buruma's plug for "classical purity" and Mobilio's "stability of expectation." Much like Mobilio, who accepts pouring serious fiction into genre expectations, Buruma would like multicultural writers to cater to readers weary of complication, to cleanse narratives of irony and exoticism. Notice how the terms are posited in his argument: it's the same old story of anti-intellectual contamination, with foreign influences tagged as obstacles to classical purity. The "global writer" assimilates to the great tradition by shedding cultural particularities.

Yet the strength of literature from around the globe often lies in its revelatory local details. In the May 20, 1999, issue of *The New York Review of Books,* Pankaj Mishra argues for the value of Indian authors "whose identities are rooted in their regions, and who for that very reason are alert to the fine discriminations and nuances of their subject in a way a reader in the West would find difficult.... In this sense, parochialism—which Rushdie calls 'the main vice' of literatures in Indian languages—is not such a bad thing." For Buruma the parochial—cultural material the Western reader will find baffling or extraneous—is not a good thing. Not because he views the exotic as the "Other" to be feared or ignored by Western imperialistic culture, an argument whose power fades with the continual mixing of races and cultures in the West. But for a more dangerous critical reason: Buruma's stripped-down requirements for novels that tap "the ground of our shared human condition" lead to a desiccated sense of fiction. The radical newness of the best fiction has been rooted in its grand peculiarity, its loyalty to the parochial. Buruma suggests that cultural allusions in novels endanger their universality. But that local density is also a way fiction eludes the spreading boutique multiculturalism of McWorld, where cultural differences come down to a matter of diet and food preparation.

Irony and parochial details are necessary tools in exploring the complexities, "the newness" of modern reality. Yet today the ironic has become as stigmatized as the exotic; increasingly the exotic is as unwelcome as the ironic. (Novels about the arrival of new groups in the suburbs have their limits—they must not be *too* alien.) Some critics would argue it has always been this way, justifying their kowtowing to the whims of fashion. But should those concerned with the power of fiction to take the reader outside of him or herself into other selves, to dramatize challenging ideas, and to reinvigorate language accept this domestication? Are American novels chockablock with irony, or is it quickie-mart snickering rather than the cutting skepticism of Swift and Voltaire?

Critical enthusiasm for the exoticism of multicultural fiction is misleading because it is largely confined to literature produced by authors writing in English and living in America or Britain. According to *The Oxford Guide to Literature in English Translation*, "Book production [in America and Britain] has increased fourfold in the past 50 years, but the number of translations has remained the same, representing between 2 and 4 per cent of the annual total of books published." One scholar of translation, Lawrence Venuti, observes with dismay that our culture is "aggressively monolingual." It could be argued that the literary chatter about the rise of ethnic variety in American literature is an illusion—the overall vision of American writers and writing sold around the world is the half-hearted celebration of middle-class life, fables of "classical purity" centered on whether one group or another succeeds.

The rise of multicultural fiction didn't come about because of too much self-consciousness or narcissism; the movement was demanded by the marketplace because it revamps American suburban fiction, making issues of family, assimilation, and manners meaningful again. Ironically, critical huzzahs to the supposed diversity of American fiction end up condoning timidity and staleness while perpetuating cultural provinciality.

Given the political pizzazz of multicultural fiction and America's lack of interest in international news, fiction from around the world garners little attention. Aside from a handful of major authors, international fiction boasts little advertising presence, critical clout, or academic charisma. The majority of our critics and literary publications don't wander very far afield: the welcome wagon for fiction from outside our shores doesn't roll often. The fact that many of today's most interesting novels are foreign and available in translation turns few heads. Our reviewers and their publications would rather drool barrels of ink on the expedient homegrown flavor of the month.

International fiction is marginalized in the no-man's-land of aficionados and specialists; in this way the literary world aids and abets the homogenization many of its writers condemn. For example, one of the most important publishing ventures in the last decade, Northwestern University Press's Writings from an Unbound Europe—a lineup of fiction selected from writers from such countries as Albania, Romania, and Serbia—has gotten little notice. A series of novels from Eastern European authors, edited by Philip Roth and published by Penguin in the seventies and eighties, had star power and Cold War politics behind it. But Soviet Communism is dead, and that part of the globe isn't fashionable anymore, no matter how brilliantly their writers reinvent the novel to reflect the problems of post-socialist society.

Meanwhile, capitalism does what it does best: it churns out product, lumping gems in with the trash. Despite the dearth of critical coverage and interest at major publishers, over the past couple of decades presses distributing distinguished fiction in translation have been growing in number: a bare sampling includes The New Press, Brookline Books, Zephyr Press, Catbird Press, Harvill Press, University of Nebraska Press, McPherson and Company, Northwestern University Press, Marsilio, Serpent's Tail, Steerforth Press, Counterpoint, the University of Texas Press, Sun & Moon Press. Old standbys, such as New Directions and Farrar, Straus & Giroux, continue to print fiction from the corners of the world. There are quite a few disappointments, of course, with what gets imported, but the yearly crop of books in translation at least has the Darwinian distinction of being cherry-picked; someone thought it worthwhile to make a particular book available in English. A number of these novels are as rambunctious and quixotic as one could wish; modernism is extended, discarded, and blown up in rich narratives filled with history (not of much interest to the suburban novel), irony, and cerebral friskiness. Weepy critics and commercial touts haven't convinced these writers that modernism is dead. If nothing else, international fiction proves that modernism, with its stylistic and intellectual demands, isn't, as Birkerts claims, played out—it is one possibility among many for the writer to draw upon.

For disillusioned souls, tired of the creaky American merry-go-round, international fiction offers an immersion into other cultures, pasts, and selves, often by way of challenging fictional techniques that, in many countries, remain vital because they communicate new realities and ideas. The perspective of many of these novels—a playful historicism, a skepticism skeptical of itself—reflects an alternative to the innocent diligence, the earnest navel-gazing of so much American writing. The best of international fiction treats the novel as if it were a serious tool for grasping reality on the sly, not a form weighed down by fatigue and lesson-mongering. In *The Natural Order of Things,* Portuguese novelist António Lobo Antunes journeys through memory to warp time and space: "...looking at the window and seeing black miners all around me, likewise with glowing lamps on their foreheads and with mugs of cane liquor that yellow, like sulfuric moons, the evening mist...imagine a world of tunnels that end who knows where or why, or if they end at all, because maybe they hook up to other tunnels, maybe there are infinite branches of tunnels with echoing mine cars that nobody pushes, pickaxes no one uses, foreman's orders that no one remembers."

Serbian writer David Albahari does not hedge his artistic bets to fit genre expectations; his short story collection *Words Are Something Else* blends philosophical meditation and delicate lyricism: "The damp is probably getting into the clockworks, springs, probably slowing down the hands. It is hard to say what is time and what weather—all of it is nature, everything constantly repeats, there is no end, no beginning, no distinctions." Irony transforms and invigorates the imagination in such authors as Albahari and Antunes, José Saramago, W. G. Sebald, Aleksandar Tisma, Norman Manea, Rosa Chacel, Juan Goytisolo, Naiyer Masud, Breyten Breytenbach, Botho Strauss, Viktor Pelevin, and Félix de Azúa. Major reconsiderations of the novel by admirably eccentric talents—Andrey Platonov, Juan Carlos Onetti, Anna Maria Ortese, Osman Lins, Danilo Kis, S. Y. Agnon, and Raymond Queneau among them—are still coming into English. Oxford University Press's Library of Latin America series and the University of Nebraska Press's European Women Writers series are indispensable eye-openers onto different terrain.

"The translator is not just building a bridge from one language to another," argues Dutch writer Adriaan van Dis in his *Leopard IV: Bearing Witness* essay "Stolen Languages," "he is also a herald, broadcasting the words of a small language into the wider world, enriching a small country with the literature of a large one. The translator can put a country back on the map, rescue a civilization from isolation, and help it rediscover its pride and identity." American fiction and criticism is too drunk with the sound of its own monotonous drone to hear the music of foreign voices.

The mainstream literary press ignores these sounds, but its indifference should not discourage those who demand more. The highbrow gatekeeper has fallen victim to identity politics, editorial cowardice, and intellectual leveling. The waning of centralized authority offers opportunities: cultural dialogue is trivialized but critical voices are equalized. Wised-up readers must become enterprising hunters, searching for prose works that excite rather than sedate.

Of course, fiction in translation poses hazards. Politics, as often as aesthetic merit, decrees what's translated into English. Marketing trends, economics, and editorial whim dictate what writing reaches the West: Eastern Europe was hot in the seventies; fiction from Communist China has become trendy of late. And international material can be perceived as too unfamiliar, so deeply mired in the particulars of culture it risks losing the reader in enigmatic curlicues. Translation is an art few of its practitioners can master; some books don't translate well no matter how painstaking the effort.

Difficult as it is, however, the linguistic transaction is vital for cultural enrichment and survival. Modernism was largely imported to America from European countries; the black humorists and experimentalists of the sixties were influenced by writings from Latin America and Eastern Europe. Over the years the exchange between us and global outsiders has been healthy, but the increasingly insulated mentality of Anglo-American culture has set limits on the impact of foreign literatures.

American writers and critics need to go on vacation, though not on the packaged tour where the tourist guides insist the passengers sit back and enjoy the best of both worlds. Ambitious souls will break away and search for singular experiences and fantastical dives, delve into the linguistic jungles for rare plants and creepy crawlies. For the scientist, rare specimens provide cures for diseases and clues to genetic therapies; for those who care about the art of the novel, international fiction in translation has similar medicinal value as a crucial alternative, an imaginative salve, to the commercial drone of the lit-biz and the predictable shudders of the prophets.

Thomas Mann is dead; many of us can't seem to get over it. Freud might conjecture that the melancholy of Birkerts and Naipaul reflects an inability to mourn, to overcome a debilitating sense of belatedness. Unlike Naipaul, Birkerts strikes me as pining not just for Mann redux, but for the good old days of the critic-as-kingmaker. Once, giants of journalistic reviewing, such as Irving Howe and Edmund Wilson, explicated the work of difficult international writers to the literate public. The task remains worthwhile but forsaken by most editors and reviewers. The attenuation of critical authority has made such uphill literary leadership problematic in a country largely indifferent to news from around the world. Is anybody going to listen? International fiction has become a hard sell in a culture that believes it has nothing to learn from those outside of its borders.

Against the deadening mechanics of habit, Freud placed the survival value of mobility, the yen to escape from the everyday, to free-associate one's way to the new. American novelists and critics, as well as the reader unscrambled by the latest technology, need not make do grudgingly with what is blurbed in plain view. The exhilarating, if risky, alternative is to rebel and strike out for dreams tucked in nooks and crannies, poke around the world for the unexpected volume, become aesthetic researchers on a quest for the sometimes startling discoveries that small presses and university publishers bring within our reach. Searchers will be propelled by an imperiled conviction: that the essence of the novel is rooted in the pleasures of the idiosyncratic.

ABOUT GISH JEN

A Profile by Don Lee

Gish Jen lives in Cambridge, Massachusetts, with her husband, eight-year-old son, and one-and-a-half-year-old daughter, and the hectic pace of her life is reflected in her rapid-fire speech. The celebrated author of two novels and a collection, Jen is known for her humor and brimming intelligence, her ready opinions and easy laugh, her charm, and, not least of all, her volubility. Even though she remembers herself as being shy and withdrawn as a kid, she admits she was constantly kicked out of class for talking.

Born in 1955 in New York, Jen grew up Chinese and Catholic in Queens and Yonkers, where the "library" at her school consisted of a single shelf of books. When her father, a professor of civil engineering, and her mother, an elementary school teacher, moved the family to the predominantly Jewish suburb of Scarsdale, Jen finally had access to a proper library. She made feverish use of it, reading every book in the building, going from *The Island Stallion* to Camus's *The Stranger* in the fifth grade. In junior high she wrote poetry, and in high school—when she discarded her given name, Lillian, which was too fusty for her tastes, and took up Gish, after the actress Lillian Gish—she was the literary editor for the school magazine.

Still, writing was never more than a pleasant diversion for her. She was a child of immigrants from Shanghai, the second of five children, four of whom would attend Ivy League colleges. Her three brothers would become successful businessmen, her sister a doctor, and there were similar expectations for Jen. She dutifully attended Harvard, with law or medicine prescribed for her future. Her plans changed dramatically, however, when she took English 283, a prosody course taught by Robert Fitzgerald, who required a weekly assignment writing verse. "Right away I loved it," Jen says. "I remember telling my roommate I loved writing, and if I could do it for the rest of my life, I would. But—I'm the daughter of immigrants—it never even crossed my mind for one minute that I might become a poet." Fitzgerald begged to differ. "Why are you premed?" he asked her. "I suggest you consider doing something with words." Since she had just received a C in chemistry, she was open to suggestion. Fitzgerald advised that if she wasn't going to be a poet, she should at least try publishing, and arranged a job for her at Doubleday.

She worked in New York City for a year, but wasn't quite happy. "I realized I had found myself in some middle ground. I was neither doing what I really wanted to do, nor was I making any money." Once again, she opted for something more practical. "I had already been premed and prelaw; that left the one thing I'd never had any interest in—business school." She entered the M.B.A. program at Stanford, mainly because the university had a graduate writing program. As expected, she didn't have her heart in the business curriculum, entranced instead by the novels she was reading and the writing workshops she was taking on the side. Fortunately her business classes were pass/fail, and her husband-to-be, David O'Connor, prepped her the night before exams. "He would say, 'Okay, you need to know these three things,' and I would go and get a 66 and pass my exams. In the meantime I was taking really great writing courses across the street." The first week of her second year, she overslept every day and missed all her classes. "It was clear that I was never going to set foot in the classroom again, so I finally took a leave of absence," she says. (Not too long ago, she ran into an economics professor who told her that she had been a frequent subject of faculty dining-room discussions, which usually concluded: "Let's never take someone like her again.")

Dropping out of Stanford didn't fly well with her parents, either. They cut her off financially, and her mother did not speak to her for a year. Jen taught English at a coal-mining institute in China, then enrolled in the M.F.A. program at the Iowa Writers' Workshop. Although her work was received well there, Jen was fully aware that she had a difficult road ahead of her. "Maybe some people could have seen that multiculturalism was around the corner," Jen says, "but it certainly wasn't apparent to me, or to any of the Asian-American writers that I knew. Things have changed so drastically. People often ask me where the comic outlook comes from. Among other things it comes from my experience. I have seen so much social change in such a short amount of time, it seems miraculous."

Jill Krementz

After Jen graduated from Iowa in 1983, she and O'Connor married and lived in California until 1985, when they moved to Cambridge, where she played housewife more than writer. A lack of confidence about her literary career reduced her to taking a typing test for a job at Harvard. "I remember vividly the moment at which the woman at the front of the room said, 'Ms. Jen?' and I thought, 'That's me,' and she said, 'You have typed ninety words a minute with no mistakes. I'm sure we can find you a job.' It was the nicest thing anyone had said to me in about three years." Depressingly, it turned out they couldn't find her a job—at least not right away. She waited and waited, thinking a secretarial position would save her, but something else did. She was awarded a fellowship at Radcliffe's Bunting Institute. "It was quite a wonderful moment. They finally found a job for me at some dean's office and called me, and I said, 'No thank you. I am no longer interested. I am now a fellow at the Bunting Institute.'"

During her fellowship, she worked on her first novel, *Typical American,* which was eventually published by Houghton Mifflin/Seymour Lawrence in 1991. A finalist for the National Book Critics Circle Award, the book launched Jen into the literary limelight. The novel follows three Chinese immigrants, Ralph Chang, his wife, Helen, and his sister, Theresa, as they pursue the American Dream and struggle against the pressures of assimilation, greed, and self-interest. Both a comedy and a tragedy, the novel brilliantly turns the notion of what it means to be typical American on its head.

"We are family," echoed Helen.

"Team," said Ralph. "We should have name. The Chinese Yankees. Call Chang-kees for short."

"Chang-kees!" Everyone laughed.

Ball games became even more fun.... "Let's go Chang-kees!" This was in the privacy of their apartment, in front of their newly bought used Zenith TV; the one time they went to an actual game, people had called them names and told them to go back to their laundry. They in turn had sat impassive as the scoreboard. Rooting in their hearts, they said later. Anyway, they preferred to stay home and watch. "More comfortable." "More convenient." "Can see better," they agreed.

As successful as *Typical American* was, Jen sometimes resented critics who quickly labeled—and diminished—her as an Asian-American writer. Her reaction was to complicate what that meant via her second novel, *Mona in the Promised Land*, which came out in 1996 through Knopf. It surprised everyone. A sequel of sorts, the novel focuses on Ralph and Helen Chang's daughters, Mona and Callie, as they grow up in a Jewish suburb of New York called Scarshill. Mona Chang joins a temple youth group and then, to her parents' dismay, converts, and is thereafter referred to as "Changowitz." Ironically, Mona learns that her rabbi is right in telling her, "The more Jewish you become, the more Chinese you'll be." With the backdrop of Vietnam and the civil rights movement, the novel is a riotous, provocative collision of social, ethnic, and racial issues, populated by a mishmash of characters who are Chinese, Jewish, black, Wasp, and Japanese—a dizzying sendup that challenged readers to redefine ethnicity, and prompted one very confused journalist to headline her review of the novel "Matzo-Ball Sushi."

Mona in the Promised Land grew out of a short story, "What Means Switch?," that Jen wrote while trying to finish *Typical American*. She had lost her first pregnancy, and didn't know if she'd be able to see her way to the end of the novel. Then she ran into an old high-school acquaintance and was inspired to revisit her teen years in Scarsdale in a short story. "You could feel the intense liberation," she says. At the same time, she jotted down some ideas for a new book in a binder of index cards. "A year or two later," she says, "I looked at one of the cards, and it said, 'Mona turns Jewish.' And I thought, 'Oy! Can't write that,' and I laughed. Then I paid attention. The uncomfortable laughter told me that I'd hit a nerve."

Jen's next book, *Who's Irish?*, a collection of stories published in 1999 by Knopf, confirmed her mastery of the short form as well. The stories originally appeared in publications such as *The New Yorker*. Two stories were selected for the anthology *Best American Short Stories*, and one that was originally published in *Ploughshares*, "Birthmates," was chosen by John Updike for *The Best American Short Stories of the Century*.

Perhaps the most daring piece in *Who's Irish?* is the title story, which is narrated in pidgin English by a Chinese woman. Her daughter is married to an Irish American, and the woman possesses a few stereotypes of her own:

> I just happen to mention about the Shea family, an interesting fact: four brothers in the family, and not one of them work. The mother, Bess, have a job before she got sick, she was executive secretary in a big company. She is handle everything for a big shot, you would be surprised how complicated her job is, not just type this, type that. Now she is a nice woman with a clean house. But her boys, every one of them is on welfare, or so-called severance pay, or so-called disability pay. Something. They say they cannot find work, this is not the economy of the fifties, but I say, Even the black people doing better these days, some of them live so fancy, you'd be surprised. Why the Shea family have so much trouble? They are white people, they speak English. But my husband and I own our restaurant before he die. Free and clear, no mortgage. Of course, I understand I am just lucky, come from a country where the food is popular all over the world. I understand it is not the Shea family's fault they come from a country where everything is boiled.

Jen says, "I could not have written this story early on in my career in dialect, using that voice, because if I had sent it out, the assumption would have been that I didn't speak English. I'm sure some editor would have sent it back to me, saying, 'Oh, well, you know, when your English is a bit better...'"

All along the way, Jen has danced an elaborate dance with the times. She has chosen, she says, to avail herself of what freedom she could find rather than play assigned roles: of China expert, say, or of professional victim. "I have hoped to define myself as an American writer." And yet the world has continued to try to define her otherwise. In an interview on NPR, a journalist asked Jen why *Mona in the Promised Land* had "no real Americans in it." And *Kirkus Reviews* described *Who's Irish?* as "a sharp-eyed debut collection of eight tales examining America as it is seen by foreigners."

Nonetheless, Jen has pushed onward. Another story in *Who's Irish?*, a novella called "House, House, Home," shows her going in a more complex narrative direction. She hopes to carry over this impulse to experiment to her next novel, which she is working on, when she can steal the time, in an office away from house and children and husband. "This is the way, maybe, in which I am still the daughter of immigrants," she says. "It was a very long time before I was able to hear my own voice, and even to this day I need to be in a quiet place and feel I'm away from my parents, my editor, my agent, even my audience, in order to hear what it is I really have to say."

KICK IN THE HEAD *Stories by Steven Rinehart. Doubleday, $22.00
cloth. Reviewed by Fred Leebron.*

Steven Rinehart's debut collection of stories, *Kick in the Head,*
presents an ensemble of characters pushed through the edge to an
abominable and shocking other side, while at the same time giving us tales that are always magnetic, entertaining, and sophisti-
cated. In a dozen different ways, often using members of the same
cast, Rinehart artfully portrays sinister pressure systems and people who either change them or cannot escape them.

The gruesome and disturbing "Burning Luv," about a hitchhiker
bent on revenge, is both resiliently grim and yet irresistibly au-
thentic. "The cowboy hadn't said goodbye," the narrator tells us as
he is left alone in the middle of the desert, "he just took off while I
was under the bridge taking a leak. . . . It felt like the quiet you might
hear inside a bathroom, late at night in a bus station. It was a quiet that hurt, the way dying alone in the snow might hurt."

In "Mr. Big Stuff," a slyly funny barroom brawl of a story, the
recurrent character of Chris Bergman tries to rescue a woman
slugged by a fat guy wielding an empty bottle, only to have her
girlfriend try to turn him into a cop arriving late on the scene.
"Look," the cop tells her. "All I know is when I showed up this guy
was the only one doing anything. Maybe he's the good guy. You
ever think of that."

In stories with enormous stakes, and with eye-poppingly precise comparisons and laugh-out-loud humorous jabs, Rinehart
shows how hard it is to be a good guy in a world that has turned
desperate. There are men at an impromptu strip party "gathered
tight around the table, like a Last Supper of goons," and there's a
girl who is "ruggedly handsome, attractive in an oddly virile way,
like a tough cowgirl in a bad Western. . . . Even in a halter-top she
looked like she belonged in Special Forces."

The humor evolves story by story in the timing of the dialogue
and the ironic and yet deeply felt wisdom of the perceptions. "I

didn't like college at first," Bergman says in "Outstanding in My Field," "so I dropped out to go back and be with my friends full time." One such friend is "a farmer's kid, bright and healthy and strong. We didn't let him drink because when he got drunk he hit his head against walls and cars and tree trunks and cried into the crook of his elbow. 'I'm going to Hell,' he would cry. 'I'm just going straight to Hell.' He was religious and hard on himself." "It's just that I have no respect for men," a uniquely conflicted diabetic veterinarian tells Bergman in the title story, as he fails nobly in trying to rescue her from herself. "No offense, it just makes it kind of hard." "Not for me," Bergman says. "Respect is overrated."

Such sly humor is also deadly serious. The characters in *Kick in the Head* show an elegant and wise despair in the face of rage, violence, and unfairness; and Rinehart's endings are masterful, dropping the reader off a narrative cliff into a midair of resonance so thick you never quite land.

Fred Leebron is the author of the novels Six Figures *and* Out West, *and co-editor of* Postmodern American Fiction: A Norton Anthology. *He teaches at Gettysburg College.*

SOME ETHER *Poems by Nick Flynn. Graywolf Press, $12.95 paper. Reviewed by Tony Hoagland.*

Someday the term confessional will seem as quaint and obsolete as a fainting couch, and we will have a new terminology, one that feels more discriminating. In the meantime, we have Nick Flynn's compelling poems, which turn some rather extreme autobiographical details of a life this way and that, like a snow globe in the hand of the dazed survivor of a battle. Dazed but curious, connected but detached, attentive but distant, present but disturbingly enmeshed in the long sticky tentacles of memory.

The poems of Flynn's first book, *Some Ether,* revolve around the central story of a mother's suicide and the traumatized, dreamy disconnectedness of her survivor. But the book's gift is not the sensationalism of the tale, but the delicate kiltered skill with which the poems collage anecdote and metaphor into allegory: "Every day, something—this time / a French ship with all her passengers and crew / slides into the North Sea, the water so cold / it finishes them. Nothing saved / but a life ring stenciled GRACE, / cut loose from its body. / A spokesman can only / state his surprise / that it doesn't happen more often. / . . . For years I had a happy child-hood, / if anyone asked I'd say, *it was happy*" ("The Captain Asks for a Show of Hands").

I've been reading these poems in magazines for years, and still find great freshness in Flynn's arrangement of images, and espe-cially the elegant, unwinding syntax of certain poems ("Flood," "How Do You Know You're Missing Anything?"). More and more, though, I've come to realize how much this collection is con-cerned not just with memory, but with the subtleties and paradox-es of telling itself. The crucial dilemma for the speaker comes to seem how loyalty to the dead prevents ever living fully in the pre-sent. How the stories we most treasure are addictive as heroin is treated in "Cartoon Physics, Part II": "More than once / I traded on this until it transmuted into a story . . . / I'd recite it as if I'd nev-er told anyone, / and it felt that way / because I'd try not to cry yet always / would & the listener / would always hold me . . ."

One of the therapeutic premises of confessionalism, of course, is that earnest speech is a healing act. One of the integrities of Flynn's book is that it doesn't make any such promise. There is no clear indication that the speaker's damage can be triumphed over—no promise that any of us recover from anything. "Emptying Town" is just one refutation of the confessional mode: "You know the way Jesus / rips open his shirt / to show us his heart, all flaming and thorny, / the way he points to it. . . . / My version of hell / is someone ripping open his / shirt & saying, / look what I did for you."

Some Ether combines nakedness, elegance, and emotional intel-ligence. The poems are beautifully clear in their particulars and meanings. And the question of whether or not the speaker can awak-en from the dream of the past, whether telling can effect this self-redemption, whether confession *works,* is a deeply affecting drama.

Tony Hoagland's first collection, Sweet Ruin, *won the Brittingham Prize in Poetry and the John C. Zacharis First Book Award, and his second collection,* Donkey Gospel, *won the James Laughlin Award.*

THE BARBARIANS ARE COMING *A novel by David Wong Louie. Put-nam, $23.95 cloth. Reviewed by Don Lee.*

Sterling Lung has problems. The narrator of David Wong Louie's first novel, *The Barbarians Are Coming,* is a recent gradu-ate of the CIA—the Culinary Institute of America—and he has landed what he regards as a plum job, cooking haute cuisine lunches at a Wasp ladies' club in Connecticut. But soon enough, Sterling's parents conspire to import a picture bride, Yuk, from Hong Kong for him to marry and carry on the Lung line; his sometime girlfriend, Bliss, a Jewish dental student, announces that she's pregnant; his father falls ill with renal cancer; and the snotty ladies at the club, who "talk without moving their lips," want him to cook, of all things, Chinese dishes, that "barefoot food, eat-with-sticks food. Under harvest moons, rinse off the maggots, slice, and steam...squatting-in-still-water food. Pole-across-your-shoulders, hooves-in-the-house food."

His entire life, he has been rebelling against his culture and his parents, immigrants who have the droll nicknames of Genius and Zsa Zsa. Sterling grew up in the back of their laundry in Lynbrook, Long Island, and instead of becoming a doctor as they'd wished, he went to Swarthmore and majored in art history, then trained to become a French chef. "In their eyes I was a scoundrel, a dumb-as-dirt ingrate. This was the reward for their sacrifice, leaving home for America, for lean lives among the barbarians." He has proved to be a particular disappointment to his father, with whom his relationship has always been remote and cold. During one hilarious and poignant scene, Genius seems to cherish a used refrigerator more than his son, lovingly wiping it down after it has been installed: "Cut off from the rest of the family, my father basked in the refrigerator's chilled air, its silvery vapors, its measly light's glow. What I saw in my father's gentle cleaning of each egg holder's deep dimple was kindness, and the pang I felt, like fingers fanning in my throat, was envy."

As in his story collection, *Pangs of Love,* Louie draws great humor from clashes of assimilation. Some of the best moments in *The Barbarians Are Coming* involve Morton Sass, Bliss's father, a mendacious investor who convinces Sterling, after he marries Bliss and bears two sons, to host a cooking show on cable TV. Later, Sass sells the rights to the show, and it's retooled into a humiliating Chinese parody called *The Peeking Duck,* with Sterling assuming the voice of Hop Sing, the houseboy on *Bonanza,* as he gives viewers what they want: "Today I make velly famous dish...Shlimp and robster sauce! This one velly good and velly chlicky dish. Aw time peoples say, 'Wah! Where is robster?'"

Yet the heart and power of Louie's novel lies more in the tragedy, not the comedy, of the Lung men—the father, doomed by a love affair with a white woman when he first arrives in the U.S.; the son, while begrudging his father's aloofness, unable to see the selfish distance he himself creates, failing his parents, wife, and children, all in the "desperate attempt to overcome the unremarkableness of being a Lung."

FAREWELL, MY LOVELIES *Poems by Diann Blakely. Story Line Press, $12.95 paper. Reviewed by Denise Duhamel.*

In her second book, *Farewell, My Lovelies,* Diann Blakely evokes Raymond Chandler's yin and writes a decidedly female poetry—tough, stylized, and heart-smart. In the opening poem of the collection, "Last Dance," the speaker observes a gaggle of young Courtney Love fans who, during an intermission of a ballet, proclaim the performance "a fucking A-1 bore." Right away, you know whose side Blakely is on. Although her poetry does have the formal precision and grace associated with ballet, it also, more remarkably, has the roar and feistiness of a Hole concert. The girls in "baby doll dresses, worn with fishnets" are not unlike Blakely's own poems—wide-eyed, sexy, and provocative.

When Blakely spins narratives about adultery—"hashed-lace brownies with rum-&-Tabs"; " 'projects,' as if someone had made them for school' "; Ted Hughes "so handsome on TV [her] knees water"; and a girl "raped in the snowbound northwest / By six grunge-clad assaulters who crooned Nirvana's / Early hit 'Polly' "—the reader is with her. Blakely's storytelling is complex, no-nonsense, and often full of pain. Her voice is an in-your-face voice, an almost performance-poetry voice, yet her poems are full of craft and gorgeousness.

In the loosely constructed pantoum "Reunion Banquet, Class of '79," Blakely deftly weaves the movies *Farewell, My Lovely, Klute, Chinatown, Looking for Mr. Goodbar, Helter Skelter,* and half a dozen other films with the semi-tragic lives of college friends who are single moms and who are miscarrying, snorting coke, recovering from abuse. In this remarkable poem about female friendship, a "virgin" is someone who has not had a divorce.

The final poem, "Chorale," also combines several narratives: the story of a friend's illness, historical anecdotes about diabetes,

Schiller, and Beethoven. Blakely's leaps from topic to topic are genius, going from "when her lover went back home to his wife, my friend / skipped one shot, two, skipped meals" to "even out [her] bedroom / we smelled the perfume of—roses? / No, fruity and cloying, / like a sack of apples / left to rot," looping back to "our unrequitable ache to drown in sweetness."

Many of the poems in *Farewell, My Lovelies* deal with crime. In "Christmas Call," the speaker receives an eerie call from a grown woman who simply says "Mama" over and over. The speaker imagines: "a door locked / or a closet gone into, her voice muffled / by coats and stacked boxes, a husband / / with fists cocked outside..." Before the caller loses her connection, Blakely writes, "I pleaded with her, call police / or priest." And in the most disturbing poem in the book, another pantoum, "Story Hour," the speaker returns to the library parking lot daily, looking for a man who flirted with her there, even though a local rapist is on the loose: "A rapist, / or a prince, who might return with a kiss?" And then, "I'm wearing red lipstick, which I don't at home. / Catch me, catch me if you can, beneath twilit skies."

Denise Duhamel's Queen for a Day: Selected and New Poems *is forthcoming from the University of Pittsburgh Press in 2001. Her other titles include* The Star-Spangled Banner, Oyl *(with Maureen Seaton), and* Kinky. *She is an assistant professor at Florida International University in Miami.*

*Books Recommended by
Our Advisory Editors*

Charles Baxter recommends *Somebody Else: Arthur Rimbaud in Africa,* a biography by Charles Nicholl: "An eerie, brilliant, and weirdly comic story about a poet who gradually became a real-life Joseph Conrad character." (Chicago)

Madison Smartt Bell recommends *Stop Breaking Down,* debut stories by John McManus: "Would I be happy to have written these stories myself? I wish I could have written them." (Picador)

Madeline DeFrees recommends *Saying the Necessary,* poems by Edward Harkness: "The balance between reality and imagination is so precarious and the language so persuasive that the reader identifies with the speaker." (Pleasure Boat Studio)

George Garrett recommends *Graveyard of the Atlantic,* stories by Alyson Hagy: "Alyson Hagy's third collection of stories and her best so far. Praised by Charles Baxter and Jill McCorkle, among others, these seven stories all concern life on the Outer Banks of North Carolina." (Graywolf)

Mary Gordon recommends *Break Every Rule,* essays by Carole Maso:

"An original and compelling exploration of narrative strategies." (Counterpoint)

Jane Hirshfield recommends *fine,* poems by Stefanie Marlis: "*fine* consists for the most part of brief 'definitions'— poems that slip from actual definition into etymology into image, association, story, pondering. These elliptical prose poems liberate the relationship between the poet's life and imagination in surprising, precise ways, like tiny explosive charges set down in language's wide field." (Apogee)

Justin Kaplan recommends *The Edge of Marriage,* debut stories by Hester Kaplan: "Winner of the Flannery O'Connor Award and praised by *The New York Times Book Review* for the work's 'graceful, accomplished prose' and by *The Boston Globe* for the portrayal of 'articulate adults, fully aware at every moment of the agony they are in.'" (Georgia)

Maxine Kumin recommends *Hope Is the Thing with Feathers,* essays by Christopher Cokinos: "The vividly researched story of six extinct birds of the U.S.A. written by a Kansas State professor and ardent birder/environmentalist. This book deserves a wide readership and distribution. Is it possible for an author to exalt and depress his audience at the same time? Read it and decide for yourself." (Tarcher/Putnam)

Philip Levine recommends *The Trust,* nonfiction by Susan E. Tifft and Alex S. Jones: "A complex and fascinating story of the Ochs-Sulzberger families, owners of *The New York Times,* beginning with the amazing Adolph Ochs, an American success story to rival Gatsby's, and ending yesterday with Arthur Sulzberger, Jr., in command of the dynasty. For over a hundred years this family controlled 'the newspaper of record.' It's fascinating to discover who they were and are and why the record has been so badly kept. Tifft and Jones tell the story with skill and precision and no bias for or against their subject." (Little, Brown)

James Alan McPherson recommends *Don't the Moon Look Lonesome,* a first novel by Stanley Crouch: "This is an extraordinary effort by Stanley Crouch to employ the improvisational resources to the blues idiom to explore, in the novel form, the nuances of contemporary reality. In attempting to use 'riffs' to examine the emotional and psychological dimensions of his characters, Crouch has evolved a new narrative technique." (Pantheon)

Gary Soto recommends *A Mayan Astronomer in Hell's Kitchen,* poems by Martín Espada: "Martín Espada is a courageous poet who champions with grace the working class, the disheveled, the outcast, the ignored, and the imprisoned—all without sentiment. He gets better with every collection." (Norton)

EDITORS' CORNER

*New Books by
Our Advisory Editors*

Charles Baxter, *The Feast of Love,* a novel: An instant classic, Baxter's third novel is a sensual and luminous reimagination of *Midsummer Night's Dream* in Ann Arbor, Michigan—a gradually darkening comedy, powered by a dozen voices speaking to a somewhat shadowy figure named Charlie Baxter. (Pantheon)

Russell Banks, *The Angel on the Roof,* stories: A magnificent, generous collection of thirty-one stories, many of them set in hardscrabble New Hampshire, eloquently probing the lives of parents and children, husbands and wives. (HarperCollins)

Rosellen Brown, *Half a Heart*, a novel: Miriam Starobin is living in upper-middle-class Houston when she is reunited with her eighteen-year-old daughter—the fruit of an affair with a black professor in Mississippi when Miriam was a civil rights activist. A searing, provocative novel about race, identity, and ideals. (FSG)

Stratis Haviaras, *Millennial Afterlives: A Retrospective*, prose poems: A gorgeous limited-edition collection of poetic missives, each dedicated to a friend, that lyrically reflects on the passage of time. (Wells College)

Fanny Howe, *Selected Poems*: Sixteen evocative poems that are driven by metaphysical, religious, and ontological quests. Moving from Boston to Ireland, these poems show Howe at her musical and intellectual peak. (California)

Maxine Kumin, *Always Beginning: On a Life in Poetry*, essays: The Pulitzer Prize winner engagingly describes the marriage of her lives as writer, farmer, mother, wife, and comrade, including a moving remembrance of her friendship with Anne Sexton. (Copper Canyon) *Inside the Halo and Beyond: The Anatomy of Recovery*, nonfiction: Kumin, a lifelong equestrian, took up carriage racing in her early seventies, but in 1998 was thrown, and broke her neck. Miraculously she recovered, and this journal candidly and beautifully recounts her ordeal. (Norton)

Jayne Anne Phillips, *Motherkind*, a novel: With radiant prose, Phillips's long-awaited new novel portrays thirty-year-old Kate Tateman as she cares for her dying Appalachian mother in Boston while Kate bumps through the birth of her first child and her new marriage. In a single year, she must reconcile profound beginnings and endings. (Knopf)

Lloyd Schwartz, *Cairo Traffic*, poems: Schwartz extends his exploration of the intersections of character and language, of the places where common speech mysteriously transforms itself into poetry, into a series of extraordinary and compelling narratives—funny and frightening, seductive and moving. Includes several translations of contemporary Brazilian poems. (Chicago)

Gary Soto, *Nickel and Dime*, a novel: In these powerful, immensely affecting linked stories, Soto follows three Mexican-American men—two down-and-out security guards and an aging poet—as they wander through Oakland, trying to salvage their broken lives. (New Mexico)

Gerald Stern, *Last Blue*, poems: Philip Levine writes, "This is a sparer Stern than we're used to; for years he's been our Whitman for the present hour. He still is, but he's writing now with a tighter focus, as though he had to make every word count. The best news is he does. 'Ravages' and 'Against the Crusades' are among the best poems he's ever given us, and 'Progress and Poverty' may be the poem of the decade." (Norton)

POSTSCRIPTS

Miscellaneous Notes · Fall 2000

COHEN AWARDS Each year, we honor the best short story and poem published in *Ploughshares* with the Cohen Awards, which are wholly sponsored by our longtime patrons Denise and Mel Cohen. Finalists are nominated by staff editors, and the winners—each of whom receives a cash prize of $600—are selected by our advisory editors. The 2000 Cohen Awards for work published in *Ploughshares* in 1999, Volume 25, go to Judith Grossman and Jonah Winter. (Both of their works are accessible on our Web site at www.emerson.edu/ploughshares.)

JUDITH GROSSMAN *for her story "How Aliens Think" in the Spring 1999 issue, edited by Mark Doty.*

Judith Grossman was born in southeast London, England, just before World War II. Her parents were office workers, though her father was away on the Burma frontier from 1942–46. After attending local state schools, she went to Somerville College, Oxford, on scholarship. In 1961, Grossman came to Brandeis University and studied American literature with Philip Rahv. "But to Rahv's dismay," she says, "I did my doctoral thesis on Chaucer."

Before moving to America, Grossman wrote and published poetry; but the gift became lost in translation. In her mid-thirties she turned to fiction while teaching college courses and raising three children with her partner, the poet Allen Grossman. She has had no writing teachers, as such; instead, a lifetime of reading. "The disadvantage of this route was that everything took longer," she says. "Also, you can't get a recommendation letter from Virginia Woolf."

Her first novel, *Her Own Terms*, came out from Soho Press in 1988; her collection of short fiction, with "How Aliens Think" as the title story, was published in the fall of 1999 by Johns Hopkins University Press. She's now working on a novel designed to be a "last remake" of the story of Tristan and Iseult, and is also doing a nonfiction piece on short walks. Grossman has received fellowships from the National Endowment for the Humanities, Cummington Community for the Arts, and the Fine Arts Work Center in Provincetown. The Cohen Award is her first literary prize.

About "How Aliens Think," Grossman writes: "The title came first: I wanted to do a twist on anthropologist Levy-Bruhl's arrogant title *How Natives Think*, because my stories were working angles on cultural and sexual difference. Then I was teaching in Iowa for a semester in 1997, living alone in this house owned by artists, full of remarkable paintings, strange objects, and jungly plants. All I've known about estrangement surfaced there, but not as painful disorientation so much as a floating, carnivalesque hilarity. I wrote the first draft sitting under a painting clearly influenced by James Ensor, whose huge *Entry of Christ into Brussels* I saw at the Getty Museum in L.A. the year before. To be candid, I'd only known about the artist from the song "Meet James Ensor" by They Might Be Giants. A good example of how making sense of the world is still for me a fugitive thing: I must really credit this group as enabling the mood of the story. It was finished a year later, when the remembered old Jewish joke fell into place."

JONAH WINTER *for his poem "Sestina: Bob" in the Spring 1999 issue, edited by Mark Doty.*

Jonah Winter was born in 1962 in a white frame house in Fort Worth, Texas, and raised there, he claims, "by atheist wolves." "Being sensitive-artist wolves, too," he says, "my parents played Brahms above my cradle and encouraged much sensitivity, as evidenced by (a) my early tendency to sob uncontrollably over unrequited love, and (b) a premature urge to write primitive-outsider poems about leaves by the age of five, which I published in an adult magazine by the age of seven. This led to an unfortunate string of events that included going to graduate school in creative writing twice, at the University of Virginia (where I got an M.F.A.) and at the University of New Hampshire (where I got a broken arm), then becoming a llama rancher, a flower deliverer, a children's book editor, a bum, and a chronically depressed person, which in turn prompted various geographical relocations to Idaho, San Francisco, Ohio, Maine, and New York, my current home. Apartment total: twenty-three." In recent years, Winter has supported himself through writing and illustrating children's books (*Diego*, Knopf; *FAIR BALL!*, Scholastic; *Once Upon a Time in Chicago*, Hyperion) and playing various musical instruments in the band Ed's Redeeming Qualities, whose most recent CD is called *At the Fish and Game Club.*

Though Winter's poems have been published extensively in journals, they await book publication "with much frustration, anxiety, and muffled enthusiasm, peering out from the inside of my filing cabinet furtively, like absent-minded squirrels on an ice skating rink." His unpublished manuscripts include *Postcards from Paradise, Missing Panels from an Altarpiece, Amnesia, Description of the Universe,* and *Here Comes Kelby!*

About the poem "Sestina: Bob," for which he has also won a Pushcart Prize, Winter writes: "It derived its inspiration from a variety of sources. That a poet could, as I finally did, modify the task of writing one of the most complex, convoluted, prone-to-failure verse forms by simply reducing the six-repeated-end-words constraint to just *one* end-word repeated *forty-two* times— well, this seemed utterly ridiculous! It was so ridiculous, in fact, that it seemed like it *just… might… WORK*! Well, to quote Catullus, 'If a fool proceeds in his folly, he shall become wise.' Well, to quote Marlon Brando when asked in *The Wild One* what he was rebelling against: 'What do you got?' Well, to quote the airport limo driver from Philadelphia in belated response to a passenger who twenty minutes earlier had said, 'You just drive 'em': 'I just drive 'em!' "

MORE AWARDS Our congratulations to the following writers, whose work has been selected for the following anthologies:

BEST STORIES Michael Byers's "The Beautiful Days," from the Fall 1999 issue edited by Charles Baxter, and Geoffrey Becker's "Black Elvis," from the Winter 1999–00 issue edited by Madison Smartt Bell *&* Elizabeth Spires, will be included in *The Best American Short Stories 2000,* due out this fall from Houghton Mifflin, with E. L. Doctorow as the guest editor and Katrina Kenison as the series editor.

BEST POETRY Susan Wood's "Analysis of the Rose as Sentimental Despair," from the Spring 1999 issue edited by Mark Doty, will appear in *The Best American Poetry 2000* this September from Scribner, with Rita Dove as the guest editor and David Lehman as the series editor.

O. HENRY Michael Byers's "The Beautiful Days" has also been chosen for *Prize Stories 2000: The O. Henry Awards* by editor Larry Dark. The anthology will be published in October by Anchor Books.

PUSHCART Fanny Howe's story "Gray," from the Winter 1998–99 issue edited by Thomas Lux; Lucille Clifton's poem "Jasper, Texas, 1998" and Jonah Winter's poem "Sestina: Bob," both from the Spring 1999 issue; Joan Silber's story "Commendable," from the Fall 1999 issue; and Jonathan David Jackson's poem "The Spell," from the Winter 1999–00 issue, have been selected for *The Pushcart Prize XXV: Best of the Small Presses,* which will be published by Bill Henderson's Pushcart Press this fall.

CALLING ALL PLOUGHSHARES WRITERS If you have been published in *Ploughshares* and have not heard from us recently about participating in our Web project, please send your current address to us by mail or e-mail (authors@emerson.edu).

CONTRIBUTORS' NOTES

Fall 2000

ANN BEATTIE's new collection of short stories, *Perfect Recall*, will be published by Scribner in January. She is the author of six other story collections, including *Park City*, *What Was Mine*, and *The Burning House*, and of six novels, including *My Life*, *Starring Dara Falcon*, *Another You*, *Picturing Will*, and *Chilly Scenes of Winter*.

MOIRA CRONE is the author of three volumes of fiction, the latest being *Dream State*. She lives in New Orleans and directs the M.F.A. program at LSU. Her stories have appeared in *The New Yorker* and various periodicals and anthologies. "Where What Gets into People Comes From" is the title story of a cycle set in North Carolina's tobacco country, where she grew up.

PETER HO DAVIES is the author of two short story collections, *The Ugliest House in the World* and *Equal Love*. His work has appeared in *The Atlantic*, *Harper's*, *Granta*, and *The Paris Review*, and has been selected for *Prize Stories: The O. Henry Awards* and *Best American Short Stories*. He teaches in the M.F.A. program at the University of Michigan.

TOM DRURY, recipient of a John Simon Guggenheim Fellowship for 2000–2001, is the author of three novels, including *Hunts in Dreams*, which was published in May. His fiction has appeared in *The New Yorker*, *Granta*, and *The Mississippi Review*.

CAROL FITZGERALD lives in New York City, where she works for a magazine. She is currently writing a novel.

ELIZABETH GRAVER is the author of two novels, *The Honey Thief* and *Unravelling*, and of a short story collection, *Have You Seen Me?* Her work has been anthologized in *Best American Short Stories*, *Best American Essays*, and *Prize Stories: The O. Henry Awards*. She teaches at Boston College.

JESSE LEE KERCHEVAL is the author of a memoir, *Space*, and a collection of poems, *World as Dictionary*. She teaches at the University of Wisconsin, where she is the director of the Wisconsin Institute for Creative Writing.

BILL MARX reviews books for *The Boston Globe* and a variety of national newspapers and magazines. He also comments regularly on new fiction in translation for PRI's nationally syndicated radio program "The World." This year he was named, for the third time, a finalist for the National Book Critics Circle Reviewer's Citation.

GARRY MITCHELL has recently exhibited work in New York City at Art in General, Karen McCready Fine Art, and the Claudia Carr Gallery, as well as at Colby College Museum of Art, the Hyde Collection, and the Lake George Arts Project. He has a show forthcoming at ICON Contemporary Art in Brunswick, Maine.

He has received fellowships from the Fine Arts Work Center, the MacDowell Colony, and Yaddo, among other places. He lives in North Yarmouth, Maine, with his wife and son.

SABINA MURRAY was born in Pennsylvania and grew up in Australia and the Philippines. She is the author of the novel *Slow Burn*. "Intramuros" will be included in her short story collection *The Caprices*, which was inspired by the Pacific Campaign of the Second World War and will be published by Houghton Mifflin in the fall of 2001. A former Michener Fellow and Bunting Fellow, she is currently the Roger Murray Writer in Residence at Phillips Academy, Andover.

PAMELA PAINTER is the author of the story collections *Getting to Know the Weather* and *The Long and Short of It,* which came out in the spring of 1999. She is also co-author, with Anne Bernays, of *What If? Writing Exercises for Fiction Writers.* Her stories have appeared in *The Atlantic, Harper's, The Kenyon Review, The North American Review, Ploughshares,* and *Story,* among other magazines and anthologies. A founding editor of *StoryQuarterly,* she teaches in the M.F.A. program at Emerson College.

JESS ROW is a student in the University of Michigan M.F.A. program. From 1997 to 1999 he was a Yale-China teaching fellow at the Chinese University of Hong Kong, and he is currently working on a collection of stories that take place there. His work has previously appeared in *Green Mountains Review,* and recently received a Hopwood Award.

ESMERALDA SANTIAGO is the author of the memoirs *When I Was Puerto Rican* and *Almost a Woman,* and of the novel *América's Dream.* She is currently at work on the screen adaptation of *Almost a Woman* for PBS Masterpiece Theatre.

LYSLEY A. TENORIO earned his M.F.A. from the University of Oregon. Formerly the George Bennett Fellow at Phillips Exeter Academy and the James McCreight Fiction Fellow at the University of Wisconsin's Institute for Creative Writing, he is currently a Wallace Stegner Fellow at Stanford University. Born in Olongapo City, Philippines, he grew up in San Diego and now lives in San Francisco. This is his first publication. His work is forthcoming in *The Atlantic Monthly.*

MARK WINEGARDNER, a professor of English and director of the creative writing program at Florida State University, is the author of several books, including, most recently, the novel *The Veracruz Blues.* His new novel, *Crooked River Burning,* will be published later this year by Harcourt.

~

GUEST EDITOR POLICY *Ploughshares* is published three times a year: mixed issues of poetry and fiction in the Spring and Winter and a fiction issue in the Fall, with each guest-edited by a different writer of prominence, usually one whose early work was published in the journal. Guest editors are invited to solicit up to half of their issues, with the other half selected from unsolicited manuscripts screened for them by staff editors. This guest editor policy is designed to introduce readers to different literary circles and tastes, and to offer a fuller representation of the range and diversity of contemporary letters than would be possible with a single editorship.

~

SUBMISSION POLICIES We welcome unsolicited manuscripts from August 1 to March 31 (postmark dates). All submissions sent from April to July are returned unread. In the past, guest editors often announced specific themes for issues, but we have revised our editorial policies and no longer restrict submissions to thematic topics. Submit your work at any time during our reading period; if a manuscript is not timely for one issue, it will be considered for another. We do not recommend trying to target specific guest editors. Our backlog is unpredictable, and staff editors ultimately have the responsibility of determining for which editor a work is most appropriate. Mail one prose piece or one to three poems. No e-mail submissions. Poems should be individually typed either single- or double-spaced on one side of the page. Prose should be typed double-spaced on one side and be no longer than thirty pages. Although we look primarily for short stories, we occasionally publish personal essays/memoirs. Novel excerpts are acceptable if self-contained. Unsolicited book reviews and criticism are not considered. Please do not send multiple submissions of the same genre, and do not send another manuscript until you hear about the first. *No more than a total of two submissions per reading period.* Additional submissions will be returned unread. Mail your manuscript in a page-size manila envelope, your full name and address written on the outside. In general, address submissions to the "Fiction Editor," "Poetry Editor," or "Nonfiction Editor," not to the guest or staff editors by name, unless you have a legitimate association with them or have been previously published in the magazine. Unsolicited work sent directly to a guest editor's home or office will be ignored and discarded; guest editors are formally instructed not to read such work. All manuscripts and correspondence regarding submissions should be accompanied by a self-addressed, stamped envelope (S.A.S.E.) for a response; no replies will be given by e-mail or postcard. Expect three to five months for a decision. We now receive well over a thousand manuscripts a month. Do not query us until five months have passed, and if you do, please write to us, including an S.A.S.E. and indicating the postmark date of submission, instead of calling or e-mailing. Simultaneous submissions are amenable as long as they are indicated as such and we are notified immediately upon acceptance elsewhere. We cannot accommodate revisions, changes of return address, or forgotten S.A.S.E.'s after the fact. We do not reprint previously published work. Translations are welcome if permission has been granted. We cannot be responsible for delay, loss, or damage. Payment is upon publication: $25/printed page, $50 minimum per title, $250 maximum per author, with two copies of the issue and a one-year subscription.

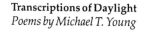

BENNINGTON WRITING SEMINARS

MFA *in Writing and Literature*
Two-Year Low-Residency Program

A. BLAKE GARDNER

FICTION
NONFICTION
POETRY

Jane Kenyon Poetry Scholarships available
For more information contact:
Writing Seminars
Box PL
Bennington College
Bennington, VT 05201
802-440-4452, Fax 802-440-4453
www.bennington.edu/bencol/writing/mfa.htm